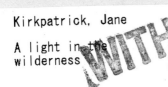

"Great characters and a strong story. Jane Kirkpatrick is an excellent writer."

—**T. Davis Bunn,** bestselling and award-winning author

"With *All Together in One Place* Jane Kirkpatrick has performed a literary miracle. She made me—a reader who seldom ventures into Western fiction by choice—struggle across dusty plains and ford swollen rivers right along with her eleven turnaround women. . . . She made me care for—no, *cheer* for—characters who rubbed me the wrong way until they polished clean my resistance and stole my heart. Finally, she made me marvel at the strength of these pioneer women of faith whose hard-learned lessons give me the courage to change what needs changing in my life, and whose collective trust in God fortifies my own. Read it and experience this miracle of kinship and courage for yourself."

—**Liz Curtis Higgs**, bestselling author
and Christy Award winner

"This beautiful novel speaks to the heart of human relationships—full in love. Jane Kirkpatrick's book is a treasure, well worth reaching beyond our genre to experience."

—*RT Book Reviews*, 4.5 stars

Praise for *No Eye Can See*

"The author brings her heroines alive with full complements of both endearing and frustrating qualities, keeping them on even footing with each other and leaving the reader unsure what they might do next. Kirkpatrick is convincingly insightful about the conflicting emotions these women experience during dramatic life change, allowing them to struggle, change their minds, make mistakes and start over on different tracks. . . . [*No Eye Can See*] satisfies overall as entertainment, as historical fiction, and as a thoughtful exploration of human character and community."

—*Publishers Weekly*

M

Praise for *A Flickering Light*

"Jane Kirkpatrick's brilliance as a storyteller and her elegant artistry with the written word shine like a beacon in *A Flickering Light*. A master at weaving historical accounts with threads of story, Jane has that rare ability to take her reader on a journey through time. You nearly feel the ground move beneath your feet."

—**Susan Meissner**, bestselling author of *The Shape of Mercy*

Praise for *The Daughter's Walk*

"Jane Kirkpatrick is a wonderful writer who creates a story full of strong, admirable characters with human flaws."

—**Francine Rivers**, bestselling author

Praise for *One Glorious Ambition*

"As always, Kirkpatrick's writing is graceful and poignant. A master of historical fiction, Kirkpatrick has long been a favorite author among fans of the genre, and for good reason. She seamlessly weaves biographical and historical facts into her expert storytelling, both here and in her many previous novels."

—*Book Reporter Review*

"Jane Kirkpatrick's ability to probe the human spirit makes *One Glorious Ambition* a soaring novel of love, compassion, and duty."

—**Sandra Dallas**, award-winning and *New York Times* bestselling author of *True Sisters*

Praise for *A Sweetness to the Soul*

"Jane Kirkpatrick's particular gift is for capturing the authentic feel and flavor of frontier life; *A Sweetness to the Soul* is absolutely true to the people and the land as they once were. This is a novel that calls up a period early in the history of Oregon marked not only by hardship, sudden death, spiritual fortitude, and physical endurance, but also by community—one person reaching out to help another so that they might all survive."

—**Molly Gloss**, bestselling author of *The Hearts of Horses*

"The best novels leave the reader changed in some significant way. *A Sweetness to the Soul* does that literally from its opening pages. . . . It is a celebration of those things that connect us, that make us what we are, that give us joy and sorrow, and understanding."

—*Salem Statesman Journal*

Praise for *Love to Water My Soul*

"Rich with sensory imagery, well-developed characters, and peppered with native words, the novel brings alive the traditional and transitional lives of the native people of Oregon in the late nineteenth century. The details about the flora, fauna, and tribal traditions bear evidence of meticulous research."

—*Christian Library Journal*

Praise for *Gathering of Finches*

"Drawing upon extensive research, including interviews with descendants, Kirkpatrick weaves a tale of a beautiful and dynamic woman who left a mark on everyone who knew her. . . . To fully appreciate Kirkpatrick's research and interest in the lives of her subjects, read her Acknowledgments and Author's Note prior to beginning this entertaining and informative novel."

—Critics Corner, *Presbyterian Magazine*

Praise for *A Clearing in the Wild*

"*A Clearing in the Wild* is Jane Kirkpatrick at her finest. The story is quickly paced and engaging from the first to the last. One of the most difficult tasks for a writer—and Kirkpatrick's specialty—is to

contemplate the lives of real people and to re-create a believable epi-
sode in those lives that is accurate yet interesting, to both inform and
entertain. The dialogue sings masterfully with perfect tone, building
characters and pushing the story line in succinct phrasing that never
overstates. Emma Wagner Giesy's story feels as genuine as if she herself were telling it."

—**Nancy E. Turner**, bestselling author

Praise for *A Land of Sheltered Promise*

"Jane Kirkpatrick has an extraordinary talent for compelling us to
explore our beliefs while telling a whopping good tale."

—**Book Reporter Review**

A
LIGHT IN THE
WILDERNESS

A NOVEL

JANE
KIRKPATRICK

Revell

a division of Baker Publishing Group
Grand Rapids, Michigan

© 2014 by Jane Kirkpatrick

Published by Revell
a division of Baker Publishing Group
P.O. Box 6287, Grand Rapids, MI 49516-6287
www.revellbooks.com

Printed in the United States of America

Library of Congress Cataloging-in-Publication Data
Kirkpatrick, Jane, 1946–
     A light in the wilderness : a novel / Jane Kirkpatrick.
         pages cm
     Includes bibliographical references.
     ISBN 978-0-8007-2231-9 (pbk.)
     1. Freedmen—Fiction. 2. African American women—Fiction. 3. Oregon
Territory—History—Fiction. 4. Christian fiction. I. Title.
     PS3561.I712L53 2014
     813'.54—dc23   2014015688

Scripture used in this book, whether quoted or paraphrased by the characters, is taken from the King James Version of the Bible.

This book is a work of historical fiction based closely on real people and events. Details that cannot be historically verified are purely products of the author's imagination.

14   15   16   17   18   19   20   7   6   5   4   3   2   1

Cast of Characters

Letitia (Carson)	an African American woman
Martha & Adam Carson	Letitia and David's children
David (Davey) Carson	Former mountain man/farmer/ common-law husband of Letitia
Smith Carson	brother of David Carson
Junior Carson	David's son from first marriage
Sarah Bowman	a Missouri and later Oregon neighbor
William Bowman	husband of Sarah
Zachariah Hawkins	doctor in Iowa/Missouri/Oregon journey
Nancy Hawkins	wife of Zachariah, neighbor of Carsons in Missouri and Oregon
Samuel, Maryanne, Martha, Edward, Laura, Nancy Jane	children of Nancy and Zachariah Hawkins
The Woman, Betsy	a Kalapuya woman in Oregon country
Little Shoot	Betsy's grandson
Greenberry Smith (G.B. Smith)	slave patroller and neighbor of Carsons in Oregon
Eliza White	slave girl under contention in Missouri
Stephen Staats Levin English	captains whom Carson traveled with in 1845
Henry Knighton Hardin Martin	drovers for Carson
Joseph and Frances Gage	Letitia's neighbors
A.J. Thayer	Letitia's attorney

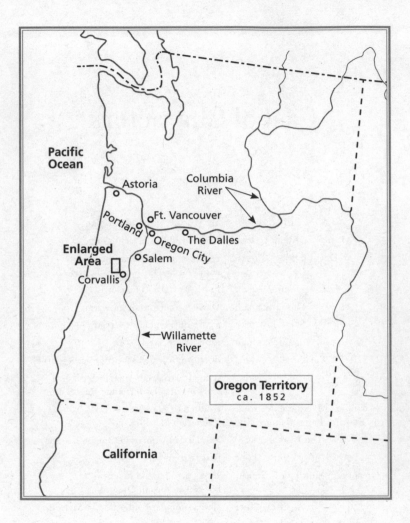

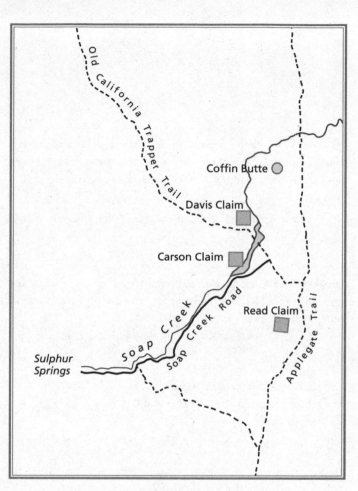

Soap Creek Valley *around 1852*

Being one of the "Poor Whites" from a slave state I can speak with some authority for that class—many of those people hated slavery, but a much larger number of them hated free negroes even worse than slaves.

—Jesse Applegate, Oregon emigrant from Missouri in 1843

The essential code must include . . . how to crawl from the wreckage when this life falters, how to plunge to the cellar of sorrow and grope for the ladder that might bring you back into some kind of light, no matter how dim or strange.

—Kim Stafford, *100 Tricks Any Boy Can Do*

She walked toward the prairie,
the unexpected promise of possibility, new grace
in her heart . . .

—Kathleen Ernst, *Facing Forward*

Prologue

She had imagined the day she would escape; it would be high noon when people least expected them to run, when the dogs lay panting in the Kentucky sun and the patrols rested, not seeking a colored woman making her way to freedom. She'd be fearing for her life. But now, no one chased her. No braying hounds barked; yet her heart pounded.

Here she was, her bare feet ready to leave Kentucky soil; and she was going as a free woman. Letitia patted the parchment inside the bond at her waist. It was secure. Then she pulled the shawl around her shoulders, lifted her tow linen skirt and her only petticoat, and pulled herself up with ease onto the wagon seat beside Sarah Bowman. Not that she was their equal, oh no, she knew that wasn't so. But she was free and free people rode facing forward. The rough cloth pressed against her legs as she sat.

"All set?" Mr. Bowman turned to his wife.

"As good as I'll ever be." The woman held a baby in her arms. She patted Letitia's fingers, held them for a moment, then withdrew them as though she'd touched a snake. "Maybe you should ride in back, Tish. Yes, that would be better. Make sure the little ones are settled."

Letitia hesitated. *Was now the time?*

"Letitia?"

She moved then without complaint under the wagon covering, the August heat already stifling, the scent of canvas new to her nose.

"Over!" One Bowman child barked at her sister, who sat on the older girl's doll. Letitia wiggled her way past the two-year-old who smiled at her even when Letitia lifted her to retrieve the sought-after doll. Like a lily pad on a pond Letitia nestled herself within the array of bags and bedding and other property of the Bowmans. She swooped the toddler into her lap when the child crawled to her, smelled the lavender of the girl's hair, then pointed so the child would look out the back arch of the opening. Caged chickens cackled their discontent on the other side of the wagon. A hot breeze pushed past them. As Letitia looked out through the wagon's bow, a thousand memories bled through the tears in her eyes.

She'd miss the Kentucky goldenrod. She wondered what flowers bloomed in Missouri, what life would bring there. It didn't matter. She was leaving this place as a free woman; she wouldn't have to be afraid now. She could own firkins, candlesticks, and kale seeds, property that belonged to her. She had papers to show.

Her heart no longer pounded as a woman running. Dust drifted up to scent the warm air. Flies buzzed. The children had settled their claims for space. A slow grin worked its way onto her face, sent a shiver down her bare arms. She brushed at the tears, rested her chin on the toddler's head, indigo-colored arms soft around the child. "Thank God Almighty," she whispered. The toddler reached up without looking and patted Letitia's cheek. Letitia began to sing, a low husky sound. "I gotta right. You gotta right. We all gotta right to the tree of life." Letitia stared out the wagon back and smiled. A free woman didn't have to face forward to know she headed in the right direction.

Part One

Having an Opinion

Letitia preferred the shadows, avoiding the skirmish before her. But the child tugged on her hand and led Letitia to the dust in front of the Platte County courthouse. Men's voices sliced the air like the whips of a field marse, sharp and stinging. The air was heavy as a wet, wool quilt, yet dust billowed around the two men as it did when bulls scraped the earth. "She was contracted for, fair and square. She failed to do the work!" Letitia knew the speaker, Davey Carson, once of Ireland, now of Carroll Township, Platte County, Missouri. Today, full of consternation. Bushy eyebrows with the tint of auburn formed a chevron of scowl over his nose. "Sure and I did nothing like she says I did. Not a thing. The girl didn't work, I tell ye!"

Letitia shrank back, grateful his anger wasn't directed at her. She tugged at the child's hand to move toward the Platte City store.

"We'll settle it in court then." The second man brushed past

Davey, leaving the Irishman like a shriveled pickle in the bottom of a barrel, no one wanting to touch it.

Davey's red face scanned the disappearing crowd. When his eyes caught Letitia's, she glanced down. Hot sun brought out sweat on her forehead, intensified the scent of coconut oil and honey she'd used to smooth her crinkly hair. She turned her head to the side. "Let's go." She started to reach for the child's hand.

"I suppose you believe that too," he accused.

She halted.

"That I'm a madman capable of beating a young lass and misusing her, slave or no! Is that your opinion, woman?"

Was he really speaking to her? She should walk away. She didn't need to get in an argument with a white man. She was in the town getting buttons and bows for Mrs. Bowman and looking after Artemesia, who had begged to come along. The child stared, slipped her hand inside Letitia's. It felt wet and warm.

"I gots nothin' to speak of, Mistah Carson. I gots no opinion. I jus' stayin' out of the way." She did have an opinion, though. He had been kind to her the year before, not long after she'd arrived in Platte County, when she'd asked him to take her money and buy a cow with it.

His voice rose again. "I may be an old mountain man not accustomed to town ways, but I know how to take care of property." He threw his hands into the air. "I never touched her. Never! It was a trick all along, I tell ye. They told the lass to run away so they'd have their property and my money and I'd be without her labor and my money both." Davey stomped up the courthouse steps past the black and white cornerstones. Letitia was dismissed.

Each American was due his "day in court," or so she'd heard. She hoped he was successful in his lawsuit. She wasn't sure why. Taking sides wasn't her way. Her heartbeat returned to a steady pace.

In the store, they waited. The mercantile owner had customers to keep happy, and serving those white people first was a given. Letitia spread her hands over the smooth bolts of cloth, the new

16

dyes tickling her nose. She lifted the lacework on the shelf, fingering the tidy stitches. Irish lace? She shook her head. People were trading their finery for hardtack and flour, getting ready for travel west.

Letitia was going to Oregon too, with the Bowmans. She wasn't certain how she felt about that. She'd learned the rules of Missouri, showed her papers when asked, endured the sneers and snarls of "free black" as though the word meant stink or worse, a catching kind of poison spread by being present near her breath. But good things had happened to her since she'd been in this state too. She'd earned money helping birth babies, enough to buy a cow. Davey Carson had in fact made the purchase for her, taking her money to acquire the cow that she paid the Bowmans for feeding—along with her own keep.

But she'd heard that the Oregon people wanted to join the states as free. She'd be free there too, and without slavery and its uncertainty hovering like a cloud of fevered mosquitoes. Maybe in Oregon she'd try her hand at living alone. Or if she married and had children, they'd be born free there and no one could ever sell them away from her. What property she had would be hers to keep. Like the cow she owned. She eyed a silver baby rattle on the mercantile shelf. She felt its cool weight. For when . . . if ever again. No, Mr. Bowman said they could only take essentials. A baby rattle wouldn't qualify.

Still, Letitia chose to go to Oregon with them, chose to help Sarah with the laundry and care of the children. She felt free to call her Missus Bowman whenever they were in public, even though at the log cabin she could call her Miss Sarah, like an older sister. Though they weren't ever so close as that.

While Artemesia ogled the hard candy counter, Letitia wandered the store, placing a set of needles into her basket, looking at a hairbrush, her face reflected in the silver back. Coal black hair frizzing at her temples beneath her straw hat, damp from humidity heavy as a dog's breath at high noon. Dark brown eyes set into a face the color of the skinny piano keys. Sadness looked out at her, reminding her of all those eyes had seen in her twenty-six years. The set was nothing she could afford.

A gust of wind burst sand against the store's windows. Outside the weather worked itself up into a downpour. Getting home would drench them. She ought to have remembered the slicker for the child, but it hadn't looked like rain. She didn't want the child to catch cold.

A sewing box caught her eye. Tortoiseshell with green and blue silk lining the inside. She opened it and saw the ivory spool holders. She could make a false bottom and put her paper there, somewhere safe and secure.

"What can I do for you, Miss Artemesia?" The shopkeeper spoke to the child. He and Letitia were the only adults now, all other customers serviced and gone, scampering through the rain with the umbrellas the shopkeeper loaned them.

"Mistah Bowman will be in tomorrow to pick up these things." Letitia handed him a list, careful not to touch his fingers even though she wore gloves. "I's buying the needles."

"This your mammy, Miss Bowman?" He nodded toward Letitia.

"Yes sir. She's Aunt Tish."

"She has money to buy needles?"

Letitia raised her voice. "I has money. Suh."

He frowned. Letitia handed him the coins. "Bowmans pay me. I's a free woman."

He harrumphed. "So you're all really going to Oregon then, Miss Bowman?"

Artemesia nodded.

"Must say, you'll be missed, little lady." He turned to put Letitia's money in the till. "Half the town seems to be heading west. I see the wagons rolling." He sighed. "Wouldn't mind a change of scenery myself now and then. Not sure though that I trust those letters sent back about all the good things Oregon has awaiting."

"We able to borrow one of your umbrellas, suh? It rainin' harsh."

"Should have remembered to bring one."

"Yessuh, but didn't see no storms walkin' in. Don't want the chil' getting' sick."

He nodded. "Wouldn't want that on my conscience either. Here you go."

Letitia didn't give her opinion of letters sent and received. He wouldn't care. Few asked her opinion. Miss Sarah didn't invite suggestions for how to clean the bedrolls of fleas or how to lessen morning sickness. Mr. Bowman acted like she didn't exist except to help break hemp or butcher hogs. But Davey Carson *had* asked her opinion of his lawsuit, now that she thought about it. She wore a little shame that she'd sidestepped his question, didn't answer that she found him to be a kind man, unlike what he was accused of. He had treated her as though she was more than a post. That so rarely happened, she'd been shocked and was now surprised at the feeling of warmth arriving on the memory.

2

The Choice

Nancy Hawkins handed her husband the wooden peg. "That finishes it."

"Told you I'd make you a quilt frame out of good Missouri oak. And you doubted." Her husband of twelve years grinned.

"It's only been two years in the making." Nancy ran her hands over the smooth wood.

Zachariah stepped back, surveying his handywork. He looked up at the rafters. "Do you still want it up there?"

"Yes, I want it pulled up out of the way when I'm not using it."

"Be as easy to store in the shed."

"I want to lower it myself and not have to get help hauling it in." She could imagine right now a Contrary Woman pattern or stitching her fifteen stitches to the inch while her friends laughed and told stories.

"Could we work on it later?" He pulled out his pocket watch.

"I don't see anyone waiting." She looked out the window. The small room at the end of their cabin served as his doctor's office, but she could see if someone rode up. No one had.

"I've some apothecary orders to put together."

She laughed. "You'll do anything to get out of finishing something, won't you?" His sheepish look was her reply. "Let's see if we can't get it all hung before Laura and Edward wake up. Samuel will help, won't you?"

Samuel, her eleven-year-old, almost as tall as her, nodded.

"Pounding around in the ceiling will wake them up," Zachariah warned.

"Go!" She swatted at him and he sidestepped and grinned. "Get the pulley and hemp ropes. We'll do the rest."

She picked up two-year-old Edward, who awoke at the sound of the door slamming. She bounced him on her hip while she stirred the beef stew. They would be heading for Oregon this year if it wasn't for her carrying a child due in October. Though the pregnancy had delayed their trip a year, she'd finally gotten the quilt frame Zach had promised her before they left Iowa, and she intended to use it.

"Here you go." The iron pulleys clunked on the wooden floor, and Nancy jumped out of the way of the snake of rope that thumped then tangled at her bare feet. "I'll work on it later. Someone's at the office door now that I need to tend to."

Nancy looked out the window. Yes, a man dismounted his horse. He stood tall, wore a fine vest and pants tucked into good leather boots. He walked like a soldier toward the door, straight shoulders, but she didn't think he'd ever served. "It's that disagreeable Greenberry Smith. Tell him your wife awaits your critical help."

"He's not the sort of man to be concerned about the inconveniences of a woman," Zach said.

That was true enough. Nancy had been present once helping her husband when Greenberry Smith had brought in a slave needing an amputation because of a foot infection gone untreated. The young slave, maybe in his twenties, had scars on his arms from previous injuries and smelled of rotten flesh. Nancy supposed it was good that Smith sought medical help instead of simply letting the man die as some slave owners might, especially when the amputation meant his value as a worker would be reduced. She clucked her tongue. Another reason to leave this place. Oregon would be a refreshing change as a free state. Power without love is never just, and slavery was all about raw power.

Nancy prodded Zach toward his office.

Zach nodded toward the pulley and rope. "Don't go standing on a stool. Most dangerous weapon there is in a house."

"Samuel and I will be fine."

Zach left and Nancy pawed through what he'd brought her. "We'll need a hammer and two iron nails. Can you find those?" Samuel trotted off in search while she put Edward in a corner with a wooden top. "Maryanne, Martha, you watch him, see he doesn't get underfoot."

Maryanne, at nine, clucked at her seven-year-old sister and younger brother like a little mother. Four-year-old Laura slept on. A sickly child, she slept most of her days away, but Zach could find nothing wrong with her. Her health was a constant worry, dark circles under her eyes. The girl hadn't nursed well and Nancy worried what might happen with this next child. Edward had nursed fine; so had the others, but there was always the lesson of Laura.

Nancy dragged the ropes to the section of the cabin where she wanted to house the quilt frame. It would be secured to the ceiling logs. Locating the stool, she lifted the first pulley. She'd need two to hold it to the rafter. She centered the pulleys above her head. Yes, this would be the best place. Samuel handed her the nails and she pounded them in, worked the rope through the pulleys and through the rings on the quilt frame. "Let's see if we've got it working."

Samuel worked one side and Nancy the other. When the frame hung snug to the rafter, they tied off their ropes at the side logs. She stood back and looked. "Well, isn't that dandy?" She did a little dance. "Imagine, I've done a man's job."

Samuel nodded. "You had help, Mother."

"Yes I did." She brushed his blond hair, sharing this little triumph. She found she needed to notice small achievements to keep from feeling overwhelmed by the everyday tasks of living.

That's when she heard the snap of the rope, saw it spin like a wild whip, leaving one end of the frame high at the rafter and Nancy's side swinging free, close to the floor—next to the pulley that smashed from the ceiling. Martha shouted, Edward cried, Laura startled before letting loose a wail. Nancy saw the knot of rope spun free in the fall as she lifted Laura. The pulley lay beside her. She brought the crying child to her chest, then checked the cheek, a bruise from the pulley already starting to form. *Some mother I am.*

Four days later, on an April morning with wild plums blooming beside the Bowman cabin, Letitia lay in her cot in the children's room, the scent of pine from the unpeeled logs tickling her nose. A small window gave her the view of the flowering dogwood beyond. The blossoms looked beaten from the steady rains, but this morning promised a clear sky. Dawn yawned in the distance as a bluebird settled on the branch, hanging as precarious and happy as a child lying back on a swing. Letitia curled back into the feather tick. How nice it would be to rise when she was ready and not when someone demanded something from her. She rose. This morning she wanted to get underway with Mr. Bowman no longer giving orders about what had to be left behind.

The children still lay sleeping as she headed to the little house, carrying the evening slop pots with her.

Her personal duties completed, she walked back past the Bowmans' window and heard Miss Sarah say, "It's too bad Davey Carson did not prevail. Now he is out both his money and someone to help him cook and clean and tend animals."

Mr. Bowman grunted as Letitia paused.

"Do you think he harmed the girl?" Sarah Bowman thought she whispered, but she never really did. Her voice carried.

"Who's to say. She had bruises."

Letitia heard the ropes of the mattress ache as Mr. Bowman must have risen. Fleshy feet hit the floor. He said something, but Letitia couldn't hear it. Then "Oregon" but nothing else.

"Oh, I hardly think so." Sarah had moved closer to the window. Letitia crept down, hoping Miss Sarah wouldn't see her. "He's vested in Missouri, no doubt about that." Then silence and Miss Sarah said, "I'll raise Tish. I declare, that girl gets lazier every day."

Letitia hurried past, entering through the outside door to her room. She heard the knock as she set the slop pots down.

"Tish! Don't forget to put the cream in the churn on the wagon and hang it from the bow. We'll let it make itself while we roll. And come get my trunk when you're finished helping the children dress." Sarah Bowman barked her orders as though Letitia didn't have a choice whether to follow or not. "Breakfast needs going now too, you know. You'll earn your wages on this journey."

Yes, she would earn her wages, though she'd receive none. Mr. Bowman said providing food and transport was payment enough.

"Yessum."

Her stomach felt root-bound. Letitia washed her face and dressed in a tow linen dress with slub knots. One day she'd spend a little of her earnings on fancy cloth with no little nubbins from a poor spinner, but no sense to spend the money now when she'd be wearing but one or two dresses on the journey west. It was said those clothes would be threadbare by the time they reached Oregon country.

Letitia cinched her belt tight with a jerk, then tied her red kerchief over the tight curls hugging her head. She knotted the cloth at the back of her neck. The morning dew wet against her bare feet, she fast-walked to the shed where Charity, her cow, waited.

Oxen bawled, ready to be freed and moved to pasture. "Not today," Letitia told them. "Today you is headin' west with the rest of us." She scratched behind Charity's ears and thought of Sarah's words. What would Mr. Carson do now? He wasn't a young man, perhaps in his forties. He walked as though his knees were knots.

Seeing him atop a mule, Letitia had thought him tall, but on h
two feet he was maybe five feet seven, shorter than Mr. Bowm
but still many inches taller than Letitia. *What will he do?* "Why
do I care?" she asked Charity. She bent beneath the cow, pulled the
stool under her, and pressed her head into the cow's side and began
to milk. The frothy warm smell rose up in comfort as it filled the
wooden pail. The switch of Charity's tail, her steady stand while
Letitia milked, always soothed. She wasn't certain why she needed
soothing today. After all, she was beginning a grand adventure,
moving to a place where slavery had never been known, and where
even if she was mistaken for a slave she could resist the slurs or
charges. She had papers. She could trust the papers.

While she worked, she thought of the young slave girl in con-
tention over Davey Carson's lawsuit. Letitia had met the girl at
the Negro church. Had he abused her? She might have seduced
the man. Had justice been served in the suit? Uncertainty settled
around Mr. Carson like flies around a carcass. Letitia finished her
milking, skimmed the cream, and put it in the cooled churn she
drew from the spring. Mr. Bowman fastened the wooden churn
onto the side of their wagon instead of overhead as Miss Sarah had
told her to do. She wouldn't disagree, but she'd likely be blamed
later. They were heading to Weston on the Missouri and would
join there with dozens of others. She wondered how many people
of color would make the trip and whether she'd find people to
gather with at a campfire. Well, she had Charity now, and at the
very least she could talk to the cow when things got tough. And
the children. She loved the Bowman children.

"Hurry up, Tish!" Miss Sarah always got short when she was
nervous. It was something Letitia had noticed from the time Mr.
Bowman brought her home to meet his father and Letitia had been
given to the new bride. "I thought you'd be ready by now."

"Yessum. I's ready as I ever be. Just gatherin' up hen fruit."

"Oh for heaven's sake, they're eggs. Why do you persist in using
those colloquialisms your mother used?"

gs in the back. Good thing you don't have
ocked to the top and we still have to pick
ston. The wagon will be inspected by the
herself. "The wagon master. We'll all be
'no marse' from now on, won't we, Tish?"
She giggled.

Letitia let the sting pass.

Back in her room, Letitia folded her dress, tow petticoats, and an extra shawl. She placed her shoes at the bottom of the carpetbag along with the candlesticks and her belt. She added clean rags and an extra pair of underdrawers. She had a few salves and herbs she pressed into paper cones in a side pocket near the paste of coconut oil and honey mix to tame her hair. Her sewing kit with needles, thimble, and pins she folded and put into a pocket on the other side. Then came a pieced quilt she'd made herself of swaddling clothes and snippets of her son's hemp shirt. Before placing it into the bag, she pushed the cloth against her nose and inhaled. She could still smell her son, though he was long passed. She once thought she might find Jeremiah but learned the boy had died of typhoid at the home of his new master. Like threads piecing her heart together, this quilt held memories. Into the bag it went. It was essential to her.

It took less than an hour to reach Weston, a busier town than Platte City where the courthouse ruled. Mr. Bowman took the wagon to a staging area while he gathered up the latest news and met with others joining the cluster of wagons. He told Letitia and Sarah to watch the cows until he knew which herd they'd be trailed with. He was also off to look for the driver they'd had to hire to go with them.

Sarah took Letitia's offered hand, stepped off the seat, and stretched her back, hands on hips. Sarah's dress of stripes and prints with columns and swirls reminded Letitia of the front of a plantation she'd lived at for a time when Old Man Bowman had put her up as a bond against a bet and lost. He'd later bought her back, but while she'd served the new household she marveled at the porch columns. She remembered the plantation whenever she saw the blue, rose madder, and yellow of Sarah's dress. Miss Sarah did love to dress up. The fullness of the design covered the reason for Sarah's morning sickness.

"You bought new needles." Sarah said it like a charge.

Artemesia must have told her of the purchase. Letitia nodded yes.

"Mr. Bowman's shirt needs repairing. He tore it loading that churn. It'll get worse if it's not fixed. Would you be so kind?"

"You have the threads?"

"Well, yes. I have thread." She wrinkled her nose. "But the baby needs changing. I'll be glad when this baby understands his call and doesn't need napkins anymore. So I thought you could . . ."

"Yessum, I use my thread."

A slow seethe boiled within her as she drew her needle through the cloth. She knew as soon as she finished, the baby would need changing again and then it would be her turn. She would always have the next turn whether she was ready for it or not.

The cluster of people with all their belongings packed in wagons was a colorful sight to Letitia. The journey would bring new ways to do things, she could see that now. Fixing meals, tending children, milking cows would all blend in to unknown landscapes that Davey Carson and others had described. She felt a lift to her steps with the unexpected and hoped she could straddle the uncertainty that new paths brought. Children tried to play, but parents shouted to keep them close. Dogs barked and scratched; a few growled, staking new territory. Oxen hung their heavy heads, long tongues licking the damp air.

Tied to the back of the Bowman wagon, Charity raised her head and her brown eyes welcomed Letitia. She patted her cow's neck. There'd been a discussion about her cow being allowed to come, with Sarah standing up for the animal's right to be along. "We can use the milk." The milk would be a portion of what Letitia would pay for the Bowmans "keeping" her on the journey. After all, there was a cost to bringing her—as Sarah reminded her often.

Smoke from cooking fires rose then flattened in the heavy overcast sky, causing soft coughing in the midday mist. Letitia kept a close eye on the Bowman children while she bounced young William on her hip, allowing Sarah to catch her breath.

"I declare if I am puny all the way to Oregon I will surely die." Sarah pressed her hand against the wagon and lowered her head to rest it, flattening the front of her bonnet as she did. She'd been sick twice since they'd arrived at the gathering site. She stood, wiped her mouth with the back of her hand. "I'll take William now. You dump the thunder bucket, Letitia. See if you can rinse it out too, and before you go, find me a bit of dried fruit to take this puny taste from my mouth."

Letitia did as she was asked. Or ordered.

As she was on her way to the makeshift latrine with bucket in hand, Sarah's brother shouted at Letitia to help his mother wrestle a barrel lid. No reason he couldn't help his own mother 'cept he was a man, busy dealing with man things.

"I'm tendin' Missus Bowman right now, suh." Letitia lifted the thunder bucket so he could see.

"You can do more than one thing, girl," he said, a bite to his words as he passed her by. She wasn't supposed to have priorities, or if she did, her priority was well down on anyone else's list.

Yes, she could help more than one person at a time, and did, with the two of them lifting the lid to cover the flour.

"Thank you, Letitia," Sarah's mother said. A child cried in the nested quilts in the back of the wagon. "Oh, could you watch James for a bit while I catch my breath. I declare I'm too old for this birthing." Sarah's mother had a newborn while her daughter dealt with morning sickness. The older woman sank back against the wheel.

James cooed in Letitia's arms, his mother sighed, and she heard Sarah calling for her. Here was the truth of it: Both women headed west. Both gave orders. So would everyone else. She'd be straddling freedom and different kinds of chains. Every day. They might be in new territory, but it would be with the same people bringing what they knew to wherever they were going.

⌒⌒⌒

"But you can't do that!" Sarah wailed. "I need your help, Tish. You were promised to me. And with the children and the baby coming, I have to have you along!"

"Don't harsh on me now, Miss Sarah. I have my paper and maybe this be the best time to let it speak." It was dusk and they remained at the staging area amidst the hustle of other wagons pulling in, toddlers crying, men riding from the port area where they'd all be boarding a ferry to cross the Missouri in the morning.

"Talk to her." Sarah struck at her husband's shoulder. "Make her come along."

"I don't know how she'll make it here on her own." He glared at Letitia but spoke to his wife. "These people think better of themselves than they are. My daddy did wrong freeing her afore he died. Me?" He shook his head. "I'm glad not to have the extra expense of her coming. Already have a driver I've got to wage." He sounded disgusted. "Her leaving is better all around."

"You'll have help with driving and the cattle, but I'll be on my own with the children? That isn't fair. It is not."

"You expected fair, woman?"

Sarah blushed a deep red. She cast a begging glance at Letitia and then, as though catching herself, lifted her chin, set her jaw, and said: "I will contest her paper and the court will make her come."

"No you won't." Mr. Bowman tore a plug of tobacco from the twist and pushed it into his lower lip. "We've no time for court doings, and besides, I heard my daddy say he gave her freedom. For the work she did. For her losses."

"What about my losses? What about what I'll have to suffer without her along?" Sarah stomped her foot, casting a puff of dust onto the white leather shoes.

Artemesia stamped her foot too and giggled, letting the dust puff up. The sound of the child's laughter caused an ache in Letitia's heart. Maybe she couldn't stay behind, not with the children tugging at her.

"You'll find a friend or two. Got your mother." Mr. Bowman patted his wife's shoulder. "Got to meet up with the wagon master. They'll be choosing up captains." He tweaked his daughter's chin, then turned and walked away.

"Can I go with?" Artemesia ran along beside him and he allowed the girl to join him.

Sarah turned back to Letitia, her dress with the pillars swinging over her crinolines. "Then go now. I can't abide the sight of you. I thought you cared about me and the children, I truly did. But now—just go."

"I care, Miss Sarah. I'll miss the children. I loves them like I loves my own before they taken from me. But I survive that, so I 'spect I survive this leavin' too."

"I never ever imagined you'd do this to me." She cried then, tears marking the powder on her cheeks. "Please . . ."

That root-bound knot tightened in Letitia's stomach. To be the cause of someone's sorrow was not what she'd been taught by her mother. It was not who she was and yet . . . "You're stronger than you know, Miss Sarah. I watch all your movin' from Kentucky to here. This Oregon be the biggest journey, but you got your faith and you got your chillun. You be all right."

"Just because I have my parents with me doesn't mean I'll have help. I'll be helping them out. Her baby's younger than mine!"

"Mistah Bowman right. Your sisters and mama take good care of you."

Sarah's sobbing grew louder, drawing a woman from another wagon.

The new neighbor put her arms around Sarah. "There, there. It'll be all right whatever it is this colored woman's done to bother you." She glanced at Letitia, dismissed her, and turned back to Sarah. "You come over here with me now. I've got hot mint tea brewing against this April chill. You tell me what that nasty girl did and I'll punish her myself. Here, let me help with that little one. So sweet." She reached for the baby's pudgy hands.

He tugged at his mother's skirts as the neighboring woman invited him to follow with her eyes.

To Letitia she barked, "You, girl, get on with what your mistress told you to do. Come along now, Missus—?"

"Bowman. Sarah."

She patted Sarah's shoulder. "These are such stressful times."

Letitia had no one to comfort her—but perhaps she wasn't entitled to such. After all, she'd made the decision. What right did she have to the reassurance that all would be well? It never had been well in her life except for the promise of the paper. The precious free paper. And now she had let it speak for her at last.

She untied Charity, picked up her bag and bedroll from the back of the wagon, when the woman came storming back.

"Where do you think you're going with that cow!"

Letitia stepped back. "She mine. This cow. I bought her."

"How could you earn enough for a cow? You leave her." She grabbed for the rope.

"Ask Missus Bowman."

"She's the one told me to come over here and prevent you from thieving it."

Letitia's eyes grew wide. "Sarah knows I bought her."

The woman slapped Letitia's face, the surprise greater than the sting. "Don't you use her Christian name," she hissed. "And don't you lie to my face."

Letitia stumbled back.

31

Sarah stood now and walked toward them, crossed arms over her narrow chest.

The woman asked, "Can she take the bag she's holding?"

Sarah nodded yes.

"But Charity is mine. You know that . . . Sarah." Letitia flinched, awaiting another slap, but Sarah held the woman's arm.

"Let her go," she said, eyes triumphant, bright. "But keep the cow."

3

Property Claimed

Letitia had made the right choice, but she was without Charity, her property. Still, Charity was the least of her worries. She had nowhere to go, no place to stay. She headed up the bank toward the back of the hotel. If she huddled down beside the barrels and bins of trash, she might hide herself until morning when she could talk with Mr. Bowman. He didn't want to take her or the cow anyway. Yes, that's what she'd do. Or better, wait until dark when everyone had settled down. She'd unhitch the cow and take it. It was hers. The property belonged to her. Yes. She'd rest and then return to make her claim.

Davey Carson set the half-bucket of water before Rothwell. The Carolina hound's pointy ears stood alert and straight as he lapped. Davey didn't hear the woman until she was upon him, breathless.

"Mistah Carson, suh."

He startled at the husky voice and turned. "Miss Letitia. Ain't you all chipper this morning."

"No, suh, I am not." She swallowed, caught her breath, her fingers resting against her throat.

"Something wrong with the Bowmans? They're leaving today if me memory serves?"

She nodded. "I needs your help."

He frowned. She was a comely woman with eyes the color of beaver fur, deep and soft. The woman wasn't much bigger than a shagbark twig. Sturdy enough from what Bowman said about her, though. Good in the field and in the house. "What do the Bowmans need?"

"It's what I need. I ain't goin' with 'em and Missus Bowman claims Charity, my cow."

"Does she now. Doesn't seem like one to take advantage."

"She . . . upset I decide to stay. But I can choose."

"You're free then? I didn't know."

"I choose to stay. I get work at the hotel, laundry and such, but Charity's all I got." She talked of the cow as though it were a family member on her way to dying.

He wasn't sure he wanted to get into this woman-fray, but the girl looked desperate. And he'd known the Bowmans to be good people. "Let's see what we can negotiate." He kicked manure from his boots, patted the hound. "Haven't had my morning coffee though."

"Please. They're at Capler's Landing and will board the ferry or steamboat out of Weston and my chance be lost. Charity's expecting a calf. I give that to you, in exchange for your help."

He'd bought the cow from Henry Knighton with Letitia's money a year ago. Davey didn't have a milk cow to sell when she came asking. He raised beef stock, for food. But Letitia had asked him to find her a milk cow and given him the money for it. Charity was the result.

"Not to worry about that. Let me saddle a mule and you can

ride pillion." She was so small she could sit behind him, both legs off to one side.

"I's grateful," she said. "Yessuh, I am."

He nodded. She must have walked the eight miles from Weston, dodging the patrollers last night.

She fingered the dog's ears as he saddled the mule, strapped on the pillion frame, mounted, then he pulled her up behind him. Part of him hoped no one would see them. If they thought she belonged to him, she should be walking, not riding. That was the code. But then people would also see that he treated slaves well—if they thought Letitia was his—not making her walk, and maybe the bad taste about that little minx Eliza and the court case would offer a sweeter aftertaste to consider.

"I tries to take Charity back, but guards around make it so I can't get at her."

"We'll see if we can't make arrangements." Davey always did have a sympathy for folks held in bondage.

Truth was, in the hinterlands people didn't wonder what place a woman took in a man's life because they could see how hard the women worked. Men took Pawnee wives and no one said a hoot. It was how he imagined Oregon to be, open to new ways, and why he considered going there himself, liked talking it up for others. It reminded him of those times when he'd been young and trapped distant rivers of the Missouri. But he was getting on in years. Forty-four already and Oregon was a place for young men and farmers. He was a stockman and not at all sure there were places that welcomed old men with that trade in Oregon. Farmers would be more successful, and he had an aversion to plows.

The sun was high when the hound started barking, and up ahead Davey saw a woman leading a cow, carrying a child with three younger ones plodding behind. It looked like Mr. Bowman's wife. Before he could howdy her by removing his hat and waving it, Letitia had slipped off his horse and hurried toward them, though she stopped well short, bent down, one of the children rushing to her and holding her at the waist. That gave Davey time to catch up.

"Mama says you're not going with us, Tish. Is that for certain?"

Letitia stroked the girl's hair. "Certain, yes. But we meet again one day, Artemesia, I feel sure."

"I'm not sure what I was thinking," Sarah Bowman said. She bounced a baby on her hip. She looked at Davey, not at Letitia. "I know the cow is hers and that you got it for her." She still held the hemp lead rope in her gloved hand. They'd walked a good mile; Davey and Letitia had ridden seven.

The cow licked its pink nose with its wide tongue, shook its head of the circling bugs.

"Mr. Bowman says it's not right to keep you from your property earned fair and square. And that Charity will be one more mouth to feed. I was just—"

"Disappointed." Letitia's husky voice interrupted. "I feels the same when that woman say I can't take Charity."

Sarah's eyes dropped. Letitia was so small, she looked up at the brim of Mrs. Bowman's bonnet.

"That was wrong of me." Mrs. Bowman cleared her throat. "I've had time to consider. Mr. Bowman said I'd erred." She smiled now, lightened her voice, stood on her tiptoes as though making a pronouncement. "With generosity in my heart, I gift Charity back to you." She handed her the hemp lead rope, the cow attached.

"Cow was never yours to have. And I spend the night fearin', sleepin' beside the hotel, walkin' through the night hopin' to come retrieve my property."

"Where you slept last night is not my concern. And she wouldn't be your property if we hadn't paid you for your work, so the cow is partly ours. Remember that." Mrs. Bowman didn't mention Letitia's midwife work, or maybe it didn't count in that woman's eyes.

Davey hoped the women wouldn't fire things up; the smoke between them was bad enough. He sat with his hands crossed over the pommel, reins loose in his fingers. He didn't like being witness to this sort of woman talk, but he did wonder how Miss Letitia might feel being told that Mrs. Bowman was gifting her back a cow she had no right to take in the first place. At least Letitia didn't have to sue her for it. Days in court were a waste, he'd found, even when he initiated a lawsuit, which he had a time or two. Sometimes justice demanded a courtroom, but there was never a guarantee that justice would be served in one. What people hankered for was an apology and a recognition of dignity, but they used the courtroom to get it. Miss Letitia would have no courtroom recourse, so he guessed she'd take the cow without an apology, though she deserved it.

"Looks like you've come to an amiable decision. I'm sure Miss Letitia thanks you." He didn't wait for her to respond. "I can offer you a ride back to your wagon, Mrs. Bowman. Curious about how the gathering's going. Though one of you girls will have to walk beside me. Maybe Miss Letitia would lead her cow back to . . . " He pushed his hat back, elbow akimbo. "Where are you headed with that bovine?"

The woman pursed her lips, then her face lit. "Could I keep Charity at your place, Marse Carson? That help me fine."

He didn't hesitate. "Sure enough. Might be nice to have a little milk now and then." Cow seemed to get on well with his Carolina hound too. The dog sniffed at the cow's nose, its fishhook-shaped tail high now in a gentle wag.

"Help me get Mrs. Bowman here to the pillion, would you please?"

Davey hopped down and Letitia held her hands like a cup. Mrs. Bowman stepped up, her shoes dusting up Letitia's pale palms. He reached to help Mrs. Bowman settle herself on the pillion, then he lifted the baby to her and then the younger girl, who straddled the mule. He stood back. "I believe there's room for you too, young lady." He helped the oldest girl sit behind her mother. His tan and white dog sat and scratched himself in his hinterlands, and Letitia caught the cow's lead rope before Charity wandered away.

"Good-bye, Sar—Miss Bowman." The graveled voice of Letitia

spoke. She shaded the sun from her eyes with her hand, her straw hat not being enough as she looked up. "Good-bye, my chillun." She patted the girls, looked about to cry.

Oh bare-fisted boxing, are tears going to pump out? "We best be going," he said. "Don't want your man to think something untoward has happened to his family."

"No, we wouldn't want that." Mrs. Bowman had a tinkling little laugh. Quite a contrast to the deep-as-backwater voice of the colored woman. The hound stood, ready to move. The children waved. "Take care, Letitia. Look after Charity." Mrs. Bowman's voice broke and Davey thought she must care for the woman after all. Or the cow.

He was surprised when the dog followed Letitia and her cow, leaving him to walk beside the Bowmans by himself.

Shadows

The rains continued in Missouri that spring.

"I trapped the rivers and streams winding their way to the Missouri River, when the idea of families bringing lives in trunks and wagons was the imaginings of a madman," Davey told Letitia as the two sat at the table in Davey's home, eating the evening meal of stewed rabbit. Corn pone and sorghum molasses sweetened the finish.

These were meals Letitia had cooked in Kentucky too, and she had found a ready eater in Davey, her work done in exchange for her cow's grazing and a mat on the floor in his larder to sleep on. Letitia listened in silence to Davey's Irish lilt as he spoke of 1844 as the wettest spring he'd ever witnessed. It was good that he had land on upper hills to graze his stock and, like everyone else, let his pigs run free. His house sat back from any creeks. He had a good spring for drinking water and that May they didn't even have to worry about it flowing well enough to water the cows. Water stood everywhere, brown lakes breeding mosquitoes. Davey was a chatting man full of stories.

He was an easy man to be around. Cheerful. He asked rather than ordered. Never made any move to touch her person in demand. He did small things that eased her day like fixing the coffee in the morning, burning the trash far from the house to reduce the smell.

Once he'd handed her a bouquet of beardtongue, white as a summer cloud and just as delicate.

"Thought you'd like a posy." His face burned red from the sun, or perhaps it had been a blush inching up on his cheeks, escaping his gray-tinted red beard.

"Spring bring surprises." She had dipped her face into the tiny flowers, not sure what to say next. No one had ever offered her flowers. Her children never lived long enough and their fathers weren't men who cared for the fancies of a woman. Such kindnesses made her wonder if Davey might have had a wife at one time, someone who like Letitia appreciated a gentle conversation over corn pone.

She spread butter on a biscuit as the rain came down. "I hear crossings be delayed out of St. Jo."

"A few made it before the Missouri flooded." Rain cascaded off the shake roof and formed a curtain to filter the lush dogwoods beyond. "'Spect the Kindreds and Bowmans and Gilliams and Fords are all on their way by now."

"And Robin and Polly and their three."

"Who?"

"The Ford slaves and their three children Ford didn't sell before he leave." She couldn't keep the bitterness out of her voice.

"Man has property he needs to manage." Davey spoke into his plate. "Cost money to take his own family plus a slave family of eight."

"He might have thought of that 'fore he decide to leave. Leave all of them here, give them their freedom. Instead he sell three Ford children away from their mother."

"How do you even know of this?"

Letitia shrugged. Davey had little knowledge of the chatter line across counties among colored people. She knew of the Holmeses who were part of the 1844 train because the Bowmans spoke of who was going from Howard or Platte or a dozen other Missouri counties.

"Well, they're off and I guess we'll know when a letter or two arrives extolling the glory of the trip—unless someone turns back. That's always possible. It takes quite a strength to keep going in the face of trial."

"A trial? Mistah Bowman's books say the trip like a walk down the cattle path."

"A cattle trail through desert and peaks. But we have to keep our tales light so as not to upset the fragile form."

"'Spect so," Letitia said. She smiled over "fragile form" and also how she'd picked up that shortened word "'spect" from Davey's lingo, sounding American in its clipped always-in-a-hurry way. Now and then a "bit o' the Irish" slipped into his speech, making her wonder how he endured the spit and stir-up against his people the way she did against hers. Did he do what he could to not bring attention to his Irish? He could hide his roots much easier than she could her beginnings from faraway Africa.

"Guess who I ran into today?" Davey took a drink of buttermilk. Like the Bowman children, he preferred it, he said, to coffee.

Letitia raised one eyebrow in question.

"Well, I'll tell you. Greenberry Smith."

Her hands shook as she lifted her cup of buttermilk.

"You don't know him, I 'spect." He continued to talk.

Letitia knew him. He was a patroller, prowling the roads at night to return property who'd gone beyond their owner's will. He "administered justice" on the road if the owners advanced their preferences, laying out lashes on bare backs, or worse.

Once he'd stopped her when her midwife work kept her out late. She was headed back on a moonlit trail, sweat dampening her hands. He'd come upon her with another man, both riding big, nervous horses that pranced around her.

41

"Your master know you're loafing in the moonlight?"

She fumbled at the knitted purse tied to her waist, grateful she'd stopped carrying it where she'd have to unbutton her bodice to retrieve it. She pulled the paper out, tried not to tremble as she handed it to him. "I's free."

Letitia wasn't sure if it was good there were two patrollers that night. Greenberry Smith wouldn't hurt her as there was a witness; or maybe a second man might urge the other on toward "doing their duty" to keep slavery secure.

"I seen her before," the other man said. His horse stomped, rested one back leg then another, ready to go home too. "Let her go. I got a gut ache and she belongs to the Bowmans."

"Does she now. So these free papers are forged?" She had seen the space between Smith's front teeth as he sneered into the moonlight.

"Nah. She stays with 'em. They give her those papers back in Kentucky, I hear tell."

"Pity if they were lost. She doesn't look like any free woman."

Letitia had lowered her head. *Must not speak up.*

The second patroller's horse switched its tail, danced sideways, ready to move. "Come on, G.B. Let's head out. Give her the papers."

"Don't be so hasty. I think we need to see if these are real or not. Take her in to Bowmans, if that's who you say owns her."

"No sense waking a man up in the middle of the night. She's free."

"Here, girl. Put your pretty hand up here if you want these back."

Letitia lifted her head and reached. He held the documents above her fingertips.

"Come on. Work for it."

She jumped then, her breast hitting his leg. She almost clenched the papers, but he lifted them higher, a grin on his face.

"Dance for 'em. Come on, pretty girl like you can dance, can't you?"

She jumped and he lifted the papers ever higher. She jumped, humiliation like hail pelting every inch of her skin.

"Here!" The second patroller grabbed the papers from behind

42

G.B. Smith, spurred his big gelding around, and handed them to Letitia. "Get on home. I ain't got time for this." He rode off.

G.B. stared at her for a time, then said, "Rescued. This time." He grinned at her as she trembled, trying to put her paper back inside her bag. "I'm not sure there is a greater affront to the successful commerce of a country than a freed slave. You are the epitome of that affront. Free and taking money from the hands of hardworking people. Someday, you'll have to pay." He'd swung his horse around, the animal kicking rock and dirt up onto her before taking G.B. away.

She felt tears press against her nose, shook as she wiped her face of them. She didn't know what "affront" and "epitome" meant, but the tone Smith used to spread the words out like a stream of spit told her all she needed. She'd never forgotten that night or others where G.B. Smith reigned. He was a man who forced others to stay in the shadows.

Davey scraped his cup on the wood table. Buttermilk edged his mustache, bringing Letitia back to the wet day.

"You know him personal?" She kept her voice light, chewed her biscuit slow.

"From my time in Carolina," Davey said. "He came up here after I did. So I sees him today and he says he's making plans to leave this country, head to where there's a territory and no laws yet on the books 'cept what citizens put there and a man can make something of himself without all the bad tales chasing him."

"Place don't make a man." She dipped out boiled potatoes, the steam filling her nose and prickling her cheeks with the wet.

"No? Well, a place sure enough carves him out so he finds out what kind of man he is."

"If he be a gambler and a cheat in this country, then crossin' mountains or survivin' floodin' rivers ain't likely to change him into somethin' different."

"Oh, woman." Davey sat back to make room for her serving, wiped his lip of the buttermilk.

She was aware of his closeness, could smell the soap he'd put in his hair. *Is that new?*

"He wondered how I bought a free black from the Bowmans." He poked the potato with his fork.

She felt the hair on her arms bristle and she stiffened in her serving, turned her back to him. "You told him I belongs to you?"

"I didn't correct him. I thought about it. But I figured it's safer for you if he thinks you're already claimed, don't you think?"

Was it? "He knows I free." Was it better if people believed she belonged to Davey? All she wanted to do was have a life, someday buy a place of her own, live without the fears of patrollers on the road. Was it any different having people think she belonged to Davey Carson, as when most folks assumed she belonged to the Bowmans? But Letitia didn't belong to anyone except God Almighty. Her mama had told her that too, before they parted when Letitia was ten. She told her that the Lord loved mercy, sought justice, and abided well with a humble person who didn't get too far out in front of herself, who knew how to fit in rather than stand out.

"Just so long as you know I's free."

He raised one bushy eyebrow. "Lookee, I know that. I'm grateful you board here. You're . . . good company." He cleared his throat.

"I'm choosin' to fix your meals and wash your clothes. In exchange for my cow's grazin'. That our deal." She turned back to face him.

"So it is."

He brushed crumbs from his beard that Letitia noticed he'd trimmed. *When did he start doing that?*

"One thing G.B. did make sense about was me becoming a citizen. Suggested I get papers. That way we movers can have enough people to push for a new state."

"We movers?"

"Yup. I've decided. I'm going to Oregon next year come high water or not. There were old folks in their forties who've gone. I figure I can too. You might think about what you'll do then. I'll sell my property and your cow's fine grass and won't be no place for you to bed down in my larder, either, come spring."

"Good to have advance warnin'."

"Isn't it." He grunted. He finished eating in silence. Then, "I got to be going now." He lifted his pistol from the corner, wouldn't look at her. "Be back before sunrise, I 'spect."

She walked toward the barn to milk, didn't let herself think about where he went on those evenings. He said they hunted raccoons, but he had yet to ever bring any back for her to stew. She knew the look of a man on patrol for runaway slaves or prowling for free black men showing up where a group of white men didn't think they belonged. She didn't want to think of Davey as a man like that. Instead she sat on the stool beneath Charity, annoyed that there'd be yet another change.

"Sho and he ain't never married," she told Charity. "No married man would give his woman a year notice of such a change as sellin' and headin' out." No, he was a man looking out for himself with some dangerous leanings as he patrolled the county. She was foolish to ever think otherwise.

Oregon Country

Flower Time. That's what the Kalapuya people called it. Her people. Small green shoots awoke and pushed up through the black earth. The Woman, known by the Others as Betsy, the name given her by the Methodist missionaries, dug with her *kapn*, pressing the digging stick against the slender shoots no taller than her finger. Later, her people would harvest larger bulbs found by their tall blooms bearing the purple color of morning skies. But now, her old fingers reached into the damp earth and sought out these small bulbs named *camas*. She soon filled the woven basket at her waist, walking back toward the rounded shelter to dump the roots into a larger basket made of willow and cedar root and shredded maple bark, the soft, inner bark. It pleased her to have the bulbs reappear each spring, a sign that the Creator continued to provide for them despite so many of her people dying of the aching disease seasons before.

Her old back ached from the work, but it was good work. Others would come soon and they would dig a pit together to bake the bulbs. She liked to be first in the morning, to feel the dew dampen her hide moccasins, make them squishy soft. With her strong fingers she rubbed dirt from the bulbs that were nearly as white as the skins of the Missionaries.

She returned to the shelter and lifted the tule mat off her grandson with her toes. "It is time, Little Shoot." The boy, nine summers old, groaned and rolled over. This boy was tall and strong and she must keep him so. He was her treasured little shoot, her daughter and sons all gone now. She did not dwell on their passing, noting only the scars left on her face from the illness they had died from but she survived. She cherished this child even more for his being all that was left. But she would not spoil him as her mother had spoiled her brother. No, this Little Shoot would learn to do women things as well as men things so when she was gone he could survive. Maybe he would have to teach his wife such things if she lacked a *kasa*—a grandmother—of her own to show her the way. Today they would see if the traps they'd set for fish the night before bore fruit.

The Woman wished she could remember the Kalapuyan word for grandmother. Instead she used the Chinookan, *kasa*, one of the trade words all the different tribes used that floated into her Kalapuyan ways. No matter. It was an easy word for the boy to pronounce and he used it now.

"Kasa. Look. Little Shoot traps a fish!"

"Ayee. Good. A trapped fish is good fruit."

He nodded, that smile lighting up his face before he turned to stand in the water and lift out the fish basket with the wiggling trout inside.

She'd shown him how to collect and dry the fibers for the weir basket, then how to twine two kinds of fibers around vertical sticks, shaping it into the cone. It had been their winter's work, along with her showing how to weave the mats they slept on. His mind was quick and his heart held the old ways from year to year. Soon, he would know all she had to teach him and he would have no more need of her. This was the way of things. A sadness fell upon her shoulders like a cedar cloak.

Fishing with a line was easier but took more time. When the fish ran thick as grasshoppers, the People could spear them and sometimes catch them in their arms. But a boy must know every way to catch a fish in this stream called Soap Creek by the trappers heading south. She did not remember the Kalapuya name for this Soap Creek that formed the wide valley and flowed in the shadow of a hill shaped like a white person's coffin. Or a whale. Yes, more like the whale she had seen once on the Big Water many miles away. She would rather think about the whale than the coffin. It was not time for death-thinking when she had so much to teach the child.

Once beaver dams formed pools, but trappers came and the stream flowed free. The landscape changed for the People, and The Woman remembered as best she could how it had been so she could tell Little Shoot, so he could tell his children one day when she was no longer here to tell the stories of the way.

The boy thanked the Creator for the fish and reached for a mat to lay it on, then went back to retrieve other weirs filled with fluttering fish. He passed by bushes, his hands swinging, and The Woman raised her voice to him. "Ayee, watch for the poison oak. Very bad for you. Remember."

Without turning around, he changed his path, but she could see his hand had touched the stinging shrub. "Come. Wash with the soap. Quick." How could he have been so foolish? They would make their way to the bitter springs so he could drink the healing water. *Ayee, he is yet young and still in need of his kasa to learn of dangers and the path through them.* This is a thing to remember.

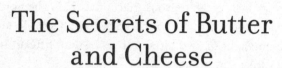

5

The Secrets of Butter and Cheese

June turned hot but Davey still chopped wood, piling it up for winter. He fixed a broken fence, reworked a gate that Rothwell had figured out how to open. He filled holes the tan and white dog dug when Rothwell rooted like the hogs for whatever he searched for in the woods. The man took long chats with neighbors, sharing stories with Letitia of a whole number of Platte County folks preparing for the journey west.

At the hotel, Letitia learned how the mistus wanted sheets cleaned and hung. She bit her tongue when the owner's wife ordered her to do her work where she wasn't seen. "Some folks don't want to sleep on linens if they know they've been touched by colored hands." In Kentucky, folks expected their slaves to do their wash. Missouri was an in-between place, especially for a free black woman.

Even if there's soap between the sheets and my hands? Letitia didn't say the words out loud, but she thought them and then chided herself for allowing the downcasts of others to turn her own good nature their way. Her touching the laundry for Davey Carson didn't displease him one bit. She'd hang on to that. But it wouldn't be so come next spring when he was gone and she was still in Missouri looking for a new place to do her wash. He had not asked her to go with him and she hadn't proposed it. She had her job. And maybe she could arrange to stay at the hotel, exchanging Charity's milk for a portion of her bed and board. She would talk to the owner that morning.

"These girls'll be taking your place, Letitia." The hotel owner stood beside the washtubs in the backyard, his body no longer blocking her sight of two girls, not more than fifteen, who sent captured smiles toward her.

"My work ain't pleasin'?"

"Your work's fine. But I bought these two at the Weston sale, so no need of you. Except for you to show them how the mistress likes things done. She's feeling poorly today. Girls," he nodded toward the two, one round as a bucket and the other thin as a mop handle, "this is Letitia."

"Who you be?"

"I'm Cora. This here's Beulah." The taller girl did the talking. "We brought from Tennessee."

"You get working, now. No idle chatter. Come by the office when you're finished, Letitia, and I'll wage you."

"Yes suh."

Cora waited until the owner had climbed the steps and gone inside before speaking again. "You free then?"

Letitia nodded. "Looks like I's free to be dismissed."

The bucket girl nodded. "Only bad thing 'bout being free I can think of."

"He treat you good?"

"He a good man. Likes things done a patterned way, but most men does."

"Amen to that." Beulah raised her eyes to the heavens and all three women laughed.

"Mistus carries a heavy stick but once you learn her ways she good."

Cora told her then about where they'd come from, sold out of a good home when their owner died. Beulah leaned in toward Letitia and whispered, "We taught to read and write, and one day we buy our way free. That how you came to be free? Earning your way?"

"I's given freedom. But I just beginnin' to earn my way."

"Best we get started." Cora spoke again. "Where you get the water from? That the woodpile for heatin' it?" She pointed with her chin. "At least we together, right, Beulah? Got someone to lean on."

In that moment Letitia longed to keep working beside them, girls who brought a lightness to their day, made do with what they'd been handed.

Letitia stopped at the owner's office, waited outside while he talked with the deliveryman bringing in pickles and wine from off the steamer. As quick as a lamb's tail her life had changed. But as the girls had said, it was a caution to being free, this unpredict-ability. Just like the slave girls, others could still make choices for your life even if you planned it out well. She had lots more ways to respond though than those girls. She vowed to make the best of it.

The owner motioned her inside his office as the drayman left.

"Hoping the mistus doing better."

The owner nodded as he pulled an envelope from the drawer.

"I's thinkin'. Maybe you still have need of butter daily. I brings it to you. Might try my hand at cheese too. Fresh is good."

The owner handed her the envelope. "No need if we get our own cow."

"That so, but then you got your girls milkin', churnin' the but-ter, and you end up with fewer hours for washin' and cleanin' and servin'."

He was thoughtful. "Bring me two pounds of butter tomorrow

and cheese as soon as it's ready. We'll see how you fare as a businesswoman. But don't tell folks, Letitia. Not everyone likes an enterprising woman, especially one who used to be a slave."

⸺◦⸻

July danced like a sultry woman, promising clear days and then ending with thunderstorms that didn't cool. The county filled with travelers like children to a picnic as more folks in wagons came from North Carolina and Kentucky, Iowa, Illinois, all talking of heading to Oregon in the spring. Davey sold beef and cord wood to them and buckets of coal as they found temporary housing to winter over. He boasted over pamphlet messages that made Oregon sound like the Promised Land.

"It's the poor market for tobacco and hemp rope bringing them this way, wouldn't you say?" Davey asked Letitia. He leaned against a fence post using a shredded twig to clean his teeth while Letitia weeded the garden she'd planted.

Fresh cabbage would be ready before long if the moles left them alone and Letitia could keep Rothwell from digging those holes he liked so well. She sold the produce along with butter and milk to the hotel. Making cheese proved a harder challenge, as she'd never done such a thing. "I's wishin' I could make cheese to sell travelers. Got enough milk."

"My older brother might know how," Davey said. "He always kept a few cows and we had cheese in Ireland, as a boy. We can seek him out, if you've a mind to."

He has brothers? Nearby?

Her earnings were but a pittance of what they'd been working at the hotel, but no one asked her to serve drinks at night and she found she liked spending more time with this man. Making cheese would add to her purse if she could do it well. And meeting Davey's brother sounded interesting. She'd see if kindness ran in the Carson blood. "Kind of you to offer."

A comfortable silence settled between them.

Then, "I do wonder what makes a man pull up roots and put wheels beneath him. Don't you, Tish?" He tossed aside his tooth-picking twig.

She wasn't sure what drew people from their homelands to the unknown, what certainty they felt compelled to set aside for the imaginations of a future believed to be somehow in a "better place." There could be no better place than where one was, and thinking there was bore a hole in a person's heart. But she supposed people could reinvent themselves, become mellow like old dogs in a new place, leave behind the recklessness of poor thinking. She'd been attempting to leave a past behind while preparing for a future, hadn't she?

Davey squatted down to tug at weeds. She must have looked surprised because he squinted up at her and said, "What? Can't a man work on the greens or is he relegated to hunting rabbits and coons for supper?"

"My mama said never turn down a helpin' hand."

"Your mama's a wise woman."

"Was."

Later that evening Davey blistered his hand on the hot kettle he'd set on the stove to heat so she could wash up the dishes. He yelped like a dog.

"Here." Letitia soothed the pain with a poultice of slippery elm she'd brought with her from Kentucky. She ran the salve over his hand with her own, aware of the wound heat and the cool of the poultice.

"Now that's a mighty help." Davey laid his good palm atop hers.

It was the first time he'd ever touched her 'cept for helping her onto the pillion. A candle flickered over their hands and Letitia allowed the calloused fingers to cluck like a hen's feathering safety over hers. No demand. No expectation like some men she'd served. She couldn't remember the last time she'd felt a man's touch without a hint of harm. Letitia let Davey's hand cluck for a bit, then she pulled back. Davey didn't grab her wrist nor persist. Instead he coughed, thanked her for the poultice, and didn't look into her eyes for some days after that.

Davey watched Letitia move through the shanty shack he'd built with his own hands, fixing supper. Her hips swayed as she brought molasses from the larder, her slender frame belying the strength he'd seen as she chopped wood or weeded the garden for hours on end. She kept herself tidy and smelled of lavender and coconut, though he didn't know why. She never complained, said more than once she was grateful for his letting her and the cow stay. What she didn't say but he suspected is that she felt safe with him. He wasn't sure she should feel that way. If she knew what he'd done on patrol—picking up colored men and under orders lashing them to within an inch of their lives for being someplace where the patrollers didn't think they should be—well, if she knew that, she might not put him on a safe shelf. But he had never pushed her to treat him like he owned her. G.B. Smith was one who assumed he'd taken advantage of her and would think him a dolt for not having done so.

There was something about her that kept him from assuming she'd stay if he tried to bed her, and he realized he didn't want her to go. On Sundays he felt a twinge of emptiness, like drinking the last drop of a good cup of coffee, when he watched her walk down the road to the Baptist Negro church. She stayed later to sing, she told him, when the slaves were allowed. He didn't fill up again until he heard her swaying down the lane singing in that husky voice of hers. He liked her cooking and, yes, her kindness, the way she tended women in their birthing. He didn't want to lose any of this comfort he'd found in her presence.

"What you lookin' at, Mistah Carson?"

"Meself? Oh, nothing." He leaned back in the hickory chair.

"Don't you harsh on me, now." She teased him with smiling eyes. He would like to bed her one day, but he suspected she'd want it done proper and that couldn't be, the laws being what they were. No colored could marry a white man. Seemed a shame to him, that separating for no good reason. Her heart appeared to be the same color as his. He rose and went out to talk to the dog. He'd have to make sure he kept his distance yet stay close enough to ensure she didn't go away.

≈∾

The August heat made her skin hot to the touch. She sat outside mending a tear in her tow linen, the frogs chirping their opinions that no one listened to. Charity had dried up getting ready to calve, so they'd made the trip north to see Davey's brother about cheese. She thought of that trip now, how Davey had spoken so little of the years between their meeting, how his brother had grunted at the sight of him and said in passing how disappointed he was in Davey for "doing like you did."

"I'm here now. Wondering if you'd advise me on cheese-making. Got meself a neat cow giving milk enough for butter and cheese."

Letitia hadn't corrected him about who owned the cow. Getting the information was what mattered.

And Smith Carson had shared what he knew, spoke of how to use the fourth stomach of a cow when butchered, how to dry the rennet in strips, and how much to use for each batch of cheese. What they ate of Smith's cheese was tasty. Letitia thought she could experiment with salt and maybe herbs, and would.

"Brought your slave along, I see."

Smith was a bigger man than Davey. He looked older than his years and not well, his skin the color of dusk. His own slave—she thought it was his slave—brought cooled water for them after they'd finished with instructions. The man looked into Letitia's eyes as he served her sitting on the steps while the men rocked on the porch above. She felt sorrow and guilt.

"She'll do the cheese-making so figured she should see it first-hand."

"Hope she's got a better memory than yours, little brother. You're prone to forget important things."

"I've got confidence in her."

Letitia heard tension in their words, wondered what important things Davey had misplaced, what eelish darkness slithered beneath the surface of this family. Or any family. They'd left with Smith giving Davey two sizes of firkin, wooden barrels in which to transport the cheese. They smelled of salt and scalded milk.

"Ouch!" Letitia poked herself with her sewing needle. She was back on Davey's porch, still listening to the frogs talk.

Charity decided to calve in the heat, starting late afternoon. "It's a good time of year," Davey told Letitia. "Calf'll be strong to get through the winter without trouble." But the cow labored well into the night, and even after the calf dropped to the hard ground, the afterbirth hung from the mother.

"'Spect we'd best get Charity up and tend to that," Davey said.

They stood outside the rail corral, Davey swinging the lantern to circle the light. Charity licked her newborn in spurts, bellowing as she swung around, mucous and blood staining her legs these hours after giving birth. The calf stood and sucked, a good sign, but Charity didn't allow him enough time before she began prancing and pacing. Davey moved then to tie up the cow that resisted being led into the barn. The calf straddle-legged its way behind its mother, bleating like a lost kitten. Letitia followed them inside.

The work was messy with warm hands inside the cow feeling what to pull and what to push back in. Charity shifted on her legs, turned and twisted but then tired, and Letitia and Davey accomplished what they'd set out to do, watched as the calf sucked.

Yellow streaks of sunrise greeted them when they washed up side by side at the wooden stand outside the house, splashing water up to their elbows from the tin bowl, blood staining the water red. Letitia handed Davey a towel. She could hear Rothwell digging and yelping his rabbit cry in the woods behind them.

"Thank you." She kept scrubbing. "Good to have help."

"'Spect so." He cleared his throat, leaned against the porch post while still wiping his upper arms, sleeves rolled up. "I know there's no way of marrying ye," he said.

"What?" Moisture formed on her upper lip. "Are you harshin' on me?" She kept her back to him, hands deep in the washbowl. She fingered a chipped place at the bottom.

"Lookee. I know there's no way of legally marrying ye, you being colored. But I wish there was. I know I'm old as those bluffs up there, but I feel a younger man around you. Able to get things done, and it's good to have a woman noticing that a man is still accomplishing. Things."

She turned toward him, hands trembling.

"Oh, I've scared you. Didn't mean to do that." He handed her the towel he'd used.

She knew her eyes must look like chestnuts in cream. Her life with him had been an easy comfort, but now . . . *Maybe I should have gone west with the Bowmans.*

"Mistah Carson—"

"I'm Davey to you." He cleared his throat, rushed into her hesitation. "I know that on the plantations a Negro man has to ask permission to take a wife, and then there's all the talk about the 'issue' and who that child will belong to, the owner of the man or the mother's master."

Letitia stood still as a rabbit with a hawk hovering above. She was startled by his awareness of what humiliation it was for a man to risk the loss of his children once they were born. Every man wanted to protect his wife and children, didn't he? She swallowed, kept wiping her arms though they were dry as tinder.

"That ain't much of a way for a man or a woman to live. In the territory, here, before the Platte Purchase had good, principled people living in it, marriage came by, well, someone saying good words over a man and his Pawnee wife or a senorita he brought up from old Mexico. No priests or pastors around. Just like it

57

ain't allowed here, being as how you're . . . and I'm . . . well, our . . . we're different."

It was the longest span of speech Davey had ever made to her. He wasn't finished.

"I don't know what it would take for you to feel married to me. Be easier to keep you safe in Oregon if you and I . . . belonged to each other."

She turned, raised that eyebrow.

"Lookee here." He tugged on his beard. "In Oregon you'd not have to worry about folks questioning your status, free or . . ." He looked away.

"You can say the word, Mistah Carson."

He wagged his finger in front of a smile that showed a broken eyetooth.

"Davey," she agreed to call him. "You can say 'slave.' I ain't one, though I was, and yes it tainted who I is, but I's free, always was even when owned. Free in my thinkin'. Free as a child of God."

"Consider my proposal then, free-thinking woman." He gave a high-pitched laugh that she hadn't heard before.

He's nervous. It made her face grow warm. "Your proposal? Your offer."

"Call it what you will. I offer my name if you choose it, free and clear and a promise to be your husband as best I can. God willing." He cleared his throat. "Think on it, would you? I gotta go chop more wood."

Letitia watched him walk away. He tripped on the step, caught himself. She grabbed her straw hat and headed for the hotel with spring-cooled butter and a basketful of thoughts burdening her narrow shoulders.

Later that day while she heated the tub of steaming water to wash linen sheets, she thought of Davey's offer. There was no love in it, but kindness. And shelter and safe-guarding, which might be stepping stones to something deeper. His power didn't rain down like hail. He'd been generous in allowing the exchange of her work and a place to sleep in return for the grazing and had not taken any money from her milk and butter, kale and carrot sales to the hotel. He'd been fair with her. Just. That too was a stepping stone to love, wasn't it? She had not loved her children's two fathers. They'd taken her. Later one sold his own child away from her. Nathan had died so young, and God forgive, at least she didn't have to see him grow to be beaten or sold.

She sank the laundry stick deep into the blob of cloth, the hickory bent with the weight. Was child-bearing a part of his offer? He hadn't said. She should be pleased enough that he proposed marriage rather than assuming she was his for the taking. And he did ask her opinion of things, which she described as a kind of respect, something else she thought necessary for love to follow. And who was she anyway to assume love would be a part of any pairing in her life. It had not been a part of her mother's. Love was a dessert. Not everyone was blessed with such earthly sweetness.

She wished she had a woman to talk to. The pastor's wife at the Baptist church who braided her hair, she might lend an ear. But subverting the law by acting married rather than owned could put those who knew of it in trouble. She hung the sheets on the line, thought of Sarah Bowman as the wind snapped the wetness against her face. Sarah would curl her nose up at the very idea of matching a white man to a colored woman and sniff at the thought there could be love between them. There'd been plenty of white men who took wenches; they could never be joined in God's eyes. But if love was there, then couldn't such a marriage one day be? Marriages were arranged all the time by owners and sometimes love flourished. Look at Robin and Polly Holmes. They'd been mated by a master but love grew where only commerce had been intended and they'd had six children together. She wondered how they fared on the trail to Oregon, how they must have grieved leaving their three children behind. But their owner had promised them freedom if Robin helped him prove up his Oregon claim. The promise of freedom could be a balm to grief. It would be a balm to uncertainty too.

Letitia pressed wooden pins over the sheet corners. Birds chirped and she heard a playful bark of Rothwell among the trees.

If she accepted Davey's offer, they'd head west. If she stayed, she'd have an uncertain road. Even though she earned money, she'd never be able to purchase his farm and have the safety of a shelter of her own, not in Missouri. Not in any slave state. Maybe one day somewhere free. And G.B. Smith would haunt her if she walked the roads at night. She'd heard of men carrying free papers who had been kidnapped, sold, the patrollers keeping the coins after destroying the papers and sending the free black into slavery. But in Oregon Davey could find new land. If he was a citizen. Maybe she could get free land too? She scoffed to herself at that. She'd always be at the mercy of people who saw *her* as property rather than her being able to *buy* property. If she bought another cow she'd have to get someone to buy it for her, as no one would trust that she hadn't stolen the money.

She was left with the next best path: having a say in what she cared about and deciding how she'd challenge any threats to that hope. Maybe those were the choices any human had, free or not.

Cleaving

Davey chopped at weeds threatening the borders of Letitia's garden. It had been a spur-of-the-moment comment to offer her an arrangement, one his fellow patrollers would scoff at. "Take the wench," they'd tell him. Assumed he already had, likely. But Tish had a presence about her, a dignity and calm. She deserved to have respect. He wasn't much of a planner. Being in Carroll Township inside Platte County raising stock was the most settled and organized he'd ever been, and he found the work less burdensome with the woman beside him. She held a steady hand, didn't faint or falter at the sight of blood or bind like most women he encountered. And she wasn't a minx like that Eliza either. *I did not hurt that girl.*

The hoe snagged a rock as he chopped and he felt the vibration through the wooden handle clear to his clenched jaws. He stopped to rest, removed his floppy hat, and wiped his forehead of the August heat. If she agreed, what could he do to make it official-like, he wondered? No minister of the Word would allow it. He might get a lawyer sympathetic to the abolitionist cause to speak some legal words to satisfy the woman. And himself for that matter. He didn't want this arrangement to be a toss in the straw. He wanted to know she'd stand with him during planting and harvest, work beside him splitting logs and raising them to roof, and, God willing, bear his children. He didn't want to have to chase her down if she took off running. Maybe he should seek out someone now. That way she'd know that he was making it as respectful as possible. Yes, that's what he needed to do.

He put up the hoe, washed his face and arms before heading out to Platte City. Here he was, planning ahead. Why, the woman had already changed his ways.

Letitia walked the path to the colored church, a tiny clapboard building recently washed white as piano keys. She'd helped pay for the stain herself, being one of the few who attended who had a little money to spare. After the service she would speak to the pastor, an old Negro man who had seen the worst of things before he got his freedom. He told his people more than once how the Lord had led him to Platte County, to open this little church in an abandoned chicken coop, and lo, here they all were years later singing and praising, the smell of chickens feathered into the walls forever.

"Oh, no, no, Miss Letitia. That'd be a dangerous thing for you to do." She and the pastor stood out under a spreading oak tree, moving the heat with chicken-feather fans. "Folks find out about it and arrest you for illegalities." He paused. "Is he a good man, Sister? There was that incident with Sister Eliza and he does patrol . . ." He let his voice trail into the unspoken.

"He been nothin' but good to me, Preacher. Allowin' me shelter and sharin' his food. That and doin' the Lord's work. Lookin' after widows and orphans as I's both."

The old man patted her hand. "Not safe—though I think the Lord would abide it, love being foremost in our Savior's heart.

But I wouldn't want the sheriff pressing either of you saying you broke the law."

"We be common law then? No word from God to bless us?"

"Best people think you belong to him but not as husband and wife. Safer that way. The two of you would know. The Lord would know. That's enough."

"Is it?"

It felt unsettled, like she was giving up something of herself to accept the proposal without the hope of God's blessing on it. Wouldn't it risk the future, being with a man without the words uniting them? She was free, neither belonging to nor the property of a father, brother, husband, or son. She wanted to stay that way, but she also wanted what binding together brought: safety, laughter, lives entering the world and strengthened inside a family. Especially if they headed west to the unknown. Others might never see her as his wife, even if they had the preacher's words said over them. But still, she'd like to know that was how the Lord saw their union.

⟨~⟩

"I agrees to your offer." They stood in the barn, watching the calf suck.

"My proposal? You do?" Davey leaned back, wanting to look at her. She had a profile as chiseled as the statues that graced the courthouse hall. He liked how she pulled her hair back away from her face in those long braided rows, leaving her high forehead clear and a lamb's frizz at her temples. She turned to him, lips plump as berries eased now into a smile; a nose rounded and promising to be as soft as a lamb's ear. Her brown eyes glistened, looking deeper surrounded by that pure white.

"Yes, I's willin' to become Letitia Carson. But I likes it to be . . . official."

He nodded. "I spoke to the solicitor, the one who handled the Eliza case." He frowned. *Why did I bring that up?* "He says we shouldn't worry over words. Say them myself maybe? And you say them too." He pushed away hay scratching at his back in the manger. "Or maybe that preacher you hear on Sundays. Would he?"

"We had words but he say no."

She was serious if she brought it to her preacher friend.

"He say it would be . . . would put me at risk. Maybe you too if folks think we breakin' the law. Even though God's law don't say no to it—God findin' it merciful to have people cleave to each other for all time."

"Funny, that word," Davey said. "Used to puzzle myself as a boy told to cleave the bogs of their fuel for our stove. Cleave is a sticking and splitting word. It's the sticking that the Bible speaks of." He suggested again, "We could speak the words ourselves."

She nodded.

She didn't seem too certain, but he'd move ahead before she changed her mind. "Good idea. What about Saturday next?" He clapped his hands. "Charity can be our witness."

Letitia frowned. He had wanted to lighten her mood, but instead his words robbed the occasion of gravity. He cleared his throat. "God will be our witness." He touched her elbow crossed over her narrow chest. "He'll see to it that we're never cleaved apart."

They planned for it on a Saturday in late August so she could still go to church the next day and none would be the wiser that she was now Letitia Carson. Yellow tickseeds bloomed along the roadway to Davey's house, and in the woods he found surprise lilies, their pale purple like a winter sunrise. He picked a few, wishing the butterfly weed with its splash of orange might bloom, but the milkweed held a hint of a later flower. It would have to be enough. He carried the posies in his wide palm. Funny what women liked. Truth was, he liked flowers too, and he held the bouquet to his nose. He wished in a way that there could be human witnesses. Letitia was a good woman and she might have liked to have a friend or two along. Maybe she had none, though that didn't seem right, her being so generous and kind. People were attracted to traits like that just as stockmen wanted good beef-to-bone ratios.

Now why was he comparing his intended to a good cow? He shook his head. At least he hadn't said it out loud to Letitia and he'd be sure he wouldn't when he handed her the flowers.

⎯⎯⎯⎯⎯ ⁓ ⎯⎯⎯⎯⎯

Davey read her the actual words from the Bible he took from the cupboard. Leathered with stains, he said he'd brought it from Ireland when he came as a lad. His mother died on the crossing and his pa never recovered, giving himself to drink, leaving his boys and one girl to fend for themselves. He pointed to the names in the Bible, of his sister, married now, and his brothers back in North Carolina. "'Cept for my older brother Smith."

"Met him." She ran her fingers over the name of Carson most real to her besides Davey. Davey had been the one to branch out, was ready when the Platte Purchase opened in 1837. He left the mountains and streams of North Carolina, settling into stock-raising. Somehow the Bible had come to his hands and he'd kept it well, considering the weather he'd carried it through. His voice held pride that he was the keeper of that family book. Letitia listened as he read the words she couldn't. She'd like to learn, but there were laws against teaching slaves, and after she was freed there were other things needed doing besides making sense of the scratches on paper. But now, it would be nice if she could read what Mistah Bowman's paper said about her freedom; and it would be good to read for herself the words in the Bible that Davey Carson said she was to repeat. She had a good memory for words. They practiced them together days before the event.

"So are you ready then. To marry meself?"

"'Spect so." She watched him smile, his lips surrounded by that fading red mustache. Looking at him made her face grow warm. She wore her best tow linen and fitted herself with a crocheted belt that showed her small waist. She'd asked the pastor's wife to part her hair in the middle, making tight twists, but had kept a braided strand to form a small medallion-like cluster centered at her forehead. The pastor's wife asked no questions about the ornate hairdo or her plan, but Letitia figured the pastor and his wife had few secrets between them. The rest of her rinsed hair she pulled back tight into a knot at the back, smoothing it with her coconut mixture. She'd bought a ribbon at the Weston store and worked it into a bow at the top of the cascading braids.

"I brought these for you." Davey handed her a blush of colors, his face a little pink as he did. "And may I say you're looking, well, like a woman should on her wedding day."

Her eyes dropped to the tips of his polished boots. "Thank you." She took the flowers. "I puts them in a jar."

"I've something else for you too." He handed her a pewter cowbell with a hawthorn leaf engraved on the side.

It was cool to the touch. Letitia shook the bell, liking the clanking sound. She turned it upside down and put the flowers into it. Her fingers rubbed the hawthorn engraving. "'Spect this'll work." She walked to the pump and filled it with water.

Davey said, "Are we ready now?"

"Yes, Mistah Carson. Davey."

"You remember the words?"

"I 'member."

He cleared his throat, took a deep breath as they heard the jingle of a bell from the road. The tinker's bell jangled, the man in his cart with buttons and bows and pots and pans making his monthly stop to sell to ladies of the house. He waved his hat at them, jostling the two curls that framed his face and stopped just at his jaws. The single horse carriage rolled forward. Rothwell barked, then wagged his tail in greeting, recognizing the man.

"May I water my horse at your spring?"

"You may, Aaron," Davey said.

Letitia took the bridle and led the horse to the trough as Aaron jumped down.

"And what's the occasion?" Letitia heard him ask. The old tinker had endured his own brand of abuse but was no slave and had never been, though his people had. Still, Letitia wished he'd move on. If there were no witnesses, the law wouldn't ever touch them. She walked back toward the men. "Pretty posies whatever the call for them. Nice little vessel you have too. Looks like it's engraved."

"It is," Davey said. "We've no need of trinkets today, but you're welcome to water the horse, then be on your way."

"Aaron Moshe doesn't intend to barter when there's an occasion presenting itself." He nodded toward Letitia. "A bride?"

Letitia swallowed, her throat dry as a corn husk. What would Davey say? *He should let the comment sink into the August heat.*

"Truth is, she intends to be one. A wife for myself."

No, no. But then the thought: a witness other than the dog would bring weight to the words. And he wouldn't likely tell others, why would he? "Well now." He looked around. "Moshe sees no preacher. But then, that's not going to happen, now is it."

Letitia's heart thumped like a butter churn. Would Moshe let the sheriff know of their breaking the law? She looked to Davey. Could he keep her safe? He'd risked their safety with his blurting out their plans. *Make the best of troublin' times.* Rothwell bumped his head up against Letitia and she petted the dog, glad for the comfort. "Maybe you see yourself officiatin' us today, suh?" Jews read Davey's book too, didn't they?

The man moved his head back as though accepting a remarkable thought.

And so on a hot day in August, David Carson once of Ireland took Letitia once of Kentucky to be his wife. Davey told the tinker the words about honoring each other, staying together in the hard times, caring for each other, and cleaving unto each other under God's watch, not letting any others nose their way in. Davey spoke them, holding the Bible, then Moshe repeated the words for Letitia, her hands quivering on the worn leather. She was glad he was there. For while she had memorized the promises, the moment flustered her. Then Moshe added words of blessing, about not allowing men to split them.

"We need a proper ending," Moshe added. He trotted to his carriage store. "Moshe has it, hold on. It's right here."

Letitia looked at Davey, who winked at her. She lowered her head, but Davey lifted her chin, his gaze making her chest tighten.

"Ah, here it is then. Let's add another tradition, shall we?" He placed a glass goblet on the ground. "Now then. No canopy, but you, Davey, stomp on it. Breaking the Jewish wedding glass is yours to do."

Davey laughed.

"Why he do that?"

"Oh, any number of reasons. That your children will be as many as the shards and your happiness also. Or that you will remember the temples destroyed in Jerusalem. And the one Moshe prefers, that the glass is fragile as is love, and marriage must be carefully cared for and never broken but in death. Go ahead." He motioned with his hands.

Davey shrugged and stomped the crystal that did shatter to a hundred shards.

"Mazel tov!" the tinker shouted, raising his hands, startling the horse who lifted its head and shook the bit and reins, and that got Rothwell to howling. "You may kiss the bride. And may the broken glass be a reminder that while you cleave together as one, the world is still broken and will always need mending."

7

Precious Promises

It was the first kiss of her husband. His mouth was soft, his lips thin but moist; his whiskers bristled against her lips and cheek when he nuzzled her. A warmth formed inside that flowed to her toes and back up, settling at her heart.

Davey stepped away.

"Moshe best be traveling."

"Lookee, let me pay you for the crystal and your blessings."

"Consider them a gift." Moshe grinned. "But I would join you for a wedding meal, if you'd planned one."

Over food they spoke of festive things—weddings the tinker had attended in Pittsburgh before coming west, though he said this was the first time "Aaron Moshe has officiated at one." Letitia served beef sliced from the smoked roast hanging in the larder. Fresh greens and beans from her garden, berry jam she'd put up. Buttermilk. Then she brought out a black raspberry pie with fresh cream she'd sugared with slivers of maple from the cone.

"You have made a good match, Mr. Carson. Mrs. Carson is a rare and opulent cook."

"I don't know what that means, but I'll take it as a compliment. On my wife's behalf." Davey raised a fork full of pie toward Letitia. "To the opulent cook."

Letitia didn't know what the word meant either, but it seemed to fill Davey's face with gladness, a sight that helped reduce the nervousness for what she knew would follow once the tinker left.

⁂

Moshe drove his carriage rattling down the lane. "I suppose I should have told him he could bed down for the night in the barn if he wished, but I was hoping to have my wedding night with my wife, alone."

Letitia lowered her eyes. She had never felt this fluttering of her stomach with the fathers of her children, but then she'd never been given the choice to have them either. She was sent to those men to enhance the owner's arsenal of labor. It had struck her as unusual; she was not a big woman and she found the taller, larger slave women produced bigger babies with less trouble, children who grew to be strong men and tall women. She didn't know how big Nathan might have been if he had lived. His father was tall. But Jeremiah, at five, when he'd been sold, sprouted up tall as a possum haw holly. But perhaps her masters did recognize that she could reason well, worked hard, fit in, and didn't carry anger around like a hot coal always burning. The gift of a marriage to someone she had chosen and who was kind enough to bring her flowers and break the wedding glass was more than she could have hoped for. There was a Bible verse about blessings being shaken down and pressed together. Today, she'd experienced it.

Davey walked up beside her on the porch. A warm dusk settled like a shawl around her shoulders, and she remembered a custom of her people with a quilt wrapped around a wedding couple as they jumped the broom together. She'd seen it done, a happy leap.

Her mother had told her it was an African tradition. She stepped inside, grabbed the broom, and the two jumped it, laughing.

"You know we won't be able to tell folks that we're married." Davey caught his breath.

"I knows."

"But I will treat you as though we are."

She'd been thinking about something all day. "We could have a contract, separate from the marriage."

Davey raised his eyebrows.

"I agrees to stay with you, to help you along the trail next year and build our land claim. Clear brush, cook, do your laundry." She didn't say *bear your children*. "I's your wife so no need to pay me. In return, you agrees to take care of me and if something happen to you, you say whoever ask whatever property you have, you leave to me. And to your sons and daughters, if we have any . . ." She looked away then. They'd never discussed children.

He plucked at his beard. "That I could do."

"And you would put that onto paper, that I could keep? And sign it, with your name?"

"I could do that." He was removing the bow at the back of her hair, sending his fingers down the sides of her cheek.

He didn't say he *would* sign such an agreement, but Letitia feared to push him too far at that moment, when they were just beginning and she'd done nothing for him yet.

"Then we agree. Together we plan for Oregon. You and me."

He moved closer to her, ran his thumbs over the medallion of braid in the center of her forehead while his wide hand held her chin steady. "I like the way you braided this little piece. It's like a tributary finding its own way out of the river of your hair." His hand was on the back of her head now, his palm warm. She could smell the coconut-honey mixture smoothing her hair. "'Spect the larder cot isn't needed anymore, wouldn't you say, Mrs. Carson? That is, if you'd care to share my bed."

"I would." She liked being asked. And when he tugged at her

ribbons and led her toward his chest, his mouth bending to cover hers . . . she let him lead her forward.

❧

She lay awake with the August moon shimmering as on a lake but through thin curtains. Davey snored beside her, contented, as was she. Who would have thought she might find joy in this cleaving together. She would discover more about this man she knew, but for now she could rest on his words of promise, like the vows they'd spoken. She had even said she'd obey him, but he had later assured her that he did not think of her as a slave needing obedience but as a wife wishing to please her husband just as he hoped to please her. This promise was respectful, new.

She tried not to wake him. She would gather new straw for this bed as they had both rolled into the impression his body had made through the years, sinking like a hammock in the middle. Straw stems broke down over time. She'd find the bed key and tighten the ropes as well. Now there were two of them and this bed needed *adjustin'*. She smiled. Like every other part of her life, she supposed, now that she had a husband.

He had surprised her with his tender loving. They whispered of where they'd come from, sent fleeting words of memories they cherished and dreams that might help them soar. Davey talked to her, told how he hated the patrolling and found discomfort with the men who didn't. She shared her greatest losses, her sons, and he assured her between soft kisses and his thumb stroking her cheeks that this would never happen under his watch. And with those intimacies of the heart shared, their bodies had folded together like the wings of a great bird wrapping itself around its young.

In the days that followed, she cooked outside during the hot month, and over meals they ate on the plank table carried out onto the porch, giving them an evening breeze. Davey told more tales of his trapping and trading times, mixed with some brief memories of his father and a sweet mother and his brother named Smith he rarely saw. Letitia talked of her midwifing, how grateful she was when she heard the cry of life. She gave him efforts of her cheesemaking, asking his opinion. She didn't tell him of the longing that she might still like a child of her own, born to a free woman.

Summer turned itself into the colors of fall, and Letitia dried vegetables and fruits, saving seeds, planning now for the trip they'd make next spring. Davey looked over his stock, choosing the seven steers he'd train to the yoke. He had thirteen loose head they'd drive west. In the cold months he planned to butcher beef and the hogs, which they'd smoke to preserve. He'd cure tobacco for trade. Davey tapped a pipe now and then but didn't chew, and Letitia told him she was glad for that. "I disliked cleanin' the spittoons at the hotel." She shivered in disgust.

Letitia sewed, making pantaloons for Davey and buying calico for shirts with her earnings. At night, she knit stockings and socks. For herself she bought wool and flax, planning on two dresses which Davey assured her was all she'd need for the trip. She'd use her tow dresses until then, and wear layers of petticoats she could tear into rags for bandages and for her monthlies along the way. She wasn't much of a seamstress. She knew that. But on Saturdays she carried the wool Davey got for her from a neighboring farm to the pastor's house, and with his wife they'd spin and weave and stitch. The subject of her relationship with Davey was never raised, the silence expected. It was safer that way. Letitia did wonder if she'd find someone to stitch with once they reached the territory and if she'd ever be able to share the musings of wives with another. Perhaps she would be alone always, even with a husband she couldn't claim in public. But his actions toward her carried love like a gentle breeze and he could keep her safe. That was what mattered.

～⁓～

Letitia found the box not much wider than her palm behind the boardinghouse stable. Should she ask if she could take it? It was in the junk heap with old wheels, frayed rope, a broken crock pot, and other miscellaneous discards. Already someone decided it was worthless. She could take it and not be in trouble, couldn't she? Moisture settled on her upper lip. Sometimes gifts arrived, her mother had told her, and one must learn to receive. Her dismissal at the hotel had been a gift in the end, giving her more time to prepare for the journey. This little box was a gift too. She would go to the blacksmith who repaired wagons and reworked wheels. He'd have a small piece of lumber already smoothed. She'd use that for the false bottom and her papers would be safe. When Davey wrote out his promise to care for her and leave any property to her, she'd put that paper there with her free papers. Now she was set to head West.

∽

In late September, someone pounded on their door. Letitia slipped out of their cot into the larder and dressed while Davey answered the knock in his underdrawers. She heard a boy's nervous voice. "Samuel Hawkins. My mother's giving birth and something's not right. She sent me to find my father. He's a doctor. He's out on a call west of here. Can you try to find him? I got to get back to Mother."

"I'll take meself to look. But my . . . Tish, here, she can help. She does midwifing."

The boy didn't hesitate. "Thank the Lord. Come along."

Letitia grabbed a bag with needles and thread, one of her candlesticks and a candle, clean rags and lantern, and followed him into the night, rushing behind as the boy mounted and began riding out, then stopped. "Quick now," he said motioning for her to hurry and take his hand up onto the horse. "We'll be faster by two."

The pungent scent from the smokehouse punched the air. Letitia rode behind him straddling the tall horse with an easy gait. She kept her bag between the boy's back and her belly. The Hawkinses weren't far from Davey's cabin, but the moon failed to assist in their travel. Letitia guessed a half hour had passed before he reined the horse into a lane leading to the Hawkinses' cabin and doctor's clinic with a large rimmed wagon parked beside a small barn. Letitia stepped up onto the porch. The door opened and several sets of eyes belonging to steps of children lined the door as she entered.

"Ma's done this afore, as you can tell," the boy said.

He spoke gently to his brothers and sisters, a lilt to his words that reminded Letitia of those betters she'd left behind in Kentucky.

"You from Kentucky." Letitia said it as she moved through the room.

"Pa is, by way of Iowa." He directed her toward the bed off to the side of the loft ladder.

She stooped to meet Mrs. Hawkins. She felt more than saw the children form a half circle around her at the foot of the rope bed. A colorful quilt with pieced circles was stark contrast to the woman's pale face. She lifted the woman's hand and squeezed. Mrs. Hawkins gave a weak tug and a smile formed on her sweat-stained face.

"Let's light this lavender candle." Letitia handed the nubby stick from her bag to the tallest girl who looked to be around nine. "Put it in that holder I brought. The scent can soothe and help your mama relax. She be workin' hard."

The girl curtsied and said, "Yes, ma'am."

"I's Letitia. " She patted Mrs. Hawkins's hand. "I helps a few arrive jus' fine. From the looks of your good family here, you know more than I does but maybe together we bring this baby to your arms."

Mrs. Hawkins nodded, then gasped. "Pains are pretty fast and sharp. They last. Very . . . different. You couldn't find your father?"

The boy shook his head. "Her man is out looking for Pa. I thought it best to bring her back to help. I'll go looking now myself."

The child set the candle with the sweet scent and Letitia placed it beside the bed on a chair pulled up there.

"That's Maryanne what brought the light," a narrow-faced child told her. She wore the same pale hair as all the girls. "I'm Martha. I'm seven already. That there is Laura. She used to be the baby and she's still puny as one. And this'n here is Edward." She bounced the boy on her small hip. "He's two."

"Grateful for all your good tellin', Martha." Letitia turned to the woman on the bed. "Now, Missus Hawkins, let's see if we can get this baby born."

"Nancy. Please. Call me Nancy." She reached out for Letitia's hand and bent forward in pain, crushing Letitia's fingers. But Letitia knew that having a hand to squeeze would help.

"I've got to do this," Nancy panted. "For goodness' sake, your father can't go to Oregon without me."

⁓

It was dawn before the sound of a baby's cry rang through the log cabin. Letitia had been able to turn the infant. Her small but strong hands proved an asset as a midwife and the salve she brought eased the child's arrival. Such a pleasure to see the baby squirm with its pinched face and wearing a cap of pale dandelion fuzz. Nancy Hawkins lay awake but exhausted, the baby swaddled in the crook of her arm as the sun came through the ripples of the glass window. "This is my last. Such a trial you gave us, Miss Nancy Jane!" She looked up at Letitia. "Thank you, Miss . . . I've forgotten your name."

"Letitia. I'm Letitia . . . Carson."

The infant, tiny as a rabbit, arched its back, discomfited.

"She don't like the blanket." The puny child, Laura, spoke. "Me neither. Makes me itch." The girl wiggled like a snake slithered down her back.

"You be right. You have a cotton cloth?"

"Here." Laura held up a doll quilt with a satin border sucked of its color. "It's my smell."

"Thank you, Laura. Your name be Laura?"

The child gazed at the quilt as though it was sugar. She'd been awake most of the night while the other children had wearied and climbed the loft to sleep and were now bustling down the ladder.

She had a purple bruise as though she'd dropped something heavy on her forearm.

"Let's see if Nancy Jane like it better."

The baby did soothe with the change of cloth. "She may be one who has special keepins. Seen those. Feet hot when others' are cold. Sun harshes on their eyes. They have finicky bellies too."

Nancy laughed. "That all sounds like me! Poor child. I hope she doesn't get my persnickety ways."

Men filled the room then. A man Letitia recognized as Doc Hawkins and Samuel, the messenger, arrived with Davey close behind.

"Ah, Nancy." Dr. Hawkins sighed. "I'm so sorry. Mrs. Johnson had a hard delivery. And you . . . you weren't even in labor when I left."

"I know it. She just arrived. A bit sooner than expected but she's here. Thanks to Miss Carson here. Letitia."

The doctor had whisked off his hat and sat at his wife's side. He held the baby, showed her to the children so each one could touch the tiny cheek, fondle the infant's fingers. He turned to his wife. Love like a soaring bird flew from the doctor's eyes to his wife's and Letitia was grateful to witness such caring. Davey smiled at her, his hat still in his hand.

"I fix eggs for the chillun."

The doctor rose and said he'd help. Even Davey lent a hand bringing in eggs along with Martha while Samuel showed his little brother how to pound imaginary nails into the floor. Everyone helped each other. Letitia liked the patterns the Hawkinses were cutting out for their sons and daughters. She had never seen William Bowman, Sarah's husband, wash a child's face of morning stickiness as Mr. Hawkins did now off Edward's little cheeks. She wondered if Davey would.

Prayers were spoken over the meal and everyone but the new mother ate at the table, Letitia included, while Nancy and her newest slept a satisfied sleep. The "frail" child, Laura, fell asleep at the table, her father picking her up and laying her beside her mother and newest little sister.

"Good peoples," Letitia said as she and Davey rode home.

"'Spect so. They're going to Oregon next spring too."

"Saw that wagon next to the barn. And Missus Hawkins say they was makin' plans." Nancy might need an extra hand with her brood that Letitia could offer. She had already been made to promise to come back the next day. She'd cook up some streaked meat and bread. "Doc Hawkins offer to pay me for my midwife work."

"Did he now? And you accepted?"

Letitia shook her head. "I said we could trade."

"What is it you'd be needing in trade?"

"I didn't tell him what it be but what I needs is . . . doctorin' of my own . . . next summer."

She let the words sink in, glad she couldn't see his face as she rode pillion behind him. It took a moment for him to pull up Fergus, the horse, and twist in the saddle to look at her.

"You're carrying?"

She nodded.

"When?"

"June."

"We'll be well on our way."

She couldn't tell if the wary tone of his words spoke of worry over her or perhaps the reactions others making the journey might have to their union or the arrival of a black child entering their midst.

He patted her thigh then. "That's good. Real good."

She accepted his words and lifted a prayer that this baby would be born healthy. That this child would be raised by a mother and a father who loved each other 'til death parted them.

She placed her hand against the warmth of his back. "You good with a chil', then?"

He nodded.

What better way to begin to mend the world than with a baby formed from love?

Seasonal Surprises

Papers. Letitia talked about her papers and pushed him for the script agreeing to take care of her. He'd write one up, in time. It was a sign of her lack of trust that she mentioned it while skimming cream or stitching his britches. Davey rode to the Platte County courthouse on an October morning, cooling mists rising from the creek. He had papers of his own to finalize. 'Course, Letitia's free papers held a mighty weight with her. Missouri was fixing to pass a law this session that would charge a $10 fine in addition to the forced departure of any colored person not holding free papers. The departure law had been on the books since 1825. Now they planned to add lashes to it and jail time too. He hoped the law wouldn't pass or wouldn't be enforced, but pro-slavers were aplenty in Missouri and a person could lose documents, even have them taken from them by an unscrupulous patroller. There was no need for her to worry though. Oregon would be different.

Rothwell did his duty, then like all river hounds, he covered his scat by pushing dirt on it with his nose instead of kicking dust over with his back feet. *Odd ways that dog has.*

Today Davey would collect his citizenship papers. He'd applied in March of 1844 and had answered the questions, few as they were. What made him squirm was having to say that he would "renounce forever all allegiances to every foreign power, Prince, State and Sovereignty, whatsoever, and particularly to Victoria Queen of Great Britain and Ireland, of whom he is a subject." Not that he held much regard for the Queen, being as how Ireland had her trials with the Monarch, but Ireland was what he knew first and there is something amputating to think that he'd be cutting all ties to his homeland, taken from him by his own signature. But it was necessary. With them heading to Oregon he had to be certain he could stand beside the Hawkinses and the Knightons and Staats and others who had stated their intentions to head out in the spring as citizens of Oregon country. Maybe by the time they arrived, Oregon would be a territory or even a state. He hoped so. He planned to claim land, but he needed to be a citizen to do so. Legally. He listened to the other cases being heard this session. Petty arguments most of them. In the mountains, men solved their problems on their own, didn't need any judge to do it for them.

As a citizen maybe he could put down the barbs about his Irish heritage that claimed his "laziness" or "ignorance." His reddish hair and accent gave him away, he guessed. In some ways, he and Letitia shared the spoken and unspoken arrows of disrespect people shot their way, just for being. As a citizen he could better take care of Letitia and now a wee one as well. He'd hang on to that citizenship paper like Tish clung to her freedom words. Still, he could lose his papers and there'd be evidence left in the courthouse. For Tish, only her single set of words existed to satisfy any who might claim otherwise about her status. That was probably why she kept them on her person mostly. Or in that small box she thought she hid under the bed. Of late she'd moved it to a tin he'd seen in the rafters. A shard of guilt pinched his throat for not yet having put in writing their labor agreement. But he was healthy and strong and didn't need to write down how he'd care for her after he died. Besides, he couldn't write all that well and he didn't want to pay a lawyer to write the words, or have her figure out he couldn't do it himself. He didn't want others knowing what he'd agreed to, either. He said he'd take care of her. That should be enough.

Greenberry Smith had a case being heard before his. The man nodded to him as he took his place before the judge. He'd known Greenberry Smith back in North Carolina and hadn't found much to praise the man for. If you disagreed with how he saw the world, well, then you were donkey dung to him. Once or twice Davey'd tried to intervene with his assaults on patrol, but it riled Smith further.

Davey's ear perked up as Smith testified about a man who'd bought one of his slaves for $1,000 and then failed to pay. He thought of that minx Eliza he'd dealt with. *Slavery. Nothing but trouble.* Smith scoffed when the judge continued the case, and when he turned, his ferret eyes caught Davey's. Smith tipped his hat, not quite masking a sneer. Arrogant, Smith was, but then most men of property and education were, it seemed to him.

"David Carson? Come forward, please."

He took a deep breath. He faced the judge. His big moment.

"Are you David Carson of Scotland?" The judge motioned him forward.

"No sir. Of Ireland, North Carolina, and Missouri."

"Hmmm." Conversation with the bailiff. Then, "There seems to be some irregularity."

Davey traced his fingers around his hat brim. "Lookee, your honor. Myself applied four years ago, nearly five." He tried to keep his voice calm. "What's irregular?"

"We have no record of your application."

"Then how'd you come to have me be here, sir?"

The judge said something to his bailiff that Davey couldn't hear, turned back. "I'm afraid there's been a mistake. There's another

David Carson who made the request and whose papers are ready for signature. In error we've notified you."

"But me application, surely it's there and processed." He knew he sounded whiney, desperate even.

"Are you certain you submitted the proper papers?"

He couldn't lose his temper. "On me mother's grave, I swear."

"Well, you're not the correct David Carson."

"But I applied. You have to have a record."

The judge raised a warning eyebrow. "All I know to do is to have you start over. I'll have the clerk provide you with an application and perhaps we can expedite your final papers."

"And when then would me papers be ready?"

The judge leaned into this clerk who whispered.

"I'd say in a year or so. Maybe two."

"Sir. But—"

"Patience is a virtue, Mr. Carson. We have dozens of people awaiting papers in this county alone."

"I'm hoping to head for Oregon next spring."

"You're fortunate that the court has the applications here. As I said, we'll move as quickly as we can. Next case?"

Outside Davey found himself tearing up. *Two years*. He'd either be long gone or they'd have to wait to leave. He needed to be a citizen in order to apply for that land. What right did the courts have to tell him to wait when he'd done everything right. He bent to scratch Rothwell's sharp-pointed ears, mounted Fergus. The horse grunted with Davey's weight. *Courts and papers. They're as unreliable as the weather.*

No snow covered the ground but the cold bit Letitia's face as they rode Davey's horse, Fergus, to the Hawkinses' to celebrate Christmas Day. Letitia wore a coat of beaver skins, one Davey had made for her from prime hides he'd trapped and kept. It was his Christmas gift to her. She'd given him a watch paid for with her butter and milk money. They'd exchanged their gifts on Christmas Eve, the memory of the evening in front of the hearth warming her still. Davey read the Scripture from what he called his Family Book, though it seemed to her sometimes he told the story more than read the words. Then they spoke of hopefulness in Oregon, of the trials and joys of making a new way in a new land. That's what Mary and Joseph and the baby Jesus had done.

"You're a citizen now," Letitia said, allowing pride to enter her voice. "Did you write that in the Family Book?" He shook his head. "I keep your papers safe with mine."

"Oh, no need for that. I could lose mine and the courthouse would have a copy. No, nothing to be concerned about." He picked at mud on his boot.

"Maybe you could write out our agreement? Mark that in the book."

"I'll get to that agreement before long, but you have my word."

"Yes, suh," she said. "I have your word, but it won't be no good if you is dead and I's still livin'."

"Me mother used to say 'The Lord takes care of the sparrow, he'll surely take care of you.' That's what we got to remember, not worry so much about papers."

He could be so loving, but he also dismissed her worries if they didn't settle in with his own.

"You like a river," Letitia said. "Ain't no good to push."

He'd patted her hand. "That's exactly so."

She couldn't push him, but she didn't have to like riding along on his raft waiting for him to shoot them through the rapids.

Once they arrived at the Hawkinses' log home, that quiet world of Christmas Eve and a cold ride swirled into Christmas Day and a frenzy of offspring, food, and festivities. Children laughed and scampered, showing their Christmas gifts, pulling from their Christmas stockings one precious orange each. Letitia wondered where Nancy Hawkins had gotten such fruit. Young Edward gripped a wooden toy in his small hand, showing it to Letitia and saying

"Mine!" as Letitia removed her coat. Maryanne stirred up biscuits while four-year-old Laura watched baby Nancy Jane as she slept on the nearby bed, Laura matching the cadence of her breath.

While Nancy and Letitia cooked beef roasts the Carsons brought and Nancy stewed four chickens and started the puddings, the men—including eleven-year-old Samuel—spoke of nothing but Oregon: who else was going, what weapons they'd take, who might be named captains or lieutenants, and all other issues of "heading west."

"I've heard that citizenship applications are backed up." Doc Hawkins tapped new tobacco into his clay pipe.

"Mr. Carson a citizen now." Letitia surprised herself by speaking up.

"Good for him. We'll all be seeking land."

"Is there an alternative for getting land? For those not so fortunate?" Davey said.

"Perhaps they could show they'd applied. Maybe have witnesses to how long they'd been in the states before coming to Oregon." Doc Hawkins lit a pipe, the scent unsettling Letitia's breakfast. "Not sure how strict they'll be. Canadians have a say, I hear. Two Canadians voted for the provisional government last year and it only won by two votes!"

They spoke then of the arrangements planned, how the groups would be set up as military units with captains and lieutenants and what-not, discussions that Letitia let fly over her without taking hold.

"The way I see it, once the captains and lieutenants get named, the real work of managing begins." Davey lifted an arm for a small Hawkins child to scoot under as the children raced around the table until their mother shooed them away. Letitia gave the children popped corn to string as the scent of roasted meat filled the small cabin. Logs cracked in the fireplace.

"The whining," Davey continued, "—and there will be whining—may be silenced by a captain's command, but like a summer stream, the whining goes underground. Shows up weeks later somewhere else but with a full head of steam."

"We need to get organized early, so we can head out before other groups," Doc Hawkins said.

"But not before the grass grows on the prairies for the oxen and mules," Nancy called over her shoulder as she cut up the two berry pies Letitia had brought.

"Who are you women talking to?" Doc Hawkins winked at Davey, and Letitia could tell he was pleased his wife was a partner in this western venture.

"Letitia hears all the chatter when she delivers butter," Nancy said. "Seems like the whole journey will be like balancing three children on your knees. Leave later so you can cross after the rivers have gone down but then wander in the dust of the earlier groups and no forage for your animals. And all along musing at length if the Indians will harass. Isn't that right, Letitia?"

Letitia smiled, pleased that what she shared was considered of value. "Gettin' along make the difference. How people settle their squabbles, make their peace, that what matter. 'Cause they is always problems."

Davey looked up at her from his hickory rocker and said, "In Oregon, we'll settle issues with fewer courts." Doc Hawkins's pipe smoke drifted up to punctuate his words. "Men ought to be skilled at negotiating with their neighbors with goodwill. After all, comes a time when every neighbor needs help without the residue of some old issue a judge ruled on smearing the need or the fixing of it."

Letitia took the now cut-up pies and put them on the window-sill, then helped Nancy lug a large crockery full of sauerkraut from the lean-to in the back before Doc saw their efforts and, with Samuel, helped bring the pot to the stove. The men left to look at the wagon Doc had purchased from the colonists at Bethel. At the barn they fed the Hawkinses's dog, Rufus. Rothwell hadn't been permitted to come.

Inside, the chatter of the Hawkins children pleased Letitia. She could see how the older ones helped the younger children. If she had more than one child, Letitia decided, she would raise them to be kind to each other and nip in the bud any signs of domineering spirits. She felt her child quicken in her womb and turned so as not to smile too broadly in her joy. She hadn't told Nancy yet; wasn't sure how people would take this union, especially with a child. It could be seen as something more and, for some, offensive.

The men returned from their wagon foray even more enthused. Davey pushed wood into the fireplace while Nancy stepped to the bed to nurse Nancy Jane, and in the lull Doc gathered his children to read the Christmas story from the Gospel of Luke, his offspring like dumplings cuddled together in a stew. He kept his eyes open while he read, unlike Davey. The Hawkinses gave her hope for what lay ahead for her and Davey. She knew spirit moments were rare and could be whisked away in a second. But for now she remembered Davey's words about the sparrow and she savored like a good stew this feeding of the soul within the gathering of friends.

After they ate, Davey offered to go home and milk Charity. "Doc here says we should stay the night and add to the game-playing. We'll sing some songs for the children maybe. I 'spect they'd like hearing your fine clear voice, Tish."

"Been a time since I sang 'Pop Goes the Weasel.'"

"Samuel, you go along and help Mr. Carson. By the time you boys are back those pies will be warmed at the hearth and be mighty tasty." This from the doctor.

"Lookee, I can do it alone. Bring my Irish whistle back and teach you a jig."

"I'd like to come, Mr. Carson. I got all my chores done. I can keep Rothwell company if nothin' else."

"Well, all right, son. We'll make a fast return. Don't you kids eat up those pies!" He shook his finger at them and they giggled. Letitia liked the way he'd called Samuel *son* and how he teased with the girls. Before long he'd have one of his own to use those words with.

The doctor went out to milk and then feed the chickens and the hogs. He came in brushing a light drizzle from his wool coat. Letitia sat in the rocker cuddling Edward as he slept, a blanket across his small body, though he still held his wooden wagon. Across from her Nancy rocked her youngest as both women took a needed rest before the final pie serving and whipping up the cream. Water heated on the stove for washing dishes later. Ah the joy of rest.

Doc settled down in front of the fireplace when they heard a tap at the door.

"Wonder what Davey forgot." Doc looked at his watch and frowned. "He couldn't be back already."

"I hope no one needs your doctoring tonight," his wife said.

Doc Hawkins eased his tall, skinny body to the door. "Can I help you?" A youngish man in his early twenties stepped inside at Doc's invitation, a fine rain drizzled on his hat that he now removed. His face was beardless and he had a hint of red in his full head of hair that curled tight from the outside mists. Letitia tensed her shoulders even before he spoke.

"I'm looking for David Carson."

"Oh, you just missed him. He's gone home to milk his cow and check on his stock, but he'll be back before long. Warm yourself by the fire. What's your business with Mr. Carson on this Holy Day, if I might ask?"

Letitia could tell by his gaze focused on the doctor that he didn't see the women. He was that kind of man. "My business? Well, he's my pa and I've come to take him home."

9

Stepping Up, Stepping Over

Letitia's stomach lurched. Edward, curled on her lap, shifted his weight with the unsettling and awoke.

"Didn't know he had kin in these parts." Doc motioned to the bench, for the man to sit, but he stood, continued to fill the room.

"I 'spect he doesn't know I'm in these parts. Haven't been before. David Carson," he said holding out his hand to the doctor. "Folks back home in North Carolina call me Junior."

Her mind swirled like leaves caught in a whirlpool, spinning, spinning, with nowhere to go. He carried on a conversation with the Hawkins pair but she heard little of it. *Davey has a son?* Why had he not told her? Could this "Junior" be a fraud? No, the reddish hair, the shorter legs and long torso, those blue eyes, they all spoke of Davey Carson. She'd thought she was giving him a family. He already had one.

Maybe Junior was the reason Davey failed to put his words into writing. He didn't want to leave everything to her and their children. He'd have to divide it, give portions to this son. Or all of it to Junior. *And what about Junior's mother?* The room felt stifling now. The smells of roasted meat or berry pies made her queasy. She put Edward down on his mat. "I needs to step outside."

"Are you all right?" Nancy's voice held warmth.

"No. Yes, ma'am. I needs air. Excuse me, suh." She had to walk past Junior, couldn't look him in the eye.

"Watch it, girl."

She brushed his shoulder as he'd failed to move when she'd excused herself to leave.

She heard the doctor's "Here, here now. She's our guest," but she kept going, wouldn't let someone's defense remove the sting of betrayal.

Outside she headed for the privy, the cool air making her cough. Raindrops mingled with her tears. She had created a dream out of nothing. How could he take care of her if he also had another family to care for? Maybe he'd abandoned them. This son said he'd come to take him home. Davey never spoke of a wife, not a word. She should have expected it. She was too happy and see where it took her.

How I miss this?

She went from blaming Davey to blaming herself, her own stupidity. Her eyes were blinded by belief in love, in a man's offer of security. His brother's words came back, carrying a disappointment of some kind. She ought to have known better. The cut-out in the privy door that she stared through was of a goat's head. She was a goat for thinking her life could be anything but loveless, hard, and alone.

<hr/>

"Letitia?" It was Nancy. "There you are. I checked the little house. You can't stay in the barn. It's shivering weather out here." Nancy pulled the heavy door behind her, hung the candle lantern on a nail, casting shadows over Letitia. She bent to where Letitia sat curled in the empty stall. Mules nickered at the woman's voice.

"I . . . I be all right."

"Goodness. You've been gone so long."

"Maybe ate too much."

A pause and then, "You didn't know. About the son."

She felt the tears come then. Nancy nestled beside her. "It's a dastardly thing, it is. But men . . . they can be dense as oxen. What is so essential to our very being they look upon as pure surprise. 'That bothered you?' or 'You wanted me to say what?' I swear we may as well be chickens to them sometimes clucking around, pecking at making their lives better while they act like we don't even exist. Yet they love us, dear and tender."

"Not all."

"Oh, yes. I've seen the way Mr. Carson looks at you. He adores you, Letitia. This . . . this hurt, it will pass. Has to. For your child's sake."

She knows.

"I . . . needs more time. Here."

"Don't get too chilled. I'll get a quilt. Take my shawl."

Nancy wrapped the knitting around her shoulders like a blessing, spreading it over Letitia's knees. "It will be all right." She patted Letitia's knees. "This hurt will pass."

Letitia nodded, let herself be taken into the warm words of this good woman. "I needs . . ." She couldn't say what she needed.

Nancy left, returned moments later with the quilt, tucked it around Letitia. She patted Letitia's shoulder and left.

In the flickering light she saw the quilt pattern, a wedding ring quilt. *Ain't that a funny thing.* A wedding ring quilt worn on the night her wedding promises fell apart. The cold didn't deaden the comforting smells of the mules and horses chewing at their troughs nor the sound of the barn door creaking open.

"Tish? Lookee here. You come inside now."

She stiffened.

"You'll catch your death. You got to worry over our wee one, so you come on now."

She sat quiet as snow falling. She heard his feet shuffle and then he squatted next to her.

"I brought your coat."

"Got a quilt. A *wedding ring* quilt. Not that it matter to you." She wanted to hurt him the way Davey Junior had cut into her. Girl. He'd called her girl. And he'd come to take his father home.

She couldn't stay there all night, she knew that. But she didn't want to go home with Davey Carson, either. "You best head back, be with your *son*. He here to take you home, he say. Where home be, Mr. Carson? Not the property down this road."

"My home is with you, Tish. It is."

"Maybe Doc Hawkins let me spend the night right here. I come get my things in the morning."

"What are you talking about? You can't go away. We're wed, fair and square. Besides, Junior won't take up much room. He can use the larder or the barn. His showing up was as much a surprise to me as to you."

She hissed, "You at least know he alive."

"You need your coat."

He tried to push it around behind her back but she resisted. Accepting anything from him would turn the tide of her anger and she wasn't ready to let it go. She pushed back against the stall boards.

"Not for me, now. For our wee one."

Her baby, yes. Her shoulders sank.

"I am sorry, Tish. Mrs. Carson. I ought to have told you. But his mother died years ago and he's been on his own for ten years or more since I've seen him. I . . . went a little crazy when his mother passed. Came to Platte County, started over." He hung his head. "Should have told you."

"Yessuh. You should have." She opened the coat to the furry inside and pulled it over her arms, wrapped it around her belly, soaking in the warmth. It didn't stop her body from shaking. He pulled her to him then, his arms a cloak until she sagged, spent.

She'd choose tending over being right. "You . . . he goin' to live with us now? Does he know that we . . . married? Have a baby comin'?"

"He knows you're with me. Nothing else."

"He think I your . . . property." She spit the words. "He call me 'girl.'"

"No, now, he don't think that far about it. He came looking for his pa and found me. I don't know what his plans are. In the morning we'll figure something out. But now you need to come in and get warmed up."

She did need to do that, for the baby's sake. But she didn't want to sleep at the Hawkinses' home now; didn't want to share a bed with Davey Carson nor have his son see them sharing like husband and wife, either. She didn't look forward to bearing the stares that men like David Junior gave women like her. And now those judgments would be right beside her hearth.

"Letitia?" It was Nancy who opened the door. "Oh, good. You've got her to come in. Why don't you folks have some pie and then we'll play a few games and get everyone settled for bed. We've floor room and plenty of feather ticks and lots of quilts. You can make your way home in the morning."

Davey said, "Mighty kind of you. Don't you think, Letitia? 'Spect we'll fall asleep like logs listening to the rustling of those children."

"We stay and thank you."

There was safety in numbers and lying nearby another woman who understood things without saying. So much better than hearing Davey Carson play his whistle and acting like life was a jig.

❧

"You'd already left before your ma died, so don't you now decide I abandoned you!" Davey and his son had embarked on their feud as soon as the Carson family left the safety of the Hawkinses' home. Letitia had gone out to the little house and upon returning heard the continuation of the words they started shouting at each other even before breakfast.

"You sure didn't come looking for me."

"How was I supposed to find you, Junior? You ran off when you was twelve and now you're what?" He paused. "A young man."

"You don't even know when I was born."

"I do so. March 1, 1825."

Letitia was surprised that Davey knew the birthday of his son. Why had the boy run off so young? No, she mustn't let herself think of him as a "boy." He was a man now, a man who interrupted their lives. But then her child had been younger than twelve when he was sold. Would he have come one day to find her if he hadn't died? Should she have tried to find him all those years before? The thought softened her toward the man, the boy.

The blaming continued, each holding up evidence enough to wear down a judge.

"They may be blame enough to go around."

"What's that you sayin', girl?"

"She's not a girl, son. She's my wife."

The words washed over Letitia like balm on a sore.

"Not like Mama was. She's a colored woman. She can't be saying vows and all."

"Well, she did. We did. And you got to accept that if you're to be in my house. Our house."

Junior glared at her. "What do I call her?"

"Mrs. Carson will do," Davey said.

"Can't." He looked away.

"Call me Letitia. I call you Mistah Carson. Or Junior."

"Don't no colored woman tell me what to say."

"Junior . . ."

The younger man shook his head. "Mr. Carson, then."

"Lookee there? We're on the road to working things out. Now let the woman fix us our breakfast."

Letitia turned away, felt Junior's glare bore into her back. She skimmed the milk of cream.

"What did you mean by 'blame enough to go around'?"

She turned to face him. A mist formed above her upper lip and Letitia risked being known. "You leave home for some reason, no stayin' to solve the problem, whatever it be. Maybe your pa not find you 'cuz you good at hidin'. Then you hear your mama's died and you come lookin' but your pa's gone in his grievin'. Guess you can find fault all around, maybe even win your lawsuit. But stayin' there won't get you anywhere you'd rather be."

Junior grunted, grabbed a chair, and pulled it to the table. "You lecturing me, woman?"

"Speakin' truths."

<hr />

They argued in a hiss so Junior wouldn't hear them, though he'd gone to the barn to tend to his horse. "He goin' with us to Oregon?"

"I don't know yet. Don't know that he wants to but I'd like him to. We'll need a second driver. It's required. And what better than to have a man's son."

"Maybe you prefer a son along to your wife."

"No, now, Tish, you know I want you going. This is our life we're creating here. But there's room for more, ain't there?" He touched her belly but she stepped away, went to scrub at the three-legged spider that needed cleaning. "He's just a boy, you understand."

"Who has man thoughts."

"He'll get used to you. Carsons back in Kentucky and North Carolina all had slaves. My brothers have 'em. We had a few. He's just not accustomed to a colored woman being free and accepted for who she is."

"You owned?"

She saw Davey's Adam's apple bob up and down. "Things are different now. You know that. I had no slaves in Missouri 'cept the one I borrowed, sort of. Eliza. And you ain't no slave. You're my wife and a partner in this Western venture. So don't go getting strange on me. I need you."

"You told him I's free? That I have papers?"

"I did." Davey lowered his eyes. "He wants to see them."

"A man can want all he wants," Letitia said. Then, "You never signed the paper sayin' you'd look after me if somethin' happened to you."

"I will. I will. Too many things to consider, but you know you have nothing to fear. Remember that sparrow." He grinned and she narrowed her eyes. "You best decide if you want what I'm offering. Marriage means change, you know."

"I knows."

"While me and Junior are going to Bethel for our wagon, you best think about what it is you do want."

Davey never even considered returning to North Carolina. The farthest east he'd go was where he headed now, to Bethel, to purchase a wagon like Doc Hawkins did. Sturdy oak. Solid wheels. Strong metal bows. He didn't think his son was all that bent on making him agree to head back to North Carolina. The boy was looking for a place to hang his hat, seeking kin. Couldn't fault him for that. It would be nice to have him on the trail west, so while the boy might press him to keep heading east, he'd press his son to head farther west.

Davey would need another driver. Each wagon had to have two men per, as he'd been told. Or he could drive the cows. He planned to take nearly thirty head. Junior could be that second drover, someone to help repair a wheel, push through muddy sections. They had a little over three months before they'd leave and by then Davey and Letitia would work things out. She'd forgive Davey for his omission and see the value in having kin join them. He ought to have told her, he knew that. But he didn't want her stepping away. Truth was, he had a son. Nephews. Brothers. Even a sister in North Carolina. And now he had another child coming on that he intended to take care of. He'd raise this one different. His son could be a good help, that was all. Letitia would see that. No way would she consider staying behind.

The trip to buy the wagon would be good for all of them, a little separation from a week of thrashing through the past then walking on flower petals hoping none got crushed. That's what he'd told Letitia. She'd made noises like she wanted to be a part of the wagon purchase, but someone had to stay and milk the cow and look after things, didn't they?

"Your son stay. I help make the choice for how some of my money gets spent."

"No, now, that's not practical. Not good for you to make such a trip to Bethel in your condition."

She'd harrumphed. "I's plannin' on makin' two thousand miles 'in my condition.'"

He grinned at her. "You're right about that. But truth is I'd like Junior along so he can learn about the wagon and see how repairs are made. Two heads knowing things would be better than one." Besides, what did a woman—even a smart woman—know about wagons? And he did want to hear about what the boy had been doing all these years. "Me and Junior'll make the trip, bring the wagon back. Time alone will be good."

She'd agreed and they'd headed out.

The January day they left was cold but clear. Days like this always gave a lift to his spirit. They rode in an old wagon they'd trade in, using the mules to pull the new empty wagon back.

"I like a good mule." Davey watched the ears prick forward and back as the team pulled.

"Uncle Andrew raises fine horses. If you came back, he'd invite you in to the business."

"No, now, your uncle and me, we're different types. He likes the steadiness of a farm and me, I like what's new out there. That's why I trapped and traded. Did you go by to see your uncle Smith before you found me?"

"He told me where to look. He's feeling poorly. He says you're going to farm in Oregon. You already have one here. Why leave?"

"If I play it right I'll have a section of land there. I'll raise stock more than crops and that means riding out, managing my herds, meeting people, maybe having a place in the community. I'll build a bigger house." And it would be safer for Letitia there.

"Looks to me like you already have what you hope to have and you're leaving it."

"We can get more land in Oregon. With hemp and tobacco dying off as crops here, not many folks buying up my beef 'cept to jerk it for the trip. Half the county is planning to move west. They got no money except when they sell their property. I'll be rich in Oregon." Rothwell moaned as he twisted in the wagon bed, finding a new way to sleep. "There'll be room for you, son."

Junior rode silent beside him for a time. Davey's eye caught the red berries of the possum haw holly. He wondered if they'd grow in Oregon.

"Can't see me living with a colored woman acting like she owns the place."

"You can see she's a loving woman. Kind."

"She's colored and she don't act like the slave she is."

"No, now, lookee here, she's a free woman."

"Uncle Smith says you came with a slave."

"Easier than explaining that she's free."

"So she says."

"Well, in Oregon she will be free, certain. She's a good help to your pa. You'll get used to her." He kept to himself the fact of his having a little brother or sister before long. Change came by a step at a time—though with Junior's arrival he'd have to say change sometimes showed up by leaps. He hoped it wasn't a sign of things to come.

Letitia scrubbed her frustration onto the puncheon floor. Now she had to negotiate with two stubborn men. Instead of the joy she'd felt planning for the trip, thinking about her baby, getting ready to change her duties, all the good things the journey promised, she was now cooking and washing for three, sitting back while the Daveys chattered and carried on acting like she wasn't even there most times, except to serve them their food or sweep out the mud their boots dragged in. She had become "their girl." The only beating hearts she felt melded with hers were this baby and Charity, her cow. Maybe Rothwell's heart, but even the hound had gone off with the men to buy the wagon. Only a bit of her money went with Davey.

She scrubbed Davey's shirt. It was getting thin. She needed to sew another, maybe two, before they left. She guessed she'd be sewing for Junior as well. Davey overlooked the little ways that Junior put her in her place. Oh, he called her Letitia now, but he said it like he had bitters in his mouth, and when Davey wasn't around, he called her "girl." And he didn't ask her to bring more molasses to the table, he ordered. And her husband never said a word of reprimand. She didn't know how much influence he'd have over his father and she didn't like the idea that he had a good week to cajole the man on this Bethel trip without Letitia's presence even in the background.

She noticed the quiet when she sat back on her heels and rested, wiping her forehead of the sweat. What if Junior convinced Davey to keep going east? She felt tears form but resisted them. She guessed if that happened, she'd stay right here in Missouri. Then, no. She'd ask if the Hawkinses would let her travel with them. Yes. She could make a new way in the West without Davey Carson if she had to. She had a cow and she had a little money saved; she could pay them for her keep on the journey. She knew how to work hard. Even with a baby she could take care of herself. She didn't need a husband. And she certainly didn't need a second Davey to look after.

Oh, she longed to refuse to go to Oregon if Junior came along, but she wouldn't. It wasn't just Davey's dream. It was hers too, she'd come to see, a solid-colored-dye dream that couldn't be washed away by anyone or anything. She heard Charity's cowbell clang outside. Davey had given her that bell. He'd been kind long before he'd become her husband. And she had spoken vows over the Bible. No, if he came back and said Junior was going with them, she'd live with that. But she wouldn't live under their thumbs. She remembered a Bible verse, one her mother spoke of. "For freedom Christ has set us free; stand fast therefore, and do not submit again to a yoke of slavery." She'd make her peace with being this step-parent, as they called it. She'd learn to step back and step aside and step away. Junior could not put her back into being a slave or step on her unless she let him. Only she could put herself back into bondage. She would step up and make the best of it. That's how she could help her child and best mend this little tear in her world.

10

Ready for Beyond

Sitting in front of her fireplace, Nancy Hawkins scratched at her hot feet while she read the letter from Sarah Bowman. It was already the end of March in the year 1845 and this was the first missive she'd received, but its arrival filled a need. She hoped Sarah would tell her of things to be sure to remember to bring.

The river they call the Columbia is wider than the Missouri and oh so much deeper. It winds for days through high, bare bluffs until reaching a narrow section where the water falls in a horseshoe shape over and among black rocks bigger than houses. The sound is deafening and you can feel the drumming of the water in your feet. Chubby Indians stand on spindly platforms built against the rocks spearing huge fish. With ropes they tie themselves to the platforms so they won't slip in, Mr. Bowman says, though someone told me the fish make the platforms slippery and if they did fall in the rush of the dalles they wouldn't survive. At least their families

*would have a way to recover their bodies for burial. I traded
my mirror for a salmon which is a tasty fish. The mirror was
broken in an accident in July when our wagon overturned.
I was poorly for a time. People call the town Wascopam, an
Indian word meaning the cascading, rushing dalles of the
river. We called it "The Dalles." I held my breath when we
were put on puny rafts at The Dalles and set afloat below the
falls. I daresay I did not breathe again until we reached the
opposite shore and put the wagons back together and rolled
on our way toward the Willamette Valley where we are now.
Let me tell you what you need to bring . . .*

When Nancy finished reading the page, she turned the letter
upside down and read on between the lines where Sarah continued her comments about the Columbia River journey from the
Dalles. Nancy shivered at the image of the mighty river falls. It
must have been frightening. Maybe there was another way across
the mountains into the Willamette Valley. She'd have to ask Zach
what he'd heard.

The 1844 group the Bowmans traveled with had arrived in Oregon in November, but they'd endured more rain than any had
imagined. Sarah had not mentioned the infant that ought to have
been born by the time they reached Oregon, and Nancy surmised
her "feeling poorly" meant she'd lost the child.

Nancy made sure *she* wasn't going to be pregnant with a child
on this trip. Nursing Edward hadn't prevented Nancy Jane's arrival.
So much for that old wives' tale. The boy had been weaned as soon
as she knew. For this hard journey, she wasn't taking any chances.
She'd gotten a sponge, and awkward as it was, it seemed right that
something from the sea should keep her from conceiving a child
who would float in the sea of her womb if the sponge didn't work.
She'd let Zach know and he had reluctantly agreed. She couldn't
afford to be carrying a child inside while toting another on her hip
and keeping five others safe on this two-thousand-mile journey.

She planned to pass Sarah's letter along to several other women heading west. Elizabeth Knighton might like to know that they could pick up needed flour or rice at the fort in Laramie. Eveline Martin would appreciate the comments about flannel shirts being used as trade with friendly Indians. Like Nancy, she'd sew extras. There'd be time to quilt another covering as well. They might make good trades to help bring comfort.

She looked up at the quilting frame hanging from the peeled logs. That frame was heading west. It held too many memories of "needles and tongues," as Zach described the activity of women quilting the blocks. Fortunately, the dropped pulley had only left a bruise on Laura's cheek. But the child had daily scratches and bumps. Her garden daisy wasn't in bloom so she couldn't use it to reduce the bruising, but Zach had Bellis, akin to the daisy, that worked wonders. She planned to take her daisy plants with her to Oregon.

Nancy heard a wagon crunch on the dirt outside. She pulled the curtains back, the scent of lavender from the soap drifting to her nose. Several people from places east had already arrived, and men met weekly to discuss this and that, leaving the women to introduce themselves and figure out how it would be traveling together for seven or eight months. Though Letitia had been invited, she never came to these gatherings. It might make the crossing easier if others saw Letitia's strength and gentle ways. Nancy's family hailed from Hamilton County, Ohio, and she realized that her abolitionist leanings put her in a rare category as one who could see past color into the heart of the person. She was required to do so by her faith. Just as Zach's experience in Hardin County, Kentucky, made him an unusual abolitionist in that slave-holding place. She'd pray that Letitia would find a few women friends along the way. Some families might settle near each other once they arrived. She hoped that would happen between the Carson and the Hawkins clans.

Nancy Jane awoke and she picked her up to nurse, ham and bean aroma washing over them both. She wondered if Zach would let her bring the small coal-burning stove. He weighed everything to keep it under the recommended pounds. Nancy folded the letter, set it aside. Sarah had made it with her six children so she could make it with hers. And at least she wasn't pregnant.

Her thoughts returned to Letitia, who was.

Letitia appeared to have resigned herself to the arrival of David Carson's son. Nancy knew a little of what it was like to be set apart by a family member. Sometimes she envied her own son, Samuel, as he got to do things with Zach while she stayed in the house with their brood. How good it would feel to take a trip to town in the wagon, just the two of them again. It seemed like eons since they'd first held hands, but it had only been thirteen years and six children ago. At least she'd be a part of what happened every day once they headed west. Maybe it would be like old times beside her husband with just a touch more uncertainty in the mix.

<hr />

"I swear, woman, if we could, I'd let you take the cabin itself but—"

"No need to swear, Zachariah Hawkins. I know. But I need my quilting frame and the spinning wheel. You made them both for me. How can I leave them behind?" Nancy's voice held a level of discontent that Letitia had seldom heard. The Hawkinses had pulled their wagon up to the house and the Carsons were helping them finish loading. Hawkins children all with hair the color of corn tassels bounded in and out, Rothwell chasing Samuel and Laura while Letitia bounced Nancy Jane on her hip on a cloudless April morning.

"Women," Doc scoffed and shook his head at Davey. "Go ahead and load the frame. It can be flooring if need be. And we can always use it for possible repairs."

"Oh no, not that fine oak." Then, "Of course. Whatever we need."

Letitia wondered if she and Davey would go through the same

thing when the Hawkinses rolled their wagon into the Carson yard tomorrow to help them finish packing up. The six oxen they'd be taking along plus Charity and her latest calf would go, that was certain. Davey was taking thirty head of stock. Men had met and prepared a list of rules to govern the journey and there'd been discussion about the sturdiest wagon types, with Bain and Shutler deemed the best. Davey and Zachariah didn't have that design but their schooner-type wagons were strong and would be pulled by four oxen with an extra team along to rest and rotate animals. Letitia had grown to love the faithful beasts who never resisted the yoke. Davey had named them A, B, C, and D. "For easy remembering." When she began to feel sorry for herself, she'd think of those oxen and their willingness to do what they were asked to do without complaint.

"Put the anvil in last," Doc told the men, and the three of them lifted it together.

"Mighty heavy," Davey said. "Mine makes us meet that 2500-pound limit mighty quick."

Doc removed his hat and wiped the sweat off his forehead with his forearm. "I know it. But to make repairs it'll be a fundamental."

"We women have to stand firm for a few of our *own* fundamentals." Nancy lifted the baby from Letitia's arms, winking at Letitia.

"Fundamentals." Doc snorted.

"How are you feeling?" Nancy asked Letitia. They stood apart from the men securing the flour and rice barrels, stashing the cast-iron cookware in a box Zach had made along with the dried beef and fruits and tobacco.

"All right, I 'spect."

"When do you think?" She raised her blonde eyebrows in question.

"Late May. Early June." Letitia hesitated, then said, "This one feel different, but I think I got it figured right."

"You've had . . . I mean, this isn't your first?"

"My third. One die as he birthin'. The other . . . sold away and then I hear he die too."

Nancy touched Letitia's arm. "I cannot imagine how you've lived through two such wrenchings." The touch of her hand brought comfort like a warming breeze. "It must have felt like tearing flesh."

"A searing burn that never quits." Letitia didn't add that traveling west meant moving ever farther away from her sons. She didn't even know the final resting place of one.

They stood together, each lost to their thoughts. "Come help me with the bedding, would you? Packing for eight is such a chore!"

"I's only got three to tend."

"The life of a wife." Nancy grinned as she led Letitia into the house that still had tables and chairs and chests of drawers that wouldn't be loaded. Rather, like so many memories, those treasures would be left behind.

"Are you carrying?" Junior posed the question to her when Davey was well out of earshot, checking the hooves of the oxen that would pull their wagon west. He faced her, legs wide, elbows out, challenging as a bull. "Don't lie to me."

"Yessuh. I's with child."

"You sounding pretty high and mighty for a Negro. See how I don't use the word you really are? Honoring my papa." He sneered, then used it anyway, looked toward his father who kept to his work. "You twisted my pa's thinking, that's what you done." He whispered with a hiss, though the sounds of harnessing, men shouting, children calling out kept Davey from hearing. "Got him into bed with you and now he's not thinking straight." He poked at her abdomen. The physical pain felt less than the sear of his touching her, using words as weapons.

She pushed him back, scratched at his face.

Junior grabbed her arm, wiped the side of his face with his other hand. A trickle of blood oozed onto his fingers and he stared at it. "Look what you done!"

"You not harm my baby nor touch my person. Ever. Again."

"I guess I can do what I want with you." He twisted her arm and she cried out.

Davey called from the other side of the oxen. "Everything all right over there?"

"Just fine, Pa."

Junior looked at the blood on his hands. She smelled anger on his breath as he hissed close to her ear. "You've tricked him to take my inheritance."

She pulled away. "Your daddy promise to care for his *young* kin and for me. But he want you in his life so we make a peace. For his sake." She looked back down. "I's not one for trouble, Mistah Carson. Seekin' good mixin' is all."

He squeezed her arm harder, then tossed it aside like kindling. He wiped at his cheek. "Don't ever expect me to mix in with the likes of you."

She lifted her eyes to his. "Then maybe one of us needs to put our feets in another direction."

One reddish eyebrow raised.

"And my feets and mixin' bowls are headin' west."

⁓

Such a fractious thing to argue about and yet they had. Davey drove the team and wagon to the meeting place in Weston. All preparations had gone well and then Junior insisted on taking only a shotgun and pistols. But the governing rules said each man was to have a caplock rifle with gunpowder in barrels as well. Junior had balked at the requirement.

"You know how to shoot. What's the matter with you?"

They'd already gathered up with two hundred other wagons near the Missouri, campfires glowing with children like puppets dancing before them. Davey and Junior had come back from a meeting to choose their captains and whatnot on April 5 at Wolf River. The Carsons and Hawkinses would be joining up with Stephen Staats

106

from New York who was under Tetherow. Davey had been elected to the executive council. He wouldn't tell Letitia yet. It would mean he'd have duties and wouldn't always be around. G.B. Smith was going too. That one had made his pitch to be a sub-captain but he'd been outvoted. Smith had no family with him, though Davey had seen him around the Hugharts' oldest girl and she couldn't be more than fifteen; such a frail birdlike child. He hoped her father would keep a close eye on her.

Everything had been going as planned and then Junior decides the rule of carrying the caplock along with a shotgun was "Stupid. I don't wanna travel with people making stupid rules."

Maybe Junior ran a fever from the bramble scratch on his cheek. It did look festered and he'd refused to let Letitia put one of her salves on it. He said as much and Junior touched his cheek, barked that his temperament had nothing to do with this. It was the guns. But then Davey had caught him looking at Tish as she crossed behind the campfire, his blue eyes dark as an angry sea. The look brought a shiver to Davey.

"I'll take the extra gun. Time comes you'll want to use it," Davey said. "That way we meet the regulations."

"Got no time for men who make policies like that. I've changed my mind about going at all."

"Lookee here, son. I need you to drive. I need you to help out. Thought we'd get our family back together."

"Looks like you got yourself one."

"You getting on well with Tish, ain't you? Why desert us now?"

"If you make it, maybe I'll come see you. Maybe travel around the horn instead of nine months with you and your N . . . wench. See your little 'family' all cozy in Oregon."

Davey grimaced. He looked across the fire to see if Letitia might have heard. She wasn't anywhere around. Seemed like except at meals she and Junior never stood in the same firelight.

"Now, son, we've got on well since you showed up. Shame having you decide to back off."

"You'll get over it. You did before."

Davey felt the blow in his chest.

Junior walked around to the end of the wagon and grabbed his pack. Then without another word he mounted his horse, tipped his hand to his hat, and rode away.

"I know you feelin' harshed by Junior's leavin'." Letitia stood to blow out the candlelight, bringing the moonless night inside their tent. "Maybe . . . my fault. We toss words back and forth."

"No. It was the rules. He was never one to follow any. If it hadn't been the guns, it'd be something else before long. Was why he ran off in the first place, having to comply." He patted her hip as they lay in the bedroll beneath the tent. A cool breeze rustled the canvas, caused a small flare in the campfire now just embers. "Wasn't your fault. Biggest problem now is finding a second driver this late. That's one rule they won't abide being broken."

She wondered if she should mention the idea she had when he first told her Junior was gone. It would be worth saying out loud. "What if I back your drivin'?"

"Doubt they'd allow that. Wives aren't permitted such things. They got to be cooking and whatnot."

"But if I's your . . . employee. Could they refuse that?"

He lifted up on one elbow looking down at her. Firelight lit her face. "But you're my . . . you know."

"Might be safer if peoples think I your slave." It would grate like rocks on glass not to say she was free, but it would be safer if they allowed the story. Her stomach clenched and the baby moved. "We gots an agreement. I cook and tend you on the journey and clear ground when we gets to the Territory, help prove up your land claim. You s'posed to write down that you provide for me and our children if somethin' happen to you. Paper could tell 'em that I work for you. They have to let you hire who you want."

"But the child . . . people will know that—"

"Child be born and I mother him. Not the first time Missouri folk see a mulatto in their midst. They find a way to avoid him. Or her. And if you sick and I drive, I put the baby in a bag like I do my boys when they's little and I work for the Bowmans. Happy as a little kitten snuggled up against me. Nancy Hawkins help with my child."

He tugged at his beard. "They might go for it. I could be convincing. And I have hired Knighton and Martin as drovers. Might find a third to rotate with driving if need be. Especially when you're, well, fixing with the baby."

"Tell 'em you have a paper claimin' our agreement."

"They won't ask." She could see him thinking. "Truth is, Tish, I don't write so well. Barely read." He cleared his throat. "I'll get Zach to write and witness it and give the paper to you. First thing in the morning. Anyone asks, you're my . . . hired-on."

In the morning Davey put a document into Letitia's hands.

"This it? It say what we agreed?"

"Had Zach write it out this morning while we were at the corrals getting our oxen ready. There's my signature." He pointed. "So you put it with your things."

She held the paper to her heart with quivering hands. *Wish I could read it . . .* "I gots room for your citizenship papers too."

"They'll do fine where they are."

Davey left to finish his work and she considered then where to put the safety papers, as she thought of them. She laid them out lengthwise onto a piece of cloth, what was left of Nathan's little baby quilt. She had a strip that would fold over the papers. She rolled them into a ball the size of her fist then tied them with a ribbon. Now where to keep it. She looked around the wagon. Maybe in her sewing kit. No, too obvious and she'd be taking needles in and out and the small ball of cloth might get tossed aside by mistake. At home, she'd put her paper in a tin hidden in the rafters, but no rafters in the wagon. *The flour barrel.* A perfect place, way down at the bottom. Nancy told her she'd put some of her best china in her flour barrel. "Zach doesn't need to even know." Davey wouldn't need to know either.

She hadn't prayed that Junior wouldn't join them, but perhaps God had heard her silent plea. That Junior had chosen to leave made it easier for her to comfort Davey when for a second time his son deserted him. Now here she was with the precious papers. A gift beyond measure. She stuffed the roll of cloth into the flour barrel. Out of the sorrow at Christmastime had come what she'd hoped for: safety. She brushed the flour away from her bodice and loosened the linen wrapper swaddling her belly. She began to swing and sway, singing, "Oh religion is a fortune, I really do believe." She had her papers, a baby on its way, and with God's guiding, she was heading toward real freedom. What more could she want?

Part Two

Oregon Country

The Woman and the boy finished burning out the rotten log.

"Now add dirt. Make sure to mix ashes good. Then we add seeds."

Before long they would have tobacco plants growing for easy harvest. They already had another burned-out log where the leaves grew tall, and they'd harvested those the year before, new plants coming back now. They'd mix the harvested leaves with bearberry leaves that were always green. Kinnikinnick, the trappers called it. They traded for more when the kinnikinnick was added to tobacco to sweeten the taste and change the smell that no one liked.

"You find the bearberry?" The Woman motioned with her chin to Little Shoot. He hunched his shoulders down, his face wearing a scowl. He stopped, stood in a low mat of green leaves with pink berries shaped like the traders' lanterns. Later there'd be red berries and stems that tangled like strands of hair over his face.

"Why do we make so much, Kasa? We can't smoke it."

"We smoke only a little. Give more to the old ones in the village to comfort their days. No, we trade the rest."

"The few trappers left?" The boy's words challenged.

"At the Big River of the dalles we meet people who trade for our tobacco. And more will come. The Others will come. Before long, we will not be alone."

"Good tobacco will make them want to stay."

"We do not own the tobacco. We only prepare it. The Others could do it and not need us to trade with them."

"Hmmph."

They gathered the shiny leaves, and with the tobacco leaves they'd harvested and dried earlier, they dumped them into water she'd heated to boiling with hot stones. The bearberry greens and dried tobacco swirled into a mass.

"I tell you now so you prepare." She motioned him to stir with the stick. "The Missionaries tell us, Others will come and many, like them, will stay. We want no trouble with them. Their coming will sharpen us."

"I am sharp enough." He held up the stirring stick in his skinny arms above his head. A boy in triumph. "Ayee. This is a thing to remember."

The Woman watched the boy gain strength. And she smiled that he was beginning to know what things were worthy of remembering.

Leaving

"I've been elected to the executive council. Made a captain." Davey returned from his evening meeting at Wolf River, a quiet stream that flowed into the Missouri. They waited for others to join them before the large group would head west. He accepted the tin cup of coffee Letitia handed him, then sat on the wagon tongue. He patted the iron, urging her to sit beside him.

"G.B. Smith made the case for himself to captain, but folks selected me."

It was the first she'd heard that Greenberry Smith would join their company. "He patrollin'?"

"No, no patrols, nothing like that. This ain't a slave train. 'Cept to guard the cattle and watch for Indian trouble. He'll be a good patroller at that." Davey bent to secure the odometer attached to the wheel. "Officers will make final inspections to be sure everyone has the necessary supplies. I'll be doing it for others, but they'll select a couple of men to check ours. No favorites being played here."

G.B. Smith and another man arrived later that day to make the inspection. She wanted them to pass without being harshed on. Tall and self-assured, G.B. wore a vest over his store-bought shirt and stiff jeans. His black beard was trimmed, unlike Davey's. Letitia stayed off to the side trying to make herself invisible. A breeze flapped the canvas opening as she tied it back.

"You got a second driver?" This from the secretary, all business-like.

"I do."

"Let's see your supplies. Be sure you have enough for three." He stepped up into the back of the wagon, checking for the tar bucket on the way. He wrote down something about the butter churn hanging from the bow.

G.B. Smith didn't move from his stand at the side of wagon. "I see you've got your slave there." The hairs on Letitia's arm shivered. "You heard that Oregon's provisional government passed a law excluding coloreds, requiring any brazen enough to stay be lashed twice a year until they leave. She won't be long in that place."

She turned to Davey to see if that was true.

"I heard. Also heard they declared slavery illegal, not that it matters. Letitia here is free."

"Is she? The worst kind of colored, if you ask me."

G.B. knows I free. He sees my papers.

"Ain't heard anybody asking you." Davey winked at her.

The clerk said from inside the wagon, "Who's your backup driver?"

"She is." Davey said it with his jovial voice. "Saving money. Don't have to hire her, just feed her along the way."

"Getting your slave out of Missouri, the way I see it," G.B. Smith said.

"She's free, I tell you. No law being broken if she stayed. Free to hire on to help me head west and so she has. To help drive and build up my claim."

The clerk jerked his head back out from behind the canvas. "Woman driver? No, no, no. Not strong enough to handle a team nor help lift a wagon wheel if need be. That won't work."

Letitia considered speaking up, though her throat felt parched as the bottom of a chicken cage. It was a constant question whether to stand up for herself or try to fit in.

"I got three drovers. Sure enough for my twenty-two loose cows and six oxen. Couple of horses and mules too making up my thirty head of stock. A drover can help drive if need be. Let's hurry along here."

Davey sounded confident. A man could stand up for himself; a woman couldn't.

"As for the woman, she's small but strong. We'll all have to help each other. It's the law of the company, I 'spect." Davey laughed then, a sound Letitia recognized when he was feeling nervous.

Rothwell huddled under the wagon; his eyes watched the men just as Letitia's did.

"Very inventive of you, Mr. Carson." G.B. Smith brushed dust from his new jeans, stared at Letitia's belly. "Using your wench as both driver and bed warmer."

How she wished she could say "We married!" Instead she looked away.

"Everything appears to be in order. Twenty pounds of lead; ten pounds of powder. Bacon—200 pounds; 600 pounds flour and 100 pounds of meal. Four guns." The secretary looked at a list.

"I added an odometer." Davey pointed. "Did you note that there on the wheel?"

The secretary nodded. "Still not sure about this driver."

"You takes on boys as drivers when they is twelve. I's good as them."

"She's right." Davey patted the wheel. "Like you said, everything is in order."

The clerk pursed his lips. "Pray you don't ever need her. But I guess if you've got drovers too . . ."

G.B. Smith leaned into Davey as he followed his partner heading for the next wagon. He whispered something Letitia couldn't hear. Letitia saw the flush on Davey's cheeks as G.B. Smith looked at her as a hound a raccoon, enjoying the hunt. At his leaving she let out a breath she didn't know she'd been holding.

"I don't cotton to that man."

"He no favorite of mine. But we through the inspection so we's good."

Davey patted her back, his hand damp against her dress. "I 'spect so."

"Didn't know I's cookin' for drovers, though."

"Didn't I tell you? Yup, Knighton and Martin, though their families are going and they'll feed 'em some, I 'spect. I'll hire a kid if need be along the way if you can't do it if you need to. With the baby and all."

"I drive the oxen. B plods good and steady." She knew those oxen and the horses and mules. "What G.B. say to you?"

"Nothing a lady should hear. Just be relieved, Tish. We passed the inspection."

This one. But she suspected there'd be all kinds of *inspections* with G.B. along.

Davey cleared his throat. "You spoke up for yourself."

"Yessuh."

He scratched at his beard. "Not sure . . . not sure that's good for us, Tish."

"They accept me sayin' I's as good as a twelve-year-old boy."

"On the surface, yes. But you challenged G.B. too. He's not one to forget that a woman spoke up to him."

Letitia wanted to keep her hands busy. It helped relieve the *cowers*—the quivers and chills of the unknown that came when G.B. Smith sniffed around. She wasn't sure why she'd spoken up at all. It wasn't her way. Or hadn't been.

Nancy Hawkins approached Letitia as she sewed on the tent they'd use for sleeping. Letitia could see a few freckles on Nancy's creamy skin. She must have had her poke bonnet off. Letitia relied on her straw hat to block the sun. Edward waddled beside her and Nancy Jane rode on her mother's hip, her bonnet bow shading her baby face. The other children had already found playmates and were chasing a hapless frog. Even Laura skipped around, dirt on her dimpled face.

"How are you faring?" Nancy brushed puffs of dust into the clear morning air.

"'Spect I survive."

"Goodness, yes. Praise God for that." She shifted Nancy Jane to the other side. "I confess I am already tired and we've only begun." When she smiled, dimples pressed into her pretty face.

"Maybe as we get into habits things be better."

Nancy nodded.

"How many there be?"

"Zach says thousands. But we'll be in different companies. And he said not to let the children run ahead to another group of wagons as we could lose sight of them and we might not see them until we reach Laramie. Can you imagine losing your child like that? One day there and the next, gone?"

Letitia could imagine.

"Oh, Tisha, I'm so sorry." Nancy placed a hand on Letitia's arm. "How thoughtless of me. I didn't intend—"

"I knows. I keeps my eyes on the little ones. You gots full hands."

Nancy laughed. "I do that. And I notice that Zach is not nearly so helpful when there are other men around to join him fishing in the evening or jawing as he calls it, when he isn't mending up some break or wound. We used to spend our evenings together, building quilt frames and planning things and laughing at the children's antics when he wasn't hauled out to mend someone up." She sighed. "Now he's surrounded by potential patients and fishing and hunting partners. Samuel's just as bad. It'll be worse when my brothers and their families join us."

"Men be different when women around."

"They are indeed." She shifted her child again. Letitia offered to

119

hold her, but Nancy said, "I'd best get back and make sure every-thing's ready. You be sure to call on me if you're feeling poorly." She watched Letitia's hands make the stitches on the tent. "A tear already?"

"No. I makin' the seams stronger 'fore I wax 'em."

"You can wax mine when you're finished," Nancy teased.

"I be pleasured to. I'd be pleased." Letitia tried to remember to speak the way Nancy and Davey did, in an educated way.

"Oh, Letitia, I was fooling you. I can do the waxing. I hadn't thought of it. You have enough to do. Sometimes you're too gen-erous."

"I be pleasured to help you any way I can. You . . . you the kind-est woman I knows." She looked up at Nancy.

"Oh, paw." Nancy dismissed the words, but Letitia could see a slight flush at the compliment. She hadn't meant it as a compli-ment but as truth. Kindness wasn't easy to find in this company of strangers, but it lived inside Nancy Hawkins.

There were G.B. Smith's slurs and those of other men who watched her with wolfish looks as she climbed out of the wagon with streaked meat for supper. She didn't tell Nancy about the woman who demanded she help lift a heavy pot onto the andirons over her campfire. When Letitia resisted, saying she carried a child, the woman had sniffed and told her, "Your little black offspring isn't my concern. Feeding my children is. Now you help me or I'll complain about you to the captain." Letitia would have offered to help if she'd had a moment, before being ordered to do it.

She didn't share with Nancy her cowers of how the women would respond once her baby was born. She hoped it would be a girl. Girl babies were less threatening than boy babies, especially if their color was black as coal like hers.

❦

The sounds along with the smells and chaos at Capler's Landing made Letitia ill. Cattle bawled their unhappiness while children cried louder than men shouting orders. Dust rose up to coat her teeth as the wagons rolled onto the ferry that bobbed in the dark swirling waters of the Missouri. The river seemed to leer at her on this "jumping off" place, as the ferry transports were called. She watched a man with apple saplings wet the roots with burlap that had been dipped in the river. He was taking hope with him.

So was she with this baby waiting to be born free. The water made her breathe prayers of safety. She'd rarely been across such a wide expanse of river with muddy waves slopping against the wooden craft that set out now groaning against the cable. The current was so strong it pushed the ferry downriver before the *clang* of the cable snapped the ferry back upstream, knocking her off balance for a bit.

She caught her breath, leaned into Charity, grabbing the leather collar that held her bell. The iron held and the oxen on the other side working the cable bent their shoulders and circled, each time bringing the Carson wagon and two others toward the opposite shore. Rothwell panted beneath the wagon, his pink tongue hanging out from his tan and white muzzle. He'd found sparse shade while Davey calmed the oxen team, mules, and horses. The loose cattle would come on another ferry, the drovers moving the other cows, oxen, and additional mules and horses mixed in with other travelers.

She rubbed her fingers on the soft velvety ears of her cow, an act as comforting as fingering her son's baby quilt. The wind whipped her straw hat and it was gone, a tiny wheat-colored circle swirling on the dirty water. She'd be relegated to the bonnet now . . . or on cloudy days one of her red scarves.

Davey stood at the front by the oxen team with each animal's newly branded horns. "So we can identify the dead ones if they get lost or stolen by Indians," he'd explained.

Davey looked back once at her. He tipped his hat, assuring her. The adventurer in him lifted him like a boy attached to a kite, not a worry in the world. She guessed that was good that one of them felt safe and lifted up like a cloud. She vowed to look ahead toward the shoreline and swallowed back her upset stomach.

Once across the big river they'd be no longer in the states, no longer under the "wing of the government," as Davey said it. She'd never felt any government protection. It was her papers that would keep her safe.

"Watch that wheel chock!" someone shouted back to Davey.

He scurried around to secure the wagon, to keep it from rolling forward. Letitia gripped Charity's halter tighter. The bell clanged at the cow's neck as she twisted her head to lick her rough tongue at Letitia's arm. Spray from the river sprinkled them. She could hear her heart pounding, the cowers making her dizzy and sick and full of prayers when the ferry struck the far bank, knocking her ribs against Charity. The wagon jerked but held. It was May 9.

"Top o' the morning, we're here!" Davey lifted his hat and swirled it. "We've left the states! Now the journey begins."

Letitia couldn't celebrate with him. She lost her breakfast over the side of the ferry.

Uncharted Sentiment

Davey watched Letitia stand in the shadows of the wagons along with most of the women. A few trotted themselves into the voters choosing up a pilot, but none of them spoke. Davey was grateful Letitia knew her place. Nancy Hawkins was a good woman, but she chatted up Zach maybe a little too much. A man can't let a woman run him even if the woman made good sense now and then.

Three men vied for the pilot privilege and the $250 to $500 fee they'd earn being responsible for taking people through to Fort Vancouver. Each family would be assessed a portion of the fee of whichever guide was chosen. Davey had done some guiding in the mountains of Carolina but never got that kind of money. He also wasn't responsible for a thousand people and all the property they brought with them. It was hard to hear all the various voices raising issues, asking for hands to be lifted for votes.

He wished Junior had come along, could have shared these meetings so they could have discussed what happened later. But maybe not having him bumping heads with Letitia was one less twisted rope he had to straighten out.

He'd just taken a seat on a barrel when someone at the edge of the group shouted, "There's been a raid! Stock's missing!"

"Those Caws! I knew it."

"Now be calm, here. Caws are friendly Indians." This from a potential pilot.

"Don't matter!" An Iowa man spoke up. "Mount up and let's go get 'em!"

Davey saw Letitia scowl as he mounted up. Fifty men—minus the proposed pilot—headed toward a quiet Caw village they'd passed some time before. Davey felt the rush inside him, of bringing to justice people stealing stock. The men charged into the village but Davey pulled up Fergus. Something was amiss. He watched as the Caws scattered, frightened as field mice, dipping under tents, running behind trees, women's braids flying in the air as they grabbed children for safety, cries and shouts ringing in the morning air. He didn't see a cow in sight. *This don't look like a raiding party place.*

"Lookee here!" he shouted. "Let's see if we can get answers rather than scalps."

Swirling mounts snorted, their riders reining up as Davey conveyed concerns to the six or seven unarmed men whose village they'd invaded. At least they were talking. The elders shook their heads. To Davey, these Indians couldn't have been the thieves. No cattle milled about. Why had he rushed to join them in the first place? He remembered Letitia's scowl.

"There's one! He just came back! I bet he stole 'em." A Kentucky man, pointing, spurred his horse toward an Indian riding a mule entering the village. Greenberry Smith seized him, pulling him from his mule. "We'll take this one back for trial."

"He's trying to give you his mule, G.B.," Davey said. "He wouldn't do that if he'd stolen cattle. Lookee here. There's no sign of stock. They're peaceful."

124

"Quit defending this dead Indian."

No one supported Davey, and the man was bound and led forward, a rope forcing him beside another's horse.

At least they aren't going to hang him on the spot. Calmer heads would prevail if he could ensure the man got taken back to the company. He removed his hat, wiping his forehead of sweat.

"Let's keep him alive," Davey said. "Give the man his day in court."

A few days out and there were already accusations and legalities and people behaving like schoolyard kids.

Back at the wagons, the chosen judge shouted, "I call this court to order." Judge Kindred, Hawkins's brother-in-law, presided at the makeshift court of wagons and ropes. "Carson, ask him if he knows anything about missing cattle."

Davey did so. The Caw shook his head, as hard as a man wrongly accused of stealing could do. "He says he knows nothing, Your Honor. And truth be, he just rode in and they were having a ceremony, so I don't think they'd have been out rustling. Mule didn't look to be rode like someone chasing cattle. Shucks, he even offered to give Greenberry Smith over there his mount. Why would he do that if he had been out stealing?"

"That true, G.B.?"

Smith hesitated then nodded.

"A man hates to be charged with something he didn't do." Davey thought of that minx Eliza who had challenged his reputation.

"Truth is, the drovers count all the cattle still here, Judge." Sheepish words from one of his own drovers.

There wasn't even a theft?

"Not guilty!" declared the judge. "Get the man something to eat. See if we take the scare out of him, poor fellow."

No one seemed to have anything more to say about the so-called trial. They resumed the meeting, though Davey thought they might have been a little shamed for riding off all wild over nothing, scaring women and children mostly. He was.

Letitia reached down deep into the flour barrel and felt the cloth tied with the red ribbon that encircled her papers. She didn't open the cloth. She needed the reassurance the papers were there. They were "evidence" of her freedom. Without evidence she might not be able to defend herself over whatever strange charges could happen on this journey. That poor Caw was at the mercy of the court, though thank goodness he had Davey's level head to defend him. She never wanted to be at the mercy of others.

She pulled her arm out of the deep part of the flour, brushed the powder from her elbow, and plopped a handful in the bowl to mix up johnnycakes, humming to her child as she worked.

In the morning they heard the guides compete again, and this time Stephen Meek stood on a barrel and shouted, "By eternal Moses, I been thar . . ." He raved about the disasters they could encounter and ride out only if "by eternal Moses you listen to me!" And for some reason, he won the Oregon Emigrating Group over. Another company said they'd go without a guide. Davey told her he just "wanted to get going. All this chattering is taking precious time and supplies."

A part of her wished they could stay a few more days and she could deliver this baby. She felt like a watermelon, every step a waddle.

On their way now, morning routines began before dawn. Nancy Hawkins thought it strange that the men kept changing companies to travel with. *That* company had fewer cattle to watch after or *this* company moved faster. She shook her head. And they say women had fickle ways. After crossing the Missouri River, the Carson and Hawkins families traveled northwest, meeting up with Solomon

126

Tetherow and Stephen Staats as captains now. Davey Carson told Zach he was happy to turn his captaining over to others, be responsible for his own instead of many.

Nancy walked beside the wagon, scruffs of dust billowing up to make her cough. When the baby slept she could quilt a block or sometimes crochet a little lace as she walked. She pushed the side of her bonnet back so she could see better to her side, freckles or not. The bonnets made her feel like she lived in a tunnel. She hated having to turn her head to see what dangers might lurk at her side or even to greet a friend. Nancy's mother and sister and two brothers—one everyone called "Judge"—and their families had joined. The gathering of more family added comfort. She had in-laws, nieces, nephews, one little niece, Mary Margaret, born in March not long before they'd left. Nancy got on well with her mother-in-law, exchanging suggestions as the two cared for infants.

Birds twittered from the bushes beside the Kansas River they followed into a hazy sky. She stepped away from the dusty road, careful not to step in front of another wagon, her eyes first scanning to see where the children were. That Laura. Such a scamp. Inside the cabin she had been all quiet and frail, while out here in the wide-open spaces the child had become a fluff of dandelion hair, racing after dogs, jumping off the wagon and back on, holding a stick to the wheel to hear it *tick-tick-tick*. She'd have to keep an eye on that girl, give her little tasks to keep her out of trouble.

She was surprised at how relieved she felt to be in a daily routine. No more planning or choosing what to leave behind. What they had now was all they'd have, and each would have to adjust to the dwindling supplies or the weather reversals such as Sarah had written of in her letter. Nancy liked the sounds of the harness and hames, the lowing of cattle, and the tick of the odometer as the wheel turned to mark their miles. She carried Nancy Jane bundled in a cloth tied to her front, patting the child's bottom as she walked talking to her sister.

On a small rise Nancy looked outward. "Oh look." She clutched her sister's arm. The world opened up before her. Like strands of oatmeal-colored yarn furled along bright green prairie grass, the wagons spread out across the landscape, not in a single line but several. The river bordered in blue. "It's beautiful, isn't it?" This would be their lives now, a steady walk through new landscapes sashaying into the hopefulness of the unknown. *One day I'll weave that image into a quilt.* She'd add a daisy or two, even though they weren't growing here.

She already had ideas to break up the monotonous days once these vistas became familiar. She'd plan special celebrations for the children's birthdays and make up flour pastes to color with wild-flower blossoms to give the children things to do when the weather turned foul and they were stuck traveling inside the wagon. She shifted Nancy Jane in the carrying sack that lodged her youngest and brushed back the tawny hair from Nancy Jane's forehead. *Hot.* Maybe from the sun. She'd have to make sure her bonnet offered cooling shade for the child. She cuddled the baby closer. At the wagon, from one of her many petticoats, she tore a strip of cloth, dipped it into cool water from the barrel to relieve the child's flushed face.

"I'm worried over Nancy Jane," Nancy told her husband that evening.

The children had been put to bed in their own tent while she and Zach and the baby and Edward stayed in another. Dogs barked in the distance. They hadn't brought their dog. Zach had said the companies didn't really want them. "They scare the cattle." But Nancy missed their old hound. Letitia helped her find a home for him at the hotel with two young colored girls.

Somewhere farther away a fiddler played a happy tune. "Seems like she's fevered even though I wash her with cool water. I hoped she'd be a healthy baby. Laura's the one I worry over with her little wild side. Goodness. Now I have two that trouble my thoughts."

"She isn't fevered." Zach touched the child's forehead. "Just the hot sun. I can get her a tincture, but the cooling cloths work best and you're doing that." He straightened himself on the bedroll. Crossed his arms behind his head.

"Tell me something reassuring."

"Everything will be all right."

She pulled her hand from his. "That's not reassuring, it's . . . condescending."

Zach rolled onto his side, the baby between them. He twirled the child's blonde strand in his finger, his elbow sustaining him. "'Eastward I go only by force, Westward I go free.'"

"Thoreau," Nancy said.

"Yes. And children get sick no matter where they are. Could have gotten sick back home too."

"I know."

"There are all kinds of unknowns out here, but I carry with me the absolute belief that this is what we're supposed to be doing, that our going is part of some larger plan. So I can't let worries bring me down."

"I don't want them to bring me down either. I'm—"

"A mother. I know. But I also know you will do everything in your power to care for our children no matter where you are. You love, Nancy. No finer healing balm than that. I'm blessed with the results of that myself." He leaned in to kiss her, held her chin in the palm of his hand. He smelled of leather and the laudanum he'd administered to a patient, comforting smells. "You haven't changed your mind about having another, have you?" He grinned.

"No!" She laughed as he ran his fingers down her shoulder, creating those happiness chills. He did make her feel better, reminding her that they were in the palm of God's hand, that she came freely west.

The warmth of his hands along her hip made her weak. Zach lifted Nancy Jane and put her on the far side of him on their bedroll next to three-year-old Edward snoring softly. Then he reached for Nancy.

"I have so little will," she whispered.

"You're being an obedient wife. Trust me. Everything will work out as it should. Nancy Jane will be better by morning."

"That's my prayer."

"That, and that you will always love me, is mine."

She let herself be pulled to him, her face warm in awareness that other people were close and might hear them in their tent, and yet that thought added to the happiness chills Zach brought again with his kiss. She kissed him back. *I am so very weak!*

Guarded

The companies hadn't been out but a few weeks when Davey told Letitia, "They're posting double guards tonight. I'm one." He pushed his knee into Fergus's belly to make the gelding let out air so Davey could tighten the cinch on the saddle. His pat on the animal's rump was friendly.

"Don't let them take Charity." Letitia bit at a piece of hardtack hoping it would ease the discomfort in her belly. It didn't. Her back ached when she walked, but walking felt better than riding in the wagon and having her bones jerked about by the rough trail.

"Oh, now, I shouldn't have worried ye. I'll make sure your ol' cow's good. She'll be chewing her cud at the moon." He rubbed her shoulder. "I have the first watch. Be back in a few hours." He looked around, then pecked her cheek.

Letitia held Rothwell's collar and they both watched Davey ride off. "You stay with me, Roth." She scratched the hound's ears. Not that she had to tell the dog to stay. He'd been a faithful companion to her, more so since they'd been on the trail and the guards didn't want dogs loafing around, which seemed strange to her. The animals would pick up false sounds more easily than men would. She liked Rothwell's company, liked how he chased a rabbit through the sage, then returned panting with joy despite never catching his prey.

Watching Davey ride off she realized she'd be alone much of the time on this journey even if Davey no longer captained. He'd be flitting here and there like a horsefly lighting then disappearing. Davey drove the wagon, but anytime they stopped he was off helping others, talking up a canyon with resulting goodwill, so she didn't complain. The dog was untroubled company. Davey was a good man, she knew, but sometimes, like tonight, she wished he could have stayed here with her. She stroked her stomach, her fingers catching on the rough tow.

They'd circled wagons not far from a river whose name escaped her. The prairie had a dozen streams marking the dusty trail. She and Roth walked toward willows offering shade for rabbits and women tending their dailies. Instead of feeling comforted by the dry air, clear skies, and bird-chattering shrubs, a cower visited. She created it herself, as she'd never noticed any dangers there, hadn't seen anyone follow her. And if she turned quickly when she felt a stare, no one was ever there. The cowers in such places arrived on old memories, she decided, when being alert to potential danger was a matter for living and dying. Here she needed to sweep those thoughts with a new broom.

She decided it was a mother-worry. She patted Roth's head, and with a bar of soap she filled the bucket then nestled herself in the cover of the shrubs. She slipped the wrapper over her shoulders, letting the top fabric hang over her waist, exposing her arms and white undershirt. She bent awkwardly to dip her rag into the water and let the cool liquid cleanse her neck, her shoulders, her arms. She poured cool water over her feet. The dust. At times it was like walking in yellow moonbeams, the powdery earth washing her feet. But it felt good to rid herself of that powder too. Roth sniffed at a distance. She wiped her bodice and replaced the wrapper top. She spoke softly to her baby, words of love and comfort and welcome for when that baby would arrive. Finished and refreshed, she walked out of the willows.

"Oh!" She bumped into Nancy Hawkins. "Goodness."

"Scare me to dyin'."

"I saw a man come out of the bushes. I didn't think anyone else was here."

"He near?" Letitia felt her arms shiver.

"Close enough. You'd best let me know when you're taking your toilet. If for nothing else so I keep from scaring you!" Nancy searched her face. "Why, those beautiful arched brows of yours like to disappear into your hairline, I frightened you so. I'm sorry."

Letitia laughed, relief washing over her. "Come on, Roth. We stand guard for you."

"Much obliged."

When Nancy finished, the two women walked back to Letitia's wagon where Letitia picked up the milking bucket and stool, then she and the dog dropped Nancy at her wagon some way back from the Carson camp.

At the rope corral where the neat cows waited for milking, there was no Charity. They had lost stock. Her eyes searched the growing dusk. "We needs that cow," she told her baby.

She waited up for Davey, the dog snoring beside her as she listened to the sounds of families settling in for the night. There had been a man watching in the willows. Nancy had seen him. Stock was missing. These cowers were real. Letitia located one of the pistols, held it in her lap. She would take care of herself if Davey didn't return before she fell asleep. Or if he never returned at all.

⁓

Davey's face was hot and his wrinkles grimed with dust and sweat, but he was riding high in his saddle. "Old Charity saved the day," he told Letitia.

The sun cast its morning light on Letitia, who waddled out from their tent. He'd enjoyed this stock search, even though there'd been one slight discomfort. Not the right word. *Problem.* "Yes sir, I 'spect we'd never have found them without your Charity and the bell around her neck. We're the earliest companies coming through, so those Indians got to get themselves clear about what's going to happen if they sneak in and steal cattle at night. We'll go after them and we'll get our bovines back."

Letitia spread her fingers on her back that must be aching. The cow wouldn't need milking, pushed hard as she'd been. At least she wouldn't have that task.

"Kept shaking her neck like she does. Glad I gave you one good solid bell."

"Indians steal 'em? They plow through ropes?"

Davey swallowed. "Some guards fell asleep." He hurried on. "I didn't actually see any Indians, but the other search party heard a noise up in a tree when they were bringing cattle back and thought it might be a bear or meat and, without looking, shot." He whacked dust from his floppy hat. "And guess what? An Indian fell out."

Letitia gasped.

"You got some vittles I can take back to our drovers?"

"They kill him?"

"Who? Oh, that Indian. When I heard, I told them that wasn't a wise thing. We don't want no trouble with those folks. We're passing through, and chasing after our cows is a small price to pay for crossing their land, I 'spect."

"They bury him?"

Davey shook his head. "Left him, I hear."

"He stole Charity?"

"Doubt it. He was on foot. Probably crawled up there to be safe." He squinted at her. "You all right? Should I get Mrs. Hawkins?"

"I . . . lies down for a spell."

"Sure, sure. Didn't mean to upset you. Thought you'd be happy to know Charity was back. I'll get the biscuits and bacon for the drovers."

He never could figure out what upset a woman and what would make her happy. He guessed he could use a different path in his telling maybe, but he didn't think keeping bad news from her was wise either. There'd be lots of bad news in the days ahead and she'd have to learn from it. Not like she hadn't known trouble in her life before him. Still, maybe he'd been a little brash in sharing about the shooting. He threw away what was left of his coffee, the liquid beading up in the dust.

He approached their tent. "Letitia? You doing all right?"

A steady drizzle fell on her as she removed the tent from the wagon, then helped Davey unharness the oxen. The baby stirred but wasn't planning to enter the world this cool evening. It had been a long day with a late start due to the men helping repair a broken wagon wheel. It wasn't their wagon, this time. Letitia carried the bucket and her stool to the makeshift corral for the milk cows. Charity chewed her cud, looked at Letitia with placid brown eyes. Charity was safe. Little Nancy Jane's fever had broken. Something worried Letitia, though. *That Indian*. He'd been shot and they didn't even bother to bury him. He might have been someone's father. A mother would grieve him. What had Davey said? *Crawled up there to be safe.* As the warm milk hit the bucket, Letitia got lost in the rhythm and scent.

She remembered a man on the plantation she'd been contracted to, a man who crawled up a sycamore tree, hiding. The field marse lashed him out with his long black whip, then beat him to death in front of the slaves. "Let him be a lesson to you." She'd never forgotten the sounds, the thump and slash and wails. He was property, and the marse told them he could do whatever he wanted with his property.

May my baby's skin match his daddy's more than mine, she prayed. Maybe her son or daughter would pass as white. Davey would be more likely to love them, wouldn't he? Tears welled up;

she brushed them with her wrist. She needed to tell herself the truth. A child who could pass would be easier for Davey to claim as his own and better for keeping the story that she was his employee . . . at least while they were on this wagon train.

She stripped the teat to make sure no milk remained, dipped her fingers into the warm white as she lifted the bucket. Maybe there was no place safe.

The Fundamentals

"Some of us are gathering in a circle for our morning fundamentals," Nancy told her. "Come with us? Maryanne's watching Nancy Jane for me."

"Until you mentioned it, I's doin' well." Letitia rubbed her belly. "But now I's feelin' the pressure." She grinned. Davey told her she needed to get more kindred, as he called it.

They followed a group of women laughing as they formed a loose circle, their backs to each other holding wide their skirts fluffled with many petticoats, making their waists look small as a wagon hub. As they approached, Nancy waved at her mother and introduced herself to the rest of the group.

"Come on over." One of the women let loose her skirt and motioned them in. She had a pockmarked face and a broken front tooth. "Slip in right over here." The woman moved to make room.

"That's my daughter," Patsy Hawkins said, turning into the circle. "By marriage. Couldn't ask for a better one."

"I didn't see you over there, Mama Hawkins."

"You didn't recognize my backside?" The women laughed, a banter like quail chatter pecked the clear air.

"This is Letitia Carson." Nancy settled in beside her mother, motioning for Letitia to join them.

Letitia felt the pressure of making water and took a step forward.

"She can wait 'til last." A stout woman with a clean white apron over her pink-flowered calico held up her hand to hold Letitia back. "Out there." She pointed.

Letitia felt a burn rise up. She'd forgotten for a moment, thought she belonged when she didn't. The baby kicked at a greater need to relieve herself. *Just step away; hold your water.* She adjusted the kerchief she tied at the back of her neck, lifted her thick hair off her neck, willed her body to comply. *Please. Not now.*

Then the first trickling down her legs. She wanted to disappear into the dirt beside the hot water from her body.

Unaware, Nancy said, "I don't know that our bodies always do what we want when we want them to. That's why some of us have children we didn't expect." She said it cheerfully and several women laughed, but not the stout woman. Nancy added, "She may not be able to wait until last is all I'm saying."

"I'm not about to expose my privates to no black slave woman parading as a wife. She don't belong in this circle."

"She's not a slave, she's my friend and—"

"I's all right. You stay." Letitia stepped farther back to a desert place without shadow.

"This is ridiculous." Nancy moved back toward Letitia. "Oh." *She smell me.*

"Please. It be easier. You go to circlin'." Letitia motioned with her hands, then squatted, finished relieving herself, alone.

Nancy's hands gripped her hips. She set her jaw, then accepting Letitia's plea, stomped back beside her mother. The stout woman curled her lip in a sneer and turned her back to the circle's interior, held out her skirt to offer protection to the first woman who stepped inside the circle of safety. A skinny woman leaned in to

Nancy and said something Letitia couldn't hear, but Nancy nodded. Her shoulders dropped a little. When each woman had tended
to her personal hygiene needs, "the fundamentals" Nancy called
it, the stout woman broke from the ring and walked back to the
camp without a backward glance. A few others joined her, looking
back, shaking their heads. The women in Nancy's family stayed, as
did a few others who at Nancy's insistence moved toward Letitia.

"I's finished."

Letitia dropped her bundled skirts that brushed the dirt. Hot
tears pressed against her puffy cheeks. Nancy wrapped her arms
around her and mercifully, said nothing, just held her. Through tears
she heard two women agree to exchange a spice. A grandmother
told a story about her littlest grandchild finding a frog. Nancy
patted her back, released her, as Letitia wiped her eyes, "Anyone
know how to keep a fever down?" *These be fundamentals. Tendin'
and mendin' and befriendin'.*

Walking back, Nancy took Letitia's hand and said, "You should
have let me argue on your behalf, Tish. People won't change their
ways if they aren't confronted with their prejudices. They need
their sensibilities confronted."

"I knows my place. I jus' forgets sometime 'cause you so kind.
Don't stand for me. It make trouble for you if you seen as befriendin' such as me."

"If they knew you, they'd soon see that your soul and your spirit
are the same colors as theirs." Nancy said it with a huff.

"People don' change 'cause you ask 'em to. They change if they
let the Lord make a safe place for 'em. They don' feel safe with me
. . . like I don' feel safe with lots of them."

∽

They made their way through prairie grass and swollen streams
lulled by the harness shakes of A, B, C, and D bearing their heavy
yokes. Pale yellow clouds wisped into dusk as Letitia prepared a
light meal. There'd be a wedding this evening. The pilot, Stephen

Meek, would take a young bride, already eighteen, whom he'd known for three days.

The night before, Letitia and little Laura had walked to the river and found turtle eggs they brought back to make the bride's cake. The bride was a new orphan, her father having drowned days before. She had no one. Letitia baked the cake, the pleasant aroma pouring from the reflector oven.

After the vows were spoken before a Mississippi Baptist minister, everyone danced and laughed and told stories and ate. Letitia tapped her toes to the music but stayed well away from the partying. Her own wedding came to mind. Love didn't always draw two people together. Sometimes it was security as she suspected it was for the new Mrs. Meek. But like a good garden patch, security was the soil that made love grow strong. Marriage, spoken over sacred words, was meant to last a lifetime and she hoped that would be the case with Davey and with the Meeks.

She watched Davey stand off with men laughing and talking. Once he looked up to where she stood in the darkness. She was out of campfire light so she knew he couldn't see her well, but it pleased her just the same that he'd taken the time to seek her out. He gave a little wave, his white blouse sleeves ballooning in the evening breeze, the wide black belt showing his slender frame. She lifted her hand from her belly and waved back when Davey started across the dance boards loaned from someone's wagon bottom. "Care for company?"

"I's obliged."

He slipped his arm around her plump waist. She leaned her head on his shoulder. Sometimes a body didn't know what it needed until someone else made the offer. Marriages were made up of those small moments, she decided; she would learn to inhale them.

～✑

"We're going to split into three groups now." Davey talked while she cooked a rare turtle egg in the pan.

She wished they'd brought chickens along. Davey called her streaked meat "bacon." It bubbled beside the egg.

"Meek is taking the group without cattle and they'll go ahead. Joel Palmer will take the small-stock division—where we'll be—and the rest will go in the large stock company. We'll rotate being in front a week at a time. Maybe there'll be less arguing that way about who travels in whose dust." He adjusted the wide belt at his waist. "I think I'm slipping pounds, Tish. Get me another slice of that bacon. How you feeling?"

"I like slippin' a few pounds." She patted her stomach.

"All in due time. All in due time."

That week they saw wolves trailing large buffalo herds raising mountains of dust in the distance. Debate about hunting them ensued, but the company voted to keep going. They encountered a group of trappers taking hides to St. Louis who offered to bring mail back to the states. The companies shut down early so letters could be written and sent off. They were also joined by a platoon of nineteen soldiers out of Fort Leavenworth pulling two wagons of howitzers along with their sidearms and rifles. "Sent for security and to be a show of force to the Indians, I 'spect," Davey said.

They went to bed knowing the dragoons camped not far from them. Additional security. Letitia woke with a start. The tent floor felt wet. Had her water broken? No. The crack of thunder again. "Davey. We get up and sleep in the wagon. It rainin' hard."

The night lit up then, flashes of lightning split the wide sky horizontally, the boom and roll of thunder forcing her hands to her ears.

"I'll pull the tent under the wagon out of the rain."

In the flashes as she crawled under the wagon, she watched others scurrying from their tents or tying the canvas down and quieting the cries of children. Cattle bawled. Hail came then, as large as a baby's thumb. One hit her leg and she winced. Rothwell pushed into the tent with them. Once assured that Letitia was covered, Davey moved off through the rain toward the cattle. The drovers

141

would need help. He yelped when the hail hit him as he ran toward the rope corral to find his horse, pulled his greased hat brim down tight against the storm.

Wind whipped up the tent side flaps, forcing water to gush onto the oiled pad. Being under the wagon was foolhardy. She was as wet as being outside. "You stay here, Roth." She scrambled out as best she could and was drenched to the skin by the time she pulled her bulky body up into the wagon. Inside, she tugged the ropes tight at each end, shook her arms and fingers of the rain. Ran her hands over the cornrows, feeling their nubbins, then found a dry tow linen to slip over her head.

Inside, she stared out at the vast night through the O with its puckered opening. She'd never seen such a storm as this, wind whipping the whole wagon as though it might tip over, then rocking back on its wheels. Her skin quivered with a lightning flash. The sky was so vast and their little wagons as vulnerable as rabbits beneath a sky full of hawks. The hail split a hole in the canvas and she stood to pull it tight, to keep it from tearing further. She looked around for her needle but it would have to wait. She grabbed a wooden bucket and collected the rain beneath it. She wished that Davey would come back. She didn't like weathering this storm by herself.

"Roth! Come!"

He only had to be called once. She pulled the strings to the O, letting the dog soar in. The two hovered together in the rain, shivering but neither alone.

❧

In the morning Zach and Nancy looked out at the devastation. Wagons tipped on their sides, with blankets and barrels and children's stuffed dolls, and a boy's small boot spilled out into mud so thick that people grew two inches with it stuck to the bottom of their shoes. Broken wagon tongues and wheels meant a day or more of repairs. Dozens of horses and cows had been lost and a party formed to search for them. Zach left to check for wounded.

Nancy saw Letitia sewing patches on the hole in the canvas, her face warm from the drying sun. Clothing lay spread on the wagon seats to dry. Nancy had attached a clothesline to her wagon and hooked it onto her mother's so they could lay out drenched quilts. Then she headed toward Letitia.

"Quite a tirade last night." Nancy carried her youngest on her hip, bouncing the child while Laura clambered inside the Carsons' wagon. "Careful," Nancy warned her daughter. "Martha, go with her and get her back. Her feet are muddy as the Platte and don't need to be crawling over Mrs. Carson's things."

"It hard to believe the storm bring such trouble and then be all sunshine and warm right after."

"Guess that's what we're supposed to remember about hard times." Nancy swatted at a bug near the baby's face. "They're always followed by the warming sun."

"At least this baby stay put." Letitia's voice caught.

Nancy reached across and patted her hand. "You call on me. Send Rothwell if you're alone. That Davey busies himself." The dog's tail began to wag at the sound of his name. "Our wagons will never be that far from yours."

She'd make sure Zach knew that they should be close to the Carsons. That Davey looked after the cows all right, but goodness, he wasn't always aware of what his wife needed.

Nancy lifted her face to the sky and inhaled. "Air is fresh too. Good day to wash off the mud. Laura, get down."

Letitia reached for four-year-old Laura from the back of the wagon.

"Oh don't you lift her," Nancy warned.

"I'm too big to carry." Laura jumped through Letitia's hands and landed with a splat in the mud. Laura didn't even cry. She slapped the mud with her hands, tossing up black blots like freckles onto her face.

"Mama," Martha complained as she stepped back from the splatter.

143

Nancy shook her head as she pulled Laura up and swatted her behind, then she sent her and Martha off on a task. "Time to fill the buckets, you two. See who can bring back the most water. Martha, you look after that scamp. And maybe find a little dry wood for us."

"Slim chance they find anythin' dry." Letitia shaded her eyes of the sun. "You think it safe to let them fill buckets from the river with the rains? It so swift."

Nancy looked. "They'll be all right." She turned back. "We've made a game of the bucket-filling. You feeling all right? You look a bit peaked."

"I's not feelin' tops." Letitia sank against the wagon wheel. Both the Hawkinses' and the Carsons' sturdy Bethel wagons hadn't been tipped over nor had anything broken. Only the tears in the canvas and soaked bedding testified to the deluge. Letitia put her hands to her cheeks. "Jus' hot. And wishin' this baby would arrive. Overdue by my figurin'."

"It's a girl then." Nancy spoke with certainty. "We women are always late."

Letitia's laughter was interrupted by a child's cry of "Mama!"

Nancy turned toward the river. *Is that Laura screaming?* Nancy hesitated then started to run.

"Give me Nancy Jane."

Nancy nearly threw her infant at her friend while she picked up her skirts, rushing.

"Martha? Laura!"

Martha spurted out through the willows, sobbing.

"Where's Laura? Where's your sister? What's wrong?"

Martha's eyes were washed with fear.

Nancy looked beyond. "Where's Laura?" She brushed past her daughter. "Laura! Where are you? Laura?" There hadn't been enough time for her to get into trouble, had there?

Martha followed her mother through the willows and stood sobbing as Nancy rushed up and down the riverbank, calling out, skirts in her hands. One empty bucket lay at the riverbank. Nancy

144

felt more than saw her mother. Her mother-in-law. Letitia. Her sister. *The river is high and swift.*

"Martha." Nancy turned, grabbed Martha's shoulders. "Where is your sister?"

Martha pointed to the river, her sorrow broken with hiccups of pain. "She were there. And then she weren't. I'm sorry, Mama. I'm sorry."

And so am I.

15

A Time to Weep, a Time to Laugh

A pall like a black lamp shade in an already darkened room fell over the camp. Letitia heard that a child lay ill with typhoid and another had been run over by a wagon but had been saved by the soft mud sinking him beneath the wheels. Heavy rains take one child; another is saved by the same downpour. Doc Hawkins had set the two broken bones. Letitia heard the hacking of a child with whooping cough. Laura was gone. Not a trace of her.

When the men returned, they too rode the riverbank seeking some sign.

Meek, the guide, said, "By eternal Moses, that thar river is full of swifty currents enough to swirl a grown man beneath them and hold him thar for weeks afore spitting him up."

Nancy's family surrounded her in her grief, but she sat dazed, seeming unaware that an infant patted her tear-stained cheeks. Laura was a child of the river now. Memories like wisps of sunset were all that remained.

Letitia offered to milk the Hawkinses' cow. It was what she could think to do to help. Zach nodded his thanks, his eyes red and pinched.

Nancy repeated, over and over, "I sent her to her death. I sent her to her death."

"No you did not." Doc pulled her to his chest as they sat on the quilt in the wagon shade. He patted her back as she sobbed. "These things . . . we don't control life or death." He cleared his throat, nodded to Letitia.

"But I told them to go to the river. Letitia even asked if I thought it was safe. I should have known it was dangerous. I was so . . . cavalier about it. I killed her!"

"It was a terrible accident, Nancy. I could say I should have been here helping, so it's my fault. Or we never should have left Missouri. That's my fault too. Poor Martha's blaming herself. There's no place to mark blame or go back on this map. Here is where we are."

Letitia touched her friend's shoulder and squeezed. She picked up the Hawkinses' milk bucket and stool. She waited a moment, trying to find something to say. What had anyone said to her that brought comfort when Nathan barely breathed a day?

"'They is a time to weep and time to laugh; time to mourn and time to dance.' I trust that promise, livin' it. Things go better when weepin' and mournin' pass. I pray you is goin' laugh and dance again. I walk beside you 'til you do, Miss Nancy. You not grieve alone."

Nancy took Letitia's hand. "You've lost a child. I'd forgotten. I'm so sorry. Your boy sold . . ." She turned back to her husband. "There's no . . . body. Nothing to bury." And she wept again.

For Jeremiah, sold away, there'd been no body either. A living death is what Letitia mourned; Nancy too, and those were hardest.

Doc whispered something about sorrow. Nancy nodded, wiped her nose still buried in his chest. Letitia could see the love Doc held for his wife, delaying his own grief while he worked to untangle hers.

147

Later that evening the company held a memorial for Laura Hawkins. Doc took one of the quilt frame sides and cut it, transformed it to a wooden cross, and carved Laura's name on it. They pounded it into the soft ground not far from the river. The great sadness brought back Letitia's old feelings of wondering if she ever should have left Kentucky. Maybe her son hadn't died, was waiting for her to find him? She spoke a healing prayer for the Hawkins family. What had Doc said, that there was no map to go back.

The companies started wearing cantankerousness like a yoke around their necks. Davey tore at a piece of tobacco. It was worse than the town meetings squabbling over neighbors' dogs or loose cattle in the commons. Company members complained about who got to follow whom, about whether to form two lines and let the children and women walk between them or form one long line. Either way, what to do about the dust—as if anything could be done about dust. The first time they'd actually been threatened by what someone thought was an Indian attack, chaos reigned like men riding unbroken horses in the middle of a mercantile. Women and children screamed and men ran around without ammunition close by, kids hid under the wagons as though they'd find safety there. No one seemed to be in charge or everyone was. They'd lived through that and there hadn't even been an Indian in sight. Just a voice of panic from someone seeing things that weren't there.

"There's so little grass now," Davey told Letitia, "the cattle are roaming farther and farther through the night and it's taking us half the morning or more to round 'em up."

Letitia scraped the tin plates of breakfast scraps for Rothwell.

"We have to have more than a few hours in the afternoon to travel or we won't get to Oregon 'til Christmas. Now what's that?"

He stood to the sound of a braying donkey.

"Lookee there. A little donkey's got buffalo tails high to the wind heading west! Tish, they're making better time than we ever will." Davey laughed despite his annoyance. "That little donkey has guts." He sighed, poured himself another cup of grain coffee.

Letitia grinned watching the donkey's antics, the big-headed buffalo running like frantic chickens.

"Lookee. We need to move ahead with the first company, Tish. We could be on the trail right now instead of sitting here while the guards round up the cattle. There was a group far behind us that's moved up. We best do that too."

"Don' people count on each other? Aren't you standin' guard in, what you say, rotation?"

"We'll find new people."

Tish was quiet. He knew she was thinking because she sucked on her bottom lip when a thought worked its way to her tongue.

"We'll be fine. We don't want to get caught in the mountains at an early storm, so we got to go faster."

"I needs to stay with the Hawkinses."

Was this woman suddenly going to get demanding? "They've got two wagons and their cattle and kin. They can't move much faster. We can."

"We know them. They friends. They needs us."

She chewed that lip again and absently rubbed her belly. *Maybe she needs them.* He couldn't be giving in to every woman whim. Still . . . he didn't want her troubled with this baby coming. She was good help and, besides, he liked her and maybe even loved her. He knew he liked her best when she wasn't soured on something he'd done. He decided never to tell her that he'd been left off guard duty from now on because he'd fallen asleep. He was lucky he didn't get lashed.

"Alright. We'll wait until the baby comes. Then we move forward." He supposed women did need each other at troubling times, unlike men who could go it alone.

The fiddler played "Turkey in the Straw" on a cooling-off evening on the first days of June. There'd been a wedding earlier in the day with dancing and jerked buffalo meat to eat. Letitia and Nancy and her relatives had hung the strips on the poles the men set over a fire pit, smoking the meat in five hours or so. The men had come upon a buffalo herd and decided it was time to harvest a few. That's what Davey called it, a harvest. Letitia boiled meat strips in a heavy salt brine, her mouth watering in anticipation. This meat would keep them for months, but the work had tired all of them. Some women didn't even know how to cure it, nor separate the hide from the muscle.

Nancy's family had worked beside Letitia, and even Nancy smiled once when Nancy Jane put her pudgy palm into the salt box then licked at the grains. The face she made looked like a punched-in peach. Letitia noticed that Nancy kept Maryanne close by and Martha even closer. Forgiving herself would take even longer than discovering there was no way to move her heart around to fill the empty space that Laura left.

It wouldn't be long before the wagons reached Fort Laramie where they could resupply flour and corn and get iron for major repairs. Letitia planned to get new salve for the oxen and Charity's hooves, split by the hard, dry ground. When the short bristled grass pushed up between the cracks, the hooves festered though Letitia washed them every night hoping to keep the faithful beasts from going lame. She struggled to bend and lift the heavy hooves, sat to do the washing. Fortunately, the animals were docile, but she still used caution lifting their legs. One jerk and her baby's . . . well, she wouldn't think about it.

Walking to Nancy's wagon for her evening pause, Letitia caught an image of herself in the broken mirror Nancy'd hung on the side of her wagon. Letitia's face had grown darker in the hot sun despite wearing the bonnet. And her cheeks looked plump as a gopher's. When would this baby arrive?

"It feel good to have a full larder." She nodded at the dried buffalo meat.

Nancy sighed. "At least I can keep the children fed if not safe."

Letitia didn't respond, ran her fingers through the daisy fuzz on Nancy Jane's head. After a bit, she said, "I not sure we keep our chillun safe, not forever. We jus' asked to prepare 'em for the dangers."

"I didn't do that well."

"I hear you tell your girls be careful. But chilluns . . ." She raised her palms. "No holdin' chilluns back from explorin'. It their nature."

"Will it ever stop hurting?" Nancy looked at Letitia, wearing an ache so cutting, Letitia's thoughts sank to a deepening well.

"Wounds heal, even ones made with sharp knives. But they be leavin' scars."

"Especially on the heart. My sister-in-law tells me I need to stop talking about it. 'You're not the first woman to lose a child,' she says."

"Grievin' a personal thing. Can't move on till you witness to the loss and that be different for each of us."

"I pray, I do."

"He listen. Maybe he send me to listen too."

Nancy looked up. "Thank you for not telling me to be silent."

"A grievin' cloak wears different on ever' body. When you ready, you put on a different one. 'Til then, I be here holdin' your grievin' shawl."

"You and Zach. He never tells me not to talk about Laura or the emptiness."

"He lovin' you into healin'." Nancy nodded and the two sat together with the fiddle playing in the distance.

Letitia hadn't had anyone to help her being loved to healing, but she somehow knew how to do it for another. She guessed that was the Lord's provision.

Walking back, Letitia felt her water break. "This good as any evenin' for you to arrive." She turned back to get her friend.

151

They named the girl Martha. Davey said it was his mother's name, and Letitia liked giving Martha Hawkins a namesake, something to remind the child that life went on.

"Her skin's like Mama's coffee," Martha told Letitia as she ran her small finger down the baby's cheek. "She puts lots and lots and lots of milk in it."

"A weak coffee." Nancy gazed at the child. "She's beautiful. Look at that head of hair, so thick and sticking straight up, and those lashes. Goodness. What I wouldn't give for those!"

Davey had stayed outside the wagon and was there when Doc Hawkins delivered Martha near dawn on June 9. Letitia heard fiddle music at the beginning of her labor, the strings still vibrating when Martha arrived a few hours later.

"I'm not sure it's fair that your labor was so short," Nancy teased, her eyes on Martha, the child now holding her namesake.

"Ain't nothin' fair 'bout child birthin' except when it over."

"Amen to that." Nancy looked wistful. "Laura was a hard birth, hardest of all of them. So frail in the beginning, I even wondered if she'd live past the night." She swallowed. "But she did, weak as a wilted bachelor button until we started on this journey. Then so lively and full of life until—"

"Best you think on that healthy chil' and the good days you have with her."

"Of course. I'm sorry. Here's your joyous time and I'm mixing it with misery."

"Can't mix it unless I lets you. Good to let memories be salve instead of sorrow, though." She hadn't known she knew that before she said it. A good thing to remember for herself. "You be god-parentin' for her?"

"Why, I'm sure Zach and I would be honored." Nancy's eyes teared up. "I'm happy for you, know that I am, Tish."

"I knows. Tears mingle. Help us fly like sparrows out of the cave of darkness into a sky of light."

Nancy squeezed Letitia's shoulder, wiped her eyes of sadness.

Martha Hawkins spent the morning riding in the wagon with Letitia and her baby, but by noon Letitia was ready to walk. The little girl kicked dirt beside her and that was how their days went, with Martha tending to Baby Martha any way she could and Letitia loving the feel of a child in her arms and another near her knees.

"You're a good mama." Davey watched the child nurse. He'd been fed by the Hawkins clan and brought back a cup of soup for Letitia that he set on the wagon ledge.

"I's practiced. You wanna—want to—hold her?"

"Aw, I'm not so good with little ones like that."

"She don' break."

"She's so . . . fragile."

"Good-sized ham and as solid, I 'spect." Letitia watched Davey's eyes go from a moment of uncertainty to soft like a sunken cake as she handed the swaddled baby into his calloused hands.

He bounced the child who promptly burped up her supper. "Oh, here." He handed the baby back.

"You just beginnin'. She make a papa out of you." She paused. "But then you already one."

"Now I have two. A lucky man I am."

Davey picked up the rib of a buffalo skeleton with currant berries growing around it. They were a few days out of Fort Laramie.

"We can use it to write a message on if we need to, to those coming behind."

She frowned. *He still hopin' to join the faster groups if he plannin' how to leave messages for others. And I thought he couldn't write much.* She adjusted the bonnet on Martha's face to keep out the sun.

"Or better, use it as a back scratcher." He demonstrated and they both laughed.

Later that day they came to a deep ravine and men began the tedious task of locking wheels and lowering the wagons with ropes to the bottom of a narrow canyon bordered by a dry riverbed and steep cliff walls. Cattle had been taken a different route where the wagons couldn't pass. They traveled beside cliffs taller than any Letitia had ever seen. Small trees grew from the crags and she could smell honeysuckle blooming on sturdy vines pushing their way through cracks far up toward the top. They'd been careful with water, but for the entire day they did not cross a stream and their throats were parched as old paper.

Davey said they were all supposed to wait once they got to Ash Hollow, but forward groups had gone on ahead. "We may as well keep going ahead too," he said.

"But Nancy—"

"Hawkins can decide on his own. They'll follow the north fork same as us and we'll meet up again. In Oregon if nowhere else."

"I thought . . . she a big help." How could she tell him about the rare and pleasant feeling of having a woman treat her like a friend.

"We'll hold over at Fort Laramie. You're more a help to her than she to you anyway."

"No. She—"

"There's no arguing about this, Tisha. You say your good-byes. We'll head out at first light to catch up with a forward group. You do as I say now. That's the way it is and I'll not have an argument. Remember you're working for me. Man has to be the head."

"We leavin' you. Davey got his mind made up." Letitia had left Baby Martha sleeping in the wagon, settled for the evening, but she felt undressed without the child in her arms, as though she'd left her apron off in the middle of the day.

"Oh, Letitia!" Nancy hugged her. "I'll have Zach talk to him."

"It won't do no good. He get his back up about somethin' and—"

Nancy sighed and nodded. "The life of a wife. Maryanne, get Tish a cup of my tea."

"I'll miss Martha helpin' me and all you do." Even now Martha sat in the Carson wagon making sure the baby didn't tumble off of the cot, the child not believing that a baby that young couldn't roll over. Even Rothwell felt safe enough to leave the baby in Martha's care. He'd trotted along with Letitia to the Hawkinses' wagons.

"Have you told Martha?"

Letitia shook her head no.

"She'll be at a loss, poor thing. She's found a balm in looking after your baby. I'd let Martha go with you 'til Laramie but—"

"No, no. Too hard for you wonderin' about her."

"She'd be in good hands with you and I wouldn't have to see those sad eyes staring guilt into me like an arrow to a target."

"You keep your kin just fine. Martha need you."

The women hugged again. There were still leavings to deal with and would be their whole lives.

"I hopes there are lots of trees so I bypass that fundamental circle." Letitia made it sound light but she chewed on her lip. She wasn't sure she'd find people to be a shelter with. And now, with a pecan-colored baby, there might be even more raised eyebrows and painful words spit her way. White folks didn't like seeing more black folks join the world unless they owned them.

"Maybe . . ." Could she ask to travel with the Hawkins clan instead of with Davey? Davey would do fine without her. He had for years before she came along and even on this journey he handled the oxen himself. She'd been of little help of late because of her carrying and then the new baby. He wouldn't have to deal with any comments about his "black woman" and child if she wasn't around. Nor would she. Folks would assume for certain that she was a nanny of the Hawkinses and she could disappear inside their large family. She could offer comfort to Nancy and Martha too. She could milk the cows, Charity included. Davey would let her take Charity.

"Maybe you could come with us," Nancy said.

Had she spoken her wish out loud? Letitia chewed on her lower lip.

"I was thinkin' to ask." She looked down. Some things are better left as wishes. "But truth is, I takes a vow and now I gots a family of more than Davey. And he makes a promise to me too. We get mixed up with you again in Oregon, Davey says." She'd pray for that.

Oregon Country

Ducks flew overhead as The Woman dipped water from the bubbling springs to give to Little Shoot to drink. The smell pricked at her nose. "Those leaves are not friendly," she told him.

"They grow thick like mosquitoes."

"Ayee." Poison oak did grow thick in this place, but so did many good plants. "One must learn ways to live with good and bad."

Little Shoot still suffered from the poison oak, though the scratching lessened and the bubbling water at the springs seemed to help. For many days now they had eaten the trout from the streams by taking all the parts, the head and eggs, and then drying the flesh. Today she put one of the dried fish heads in a basket with hot rocks to make a boiled soup. Then she added a ball of baked camas into the bubbling mix. They would eat well, the entire clan spending a few days at this place of encircling hills.

The fish eggs they'd save and eat in the winter, along with long strips of dried fish flesh. These fish were not big as the salmon on the Willamette River, but added up they would be enough for a long, rainy winter.

"You are well enough to do more?"

Little Shoot groaned. "I still need rest."

She wasn't sure if he teased her or not, but perhaps they had accomplished enough for one day. They made their way back toward the encampment where several families had built rounded shelters of hazel branches covered with tule mats and grasses. The Woman knew all the people were needed when they prepared the camas bulbs they'd dug or to grind the acorns into a meal. But she also liked the time alone with her grandson where he learned from her and not from the boys who knew better how to play than how to feed themselves.

Back at the camp, a pig snorted into a clearing. She had seen such an animal at the mission. This one must have escaped from far away. It sought acorns and belonged to the land. Little Shoot and several other boys chased it.

"Ayee. My grandson is feeling better."

The Woman set about showing the boys how to make a fence from the saplings and grasses. "You will watch him and move the fence with him so he can eat the acorns. He will give himself up to us this fall, if we can keep him around."

The boys did not look happy. Little Shoot told her later that the chase was more fun than what happened after the capture.

"It is good you learn this now and maybe, if you are wise, you make the capture interesting too. There is always room to find a new way to treasure a gift arriving unexpected."

Carrying On

The next weeks felt harder to Letitia as she walked the trail without Nancy. They passed a wagon now and then, and she asked Davey if she and Martha could ride then. "It keeps the dust from the baby's eyes."

"Doesn't take that long to pass a wagon." But Davey agreed, stopping the ox team for her to get into the back under the bows as they came upon another family.

Inside, she didn't have to feel the piercing hurt when a woman "hallo-ed" her and then stopped waving when Letitia turned her dark face toward the westerly-heading wife. She had yet to see another colored woman in all the wagons they'd passed. She longed to share a mother's stories, how Martha curled herself into Letitia's breast, how she nursed, soft and gentle, never greedy, as though she knew her mother had more than enough to give this child. But the women had turned aside.

Letitia wondered if she'd have any colored neighbors once they reached the territory, not that having them meant they'd be speak-to neighbors. Or if she'd have any speak-to neighbors at all.

Somewhere east of Laramie, Davey developed a cough and sore throat that she treated with an herb tea. He improved and told her he was grateful, patting her hip as they lay beside each other in the tent, Martha cooing between them in the crook of Letitia's arm. Davey hacked through the night while Rothwell snored his level of concern outside the tent.

New challenges of the trail hardened the demand on the overlanders. One long route of fifty miles was made without any water for oxen, dogs, or people. The guide book Davey read from said it would be thirty miles. High clouds did little to soften the heat, and trees became scarce through much of the landscape before Fort Laramie. A strange high-peaked rock shot out of the land like a giant chimney in the distance and she didn't have to ask its name. Davey had been saying they'd see Chimney Rock before long. She wished she could be there when the Hawkinses' Martha first saw the pillar. The child's eyes would be wide with wonder.

She found she talked to Baby Martha as though she was Nancy, holding her up to the landscapes, chatting away about the weather or Davey's mumbling as he harnessed the oxen; even when she milked Charity and the baby stared with wide eyes at her from the cradle basket, she talked. "I spend more time talkin' with you than your daddy. Guess you know afore him we still got cornmeal but gettin' low on flour." It was easier discussing a meal or dwindling supplies with another woman. Davey pooh-poohed any worries she raised or told her how he'd fix whatever troubled her. It was a part of him that annoyed like a too-tight shoe. She didn't want to take it off, but she wished it would stretch a bit, give a little more room for the walking.

"We'll resupply the flour at Fort Laramie."

"What if they out or the price too high?"

"Then we'll get corn. You can fix corn pone instead of biscuits. I'll live." He lifted her chin and smiled. "You worry overmuch."

Sometimes she didn't want a concern she raised to be fixed; she wanted someone to listen to her thoughts spoken out loud without dismissing them because the listener didn't feel they carried any weight.

Teepees with decorations of feathers and black drawings on hides welcomed them as they approached the fort. The triangle-shaped structures sat like cone hats surrounding the adobe buildings of Fort Laramie. Davey and Letitia arrived with Captain Rigg's group following another terrible wind and hailstorm that left their Bethel wagon with a split wheel. While Davey sought out the blacksmith, Letitia wandered across the courtyard to the bakery, the scent of fresh-baked bread with poppy seeds watering her mouth. If they stayed three or four days here, she'd look big as when she carried Martha.

But the Hawkinses' wagon might well catch up too.

The baker hesitated before giving her the bread but must have decided her money was as good as any white person's. "Ain't seen many like you." He handed her the string-wrapped package.

"Ain't seen many mothers? Our camp full of 'em."

The baker grinned. "I had that coming."

She'd save the package wrapping. Maybe Davey would write a letter for her, leave it for the Hawkinses. No, he didn't write well, he'd said. And she had no one else to ask.

Later she carried her washboard and a basket of clothes on her head to the Laramie River while Martha snuggled at her chest. She heard stories while she ran Davey's pants against the washboard, her knuckles catching the rough tin now and then. At least they hadn't lost an ox the way one of the travelers had, the poor animal breaking its neck in the midst of a stampede.

One woman told of trading with the Indians for a beaded purse she planned to send home to her mother in Iowa. Letitia had seen the Indian women carrying their babies in a wood-framed cradle on their backs, and she thought she might go there to see if she could trade for one. But she wasn't sure what she had to trade except one of Davey's flannel shirts. She listened as she worked, to stories of escape during a stampede and runaway.

"Captain Barlow yelled for people to drop their wagon tongues to hold them back, but by then it was too late. They overrun us all," the woman who had escaped told the washing women.

"It's a wonder any of us lived." A slender woman snapped an apron, laying it on the shrub beside the river. "I declare I would not have come if it hadn't meant I'd have stayed in Kentucky alone, that man was so committed to this journey."

"I heard one company was exposed to measles," Letitia offered, working up her courage to join in the conversation.

The women turned as one to her. Several frowned.

"Ain't heard that," the Kentucky woman said.

"Don't even mention such a thing, girl. That's all we'd need way out here."

"Who's got a good pie recipe for dried currants?"

A breeze cooled Letitia's hot face. Martha cried from her sack then and the women returned to their chatter, their voices lower but still carrying across the water. Maybe talking about the terrible things that could happen and putting worries in a bucket to carry around to share wasn't a good idea. Listening to the women's laments, Letitia decided she was in a better place than many of them. She had chosen to come with Davey, chosen to make a new life with him.

She spread her wet laundry over the bushes, watched as the sun shimmered against the water, the reflection fluttering the leaves like a mist that never disappeared.

The Kentucky woman carried her basket of wet clothes on her hip, but she stopped and looked at Martha. "She's adorable. She'll crush some man's heart with those long eyelashes flashing."

"Yes ma'am, she will." Letitia wiped her daughter's chin of drool.

The woman moved away, leaving behind a wake of kinship. Letitia would savor those ripples in her sea of uncertainty, reminding herself that she'd made a choice to come.

———※———

"We'll be leaving tomorrow morning, with Captain English," Davey told Letitia as she moved a firkin so she could put the scrub board away. He hoped she wouldn't resist his decision. "English has but twenty-six wagons including ours and 300 head of cattle. We'll still be part of Tetherow's main group under Meek's guidance but able to move faster. I've picked up flour, sugar, salt, tea, coffee, and tobacco. And lead. It's good we're here ahead of others." He pulled up his neck bandana and coughed. "Dang dust here. They'll run out of sugar sure thing and the hind companies will have to pay twice my eight cents a pound for flour."

"You done a good job of tradin'." She lifted the flour barrel cover. "Good to see a full supply. I tries to trade your shirt for one of those cradleboards the Indians use."

"You went to the Indian camp? So that's where you were. Brave of you." He poured himself fresh coffee, the scent rising in the morning air.

"Jus' curious. Mrs. Meek go with me. Her husband say it safe. She speaks like she from the provinces, north."

"I 'spect she's French."

"A board leaned against the teepee. I shows 'em your shirt but a woman shakes her head no."

"Those boards are pretty special. Made for an individual child. Probably didn't want to part with it."

Then she pressed the point he'd hoped to avoid. "Can we wait? One more day? For the Hawkinses?"

"Now lookee, Letitia." She could be as persistent as a mosquito once she got something into her head. "We got to keep going."

"We makin' good time. Mr. Meek say so."

"Letitia. I've decided."

But in the morning Davey awoke with swollen eyes, a sore throat, and a persistent cough. Letitia went with him to the fort hospital.

"Measles?"

"Buried a boy from an earlier party and a company just came in has the disease as well," the fort doctor told them. "Your master could get pretty sick." He nodded toward Letitia.

"Maybe we stay. I finds out if Nancy with the group of last evenin'. You have treatment?"

"Very little." The doctor washed his hands in a basin. "Keep the temperature down with cool baths. Keep your baby clear of him. If you can. Blotches will appear in three or four days. They'll itch. Try not to scratch them. It'll prolong the disease. I'd recommend staying here until the fever breaks."

"Yessuh."

"Lookee here. We got to get going." Davey let Letitia help him back to the wagon.

"Doc Hawkins treat you if we wait."

"We ain't waiting, Tish." Speaking tired him. "You'll have to drive. The drovers are so far behind. It might be three days before they catch up. I want out of here now. And don't say nothing to nobody about measles."

"Can't tend you well if I's drivin'."

"It's the end of June and we're only 650 miles from home. I'll push through this. May not even be measles." His breath came short. "You drive."

"You too weak today."

He cursed and Letitia startled.

"Sorry."

She rarely stood up to him. But maybe she was right. "OK. For a day. I don't like this delaying."

"You be stronger come mornin'. Maybe somethin' good come of it."

He knew she spoke of the Hawkinses or the drovers catching

up. Maybe she was right. "We're only waiting 'cuz the day's nearly passed."

Letitia settled Davey in the wagon. In the morning she brought him a thin soup he fed himself while she hitched the oxen. She did it alone but her eyes throbbed with the effort. This would not be an easy journey, and truth was, she wasn't sure she could handle the teams. She wasn't that strong and there was Martha needing feeding and rocking if she cried. Her heart beat faster when she remembered the stampedes or quick orders from the captains to "Circle up!" She so hoped the Hawkinses would catch up. Troubles seemed lighter with someone to share them, even if they couldn't change the trial.

"Thank ye."

Letitia knelt back, setting the bowl aside.

He was up on his elbows. "Lookee who's here."

Letitia twisted to look. "Nancy?"

She watched instead as an Indian girl and Meek, the guide, approached.

"One advantage thar be of a colored soul is she's easy to find in a crowd," Meek said. "Come on out here, Mrs. Carson. Want to say thanks for spending time with my Elizabeth. Missus Meek. She gets lonely. Likes woman talk."

Letitia scrambled out, stood facing an Indian girl, her eyes red from weeping. The girl held out the cradleboard toward Letitia. She was young, not the older woman who had said no to yesterday's trade.

"I gets my shirt."

Meek put his hand up to stop Letitia from leaving. "No trade. Wants you to take it. A gift. She's Arapaho. They're a generous people."

The girl pushed the baby board toward Letitia again. "Take."

"She wants you to have that thar Indian cradle for your little papoose. Came looking for you. Scared half the camp walking in."

"Her baby's?"

"It were."

"I gives something."

"You give when you take that thar gift," Meek said. "You pass the gift-giving on. Maybe not that thar board but something else what's treasured. The way it works here. Her baby died and she gives everything away so the papoose travels to the spirit world with nothing to hold it back. Frame's wild rose. Moss for the pillow thar and beneath that little baby bottom." He fingered the greenish fuzz sticking out from the soft leather patch that covered it. "We head out promptly now. You takin' it?"

"Yessuh." She clutched the cradleboard to her breast and wanted to touch the woman, to thank her with motion. She opened her arm then and the girl walked inside the one-arm hug. She leaned into Letitia though she was taller. Letitia felt her grief, no different from her own when Nathan died an infant, nor Nancy's mourning over Laura. Tending and mending used threads of many colors.

Letitia found she could lift the heavy oxen yokes to hitch the wagon, run the reins through the rings and attach them. It was awkward and tiring, but she could do it and the success pleased her. She could set the team of four oxen off with a flick of the reins and her words "Go, A; go, B." They'd plod out. Sometimes she'd hop off and walk beside the steady beasts as they followed the wagon ahead. The wagon seat brought no comfort to her back even though the sun warmed it. She hadn't thought having to sit on it for long hours driving would be so miserable. She had new appreciation for Davey's part of this trip.

If she kept the baby outside in the fresh air, she'd have a better chance of avoiding whatever Davey had. But if Davey was exposed enough to get measles, she could get it too and then dear Martha. She wondered why they hadn't yet. She ran her hands over his hot forehead. He had no little pocks on his face. Maybe it wasn't measles. She'd prayed it wasn't.

"Easy now." Davey groaned from inside the wagon.

Easy? Not with the rocks and riddled trail no more than a hard-packed track. Every little bump must hurt him. But there was nothing she could do except proceed. She would allow others to pass. He wanted to keep going, but she doubted he'd complain about the slower pace today. While the oxen behaved, they could continue with the company he'd chosen to go with, though they'd be in the hind group.

The third morning G.B. Smith approached. "You can use a hand."

They'd somehow caught up to him, of all people. G.B. had his vest buttoned up like he was going to a gambling hall. She hadn't heard him approach as he wasn't riding his big horse. Rothwell came out from under the wagon and barked. *A little late.* G.B. brushed his boot toward the hound and the dog scurried back under the wagon, his big head resting on his paws, eyes focused on the man, pointy ears laid back. He growled low.

"I manage." Yes, she could use a hand with the yokes—but not from him. Milking Charity morning and night along with everything else tired her. Even giving milk away or trading it for dough risings and eggs proved a chore. But at least women traded with her even if they didn't carry on a conversation. Bathing Davey when his fever grew; fixing a weak meat soup. She had to eat and keep her strength up too, for Martha, so preparing a meal of jerked buffalo and hardtack was all the energy she had left.

"Don't be stupid. I saw you struggling. Carson!" He shouted toward the wagon bed.

Davey came to the opening, still fevered but no blotches. She began to think the fort doctor was wrong.

"Sure and it's me."

"Your *girl* here resists my services." He rolled the word *girl* around his tongue like he was chewing poison. "Tell her she needs help."

"Tish, let him."

"There, you see? Your *employer* wants you to be a wise woman. You can pay me back sometime." He raised one eyebrow, then moved in close enough she could smell his tooth powder.

"I's able. I sign on to work."

"Ah, yes, I remember. Carson's extra driver. And other things."

"Tish, let him help."

Pride goeth before a fall. She could be right or happy.

Together they lifted the yoke, the one she'd been lifting on her own all these days. She never looked at G.B. She made certain her hands never touched his, though he moved his body closer to her than necessary. He made no move to touch her. Maybe he was just trying to keep the company moving.

"All set." He tipped his hat to her as though she was a lady. "Glad I could assist, Carson." He sauntered off, leaving behind the scent of caution.

<hr />

When Davey asked for a pie a day later she knew they'd passed the rough edge of his ailing. The next morning she rolled the dough out on the smooth wagon seat, filled it with the berries she managed to pick the evening before, trading a cup of them for an egg. She rolled the extra dough over for the top crust and put it in the reflector oven and let the pie cook as they rolled along. At least he must be getting better if he was hungry for pie.

They approached Independence Rock, which Davey said reminded him of a picture of a whale he'd seen once. It was covered with names of emigrants who had passed by. Letitia wondered if Sarah Bowman's name from the 1844 journey was there or if Polly Holmes signed it. Did Polly make her mark to stand out, or like Letitia was she too hoping to fit in? She was too exhausted to climb up and see.

But as she waited for Davey to make the climb, someone began to sing "America" and others joined in, their voices filtering back across the plains, settling onto the travelers as they stepped back up onto their wagon seats or began walking beside.

Letitia broke out the next song. "I want Jesus to walk with me." Voices joined hers, and Letitia was aware of a warmth growing within her both for the prayer of the words and the comfort of being a part of others making this trek.

It wasn't the same without Letitia to walk with, Nancy decided. Oh, she treasured her sister and mother and she enjoyed chatting with other women from parts of the states she'd never been to. But there'd been an ease with Letitia. They could walk for hours and rarely speak and other times chatter through an entire meal-preparing. Letitia laughed when they were together and seemed more confident, less afraid to share her thoughts than when she was part of the large Hawkins family gatherings. Goodness, she'd even sung one evening and Nancy heard that low, clear voice and was comforted by it. Knowing she'd lost a child helped her feel less alone, the way she felt now.

She and Zach didn't talk about Laura. He assumed she had "moved on," as her mother-in-law said she must. But she couldn't move past that place where Laura lay nestled in her heart.

"Do you think we'll meet up with the Carsons again?" she asked Zach that evening. Maryanne had taken over fixing suppers under Nancy's direction. Martha needed more of her time. The child had lost more weight than the rest of the family, picked at her buffalo meat even when it was fresh. She ought to have let poor Martha go with the Carsons. That way they'd have been certain they'd meet up again and poor Martha would have her namesake around, someone to feel responsible for and earn her confidence back.

"Maybe when we get to Oregon. Carson spoke of settling south of Oregon City. He'd heard much of the good land was already taken by the French Canadians and their Indian wives."

"Maybe they'll leave a message for us at Laramie. Or Fort Hall. Didn't you say those were major stopping points?"

"I did. Might even pick up something along the way. A bunch of trappers heading back brought messages for some. None for us, though."

The disappointment at not hearing news was almost as sharp as the thoughts of Laura that pierced her when she least expected it. She longed to find comfort in the future, even with Laura in it only as memory.

Most of all, if Letitia walked beside her, Nancy would have someone to confide that she believed she was carrying another child. Her feelings rose like a boat on a lake. Sometimes she found smooth sailing in the hope. Other days the guilt over feeling joy while her family had been eclipsed kept her bobbing on rough seas. She didn't want Zach to hear her crying. She wished she could ask Letitia to tell her again that one day the pain would end.

What Matters After All

On the Fourth of July the English company Davey joined celebrated with fireworks and gunshots. *Men made room for fireworks but women had to leave their good dishes behind.* Letitia had no one to tell that opinion to, not even Missus Meek who kept up on horseback with her husband now. They crossed streams and rivers and moved through red bluffs where stands of timber offered shade and shelter for her lonely "fundamentals." Several members suffered from a fever and bone aches, and Letitia worried it was measles, but it must have been the same fever Davey had recovered from.

"Dengue fever," she overheard Captain English tell Davey. "We're staying here a few days, hope to give relief."

Time for the Hawkins wagon to catch up.

"Will you come help my ma?" A boy with freckles the size of peppercorns dotting his nose stood at their wagon. "Pilot says you deliver babies. My ma sent me."

"I do. I gets my fixin's." She slipped back into the wagon, grabbed her basket of needles, thread, lavender candle. She decided to leave the candlestick buried in the corn bin. She picked up the board with Martha in it. "I's ready. Which wagon?"

The boy pointed and she hurried ahead of him.

"Missus, I's here. How far you comin'?"

"Oh, thank God. Bennie found you. Oooooh."

Letitia scanned the wagon, saw that clean cloths had been laid out, a tin basin filled with water sat beside the narrow cot. "When the pains start?"

"Three hours. Coming faster now. Oooooh."

"Lord's bringin' you a baby, Missus. We see you taken care of, do this together." And she went to work.

Martha fussed during the time of delivering and Letitia spoke to the child, telling her she'd have to wait. A good midwife tended to the mother, giving her confidence that she could bring this baby forth; had to put her own family's needs aside. Martha soon fell asleep.

The candle Letitia sent Bennie to light and place in the brass holder burned halfway down, filling the canvas with the sweet scent. She told the boy to let Davey know he'd have to scrape up his own supper. "And tell your papa he need to fix his own meal tonight. Yours too." There'd been a pause in the frequent contractions, and Letitia reminded the mother, Ava was her name, that this was normal. "Things go good and you rise high, then they slow and you go low, and then they rise again. You remember."

"Like music."

"Yessum. Baby music."

A healthy baby boy arrived to the sounds of a rooster crowing in a forward wagon. Ava Rinehart soon held the swaddled child against her breast, her finger gentle against the pink cheek. She looked at Letitia. "I don't know your name."

"Letitia Carson. This be Martha." She had taken her baby from the cradleboard.

"That's a fancy carrier."

"A gift."

"For helping birth a baby?"

"No, ma'am. To salve a grief."

"It's mighty fine. My husband will pay your owner for delivering Andrew here."

"If he's willin' to pay, he pay me. I's free to accept."

"Oh, I didn't . . . I'm sorry. Of course. Your husband? Well. My goodness."

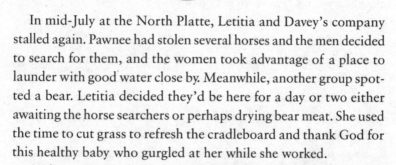

In mid-July at the North Platte, Letitia and Davey's company stalled again. Pawnee had stolen several horses and the men decided to search for them, and the women took advantage of a place to launder with good water close by. Meanwhile, another group spotted a bear. Letitia decided they'd be here for a day or two either awaiting the horse searchers or perhaps drying bear meat. She used the time to cut grass to refresh the cradleboard and thank God for this healthy baby who gurgled at her while she worked.

And it was a good time to make biscuits. The air was clear and the sound of the rushing water gave a lift to her spirit. She sang "Pop Goes the Weasel" to Martha as she worked. Letitia lifted the barrel lid from the flour. It seemed heavier than before. Maybe she was getting weaker instead of stronger with all the work of helping Davey lifting the oxen yoke, the miles of walking. Maybe she wasn't eating enough. Her clothes did hang on her. Fortunately her apron tied tight.

Martha gazed with big brown eyes at her mother, kicked her feet and smiled. Letitia was certain it was a smile and not some kind of stomach fuss. She had Davey's little mouth and her own small nose. Martha loved her board, would quiet down as Letitia tied the sinew strings over soft leather to swaddle the child. In the frame, Martha leaned up against the wagon wheel and watched as Letitia prepared a meal and could be out of sight for a moment without worry that the baby would topple over. And it served well to care for the child should she be called for midwife work.

She lifted the measuring cup, scooping the flour out of the barrel. She finished the biscuits, put them into the tin oven she'd pushed into the side of the riverbank to create the proper draw over the coals. She loosened Martha from the board, nursed her, then burped her as the child's eyes drooped. Back in her board, Martha slept and Letitia opened her sewing basket to work on a quilt block. She could hear the chatter of other women in the distance. It would be nice to be sharing a few minutes with friends. Maybe Ava would exchange a word or two with her outside of the intimacy of birthing.

She got inside the wagon for more red thread and stopped when her eye fell again on the flour barrel. The iron cooper's ring wasn't rusted in that spot before, was it? They weren't in rust weather. Maybe it had gotten turned around when Davey refilled it. She checked on Martha, then removed the barrel lid. She reached down inside, her hand seeking the rolled up material that held her papers.

Nothing.

She put both hands in deep, the yellowish grainy fluff puffing up to her elbows. *Nothing.* Maybe she'd put her papers in the rice barrel. She clawed in that barrel, pushing the grains up against the side, the dusty scent tickling her nose. *Don't worry.* Had she moved it? She dug into the corn barrel, felt the candlesticks there but nothing else. She returned to the flour. She always had the rolled papers in the flour, didn't she? When was the last time she'd looked? Long before Fort Laramie. Could Davey have moved them? But did he even know that the papers were rolled up in the flour barrel? He would have told her if he'd moved them. If he'd remembered. Did he put it somewhere else when he filled the barrel in Fort Laramie? She chewed her lip, the palms of her hands damp. She rubbed them on her apron. *Freedom.* Her freedom and security. Missing.

She jumped down from the wagon. Where would Davey be? He'd said he and several others were going to hunt a bear. She checked the biscuits. Paced. Held Martha. Couldn't concentrate to stitch.

Where could the papers be? Davey understood more than anyone what the words meant to her. Would anyone steal them? No one knew of them but she and Davey. *Give me peace. Give me peace.*

Dusk rode in with the men when they returned bringing a bear if not all the missing horses.

Davey unsaddled his mount, began rubbing Fergus down. She didn't wait to ask, coming up behind him. "Did you . . . my papers, they's missin'." She spoke low so others wouldn't hear her.

"What? Your papers?" Davey frowned.

"My freedom papers. Your agreement." She tried not to sound frantic but her chest felt tight. Her cheeks were hot.

"Oh, those. Not seen them since you kept 'em in the jar in the rafters back in the states. Or in that box."

"I puts them . . . I rolls them in a cloth and bury them in the flour barrel."

"I didn't take 'em out." But then his eyes got a faraway look. He stopped brushing his horse. "Flour barrel?" He returned to brushing, harder. "That's where you had them?"

Letitia nodded. "Down deep. Top peekin' out when we got low on flour but enough to cover. Covered more when you resupplied."

"When I resupplied. Sure now, I did." He cleared his throat, turned sideways to her. Kept brushing the horse.

"Where they be?"

"Sure 'tis a tragedy, Tish." He spoke into the horse, cleared his throat. "But ye see, I–I didn't fill our barrel. I exchanged it for a full one."

"The barrel ain't the same?"

"I didn't know, Tish. I didn't." She stumbled backward.

She couldn't breathe. Blood pounded at her temples. She held her head with one hand. Martha fussed in her board lying on the wagon seat. "My papers!" A wail of pain rose from her.

"Lookee here. It'll be all right." Davey reached for her. "You won't need those papers in Oregon. It's a free state or will be, everyone says so. No one will ask. I'll defend you."

Her mind spun, seeking solutions. Could she go back? No. Would the Hawkinses already have passed Laramie? Yes. Even if she could get word to them to ask about the papers, they'd be tossed aside or in a barrel now filled and in someone else's wagon. Then she refocused on his last words and pushed her question out swift and sure.

"And will you write another agreement, about takin' care of your kin if somethin' happens to you?" It had taken weeks to get him to ask Doc Hawkins to do it, but she could get him to do that again. She could. But no one could replace her freedom papers. No one.

"Sure and I will. I'll find someone to write it for me. But you won't need it. Oregon's not like Kentucky or even Missouri. They won't have no patrols there. You'll be safe. I'll keep you safe."

Oregon would be an extension of these overland companies with people like the Hawkinses who welcomed free Negroes but people like Greenberry Smith who didn't. She didn't see great acceptance of her color on this trail nor any who'd believe what she told them if something were to happen to Davey. The Bowmans would remember that she had free papers. Doc Hawkins had written the agreement down. She'd have to find them all in Oregon if anyone ever asked and Davey took sick and . . . she wouldn't let herself think of him dying.

A hot rock settled in her stomach. She couldn't be angry with him. He didn't know. She'd been in the Indian village when he made the exchange. Why hadn't she stayed behind, taken care of the restocking herself? She should have known better, should have told him. She had no papers. A snake made of cowers worked up her neck, threatening to choke her.

～～～

"Now things get rough," Zach Hawkins told Nancy. "We'll start up the mountains soon. Been a gradual climb but it'll get worse." They stood at the top of Independence Rock watching the sunset over the Sweetwater River. They'd made the climb together, Nancy's sisters watching the baby and younger children so the two could stand on the rounded outcropping high above the dusty plains. A hot wind carried voices of other travelers who'd made the high trek. Some chipped their names with a knife.

"Much as I hate to say it, we've got to dispense with some of our weight." Zach cleared his throat. "The oxen are tiring. It'll only get harder for them."

"Disperse? As in, leave behind?"

Zach nodded. "Some of the men call them lev-er-ites."

"Do they." She turned her face from him. "Haven't we already left enough behind?" Her thoughts went to Laura and the lone cross Zach staked at the river site. Why had he chosen this moment with such grandeur before them to bring up yet more loss? "I don't want to think about it now."

"Has to be done, Nancy."

"I know it does. I'll do it. Don't I always?" She turned aside, not wanting to look at him, fearing she'd have words with him about more than dispersal of belongings. She'd gone from blaming herself for Laura's death to blaming him—for wanting to take them west, for not being there to help as he had been back in their homesteads, for being excited and anticipating the future while the past held her hostage.

"Hate to say it but the quilt frame doesn't rise to the level of being saved."

"If you 'hate to say it,' then don't."

"Nancy."

She shrugged off his touch to her shoulder, her arms crossed over her chest.

From atop the rock the world looked so vast, like a giant quilt stitched with the blue of the Sweetwater River and green shrubs like embroidery knots to highlight the borders. Peaceful and comforting. Yet traveling through it they'd lost a child and maybe each other. Nancy scratched at the bonnet ribbon at her throat, then loosened it, letting tendrils of her hair catch the warm wind.

"We don't have to leave anything here," Zach said. "But I wanted you to get used to the idea of the quilt frame having to go."

"And your anvil? It weighs three times my quilt frame. You'll leave it behind?"

"Man needs an anvil to fix things and to form new things once we're in Oregon."

"A woman needs her quilt frame too. Good, solid oak. We may not find that in Oregon and then what would I do? I haven't heard of another woman who got to take her frame with her, one her husband made for her, then used a portion for a grave marker." She glared at him. "There must be a hundred anvils heading west."

"Which proves my point. Frames aren't essential; anvils are."

"You can borrow one. Who will loan me a quilt frame?"

"Nancy—"

Nancy's stomach roiled. She hadn't told him yet about the young one she carried. She wasn't ready yet to see Zach more happy, resenting that he had found solace before she did. *What kind of woman am I becoming?*

"You're always so certain," she said.

"Man has to be certain, Nancy. It's how I get through the tough times. I trust that we're here for a reason and right now I think it's to start a new life, to build a future for my family—our family. I thought you wanted to come." When she didn't answer, he added, "Even if you've changed your mind, there's no turning back."

There was, though. She could go back with the dragoons or the trappers they kept meeting heading for St. Louis. They'd met some discouraged travelers returning east too, with faces as beaten down as their wagons. She shook her head. He was right. She couldn't leave the children or him. She suffered from addled thinking.

"I'm not ready to give up the quilt frame, Zach. Other things maybe, but not that. Last quilt I worked on that frame was for Laura. I just couldn't." Her voice caught and a gust of wind pushed, and instinctively she protected her abdomen.

Zach stared. "Nancy? Are you . . . ?"

"Yes." She knew she sounded angry. "I am. Morning sickness and all. When I swore I wouldn't let that happen. You always talk me into things."

"You were willing, if I recall." He grinned.

Tears spilled onto her cheeks.

"Ah, Nancy." He took her into his arms. "It's a good thing, you having new life now. A reason to take care of yourself and for us to look forward to a new baby come spring."

Was it? Was it God's way of bringing her back from the brink of the sinking well? She wasn't certain about life the way Zach was. Laura's death eclipsed her heart. Nothing could cleave it back.

Zach thumbed tears from her cheeks, then pulled her to him again. "Let me think about that anvil."

Letitia poured coffee into Davey's tin and put the cover onto the flour barrel. Her stomach pinched as she did. "I's sad my papers are lost."

"Feel terrible about that, I do." He looked away.

"You rewrite our agreement? Say again you care for me and Martha by leavin' us whatever we build together. You still agree?"

"Oh sure. I'll get something writ up soon as we get to Oregon."

"Better before." What if he died on the trail? Would they take the wagon and Davey's money from her? Sell her to someone? She couldn't put that worry in her bucket, couldn't carry it around.

"Little time for such as that, Tish. Can't bother a man to write such down until winter. We'll meet up with Doc and he'll be able to write it from memory."

"I knows what it say."

"You worry too much. Any more fish?"

She served him and they ate in silence.

"We've been lucky so far, Tish. We'll make it through, and like I said, you won't need to worry about papers telling that you're free. I'll defend ye." He grinned. "I plan to live forever so we have plenty of time about the other."

⁓

They were six hundred miles out from Fort Hall and the oxen with their sore feet and sparse forage became harder to harness. In the distance Letitia saw mountain peaks, and though the oxen pulled the wagon long hours each day, no longer even stopping on the Sabbath, it seemed as though they never got any closer to the snow-dusted ridges. At the headwaters of the Sweetwater Letitia heard before seeing the roiling river with its cooling mist and thundering sounds. Davey said these were "young rivers" full of drop and gouge, not like the meandering rivers of the Missouri or Platte. Days more and the world opened into a meadow with wild strawberries ripe for the picking. Six miles across and they encountered a stream flowing west. They'd crossed the divide.

Letitia spoke a prayer to Martha, then described what she was seeing. "Such grand creation, Baby." Maybe she ought not to worry about Davey's signing a new paper. The God who created sweet strawberries in the middle of nowhere, who controlled the flow of the rivers to the sea, surely such a God would tend to her child and her.

"I needs to lean." Letitia kissed Martha's tiny nose. Martha blew bubbles between lips as tiny as sunflower seeds. "At least today, I's feelin' blessed with a chil' safe in my arms and a husband whistlin' his happiness as he drive along."

Though they knew now the rivers flowed west, the way was not easier. Tall mountains loomed on either side of their travel and still more rivers greeted them, more mountains to cross. This land made Letitia sigh in awe. She told Davey she'd never seen such vastness, such tall trees straight as spears. They encountered bighorn sheep and plenty of elk and venison whose flavors tickled the nose while they fried and satisfied stomachs when eaten. At the Green River, swollen from snowmelt in the mountains, the company took four days to cross. They built raft-like structures, then floated wagons, one at a time. No lives were lost and Letitia enjoyed the days of rest while they waited their turn. They encountered a family heading back to the states, and Letitia grew courageous and asked if they might take a message to friends behind them.

"We can try." The woman wore a faded bonnet that matched her sun-washed cheeks. "Give me the letter, dearie."

"I . . . don' write," Letitia said. "Can you take my words?"

"Who's to get them?"

"Doc Hawkins and Nancy. Just tell 'em the Carsons are well and hopin' they catch up soon." Then as the woman nodded, Letitia added, "And that we keeps 'em in our prayers."

"The best kind of friendship." The woman pushed her bonnet back. "When things aren't going right, prayer's the only thing to keep them from going more wrong."

"Even then there's no assurance." These the first words from the woman's husband. "Prayers didn't keep us heading west, now did they?"

Letitia could feel the heat between this couple, still far from a home that was no longer like what they'd left, carrying barrels of blame in their wagon. She'd work to make sure she and Davey weren't carrying similar cargo.

18

Double Deception

Near the Green River, Davey's company caught up with Tetherow's group, the one they'd started out with. *At last we're in the front group. Took us long enough.* Not far beyond they approached a deep canyon, and oxen had to be put on both the front to steer and the back to keep the wagons from careening over the front oxen and tumbling everything down the ridge. Staying in the wagons was an invitation to death.

"Sit on your bottom," Davey told Letitia. "And slide."

The success of this effort was followed by a landscape covered with crickets that crunched beneath the wagon wheels.

"Lookee there." Davey pointed to where friendly Indians had rigged a kind of cricket corral, forcing the insects into baskets.

"They eats 'em?"

"'Spect so."

Davey later learned that they'd be ground into a meal and, when cooked in boiling water, formed a thick mush lasting a year. "It would last longer than that if I was to eat it," Davey told Tish.

They encountered a section of land with several springs bubbling from the ground, one so hot Tish dipped a tin full and poured it over her tea leaves and sipped. Not far away they drank from a cold spring while geysers of water shot into the air in the distance. Tish's bread rose to a fine high with the soda springs near a rock shaped like a steamboat. A few days later they arrived at the Hudson's Bay Company's Fort Hall where snowcapped mountains awaited and talk of choices abounded: sell wagons and go with pack animals on a narrow route? No, take wagons to California where they'd be greeted like kings. Leave saplings behind. Take on bacon. Or head onward to Oregon, crossing the dangerous Snake and prepare for the Blue Mountains and then the Columbia River where the Applegates had lost sons.

Davey didn't want to make a foolish choice, and yet packing mules and leaving the wagon behind sounded appealing what with all the talk about hostile Indians and even more demanding terrain. "I'm not sure what we ought to do, Tish." He surprised himself confessing his uncertainty. "I suspect the Britishers running the fort wants folk to head to California so they keep Oregon country for themselves."

"Lots of cattle here."

"Yes, they've been left by emigrants like us who didn't risk taking loose stock. We get our milk cows through to Oregon and we'll be sitting pretty. British know that."

"Could we take apple saplings?" Tish watched one of the emigrants unload apple saplings that Rothwell sniffed at, piled on the ground.

"He's leaving them because they won't grow in Oregon, or so one of the Canadian trappers told him. Surprises me. I hear tell soil is rich there, grows anything."

"I sees an apple orchard spreadin' wide on our land. Beside our cabin door." She opened her arms taking in the landscape.

He shrugged. The saplings wouldn't take up much space, and if he agreed maybe she'd talk less about the papers and the trailing Hawkins clan. Once they caught up, she'd be on him to get their contract back in writing. He hadn't decided yet whether to add Junior to the agreement or not. He hadn't broached that subject with Tish. Didn't want to think about death and dying. He held pride in Tish and the work she did without complaint and how she'd not named him responsible for the loss of her papers. It wasn't his fault; but he could see where a woman might say it was. Tish hadn't. Sometimes, he was a little embarrassed admiring of a colored woman. But if he didn't think of her as that—only as his wife and the good woman she was and the mother of his sweet Martha Ann—then the shame flowed from his ever having thought he *shouldn't* sign an agreement. Harnessing oneself to a woman caused all kinds of rough road.

"Your orchard says we'll need a wagon, so looks like we're heading to the Blues and on to the Columbia." He rather liked that they shared that decision. "Since he's leaving the saplings, maybe he'll give us a couple rather than my having to trade him for them."

"I's grateful." He could tell when she was moved by the grin on her face and a look of sparkle in her eyes. She had a dimple back now that her face wasn't so puffed from her carrying the child. He liked the warmth in his belly when he saw that burst of gratitude. He'd have to try for more of those occasions—so long as they weren't dancing around papers.

The evening before they planned to head out, the Hawkins clan rolled in. "Tish! Tish!" Martha's tiny voice rang above the sounds of pounding wagon repairs, cattle lowing, men laughing, and dogs barking.

Letitia stepped down from the wagon and slipped Baby Martha on her back. She squatted and Martha Hawkins, arms open wide, plowed into Letitia, a dirty cheek pressed velvet against Letitia's as she squatted.

"Goodness, Martha." Nancy spoke from behind her. "Don't knock the woman over."

"She fine, jus' fine." Letitia stood, rested her hand on Martha's head. The evening breeze ruffled the girl's skirt, the hem hanging low. She wanted to hug Nancy but wasn't sure she should. During grieving maybe, but out of friendship? Yes, they were friends, people who had shared sorrows and joys.

Nancy wrapped her arms around Letitia. "I'm so glad we caught up with you." She whispered now. "I needed someone to complain to about my sister-in-law and my mother. It's been a long time since I've spent this much time with them and I declare, Tish, if I wasn't crazy before I must surely be there now. You can catch bouts of craziness from your children and your parents!"

Letitia laughed, the sound coming from her belly. It had been a long time since she'd laughed so deep as that.

"Let me see that little coffee cup. What an ingenious contraption you've got for carrying her." She leaned in. "Better be careful. I might come borrow it sometime. Nancy Jane's weighing a ton carried on my hip."

"We makes one for you."

"That would be grand. Not tonight though. I'm tired as an all-day-hunting hound dog. Speaking of which, where's that Rothwell?"

"He's off with Mr. Carson rootin' holes like he does. He more pig than dog. How you manage to catch up?"

"Wasn't easy." She perched against the wagon wheel, let Nancy Jane crawl on the quilt Letitia laid down. "Folks like having a doctor in their company. But Zach knew I wanted to hurry along. He pushed my in-laws too. And Martha, well, Martha grieved your leaving so much I think he was willing to do most anything to put a smile back on that child's face. We put our few stock in with others and it took us but a few hours to cross Green River. We heard it took one group four days."

"That be us."

Doc Hawkins sauntered over then and Martha ran to his knees and hugged them. "Baby Martha's growed up."

Nancy pointed to the cradleboard as Letitia took Martha from it.

"Looks healthy. And you, Miss Letitia?"

"Not a day of sickness. Davey had Dengue fever."

"That can be fatal. Good he endured. Where is Davey?"

"At the horse corral." *Should I bring up the lost agreement?* "Doc Hawkins, suh, you remembers that paper you draws up, one Davey sign? About his agreein' to look after me and our chil' in return for my workin' with him, cookin' and farmin'. It got lost."

"Oh no," Nancy said. "You had a written contract?"

Letitia nodded. "Lose it and my freedom papers."

"Oh, Letitia!" Nancy touched her arm.

"Davey say Bowmans say I's free so I needs to find them in Oregon. But I needs another agreement paper signed, case Davey dies and I still livin'."

Doc Hawkins frowned. "I don't know what sort of paper you're referring to, Miss Letitia."

"Davey say you write out that he care for me and my chil'. His property come to us when he die. He say he sign it in front of you."

"There's no such agreement that I prepared." Doc Hawkins's eyes held sadness. "Maybe he had someone else do it. I'll bet that's it."

"You didn't draw up the words?"

"I did not. I'm sorry."

"Oh." All sorts of rumblings tumbled through her thoughts, none of them bringing cheer.

❧

"Doc Hawkins say he know nothin' about no contract." Letitia hissed at Davey when he'd sauntered back from fishing, poked his chest with her finger. "What you show me with your name on it? It weren't no agreement. Someone else write it for you?"

Truth was, he never had signed any agreement. He'd signed a paper certifying the list of supplies he'd brought along. He didn't want any other white man to know what he'd verbally agreed to with a colored woman. They'd think him daft probably, committing to caring for a colored woman and child even if he did think of them as his family. His second family. Davey had another son, and now that he knew where Junior was, he felt he ought to provide for that child as well if something ever happened to him. He'd shamefully been a little relieved when Letitia stopped asking about written words to match what he told her and a little more ashamed to know she hung onto a worthless list thinking it was gospel. Now the roosting chicken roasted in the fire of his own making, as his mother might say.

"I . . . my word to you ought to be enough." He puffed up his chest, lowered his voice. No need to let folks know about their squabble. "What's the use of papers anyway. They just get lost. Like yours. You have my word. That's enough for any man; should be enough for you, too."

"You lie to me about what I look at and keep so careful 'til you toss it away."

"Now Tish, I didn't mean to do that. You know that."

"Do I? My man say he care for me then deceive me like I's some chil' he stealin' candy from, tellin' it sweet when it poison. I gots a sweet paper but it nothin' but stink!"

He did hate to see her eyes filling with tears, but a man ought not be challenged over every little thing. "Lookee, I can get one written, but I resent the need to. I told you I'd care for you. I did. I will. We got a *verbal* agreement." He leaned in close. "It still stands."

"Sho if somethin' happen to you, what Martha and me do then?"

"We'll be in Oregon. We'll prove up the land. It'll be a state one day." He kept his secret about his citizenship papers. He held up fingers he counted out, his voice like he was teaching a child. "Truth is, I don't know that you can inherit."

"I can earn money you pay me, and I get to keep it if you dies, if you puts that in a paper. Laws change. Maybe one day a woman inherit land, even a colored woman."

"I told you, Tish, not to worry."

Martha started to cry.

"There no witness to what you tell me. You say it in front of Doc

Hawkins, then I believe." She carried the child on her shoulder, patting her back, and turned away.

"No witness? Sure there is," he called after her, not caring if others heard. "That tinker who read the words over us when we . . . you know." She stopped. "He heard me promise."

"Not abouts you payin' for my laborin'."

I wish she wouldn't talk so slave-like, dipping into words without finishing them. "Well, no. But promising to keep you in sickness and health and all that. God's my witness. None better." *That should quiet her and comfort her too.*

"I want a man to witness your words. Doc Hawkins. You say this in front of him, then I rest. If I need, he can be the one to tell if I needs a day in court."

They stood in the shade of a large cottonwood tree near the fort. Doc Hawkins nodded while Davey declared that he had an agreement with Letitia from the time they left Missouri until his death that if she would help him, care for him and his children and help work his claim, he would put her name on the deed if allowed. Or that when the land was sold, the money would be hers in return for her labor. Davey glared at the ground.

"I can easily write this down for you, Davey. You could sign and Tish could keep it in your Bible."

Letitia raised pleading eyes toward Davey. "He say it easy to do."

"My word's as good as gold and you need to trust that, Tish. Bad enough I agree to have another man involved in our little . . . arrangement." He held his hands on his hips, elbows out.

It wasn't such a little arrangement, but she'd pushed him to his limits. He didn't like others knowing he was beholden to her. She was fortunate he allowed a woman to require him to do anything. She had pushed this for her Martha. Or for any other children they might have, though at the moment she couldn't imagine coupling with him to have another. It would take time for her to trust him again, and trust came first before a shared cot. Still, if she did and they had another son or daughter, she had to be certain he wouldn't—she could barely think it—sell his children the way the father of Jeremiah had. Doc Hawkins's witness might not prevent that, but it could slow it down. Davey had promised to care for his children and her in front of Doc Hawkins. She'd promised to care for him too, before God, so they had another witness to it all. She'd get no better than that. She'd keep that marriage promise and trust that God would fill the empty spaces that lay between their history and her hope.

Letitia and Nancy pushed the dust beside each other, stitching quilt pieces, patching pants, renewing tender ties. Martha and Maryanne ran ahead to be with other children but stayed within the company, not moving too far away. Martha always came back first, often walked between the two women, carrying Martha in her board for a few steps until her arms tired. In one lull, Letitia told Nancy of the agreement.

"Zach makes a good witness should you ever need it. He's such a good man."

"You can witness."

"Oh, I don't think they'd allow that. I mean, I can speak to your good character, but anything I didn't hear myself they'd call hearsay evidence. But Tish, Davey would have to be dead before you'd need a witness for your character or Davey's words. I'll pray for long years for the two of you together so no one would even question that he would make such a promise to his family."

South of Fort Hall on the Raft River, a large group of travelers headed south into California, and Letitia was pleased the Hawkinses didn't go. They traveled now above a massive river called the Snake, looking down steep bluffs with deep ravines gouged out and peppered with ragged rocks. Eagles perched then plunged below to dive for fish. On August 9, as they camped at Rock Creek,

Letitia and Doc Hawkins helped deliver a twelve-pound baby. And a day or so later, at Salmon Falls, another infant joined the world. Yet right after, Davey's and Doc Hawkins's companies made plans to separate again.

"They're choosing to go with Parker's party and I'm committed to Captain English. Twenty wagons. He moves faster." Davey greased the wheels, the smell of oil strong to her nose.

Letitia wrapped the apple saplings in wet burlap, then soaked them. All six were still alive. "Our oxen all beaten up. They need to go slow."

"You keep their feet good. And we packed light so nothing more to unload. 'Cept your candlesticks."

She didn't respond.

"You'll meet up with Mrs. Hawkins in Oregon."

That evening she lamented to Nancy of the company's division.

"Best I tell you my latest secret then." Nancy leaned into Letitia. "I'm carrying."

"You is? Lawd woman, you said Nancy Jane be your last."

Nancy giggled. "I have an available medical man to help deliver."

"Get him to hep you figure out what cause it and maybe put a stop to it too."

Nancy laughed, then took a big breath. "It's helped me, with Laura. Finding new life, new hopes, that's what heals the wounds. That and believing as I do that God is in all things and wants the best for each of us. I have to keep moving toward the light, even in the darkest days." She stroked the cloth over her belly. "Besides, it got me the quilt frame. Oh how he hated to leave that anvil."

In the morning they said their good-byes.

"Zach says we'll head south of Oregon City to find good land not already being farmed in the Willamette Valley. Goodness. How big can a valley be? We'll find each other."

"Yessum, we find Doc Hawkins's shingle easy." Letitia held Nancy Jane and now she exchanged her for Baby Martha. Martha played with the baby's toes. "We see you in Oregon." Tish ran her hand over Martha's hair, smooth as corn silk. "Maybe before if we stall and you catches up." Her voice caught, but she kept from crying.

Nancy grasped her hand. "We'll pray for that and for safekeeping. It'll all be better on the other side of these last mountains." It was every pioneer's hope.

Oregon Country

They would do it as a people, all together. Children would learn to use the flames to move deer into chosen places so they could be brought down more easily, brought down to feed the People. Later, the flames would push farther, taking the low shrubs, clearing the underbrush of trees whose trunks would sometimes blacken but not burn, keeping the oak leaves as shelter for both animals and people. After burning, women and children gathered up grasshoppers in baskets, their crisp forms already cooked and ready for the grinding stone.

"When will we go to the lake, Kasa?"

"You like *wapato*." Little Shoot nodded. "Or is it the muddy streams your toes miss?"

The boy grinned, making his face round like a moon. She was glad his father had not insisted his head be flattened like so many of the People along Nch-i'-Wana, the big river with the dalles. She didn't understand that custom, the slow crushing of a baby's skull until over time, the baby's forehead sloped like the end of Coffin Butte. Not that she would say. How one does a thing that's different does not require comment from another except to prevent injury. She saw no evidence a child was injured with the changing head shape. And she had heard that the sloped heads were considered beautiful and distinguished them as slaveholders rather than slaves. Little Shoot was a handsome boy. When they visited along the river, a Kalapuya boy with a round, handsome head stood out.

The scent of smoke drifted in the air as they walked a line with the others, making the flames behave. This first day of the People's year the wind stood still. A good day for burning. Tar seeds would be charred and women would collect then peel the seeds from the blackened stems and grind those too. With blackberries they'd make a paste that would keep through the winter but would still blacken their gums as they chewed. They had so many baskets full of camas and wild onion and cat's ears that they might remain in this valley through the coming winter, not make their way north toward the mission. Here, a spring on the side of the hill burbled out like a treasure basket left for them, a sure sign of the Creator's blessing. She and Little Shoot might even find *wapato* in the swampy lower land near Soap Creek. The white tubers were tasty, and when many women gathered together wading into the warm water, digging for the roots with their toes and kicking them up like dogs covering their scat, there was always much laughter. One needed laughter. Like one needed fresh spring water close by. Both, every day, allowed the People to survive the disappointments offered along the way. That was why she teased Little Shoot sometimes; why he teased her. The laughter caulked the People, held them together and kept out the heaviness of the rainy season and the uncertainty of the unknown.

"Ayee." She shouted to her grandson. "Watch that flame. It makes its own way."

The boy turned from his friends where they huddled over something in one boy's hand. He looked where she pointed, startled, and sprinted with his shrub, pounding out the errant lick of fire.

"*Kloshe*. Good." She waved at him and motioned for him to

remain near the fire's edge. She would have to watch that child. He could let boyish things steal away his judgment, send his mind to lesser things. As a child, the Missionaries had warned her of the same thing when her mind took flight to the empty times of her family perishing instead of her thoughts staying on the full basket the Missionaries promised if she kept her eyes on the Creator or his son. She saw all points of view now: the People, the Others, but most of all her grandson. Teaching him was what kept her alive.

What Once We Loved

In what people called the Boise country, a trail led down a gradual incline to the Snake where Hawkins's party would cross. At the bottom of the canyon, sweet grass and clear water fed the parched animals who yesterday had looked longingly from atop the ridge. Now water was at hand.

"Must you go off hunting with Mr. Hinshaw? You're a doctor. What if you're needed here?"

"We can see game on those islands. I haven't had much chance to hunt." Zach lifted her chin with warm fingers. "I'll be fine, Nancy. I can help George bring back his game if nothing else."

"Oh for heaven's sake, you men. Always with your hunting. Why weren't we smart and bring along a pig or two so you wouldn't have to hunt?"

"Food on the table, woman." He grinned then kissed her hard. "It's good to see you back, my wife." His gaze warmed her. "I love you, you know."

"I know. Go on." She pushed against his chest. "Bring back something besides venison or bear. How about a good goose?"

Zach saluted her. "Yes, ma'am. Anything for the captain."

"Go and hurry back." She gave him a light kiss. Nancy Jane fussed and she set her on fours on a quilt top. The child rocked and moved. She'd be walking before long. Three-year-old Edward waddled past carrying a grass snake. Soon they'd both be a handful to watch.

Davey smelled the acrid scent of the hot springs, a lake they approached at the edge of a large valley surrounded by rounded, tree-lined peaks. The company had rested there and the women washed in the nearly boiling hot water. A party of tall Indians with their wives arrived, bringing fresh vegetables and other items they hoped to trade for. They wanted cows or calves. "Keep close watch on Charity," Davey told the drovers. He'd be in the hound house for even longer if something happened to Tish's cow. A lot of things had gone wrong on this trip and he knew his way of handling things was part of that. Tish hadn't let him curl close to her in a night ever since they'd separated again from the Hawkinses' party. That's how she displayed her "mads," going away while her body was still here. He hoped to overcome those mads before they reached the Columbia River, because he knew she wouldn't like what he'd be saying to her there.

So he kept up a cheery chatter explaining things as they left the hot springs and rumbled into the Blue Mountains, as they were called, "from the smoke where the Nez Perce and Umatilla Indians burn the underbrush to keep the meadows clear. Burning brings out elk and deer to feed." Letitia nodded. "Don't know if the Indians where we're headed do such things."

"We wait and sees."

At least she's talking to me again.

The journey was demanding but not disabling, and in the four days it took them to traverse the Blues, they were near a stream each night shadowed by dense forests. Evenings drifted cool. Davey played his Irish flute and Tish drummed her hands on a pan to set the rhythm while Martha's big brown eyes followed her mother's moves. Davey stayed at the wagon in the evening rather than jawing with others. He played with Martha while Tish cleaned up their tin plates or took care of her fundamentals, as she called her walk into the timber. He was being there for her. He hoped she noticed.

One evening, four children about the same age as the Hawkinses' Martha wandered over and introduced themselves. They asked to hold Baby Martha. They gentled the child and afterward Letitia asked if they'd like to play "Hot Tater" to pass their time.

"What would that be?" The tallest boy had a New England accent.

Letitia reached for a knitted sock from her sewing basket, rolled it into a ball, and tossed it to the girl.

"It's a sock." She frowned.

"It also a hot tater. Quick, quick. Toss it to your brother 'fore it burn your hand."

He picked up the game and sent the sphere spiraling to a different girl. "Ginny, careful it's sizzling."

Ginny jumped up and down as though the sock burned her palm and her feet, then tossed it to Letitia, who blew on it to "cool" it before sending it to a shorter boy across the circle that had formed. The children laughed and spoke of the "potato" that was "blistering" and "searing" their fingers. "See how long you keep it goin' with just your mind turnin' it into something fun, takin' that old sock to a new place. Your mind too."

Baby Martha laughed at the action and even Davey left the fire to watch. Rothwell howled his approval.

After the children left, Davey said, "You're good with wee ones. I didn't know."

"They gives me a pleasure."

"You're pretty inventive too, taking a sock to new heights. You have a good imagination, Tish." He put his arm around her shoulder, kissed her. She allowed it.

"Didn't know that what it called, lettin' a mind take us to faraway places, movin' our hearts at the same time. Imagination. A good word."

At one point they met an Indian agent named Doc White heading east with a small party guided by a Negro named Moses "Black" Harris. Davey remembered that Harris had left Missouri with National Ford's company the year before. Letitia stared at the fine specimen of a man while he shared information their company could use, his voice deep and well-spoken as a learned man. Davey felt a flicker of something, he wasn't sure what, but after watching Letitia's attention to Harris, how she listened with her eyes on the man, he was happy to see the rear of that party as they continued on. Letitia said nothing about Harris, but it must have pleased her to see her own kind at least once on this journey. "You notice, Tish? No one asked for that man's papers."

She nodded.

"Coming to this country's a good thing."

"He lookin' like a good man."

"Does he?" He ought not be grumpy about her interest but rather see if he could target those admiring looks his way instead.

They passed graves, and grasses already grown up beneath discards of dressers still holding china that had made it that far but no farther.

"We're fortunate, wouldn't you say, Tish?"

She asked him to stop at a marked grave site. He'd let another wagon pass them because she seemed not to want to leave that lonely spot, though they had no idea who was buried there.

"Best we be going, Tish."

"Always good to give honor to those passed on."

"Yes, well, I 'spect so."

On the fourth day through the Blues, coming out of the timber they saw the snow-capped mountains rise up from the valley floor in the distance. He could almost feel Oregon. "Lookee, Tish. Ain't they beautiful?"

"Yessuh. They's beautiful." She corrected herself. "The mountains are pretty as a painting."

He grinned, his hands still holding the reins but patting her thigh as she sat beside him. He'd said something to her about listening to how other women spoke, putting words down different, and she'd been learning. On her own. Another sign of her intelligence. And she'd chosen him. He had to remember that. And he'd chosen her.

After descending a long and treacherous hill where trees grew in small clumps, leaving much of the landscape bare, they reached a rolling plain. As they traveled beside a good-sized river, Dr. Whitman, the missionary, and his pretty wife came out from his mission and met their party. "I'll guide your wagons through hostile Cayuse and Walla Walla Indian territory," the doctor said. He drove a wagon full of small potatoes, meal, and unbolted flour. Their company accepted his offer and at the mission they resupplied.

Davey filled the flour barrel. "Eight dollars for one hundred pounds." The price galled him, but the flour pleased Tish; at least she thanked him. He wondered if he'd always be reminded of Tish's lost papers and his part in it whenever he looked at flour.

"I'd suggest you leave your milk cows here." Dr. Whitman spoke to the group. "Getting them over Mount Hood will be a challenge as weakened as they are. You can buy more at Fort Vancouver."

"He has a point," Davey told Tish that evening. "The last part of the journey over the Cascades could be the worst, they say."

"Charity is mine and that's how we build our life. That what you always sayin'. We got twenty cattle comin' behind. Already lost too many. Not likely neat milk cows where we goin'. Charity has to come."

He let her think she'd convinced him, but Davey agreed. At Fort Vancouver he guessed there'd be few neat cows to buy for milking. Nor would the British be willing to sell them. Besides, he had no plans to go that far north, would head south into that lush valley as soon as they arrived. If they left their milk cows here, they'd be stuck with the wild cows he'd heard had been driven up from California with their long horns and dastardly ways.

"We'll hang on to Charity, Tish, and her heifer and the cows and oxen teams."

Their company crossed rolling hills, sometimes camping above high basalt cliffs with no wood for cooking fires. Davey was getting tired of hardtack and dried patties Tish had formed of the cricket meal weeks before. "I said these would last longer than a year because I wouldn't eat 'em, but here I am." He bit and chewed. "Only Martha there has the best meals."

With each new river crossing there were always challenges. The muddy banks of the John Day grabbed at the wagon wheels and the steep incline on the other side tested the tired oxen. The fierce current of the Deschutes stole away some of the company's weaker cattle, but Charity and their other cows made it. They dealt with Indians who stole horses or demanded calico shirts in return for taking people across in their canoes. With each success Davey reminded Tish of their good fortune. They'd met all the trouble rocks that had to be crossed over or gone around. Mount Hood stood before them now. Maybe he hadn't made so many bad choices. "The Good Lord is blessing us, Tish." He kissed his daughter's forehead. "We're going to be all right, have a good long life ahead of us. Together." She didn't disagree.

* * *

Nancy heard ducks and birdsong and the mournful call of geese flying overhead, circling before settling down on the shoreline. When night fell and Zach hadn't come back, she'd sent Samuel to find Isaac Hinshaw, George's brother, to see if George had returned. He hadn't and that raised the alarm. It wasn't like Zach to worry her like this. Maybe George had fallen and hurt himself and Zach had stayed, planning to come back in the morning. Maybe Zach had shot himself. He wasn't all that familiar with guns. *Oh goodness, that's it. He hunts so rarely. George has a wound that's kept them there. They'll show up in the morning.*

They hadn't. So Isaac and three other men crossed to the island to look. Now it was noon and they were back. With George's body. "He died shortly after we found him." Nancy heard the words but they made no sense. "There's no sign of . . . Doc Hawkins."

"But Zach . . ."

"We found evidence of him . . . some blood."

Nancy's mother stood beside her, a woman widowed herself years before.

"We followed, but the trail let off at some rocks and we never did pick it up though we tried." Isaac turned his hat brim in his hands, knuckles white from the telling, his eyes red with his own grief.

Nancy focused on the white knuckles, couldn't bear to look into the depth of sadness in the man's eyes. "Can't you look more? Maybe he's waiting for rescue. Please."

The captain stood beside Isaac and he turned to the leader now. "We'll bury George, but then we got to move on."

"But . . . a few more hours of searching . . ."

Zach's parents came to be beside her, holding her up it seemed, the three in shared grief like windblown trees not allowing the others to reach the ground.

"It's not just delaying further because of the season, Mrs. Hawkins. It'll risk the entire company to remain. We don't know how many Indians are around, but we know they aren't friendly from the . . . condition of George's body. We need to move out."

"Condition of the body?"

"Not fit for the sensibilities of a lady," Isaac said. "I'm so sorry, missus."

"I know you are. Your brother. Gone." She turned to her in-laws. "I'm so sorry. Your son . . ." She was tending to everyone's grief, delaying her own.

Nancy's brother-in-law said he'd help drive the wagon, but

Samuel said he could do it. He'd done it before, he told the men. "All right then, we head out right after we put George in the ground."

Leave her husband? No body? He might be there still, waiting for them to bring him back. How could she lose Laura and now Zach? No, it wasn't possible. There had to be a mistake.

"Samuel, take me across. Let me look."

The boy's eyes were large as rocks. "No, Ma. It's not safe for you." He paused. "I could go."

"No!" Judge White, Nancy's brother, overheard them. "You must accept what is, Nancy, not risk my nephew." He placed his hands on the boy's shoulder. Edward stared up at his older brother.

Nancy didn't want to lose Samuel either, and resentment like fire flared, but she pleaded, her voice scaring Nancy Jane, Martha, and Maryanne. "Would you let me go?" She paced, walked back. "We can't leave. I have to see him, touch him one last time." Her fingers pressed against her lips. "How awful for him to think we'd left him behind!"

"You don't need to see him." Zach's father took in a deep breath. "George's body was mutilated almost beyond recognition, Nancy. He'd been tortured. Scalped. His fingernails were cut to the quick with sticks driven under them and then set afire. My son has met the same fate. He's dead and probably prayed thanks that it came as soon as it did."

She collapsed against Zach's mother then, just before she felt the stabbing pain in her belly. Zach's last child.

Then her world went black.

20

One More Crossing

Letitia ate dried salmon at the river's edge, the thump and roar of the water blocked out all other sounds, even the soft cooing of Martha whose mouth opened and closed in silence like a fresh-caught fish. The water surged against the rocks making the ground tremble against Letitia's thin-soled leather shoes. No more bare feet. It was the first of many changes she'd now face. The thundering noise that covered all noise at these dalles allowed her to consider what Davey offered—or ordered as they walked to where they could talk.

"You and Martha got to go on the Columbia. We'll meet up again at Linnton. I've secured a Hudson's Bay craft to take you and Martha and the wagon. Thirty dollars for the wagon and five dollars for each of you." They drank weak coffee in the chilled morning air. By noon it would be hot as a Kentucky summer if the day before was any indication. September was apparently not a cooling-off month in these parts except at night.

"We goes with you."

"It'll be too hard on a woman with a child. Lookee. I'm taking the 'walk-up trail' with the cattle. Knighton and Martin are coming along. It's too dangerous for you, and if we get an early snow, you won't survive it; Martha neither. It's my good money managing—and your careful tending of supplies too—that gives us cash so we can pay your passage. Besides, someone's got to make sure my goods get to that valley. And that wagon will be worth gold."

"Where we meet up?"

"I'll come out at Oregon City, cross over and find you."

Lord willing.

"Some say they staying here at these dalles, buildin'—building—winter cabins. Others leavin' wagons and supplies, say they come back in the spring. Will come back in the spring." Sometimes forcing her words to sound like Nancy's made her tired. She was very tired now.

"That ain't us. We've come this far, made good. Still got our cows and oxen, a good wagon, and enough supplies. They'll serve us well when we settle in the valley."

"Transport money be spent better *in* the valley."

"No. Sometimes you got to spend in order to make money. Tish, I want you safe. That's why I'm sending you by water." It was hard to argue with his goodwill.

"Barlow goes south through the mountains. With wagons. Why can't we—"

"Barlow's making his own road and there's no guarantee he can do it." He stood up. Fluffed Martha's kinky hair. "Look at that mountain." He pointed with his tin cup toward the triangular snow-covered peak taller than any Letitia had ever seen. "It would be dangerous to try to make a road through that."

She could see that for herself, really. But why should he decide things and then *tell* her about it?

"I've decided how we'll do this," Davey continued. "I paid for Hudson's Bay crafts. They'll take you and Martha, the anvil, tools, your . . . things. Wagon is almost taken apart. Knighton and I'll finish that today and wait to head out 'til I wave good-bye to the two of you. You're on the Bay's list for transport. It's all settled."

"I gets no choice."

"No, you don't."

"What happens to Roth?" Someone chased the dog away from salmon drying on sticks near a fire, and he headed toward them, tail between his legs. He stopped on the way, sniffing greetings to the numerous Indian dogs running about.

"He'll come with me. He can help with the cows."

Letitia thought that he might not come back for her and Martha, but he would for the dog.

"I hope they get you out of here before you take on mountain fever. Or I do. Place is rampant with sickness and I can hardly hear myself think with the roar of these falls."

That conversation had taken place two days before. She'd spent a sleepless night beneath stars so close she could pluck them. Now she took another bite of salmon, liked the firm pink fish. Another immigrant told her not to let the dog eat any raw fish as it would kill him. She broke a piece of the smoked fish off for Martha, softened it in her mouth before placing a touch of it on the baby's lower lip. She gave another swatch to Roth. Letitia smiled at the expression on her four-month-old daughter's face. "Is it good? Jus' different."

She watched as the Indians stood on rickety platforms with spears and nets, stabbing at fish roiling in the thunderous falls. They did what they had to do regardless of the danger. So would she. It would be her and Martha going on alone because Davey said it would be safer. But she couldn't let where they'd be meeting stay floating in the air like leftover chicken feathers.

She walked back up to the area where Davey disassembled the wagon. Others in their company had cut trees they were strapping together to make their own rafts, crafts that looked more frightening than Hudson's Bay's. The British boats were the best she could hope for and Davey had paid their way. They would leave in the morning.

Back at their camp she said, "We meet up at Oregon City, not Linnton."

A man lifted his head from his work, looked at Davey and scowled.

"What?" Davey turned. "What's that you say?"

"We meet in Oregon City."

He stepped away so the men couldn't hear. "Lookee. I think you might be better waiting at Linnton or even go on to Fort Vancouver. The Chief Factor at the fort is known to be partial to caring for women and children. At Oregon City . . . don't know if you can find a boardinghouse that'll take you . . . but at Linnton you can stay in the wagon. Safer. I don't want to be worrying over you."

How much had he run interference for her with others that she didn't know about? Maybe he was right.

If he didn't come for her, she'd have to begin a life on her own. He didn't seem to grasp that. But for now, she would comply. "I gives you two weeks after I makes it for you to come for me. After that, I sells supplies what I don' need and me and Martha begin a life on our own."

"Fair enough. But I'll come. Trust me."

"You gots Charity. I feel better if I have Roth."

Davey hesitated. "All right." He scratched the dog's neck. "Roth can go with you."

Letitia was about to follow the two other families boarding the raft behind their wagons when she thought she saw someone familiar. *Yes.*

"It Martha Hawkins," she told Davey and rushed toward the girl, carrying baby Martha in her board. She didn't want to lose sight of the washed-out ruffled dress. "Martha!" She shouted and the girl turned, then was lost behind a team of oxen pulling a log. "Martha Hawkins. That be you?"

Davey called after her. "Letitia! You got to go."

She rushed around the log to see the girl still standing, eyes as hollow as the holes that Rothwell dug. The dog barked as he followed her. Breathless, she reached for Martha, who shrank from Letitia's touch. "Martha? It be Letitia, Letitia Carson. And Baby Martha. Where's your mama and papa?"

Martha pointed toward a group of men resting beside unpeeled logs. Letitia didn't recognize Doc among them but saw his father and Nancy's brother, Judge. None of them looked well: thin as oars with clothes even more threadbare than her own. Mountain fever? She didn't want to expose Martha to it.

"Your mama?"

"She's crying. Always crying."

"Why she cry, chil'?" Letitia squatted to look into Martha's eyes, held her shoulder. She was thin as a chicken leg.

"Baby dies and so does Papa. And Mr. Meek left us and we almost died too."

Then, as though she just now noticed Baby Martha, the girl's eyes flooded with tears that ran down sunken cheeks. "Baby Martha." She said it as a sigh.

Chil' needin' comfort from a bad, bad time. So will her mama.

Letitia took Martha's hand. Her troubles were pebbles in this child's rocky trail. "Show me your mama, baby."

"Letitia!" Davey had caught up with her, breathless. "You got to go now."

"We gotta make things better first."

⁓

Nancy lifted vacant eyes to Letitia and patted the ground where she sat on a faded log cabin quilt. She nursed Nancy Jane though she had almost no milk to give her baby. She considered getting up to hold her friend but didn't have the strength. She wanted to sleep and never wake up. The company they'd traveled with sought a shortcut, and though Meek had warned them against taking it, the men had insisted that he guide them. That Greenberry Smith the most vocal.

"Letitia!"

Nancy watched Letitia turn toward Davey. "You give me a time here with my friend. I be along."

Davey puckered up his mouth, but he stomped away leaving the women alone.

Letitia turned back to her. "You not doin' well. Nancy Jane . . . she hungry." Letitia nodded to the child who fussed in her arms. "I's milk enough."

"Oh, would you?"

Tears pressed behind her nose as Nancy handed her child to Letitia. Something substantial for one of her children at least. They were all starved.

"Judge and the others blame Meek for getting us lost. But he'd told them he wasn't sure of the trail before we even left the Boise country. But after Zach . . ." Her arms lay limp in her lap. "I didn't have the interest. Or will. Or faith or anything to put my two cents into the discussion. Not that the men would have listened." She gasped for breath. "People started dying. Twenty they said. I wanted to survive. I don't know why. Zach's gone, Tisha. Or maybe he's waiting for a rescue." Her throat caught. Her friend didn't ask questions. She was so grateful. They'd arrived at the place Sarah Bowman described in her letter. Pounding waterfalls, bare brown hills. "There's nothing to look forward to now, is there? This has all been a terrible, terrible mistake." She coughed, the words draining her as they had since she'd lost the baby. The last child she and Zach shared.

"But you makes it here, thank the Lord." Letitia's dark finger stroked the cheek of Nancy Jane nursing beneath an apron Letitia pulled over her.

"I don't know about the Lord, unless he sent Major Moses 'Black Squire' Harris." Saying the long name tired her. "Meek said he'd get help from the missionaries. They declined. But Meek spent his own money getting food and pulleys and axes—and got this Major and some Indians to bring them to us. He guided us across the Deschutes and brought us here. Thank goodness a good man was willing. Maybe it will change a few minds about the hearts of black men, though I doubt your G.B. Smith will change his."

"I's not claimin' Greenberry Smith."

"He was one of the ones who insisted Meek lead us and then . . . we got so lost." She put her palms up to the sky. "It was . . . there are no words."

Nancy wanted to ask how she was and where Davey wanted her to go. He paced off to the side. She was too exhausted. Letitia had taken the tiny rows of braids out of her hair and held the thick tight curls now with a strip of petticoat tied back away from her pretty face. She didn't have that hollow look of Nancy's children nor of the other men and women who'd followed Meek. Sighing, Nancy asked, "How are you faring?"

"We have trials but we weren't long hungry. Doc Whitman helped resupply. We met that Major Black Harris. Good the Lord turn him aroun' so he be here to help you."

"Maybe. Oh Letitia, what will I do now with Zach gone? If it weren't for the children, I wouldn't care but . . . Judge says I need to marry quickly. Says I won't survive otherwise. Then I can have half a land allotment. As though I cared."

"A wife own land?"

"So they tell me. But I can't marry again. You understand that, don't you? Zach is all there'll ever be for me." She looked at her daughters, all sitting listless, close to their mother. Maryanne, her face as pale as a fish bone, lounged against a wagon wheel while Martha stared into space. At least when Baby Martha squealed, Martha paid her attention. Samuel had buried himself with the men's work, taken little Edward with him. Sometimes she felt as though she'd lost both boys. The lost Meek train held more losses than people knew of. "Zach might still live and find us. How awful if he waited and then . . ."

Nancy wasn't certain they'd have the strength to resist the mountain fever that swirled around them, let alone go more miles that people said were the worst of the trip. Maryanne was still poorly. Maybe from eating food not fully cooked when they arrived at the Columbia River. Everyone was so desperate for nutrients they grabbed at even rotten food. But they all lived. Zach had been so sure of this journey. What was it she was supposed to discover in this wilderness place of the soul?

"The worst is not having the certainty, just as with Laura. A wooden cross from another piece of quilt frame. I'll never see those crosses again. They were here one moment then . . . gone. I didn't even tell him that I loved him." She blinked back fresh tears, rocked back and forth, her arms empty, no one to hold. "We told each other those words every day. I thought I'd have the evening to say it."

"You alive. Kept your chillun alive. You still dream, for your chillun now. Later you dreams for you."

Nancy looked at the indigo face of her friend. "But I have not the will. I am so very weak."

"Just live today. Lord take care of tomorrows." Letitia handed back the satisfied infant, adjusted her apron.

Nancy had always prided herself on taking each day as it came without worrying about the morrow. Maybe now she'd have to rely on the hope of the future to keep her facing forward.

"Letitia, they won't wait forever," Davey interrupted, insistent.

"I keep lookin' for you," Letitia told Nancy. "Leave you a message, ask people going to Oregon City to tell you where we end up."

Nancy's kin would take the river route too but on rafts the families worked on building. They needed more days to gain weight back and shudder less from their weeks of meandering, burying those who didn't make it.

They said their good-byes and Letitia let Davey lead her back to the craft. "Doc Hawkins dead," she said. "Nancy wished she told him words she never get to say. So I's tellin' you words." She corrected herself. "I'm telling you words." She faced him. "I want you to make it through, Davey Carson. I's hoping we have a good life together when we reach that valley." She didn't know if she loved the man or not, but she was tied to him in her heart and maybe that's what love was. She'd do anything for him and she believed he'd do nearly everything for her. He'd paid money to Hudson's Bay men and he'd not have done that if he didn't care about what happened to her and Martha. She chewed her lower lip. "I feel for you, Davey Carson."

"Do you now." He looked at her. "I feel for you, Tish." He touched her forehead in the center where her hair came to a little peak. She felt callused fingers. His voice was soft as he said, "Do what the men tell you to do and you'll be safe. And wait for me. I'll be coming with Charity. You trust that. We've come a long way, Tish. Lord willing, we'll meet up in ten days."

His reminder of the Lord's willingness to look after them and his hopeful words comforted. So with more confidence than she'd felt in a long time, she stepped onto the wide boat, supplies wrapped in the canvas sitting in the wagon boxes, wheels stacked, saplings limp but alive, Roth standing beside them, tail wagging. On soft lips, she pressed a prayer onto the forehead of her daughter. She waved at Davey and they pushed off into the current well below the dangerous falls, headed for the other side. She said a prayer for Davey too and then one for herself, that she'd see him again and their life would finally be settled in this wilderness place. They'd come this far, Davey had reminded her. The Lord had been willing. She'd hang on to that.

The Separation

Davey and four other sturdy and younger men started pushing several families' cows as well as their own—about 150 head—up the "walk-up trail." Davey captained their small party and took as a compliment that the men called him "Uncle Davey." They were a kind of family after all this time, looking after each other, enduring trials, partying now and then as they'd come across the plains. That's what families did for each other, wasn't it? He planned to party when they reached Oregon City, that was certain. He could hear Charity's cowbell clanging as they moved through blackberries and bramble, crossed streams and found themselves in steep, narrow ravines.

On the third day out light rain fell. When the rain let up, fog took its place.

"Hello! Hello!"

Davey turned to the direction of the call. Out of the timber murk came a woman riding a horse, and a boy, maybe nine or so, and four men. One of his drovers preceded them and told Davey he'd found Mr. and Mrs. Walden and their small party whose provisions had been stolen by an Indian. "They hope to travel with us."

"Well, of course." Davey thought Walden daft for bringing his wife and children this way, but he kept his thoughts to himself. The terrain demanded too much.

The next day they spent hours going around a fallen tree. Another day an elk trail beckoned but led too high. They returned to spend the night where they'd left the camp that morning. On the seventh day, Davey frowned at what route to take. Laurel shrubbed its way beside the path and a few cows ate it before the men chased them away. But before the afternoon was out, several died. "We dare not eat the meat," Davey said. "We'll perish as they did." He didn't have enough supplies for all of them. They'd have to ration. All this way and at the end starvation threatened. Didn't that beat all. And he was responsible, the one who said "do this or that." Maybe conferring with others as Letitia always wanted wasn't such a bad idea when it came time to spread fault.

A raging snowstorm and high winds pushing against tall timber woke them in the night. The roar and biting sleet pierced their clothing and within a short time each was soaked through. They rushed about, trying to break camp, check the cows.

The cows were gone.

With cold fingers they ate a biscuit each and reloaded their pack animals with what they had left and began a descent, hoping to find a lower elevation trail. But the wind blew snow into their faces, covered the questionable path and their own tracks, and by noon their horses were giving out and had to be led. Davey held his hat in front of Fergus's face to keep the snow from the animal's eyes. Davey's beard froze, his lashes crusted with ice, and he lost sight of the pack animals forward. The group splintered.

"Go back and let the stragglers know we're ahead," Davey shouted to a drover through the din of wind. By night, the snow lit the way such as it was, and for the first time Davey felt the gall of fear in his throat. They were out of food, cold and frozen. The storm might continue for days. And they were lost. The woman, Sarah Walden, was soaked through, wearing only a blanket dress. He could hear her teeth chatter. He was the captain. Responsible. Sleet cut his face like thousands of bee stings, keeping his thoughts from marching straight. He pulled the neckerchief up over his nose. It was nearly frozen to his face.

Sarah Walden's husband placed her on one of the stronger horses. She looked to be light as a child and shivering despite her husband's placing his own blanket around her. The horse wouldn't move nor could it carry the Waldens' sons, either one, though the boys were small.

He thought about Letitia. She'd survive. Their child too. He should have gone with her, forgotten about the cattle. But he hadn't. That raft had sailed. He was here now. Here. Trying to survive. He confessed his sins to God then, wishing he'd had a better friendship with the Creator so as not to be such a surprise to him now with these trembling prayers.

<hr />

Letitia watched as a string of cattle followed along the river on what looked like a shell-covered trail. *Davey could have come this way where we could have met up at night.* But she soon lost sight of those animals and learned later the cattle would be two weeks behind, with many lost to the ridges and rivers. When Letitia saw rafts and families portaging supplies back and forth while she carried her child and her bag with candlesticks and baby-helping supplies, she realized how fortunate she was. Davey had paid for her fare and the extra work of portaging, men walking beside the barge-like crafts using ropes to wrestle it from the river until they could safely be brought back on. Davey had done right by them.

The current was swift, but they made a steady way, streaming past blue herons, and when Rothwell howled and sniffed the air, she thought she might have seen a bear on the rocky shoreline. The weather held even through the night when she slept beneath a tent, not worrying that anyone would bother them. She wasn't sure why she didn't worry; if she'd been under a tent alone in Missouri or Kentucky, she would have feared through the night. Maybe that was what freedom meant, being in a place where one didn't fear.

At the rapids of the Willamette River, they pulled ashore where other Hudson's Bay canoes waited to take emigrants on to Fort Vancouver. Rothwell sprinted around, exploring. Letitia watched as people embarked on the *Calapooia*, a small scow schooner, and overheard that the craft would take them from the foot of the rapids upriver on the Willamette to Oregon City, heading south as this strange river ran north here. They'd land a short distance from Oregon City. Davey would have to come to that city first. What sense did it make for her—and Davey—to travel to Linnton?

She had a few coins and she could sell some of the supplies to stay there, sleeping near the wagon parts until Davey arrived. They could immediately head south to claim land rather than his having to find her.

"We's changed our mind," she told the Hudson's Bay man who looked to be in charge of several people. "We going to Oregon City. That be closer. Davey Carson pay our way. We need some money back by not going on to Linnton."

"I've no author-i-ty to return cash to a madam changing her mind." He spoke with an accent.

"I knows where I'm headed. Oregon City. I needs fare for that schooner to take me and my cargo." She pointed with her chin. "And my baby." She turned that he might see the baby in the board on her back.

He scratched his bulbous nose with peeling skin. "*Oui*. I will tell the cap-i-tan and release the money to him. But it will be a cred-it given by the Chief Factor. Your husband will talk to the cap-i-tan. That is all I can do."

That was enough. She boarded the craft and watched as their goods were loaded, the few barrels, ox harnesses, Davey's anvil, and the wagon boards, bows, wheels, and canvas. As they chugged upriver, she saw tiny cabins peek out from the undergrowth of green-needled trees. She imagined she and Davey would build such a cabin before cold weather set in. A mix of mist and smoke filled the air, drifting over trees so thin at the top they could be cut for broom handles.

Arriving at the landing of Oregon City she paid laborers to begin the work of setting up the wagon, directing them when they faltered, surprised she knew more about the piecing of the wagon, even though she hadn't gone to Bethel long months before to see how the wagon was made. She had more than one offer to purchase the wagon, but she knew its value and people accepted that she had the right to tell them no. On the second day, with the wagon all pieced together, she placed her candlesticks and her bag for helping birth babies in the back; then came herbs, coconut oil, her medicines. Finally, she put Martha in her board and laid her on the backboard while she changed the child. Rothwell jumped through the front bow, sniffing in the wagon bed. They were in Oregon City, with sounds of voices reminding her of Kentucky and that nose-tone of folks from the cold north. New smells, new tastes, new everything except the waiting for Davey.

For Nancy and her family the rafts worked well carrying them and the oxen down the river, and then on the north side they hitched the animals to the wagons, driving through mud that bogged the oxen, exhausting everyone having to unhitch, unload, pull and tug, then rehitch. It was almost as bad as Meek's journey, but at least they had food. They rolled past "death houses," frame structures placed over bodies of the deceased, the houses built by Indians months or years before. People were silent through this passage but for the crunch of wheels over wind-scattered bone. At a lower landing they saw Hudson's Bay crafts prepared to take people to the south side of the river where the men pushed cattle onto barges. Judge White, her mother, and Nancy Hawkins took the barge, set up their wagons, and rolled on in to Oregon City. It was there she struggled with what to do next when her brother brought her "the way through your sorrow," as he told her.

"You're to meet Thomas Read. He's a widower with two children and he needs a wife."

"Tell him no. It's too . . . I can't."

"He's a farmer. Well-educated though. From New Hampshire. I knew his people." They stood beneath one of the big trees with needles. Fir, they called them. Around them the town crowded with the influx of worn-out wagons and equally worn emigrants trying to figure out what was next in this westward trek.

"I appreciate that, Judge. But—"

"You can't put this off, sister. Where will you spend the winter?"

"Are you saying there's no room with you?"

"No, of course not." Her brother was a handsome man with decisiveness like ink lines etched across his forehead. "You can't waste time grieving over what was. You have to move on. Zach would want you to."

"I don't think you know what Zach would want." She ought not be so sharp with him, but he didn't listen to her, he never had.

He sighed, came to her as the tears rolled out, patted her back, his arms around her. "Will you at least meet the man? He's getting ready to head south. You could marry here, then leave together."

"It's not possible, Judge. It's just not. I'll think of something to provide for me and the children."

Judge cleared his throat. "Samuel says he wants to come with us."

"Oh, does he." She pulled away. "Well, his mother has something to say about that."

"You have four other mouths to feed. And if you won't do the sensible thing, then your eldest son at least needs security."

He would take my son from me? "Tell Mr. Read we can talk. But that's all I agree to. All. And Samuel—and Edward—stay with me."

She'd not let her brother decide her future. She'd had enough of being weak.

The cows were scattered. Charity, gone. But Davey was most worried about the woman, fragile and frail. Her husband carried her over fallen trees. Davey'd carried one of the boys on his own back. They'd start making bad decisions soon. Intense wet and cold did that to a person, played tricks with the mind. He'd even known of men taking their clothes off in such states, no longer aware that what they felt wasn't heat but numbing cold. He wouldn't let that happen. He couldn't. Letitia expected him to show up. He had to.

"Keep going. The snow's letting up. We'll find flat ground and make a camp. The packers'll be calling back anytime now. Keep going." He wished for a moon to light the dark. At least the snow had lessened.

"Grass ahead!"

Did he hear that?

A shout from one of the packers. "Found flat ground!" Their words, water to a parched throat.

Gathered beneath a large tree, one of the men shot into a pile of shavings that the packers had managed to whittle from a branch and a slow flame appeared. He'd never been so happy to see fire. Davey urged Mrs. Walden toward the flames. She was listless except for the shivering. As the fire grew, they brought her still a little closer and her husband gave her a biscuit, the last of any of their food. The fire thawed the woman, torturing her while saving her. Silent tears fell as she endured the pain of her limbs gaining feeling and then she'd cry out, a sound Davey was sure he'd never forget.

He dozed, kept the fire going. He knew they'd have to find the cattle. They'd been two days without food.

The morning with its blue skies and melted snow acted like a pretty girl flaunting her beauty and forgetting she'd teased her beau to distraction the night before.

"You and your boys stay and keep the fire," Davey told Sarah Walden. He could see his breath in the cold. She nodded. She could stand now and the fire through the night had dried her clothes. "We'll find the cattle, right, men?" There were nods of encouragement.

The men backtracked and then climbed higher through brush and timber when Davey thought he heard something. "Shh!" The men stopped and he heard it again. A cowbell! "Hey boys, that's a cowbell."

Charity. It has to be Charity.

He scrambled now, following where he thought the sound came from when the men entered a ravine. "Well, lookee here." There stood the cattle huddled together under a long rock ledge, out of the wind and the snow.

"We shoulda been so lucky," one of the drovers said.

Davey approached and grabbed Charity's leather collar. He removed the bell from her neck, talked to her, then squatted beneath her and milked the cowbell full and drank his fill. He refilled it for each of the men. "Come on, boys, drink up. We need all the energy we can get afore I push this cow down the mountain. I'm praying the others will follow."

But the cows weren't having it. They'd shift a few feet then circle back, stumble and shake their heads. The men shouted, poked the bony ribs, pushed and pulled until exhausted, their faces full of sweat despite the cold air.

Davey wasn't sure what changed the cows' minds—with cows one never was—but they tired at last and let the men push them back toward the fire. It was noon. There they milked more into the cowbell for Sarah and the boys, who brought out branches of tiny blue berries, and with the milk ate a meal as satisfying as corn pone and pork. One of the men removed his hat, spoke thanksgiving.

"Right," Davey added. "We thank the Lord and hope he'll bring us by tomorrow where we'll see fires in cabins and shelter ourselves with new neighbors." And the next time he herded a bunch of cows he'd have Rothwell with him.

"Lookee, woman. What are you doing here?"

"I makes a change. A good woman thinks, don't she?" Her eyes sought his and warmed at the joy she saw there.

"I guess. But I told you—"

"I's here with Martha now. You's here. My Charity here 'cuz I see her over there, hear that bell clanging. Roth happy to see you."

"That bell saved our bacon. Not sure we would have found those cows without that." He stroked Martha's hair. "It was good you didn't come with me, Tish. We met up with a small party and Mrs. Walden nearly died from the wet and cold. No, you were good to obey me."

"I finds wisdom in what you wanted, so I chooses it."

He frowned, then his eyes lit up and he grinned. "A good way to put it." He touched Martha's fingers that were outside of the leather wrap of the board. She jerked her little arms at him, reaching. "I was getting ready to come get you but wanted to spot out some land south first."

"You have me wait weeks?"

"I knew you'd be safe."

"I safest with you. Now what we do?"

"We're crossing this Willamette River and heading south. Good land's been claimed by many here for a few years already. But trappers say this valley is long and lush, so we'll head south maybe fifty miles or more."

She hoped they could stay here for a little while, maybe see Nancy Hawkins again, but the weather would continue to get worse. Already a misty rain visited daily. They'd have snow before long. She'd pay the postman to write out a letter to be left for Nancy. Other than that there was no one she wasn't already with who needed to know where she was. That was a freedom too.

Oregon Country

The Woman and Little Shoot halted so she could bind up her leggings. She would need new sinew before long. Though the snow rarely got deep nor lasted long, the cold would find her telling Little Shoot to wear his heavier leggings too. They made their way back toward the village where they'd winter. A cold, steady mist common in this "good month" made her pull her wolf coat closed. This good month is when the Missionaries celebrated the birth of a child, Jesus. Good food accompanied this celebration and she heard the story each year with happiness in her heart. She answered to the name Betsy then, though she thought of herself as The Woman.

She heard something changing the silence. Cattle, ten, twelve, many more animals, crashing through the timber, flaring out from the trapper's trail that edged the prairie. They ripped at grasses where The Woman and Little Shoot many months earlier collected first camas. Little Shoot pointed and she nodded.

Behind the cattle rode a man on a horse followed by two mules packed with white cloth around mounds of supplies like the trappers carried. A wagon rolled behind them all, driven by a small boy. The Woman's mouth opened wide in surprise as the wagon rolled toward Soap Creek. The boy . . . no, woman . . . wore burnt-seed skin like the Kalapuya, but darker. The Woman watched the party, surprised even more by the board attached to the wagon seat. *There is a child*.

Where the spring burbled onto the grasses, the travelers pulled up their horses and mules. The man looked here and there, pointed to the butte then Soap Creek. He called out to the woman and then he dismounted, walking back toward her to say something only she and the child could hear. But when he walked toward the spring on the side of the hill she was certain his face smiled despite being wrapped as it was in a beard the color of sunset in the budding month.

"Nothing stays as we know it," she told the boy. "It is the only certainty a Kalapuya knows." This is a thing to remember.

Part Three

Settled In to Freedom

No one asked to see her papers. No one close could hear the *chink! chink!* of Davey's ax as he felled trees to build their home. The weight she carried on the overland journey lessened; here she faced each morning with a lifted spirit despite the ever-present rain dribbling onto the canvas over the wagon. No heavy winter storms pushed against them and the green beneath the trees reminded her of plantation lawns tended by slaves and grazing sheep. This was her home now, and she was reassured each day that coming west had been the right decision.

The ground wasn't frozen, so before they started any other work, Letitia said they needed to plant the apple saplings.

"I'll put the house here." Davey walked the lines to serve as borders, pointed out the merits of being close to the spring and out of any high winds. "That creek doesn't look very big so I'd say we build close to it." Letitia had washed clothes in that creek water and she could see why the trappers called it "Soap" as it bubbled her lye bar. "And if that spring dries up you'd be close to washing and drinking water. Yup, I'd say this is the spot."

"I's partial to the side hill, closer to the spring."

"I told you, Tish: if the spring dries up you'll be hauling water from the creek and it'll be quite a trip up the hill."

She wasn't sure why but she liked being up higher, to see the valley and the creek, to notice sooner when the weather changed and came rolling in over the buttes that surrounded. "Likes I say: I'm partial to hillsides."

"I told you why you don't need to be."

"I's the one spending time in the house and I's the one hauling water from the creek if the spring gives out. You can say 'I told ya so.' But I'm plantin' the apple trees by the spring and I want it near my home."

"You do that. And I'll build the house near the creek." He dug the heel of his brogans in the dirt, marking his intention.

Their disagreement sat like bad meat in her stomach. She could go with what Davey wanted just because he wanted it, but this was a new place and here she was allowed to speak her piece and now and then get her way, wasn't she? She just didn't know how to make it happen.

Within a week, Davey returned to Oregon City for more supplies and to file a claim of 640 acres with the provisional government. He'd walked the property, and with Soap Creek and the trapper's trail and the spring and Coffin Butte Peak as landmarks, he was able to tell the land surveyor enough to stake his claim until that section of Oregon country was officially surveyed. He and Letitia knew that once Oregon country became a territory, he'd have to re-register, and when Oregon became a state, re-register again. But a section of free land "put wealth on the table," as Davey described it.

He went without her to file the provisional land claim. He'd tell them he was a citizen—if they even asked. He'd heard they often didn't, just assumed if they'd come all that way across the country for free land that they'd have the right to it. Hadn't he already renounced his beloved Ireland and the not-so-beloved queen? It wasn't his fault the papers were late. He sent a little prayer that he wouldn't be struck dead for his sin—and the postman would soon erase his lie.

With Rothwell, Letitia tried to keep their stock within sight. One day, Martha would walk with a stick to bring the cows up for milking. Today, Letitia saw them and then they'd disappear as the mist lowered itself onto the bushes like an old woman sinking into a chair she'd have trouble rising from.

"What's harshin' on you, Roth?" The dog growled low. Letitia looked to see what might be out there with the cows. "Wolves?" She did hear them at night, but they didn't frighten her the way men did. Still, she'd be glad when she and Martha and Davey slept inside logs instead of the wagon. Rothwell barked then and she saw beyond the herd a man riding on the old trapper's trail Davey had pointed out.

Letitia wished they'd set the tent further into the trees. She patted the dog's head and before long he left her to do his duty, covering the scat with his nose like a house cat. She stayed near the tent and the gun Davey left her, watching the pack string make its way near their claim. Or their soon-to-be claim. A splice of sun broke through, promising a change in weather, but she'd learned that this little sun break said nothing about keeping the rain from falling within minutes.

"Howdy." The lead man wore a fur hat and clothes of skins with the fur hides turned in against him. "Where you hail from?"

"Kentucky. Missouri."

"Mighty right. Come with Black Harris? Meek?"

"Met 'em both. Meek's our pilot 'til we broke off to follow English."

"Come all that way alone, did you?"

"My man's around." The hair on her arms began to shimmer. "Mighty right."

The lead man spit onto the ground. His horse stomped, eager to move on, and they had a string of pack mules that threatened to get into trouble if they stopped too long. She'd seen that happen with other strings getting impatient, all lined up and nowhere to go.

"You got any tobacco? I could sure use a smoke and see there's lots of bearberry around to mix it with." This from another of the trappers midway in the string.

Letitia shook her head. She didn't know what bearberry was nor did she have any tobacco left. It struck her as odd that if they were newly headed out they would have secured supplies at Fort Vancouver and shouldn't be in need.

She stepped back, prayed Martha would not awake. They might be good men . . . or they might be trouble. Rothwell returned and stood beside her, his fishtail high over his back. She wished she'd picked up the pistol.

"You're always out of tobacco," the lead man said to the second.

"I lost two good twists," the other defended.

"Mighty right. You lost 'em to cards. We mean you no harm, missus." He must have seen worry on her face and offered to wash it away. "We're moving on through to California, checking our traps as we go."

"Have nothing to offer you, suh." Then, "Wait." She dipped inside the tent, stepped back out, the pistol in one hand kept in the folds of her skirt, fresh butter in the other. She handed him the packet wrapped in leaves.

"This'll make good eating. Thank you, missus." He removed his hat and tipped it at her. "You be careful now, you hear? They got a law in these parts forcing black folks into doing other people's labor."

"In Kentucky we calls that slavery."

"Mighty right. That's what I call it too, but there's lots who wouldn't and they as soon take you away to make butter for them as look at ya."

"I thanks you for the warnin'."

The men moved on then. Letitia was reminded that Davey had made a good choice staking a claim beside the trapper's trail despite her earlier wish for privacy. Yes, there was risk. But next time she would sell her butter and cheese and whatever else she could come up with that those travelers might want. She'd also keep that pistol on her person, in case the men's warnings came to pass.

❧

The Woman made her way toward the wagon set well below the spring. Newly planted saplings leaned into the windless rain. A dog barked her arrival and for a moment she wished she'd brought Little Shoot with her to charm the animal. But she didn't want any harm to come to him, so she went alone.

The dog continued to bark until the burnt-seed woman came out, carrying the "Oh" of surprise on her face. She held a baby on her hip, a little hat to ward off rain. Up close she was not much taller than The Woman was. The Woman gave her a basket filled with baked camas, pushing it toward her.

"Thank you. I's Letitia Carson. This be Martha." The burnt-seed woman took the basket, set it down out of the misting rain.

"Betsy." She pointed her fingers to her breast. "Kalapuya. We dig camas here." Palm up, she moved her hand across the meadows, her movement like a prelude to a soft-singing song.

"You speak good English. Better'n mine."

The Woman knew it was not right to wave her own feather, but she liked knowing that her English was understandable by the Others. Little Shoot had an able teacher in her and this was good. The burnt-seed woman, Letitia, wore a round and open face full of curiosity but also respect. She did not ask questions that buzzed like mosquitoes as many Others did.

"At the Institute, closed now, Missionaries teach. Dr. White leaves and everything changes."

Letitia squinted, as though the name held meaning for her.

"You know Dr. White?"

"I thinks we meet him and a colored man, heading to the states."

"You will return to the states?" It was her turn to ask questions.

Letitia shook her head. "No. We stayin'." She used her palm up to survey the same area of Betsy's camas.

"Ayee."

"You can collect your camas, still. Other plants and seeds too. Maybe you show me."

There were no words to make the Others go away once they decided to stay. She had heard of people who tried this and many died, and still, more of the Others came. A thing to remember was to bring the Others the wisdom of the People's ways and so live with peace in the shadow of these hills.

She looked with curiosity at Letitia's face. She had not seen an Other with such dark skin. None of the Missionaries had burnt-seed faces.

This Letitia warmed her baby's hands at a small fire.

The Woman noticed then logs laid out not far from the creek, marking a lodge, she imagined. "The creek." She gestured. "Rises in budding time. Water fills this place we stand on."

"It overflow?"

The Woman nodded.

"I want to build higher up. Near the spring."

The spring. Not "our spring," not yet. The Woman hoped the sadness on her face didn't show. "You will let the People use the spring."

"Yessum. And when we have apples you'll eat." She nodded toward the six new mounds surrounding the apple saplings. "Building nearer the spring keeps us safer?"

"Ayee."

Letitia chewed her lower lip, adjusted the baby on her hip. The child looked with curiosity, big eyes the colors of a grey wolf and a bear.

"Betsy, you helps me pull these logs up the hill? We lays 'em where the water don't reach."

The Woman nodded. Letitia put Martha under the tent in her board. Then together the women pushed and pulled the logs toward the hillside. They should build into the bank. The earth would keep them warm; dig down too, the way the People built their lodges.

The Woman said as much. "Yes. That be a good idea. Let dirt act as walls."

By the time they finished, the child cried from the tent, hungry for its mother. Rain fell again and The Woman took it as a sign to leave. She fingered the sapling leaves.

"Apples. One day. Today, I gives you this." From the tent Letitia handed The Woman four biscuits and a jar of jelly. "Pear-apple jelly. Brought a long way."

"Ayee. *Kloshe*. My grandson Little Shoot will like these with his eggs."

"You have chickens?" The Woman nodded. "What can I trade you for a laying chicken?"

"More of this." She held up the jam.

The Woman left, pressing her walking stick into the soft ground. She tired from the effort of dragging the logs, but grateful that here, there was nothing for her grandson to fear.

Four able men returned with Davey to help him fell more trees and set the center beam for their house, form a roof he'd make shingles for.

"You moved the boundary marks."

"Yes suh."

"You did this by yourself?"

She shook her head. "A woman, Betsy, come by. She a Kala . . . Kala-puya and said the meadow floods. Every spring. Where you put the logs will be swimming in two feet of water. She marked on her leggins."

"Flooded? Every year? That creek doesn't look to have it in it."

"We dig into the earth and have dirt for part of the walls. Build it faster and stay warmer."

"She's got a point," one of the men said.

Davey frowned. "Had my heart set on looking out at the stream, dropping a line off the front porch."

"It ain't that far to the hillside." Another man took a twist of tobacco from the braided sections. "Let's get this thing going."

And so they built their home on the side of the hill, using the earth for warmth as Betsy advised. One of the men helping said he thought Davey had picked a fine place to claim. He planned to file on the section south. "We'll be neighbors," he said.

"You have family, suh?" It would be nice to have a woman close by . . . if she was a woman who'd accept the likes of her.

"Not yet. But I'm courting."

"May you find as good a helper as my Tish."

⁓

Davey split rails for potatoes that winter, though he announced the camas "tasty" and hoped next year they'd have a supply of their own. A chicken appeared, and while the darker days kept the chicken from laying many eggs, it was still something Letitia looked forward to, the wondering and then picking up the warm egg and carrying it to the cabin.

The following spring and summer Betsy became her teacher, showing her plants and what they did, which to eat and how to dry them. They dug out a rotten log, burned it, then planted tobacco seeds, Martha watching from her perch, outgrowing that board. They climbed Coffin Butte and Betsy pointed out landmarks with the Indian names she could remember. The view was of a splendid valley, meadows and small plots of trees, but no other homesteads that she could see. It was a vast beyond and Letitia took in its promise.

Her days, like the winter rains, found a steady joy despite the work. Davey laughed and tickled his daughter, bounced her on his knee. They decided not to butcher any cows but build up their herd, so they lived on venison and raccoon and once an elk. When Letitia decided it was time to make cheese, they used a deer's stomach for the rennet. She stretched and dried it, but Letitia had to experiment with amounts to make cheese. Davey helped wash up dishes and said more than once how good it was to be close to the spring, especially when the meadow flooded as it did that next spring. "You were right."

Letitia grinned, remembering Nancy saying once how rare it was for a man to admit that his wife was right, because it always meant admitting he was wrong.

Betsy learned how to make cheese too, Letitia grateful to have something to give back to the Kalapuya woman. Little Shoot joined them, a boy with long black hair Letitia envied for its straightness and easy care. Betsy's too. Martha's fingers were always getting stuck in the thick nap of Letitia's hair if she left it unbraided, which she did most often, the coconut oil and honey mixture keeping the tight kinks in check. Martha's hair was soft fuzz, black as earth.

"First we heat the milk in a copper pot. When it warm, we takes it off the heat and puts in this itty-bitty piece of a deer's stomach. Always save the stomach, stretch it out like a banjo."

"A drum."

"Dry that stomach, then roll it, and it keep and give us a piece the size of my Martha's thumb to make the milk jell."

Betsy nodded, seeming to memorize as they worked. While they waited for the milk to heat or cool, Betsy told stories. She reminded Little Shoot to listen and to sit. "If you stand, you will get a hump back. We should have three storytellers."

Letitia handed her the spoon.

"That way they correct my telling. But there are few storytellers left so I teach Little Shoot. And with your baby, there are three to listen. I tell today of pine squirrel and deer and of hope and fear." She gave a little cackle and Martha giggled.

"Now we waits until the milk gets thick and jiggles like a fat man's belly."

Betsy shared a story of a boy becoming the moon and another of how a coyote outsmarted a frog. The stories reminded Letitia of days before her mother was sold when they sat around a fire pit in an evening while men and women sang and swapped stories to make the children laugh and sometimes the parents cry.

"I cuts the thick milk now into small pieces and then breaks it." Letitia liked the squishy feel of breaking up the cheese until it was the size of grains of corn dribbling over her dark fingers. She could transform milk. A woman was always transforming. "It like a custard all broken apart. Now we heat again. Keeps stirring. Don' let it boil. Good." She hovered behind Betsy. "Now we lets it cool and hears more stories. Or I teaches you to pun jab, tell stories with pats and claps of hands."

Little Shoot laughed as Betsy tried her hand at the claps and slaps. She shook her head. "No good!"

Letitia strained the cooled milk, then let it drip through one of her old petticoats before returning it to the pan and kneading in the salt. When she pulled out her quilting hoops, Betsy's forehead furrowed.

"I gots cloth and this be the shape of our cheese. Wrap this cloth around and we store it in the firkin I bring all the way from Missouri. Keep it cool and dry. It gets a hard crust and tastes *kloshe*." She was proud of her use of Betsy's word for "good."

"You trade it."

"Sell it to the trappers and anyone else achin' for a good bite of cheese. Closest neat cows are in Fort Vancouver, Davey says, so we good. We very good to have our cows. We wily as your coyote changing milk to butter and cheese to money."

Davey went to town alone. Letitia preferred the shadow of Coffin Butte, singing hymns and trail songs to Martha as she skimmed cream, transforming milk into cheese. At the cabin, Davey appeared settled, happy to be splitting rails to mark his property, keep the cows from wandering. They'd bred Charity and her heifer. Old B was fit to the plow and they broke ground for a garden. "We're not raising wheat, nothing like that. We're stockmen."

A lean-to kept Letitia dry while milking cows. She called each in by name. "Here, Charity." She'd milk, then with a gentle slap, send her out, her bell clanging, then call in Blue, Charity's calf, now with one of her own. Martha could say "cow" and worked on "baby" as though she knew that was her name too.

The days rode up and down, filled with the ordinary: stuffing a mattress with bedstraw, examining a plant Betsy shared with them, eating watercress near Sulphur Springs. Little Shoot learned to aim with Davey's pistol, the two males laughing together. Martha took her first steps. Cheese crumbled off their chins on a frosted morning. This was freedom both inside and out and Letitia relished it, even letting herself stand out to the passing trappers who bought her cheese and butter, gave her security in her earnings.

Davey's citizenship papers arrived in the fall of 1846. He did a little jig outside the store housing the post office in Oregon City.

When he arrived home, he shouted, "Tish! Guess what? My papers are here!"

"What papers be those?" She wiped her hands on her apron, walked out to where Davey grinned.

"Why, my citizenship papers. I was waiting on . . . Oh."

How could he have forgotten that she never knew?

"You just now getting those papers? How we have this land then?" She spread her hand to take in their homestead. "You lie?"

"No. Now, lookee here. They knew I'd applied. Came all this way. Only a fool would come to claim land without being certain he could."

She stared at him. Was that disgust he saw on her face?

"Now Tish—"

"You risk this land, this place you leave us if something happen to you?" She narrowed her eyes, her words a hiss.

"But see, everything worked out fine. The sparrows are being looked after."

She shook her head and went back inside. So much for sharing a happy thing with someone committed to loving you. He led Fergus into the barn. Might be a good place to stay the night.

⁂

Later that October, Davey was asked to help build a cabin on a claim south, one taken by the man who'd helped raise their cabin. Letitia brought along a berry pie, egg noodles, fresh bread, and cheese. The day was balmy like spring without the winds, and there'd be people there, some from the wagon train she hadn't seen for a year, Davey'd told her. She smelled distant burning smoke. As they pulled off the trapper's trail, she saw children. Then closer she recognized little Martha Hawkins walking with Nancy Jane. Her heart swelled.

"Martha? Is that you, chil'?"

"You know my soon-to-be stepchildren?" Micah Read took the pies from Letitia's hands.

Nancy Hawkins stepped out of a wagon. "I know that voice." She opened wide her arms.

Martha ran toward them while Nancy asked, "You live close?" Then to Micah Read, "Why didn't you tell me who had the claim north of us?"

"You never asked."

"We's neighbors." Letitia couldn't control the wideness of her grin nor ignore how good it felt to anticipate a neighbor she so loved. "The Lord be good, so very good."

A month later for her November wedding, Nancy Hawkins readied a dark blue dress borrowed from Sarah Bowman with whom she'd spent the winter. But the lace she'd stitched to it was a piece she'd worked on while walking across the trail.

"I never expected to fall in love again, ever, but that Thomas Micah Read . . . he prefers to be called Micah," she whispered to Letitia as Letitia helped her dress. They were in the cabin Micah had built with Davey's and other men's help. "He's been as kind and gentle as any man could be."

Letitia glimpsed out the window at Coffin Butte, a different angle from the one she and Davey shared, but one she'd come to appreciate and hoped Nancy would too.

"He's a few years older than me but widowed nearly two years. He said he was 'waiting for perfection and found it in me.' Isn't that sweet?" Nancy pulled her shoes off and wiggled her toes inside white silk stockings. The white leather shoes were borrowed too.

"Nancy," her mother cautioned. "You'll pick up slivers. This floor is well adzed but nothing keeps all those splinters out."

"I'll put them back on. They make my feet itch." She rubbed the arch of her foot with her toes. "He has two children, but he's happy to add my six. Is it all right to still count Laura?"

"'Course. She your little girl always. He make you happy?"

"He does." She clasped Letitia's hands, looked into her eyes. "And do you know what he gave me for a wedding present? Guess. Don't tell her, Mama."

Nancy's blue eyes twinkled. She reminded Letitia of a young Sarah Bowman, the woman she'd been given to years before, teasing with her friends. She had only seen Sarah at a mercantile once since she and Davey had arrived in this country the year before. She'd been laughing with friends and didn't acknowledge Letitia, though her eyes said she recognized her. The incident with the cow still stood between them.

"Come on, Tish. Guess."

"He give you a razorback pig. They hard to come by. Be a mighty fine present."

"Oh you. No, he made a brand-new quilting frame for me. One I can hang from the ceiling like I did back home and lower it when friends come to stitch. The first thing I quilted was a wedding ring pattern I've already put on our bed. Seemed fitting." She leaned her head back into Letitia's stomach as she stood behind her, working Nancy's hair. "He's a good man. I think Zach would like him." She swallowed, her eyes catching Letitia's in the mirror. "I do miss that man. My best friend . . . I feel like he's here giving me away on this, my second wedding day."

"That a good way to feel. A blessing from heaven. Laura be clappin' her hands too."

"I like to think so."

Letitia wished she hadn't brought up Laura's death. "Maybe Nancy Jane won't be your last chil'."

"Oh, I think I'm finished."

Nancy's mother herded the girls out. Samuel and Edward would come to the wedding, but they lived now with Judge, Nancy's brother, north, across the Columbia River. Letitia wondered how it grieved her having her sons so far away.

In the silence Letitia wove a green plant with red berries into Nancy's blonde hair. Patches of the pretty stuff grew close to their cabin. Betsy called it *kinnikinnick*.

"Maybe we'll have children, Micah and I. But I'll never forget Laura. Or Zach. Nor the baby I lost. But this is a new chapter in my life."

"You all brand new."

"Oh, that looks lovely, Tish." Nancy smiled into the rounded mirror she held. She turned her head back and forth. "A better use for kinnikinnick than mixing it with tobacco. Micah doesn't smoke, not even a smelly pipe. I think we're going to get along just fine. Why, do you know he's already written out a will." She frowned. "I need to probate Zach's will. I guess I haven't wanted to admit that Zach is gone. I keep thinking he'll walk back into our lives and—but now, I need to get the estate handled."

"It be good Doc wanted to care for you in the future whether he in it or not. Your Micah too. A will be a good thing."

"Yes. It is. And your Davey ought to remember that. Maybe I'll get Micah to urge that action."

"That be a great gift, Miss Nancy. I supposed to give you a gift."

"The cheese you brought will be present enough. And your friendship." She grabbed Letitia's hand, held it to her cheek. "There's no greater gift than having a good friend to share a woman's wedding day."

Letitia helped Nancy get her shoes on and went out first to join the gatherers. Davey held Martha in his arms, her little bottom hanging below his forearm, her hand patting his head. He looked happy and content. She almost didn't want to break that mood, almost. She slipped in next to him and said, "Nancy giving me a present on her wedding day."

"Is she? What's that?"

"She talking to Micah to tell you to write up a will." She felt him tense. She whispered, "Micah give her a written promise, wants her not to worry about her future. Don' you want that for me and Martha?"

"Ain't the time, Tish," he whispered back to her. "Not now. I like the way you're letting the ends of those cornrows flail. Looks like water flowing."

"Sayin' pretties won't keep me from askin' again."

Letitia feared it never would be the right time. She kept wishing it didn't matter. But it did.

<hr />

They did well with Davey's proving up ground, planting potatoes, and splitting enough rails that the cows didn't wander so far. They covered the spring where she cooled the cheese and other promises from summer that she served in winter. Letitia sold butter and cheese to trappers and new settlers, many heading south. She spent time with Nancy, who needed a midwife eleven months after her wedding and again twenty months after that.

Letitia's days filled with labor bringing purpose to her life. Eggs filled her apron in the morning; pigs grunted greedily at the acorns and potato peels she tossed them. Martha grew happy under the pampering of Betsy and other Kalapuya women who teased Letitia, saying, "Martha a Kalapuya, just like us. *Kloshe.*"

Letitia found rest instead in Davey's arms. More than once she sat beneath spreading oak trees to listen to a circuit rider preach while even Davey sang the hymns, and neighbors north and south accepted she was there. She was a cared-for sparrow. When she knew she was carrying a child again, she took it as a blessing, a double blessing, to have Davey say, "Sure 'tis a gift" at the birth of Adam. Their son arrived in First Month, as Betsy called it—September by all others—in 1849.

Then Davey made his pronouncement, startling the cowers back. Adam was three weeks old.

23

Where Safety Lies

"No reason I shouldn't go to Sutter's. There's a ton of gold there, and when word gets out, half the men in the states will head west. I got to go now."

"We have enough. Herd's growing. Garden sendin' up shoots. We selling butter and cheese and beef this year. Can sell bacon and hams too. Why you want to leave all that when you might not find gold? You got a new chil' to look after. He need his daddy." She held Adam to her breast. He wasn't even a month old, October around the corner. She shook her head. No arguing with a restless man.

She thought Davey was pleased with his life. Only one thing bothered her—until Davey said he was planning to leave.

"Truth is I's worried about that exclusion law."

"Nothing to worry over, Tish."

"Nancy say it means anyone of color has to leave Oregon. No Negro or mulatto can stay here. That mean your daughter at risk too. Anyone come and say we got to leave. If you go on to California, what we do if they make us go? What happen to this farm?"

"I tell you, nothing will come of that law. Just a few slavers wanting to puff up their chests in a political way. Anyway, it don't speak to coloreds already here, just no new ones coming in. What I hear is voters don't want Oregon to be a slave state when we come into the union. No one thinks they'll enforce the crazy law."

"Those slavers have a way with me and Martha and now Adam, too, they puts their mind to it."

"I picked this place way far from the government. No one even wanders down this trail 'cept trappers and they're leaving the country or coming back and show no political interest as far as I can tell. Most are British anyway. Those that buy your butter and your cheese, why would they object to you? You're one of the country." He finished putting a chunk of cheese in his pack. "Sure wish you'd make that faster-eatin' cheese like you did that one time."

"If you stay home from California, I make it every week for you."

"Bribery, woman, will get you nowhere." He leaned across his pack laying on the bed and kissed her nose.

"I's not so easily smoothed." She crossed her arms. She could smell the coconut oil scent heightened by the perspiration at her forehead. "You write your will or our agreement, Davey Carson, before you leave or maybe we not here when you get back."

"You wouldn't leave, would you? Now lookee here, this is a great chance for us. I'll be back in a few months." He came around to her. "It's a law, but it don't mean anything. No one has the time to act on it."

"I hears of a black man who went north he so worried about that earlier exclusion law. Oregon keeps repeatin' that rule like they never get it right the first time."

"See, no one made him go. They rescinded the one passed in 1844. And the one in 1845. This 1849 one, it'll go by the wayside too. It's just some people with nothing to do coming up with this latest one. No one will enforce it. Where's that faith you say you have?"

When she spent time with Betsy, she calmed, the light of kindness shining through the woman reminding her that she had all she needed to survive. Thrive, even. Learning the Kalapuya ways reminded her to "remember the sparrow" and not worry about whether she could be taken care of if something happened to Davey. But still . . .

"I not promising I be here when you get back."

"Well, I know you ain't going far, with two wee ones. No, you'll stay close to Nancy or Frances Gage."

"Both those women have husbands at home helpin' with work and their chillun. Nancy got a new girl, Theresa, and her boy Perry. You think Mr. Read leave her by herself? Mr. Read running an inn so he able to be around to help his wife and chillun. But you leave me with a new baby and no papers?"

He patted her hand. "I'll come home with gold and we'll be able to influence any who might want to act on that exclusion law. No, you don't worry."

As she watched him ride away with the pack animal trailing behind him, she tried to sort out if his unwillingness to put her safety in writing was a lack of trust in God's provision or a constant nudge to trust that his care for her was sufficient. If he loved her, would he not do a simple thing that could make her happy and ease her future worries? Wasn't that part of what love was all about?

He left. That was her answer.

Micah Read stopped by each week to check on her. She paid the man in cheese when he would take it. Little Shoot rode the Carsons' horses with the ease that young men often had and helped with the cattle. Letitia thanked both man and boy for checking rails and repairing them. When it came time to dig potatoes, Little Shoot dug beside Letitia while Betsy sat on a quilt and played with Martha, giving her a tule-dressed doll stuffed with goose down and singing to Adam.

"More fun to get *wapato*," the boy said.

Letitia and Martha had gone with them once to a murky swamp area and stepped into the water, feeling for the potato-like *wapato* with their toes. Even Roth got in the effort, burying his nose in the water and coming up with a tuber. But Letitia liked the garden potatoes too.

By the time snow fell and water in the tin bowl wore an edge of frost, Davey had still not returned. She didn't want to admit it, but a part of her liked being in charge of things. She was alone but not lonely; she'd been left behind but wasn't abandoned. In some ways, this described her life of faith as well.

She thought it was either Little Shoot or Micah one morning when two horsemen rode up. One wore a new red vest she could see leering out from behind his store-bought coat.

"Well, look who's here," Greenberry Smith said.

Letitia stood in the doorway, out of the slow, cold rain. She did not invite them in. "It's Davey Carson's wench. Where's that brat of yours?" He stretched his neck to look behind her and she felt the bile rise up within her, her palms sweating though the air was cold.

"What you want?"

"Why, I'm Greenberry Smith, in case you've forgotten. This here's my brother Alexander. We're helping the sheriff out, and wondering where that Davey Carson is?"

"He around." The lie was a small one and didn't ease the pounding in her ears.

"Is he? Well, maybe you'll ask him to come on out."

"Nothing you need here. You best be goin'."

"You challenging me, girl?"

Rothwell started to bark his hound sound and pushed in front of her. He stood in the doorway, hair on the back of his neck raised and ruffled, his tail up and stiff.

"Call off your dog. We're here doing the law's work," the brother said.

Greenberry looked at Letitia. "You're in Oregon Territory now, woman. There are laws, a fact you might be ignorant of. And you're violating one of the Territory laws by being here, you being a Negro and your brats being mulatto. You got to leave."

Her throat was dry as a corn husk. "Where are your papers sayin' I gots to leave? That law only for newcomers."

"Ooh, she is something asking for *your* papers, G.B." The brother grinned, his hands resting on the pommel like he was passing the time of day.

The dog continued barking, jumping forward, then back, his tail rigid as a scythe. Smith raised his pistol and aimed.

"Roth! No. Come!" She croaked the words, grabbed at his collar.

"That's better. OK now. You need to git." G.B. Smith growled out the words, revealing the space between his two front teeth. His horse began to dance around and he yanked at the reins. He held his pistol out. Rothwell growled low, tugged against her hold. "Take those brats and leave. That's the law."

"We in a county now." Her voice shook. "I knows that. I wants to see the county sheriff. Not his . . . patrollers."

She stepped back, heart pounding, and lifted the pistol from a shelf above the door, both hands pointing as steady as she could. "Roth, inside." The dog complied but still stood beside her, growling low at her skirt.

"Ain't no wench gonna pull a gun on me and not feel the pain of it."

G.B. leapt from his horse then. Rothwell barked, barked, jabbed toward him, then bit his leg. He struck the dog with the grip of his pistol, lurched toward Letitia, jamming her arms into her chest as he pinned her up against the door. Spittle formed at the edge of his thin lips. He smelled of sweat as he wrenched the pistol from her hand.

Martha cried, "Mama. Mama." Adam gasped a hiccoughed sob.

G.B. hit Letitia on the cheek with the butt of his pistol, shoved her backward, and she tripped over Rothwell, fell against the table. "Don't you ever defy me, girl. You know your place and it is not to challenge a white man. Ever. Now you get out of this state."

She heard a horse from a distance.

"Let's ride," G.B.'s brother shouted.

Greenberry Smith hesitated, then mounted and the two rode off with Rothwell moaning, her children crying, and Letitia shaking as they fled.

"I'm still so mad at Davey Carson for leaving you, I could spit." Nancy put a cold press on Letitia's cheek. "That needs to be stitched up." They were at the Reads. Micah had helped Letitia and her children mount a horse and then laid Rothwell across his pommel. It was pure chance Micah had happened by when he did.

"They coulda done more harms than they did. Left Martha and Adam alone. And I think Roth gonna be all right. You think so, Mr. Micah?"

He didn't look her in the eye.

Nancy got out her sewing needle. Letitia flinched but allowed the stitching. "This'll still leave a scar."

"You know who they were?" Micah asked.

It will do no good to tell him. Maybe he didn't know, being from New Hampshire, that the word of a black woman accusing a white man would only bring her trouble.

"I needs to get back, tend to the stock. Little Shoot might not come 'til later. Cows need brought up to milk." She patted Martha on her lap, who reached up with feather fingers to linger at the stitching. The throb pushed at her cheek. Adam slept swaddled on the Read daybed.

"You shouldn't be alone there, not with the exclusion law in place. I can't believe they passed such a despicable act."

"My tongue got loose, maybe egg him on."

"You are not at fault here, Letitia. Goodness. Not one bit."

"They can't make me go, can they? Don't they needs the sheriff?"

"If they'd been deputized, they would have said so. It's winter coming on and men need things to keep 'em busy instead of riding around enforcing laws without a license," Micah said.

She hated bringing her children up into a world where just being alive caused her to be in trouble with the law. Only written words of white men seemed to matter. "Would you . . . would you write up a paper that Davey sign when he get back saying I work for him, have since '45. Maybe they see I his employee they be less willing to send us away."

She could feel the sting of tears in her nose. Pitiful, that's what she was. Pitiful and chained by something she could never change.

"He hasn't written out a will?" Nancy turned from putting her scissors back.

"Not sure it do any good now, but maybe I get his property in the state if something happen, even if I is colored."

"There is something in that law that honors contracts between the races, isn't there?" Nancy asked.

Micah nodded assent. "Where do they think black people or the Hawaiians are supposed to go? North to Puget Sound?"

Nancy picked up her youngest, paced. "Maybe she should stay here, until Davey comes back," she said.

"I don't think she'll be bothered. Sheriff won't be out, that's for sure. Hofins left for the gold fields. I don't know who they appointed, but there's enough crime and land grabbing to deal with, without taking on the exclusion law full force. Haven't heard of any judge wanting to hear such a case either. Maybe your tormentors, whoever they are, will head to California too. Let all the trouble-makers end up there."

"I's not leavin' my home." She had nowhere to go. "I talks to Little Shoot. Maybe he stay. But first, you write out the words for me? I get Davey to sign when he come back. If he come back."

❦

At her farm—as she thought of it—she could see ahead that Little Shoot had finished slopping the hogs as she rode in. She held Martha in front, Adam was in his board. She tried to leave Rothwell behind until he was better, but the dog slinked along, his head tipped to the side. Once at home, she'd put a basil poultice on it or get him to drink water from the Sulphur Springs. Both could help.

What was she going to do about being alone here? G.B. Smith could come back any time. Little Shoot took Martha from her arms and then helped her dismount. "I'm thinkin' I can use winter help." She spoke to the boy, who was as tall as a sapling though he couldn't be more than thirteen summers.

"You have trouble." He stared at her cheek. "We go toward our village in this season, longer time away from you. But not so much work now either."

"Havin' folks here keeps the unwanteds away."

"An unwanted hurts you." He looked at the stitches on her face and she raised her hand to her cheek.

Maybe he gets harmed too. A shot of fury coursed through her, aimed at Davey for leaving them; at G.B. Smith for showing up after four years of not worrying about him; at the territorial government for passing such a law; at being born a colored woman without any power.

"Would your kasa let you stay here? It may not be safe."

"Maybe you ask her to stay too." His round face filled with his grin. He swiped his straight black hair away from his face. "More cheese, faster. You ask?"

"I will."

"*Kloshe.* Good."

Maybe she would never get Davey to secure her future, but she would do what she could to ensure her safety now. Strength came with the kind comfort of neighbors who looked after each other. She was powerless to change the law, but she could change how she defended against it, what stories she told herself, a slave of anger or a free woman. Her children required it. She didn't know then how much.

24

Kin

Davey returned with his arms open to her as he jumped from his horse. It was mid-December and she stood in the doorway, arms crossed over her chest, wearing her fur coat and resentment. He grabbed his saddlebag and moved into the cabin to be out of the drizzling rain. Low mists like fragile lace edged the willows along Soap Creek. He'd lost weight, his beard was shorter. His eyes held a sparkle. *They would. He has himself a good time.*

"'Tis longer than intended I've been away but I'm bringing back gold." He pulled a small sack from his saddlebag, looked disappointed when she failed to waltz into his arms, turned into the house instead.

He dropped the leather with a *clink!* on the table. "Gold."
What he values more than us.

He rubbed his hands together for warmth. Or maybe it was a sign of his greed. He opened his arms then to embrace her. She backed up.

"What, not even a kiss?" His arms dropped like branches on a snow-laden tree.

She bent to pick up Adam.

"How's my boy?"

"He already nearly four months old." She couldn't keep the bite from her tongue.

She hoped her heart would melt some of the seethe as she saw the two together. And it did. Some. Martha held back behind her mother's skirts.

"Sorry I am for leaving ye for so long. Some days I was in the field and luck was in the road. Took me a little time to get luck moved over." He nuzzled his son's neck and the boy cooed and grabbed at Davey's red beard. "Ow, ow, you little Jack." He laughed. "You can see I did good." He nodded toward the sack. "Now we can get ourselves a bull, not have to pay those breeding fees. And I'll get you some new duds. For the lassie too."

"I's fine with the duds I got. Chil' need fatherin', not featherin'."

"Got lots to share with you, Tish. Where's my Martha?" He handed Adam back and lifted his daughter, who put her arms around his neck. "Me father used to say there was no scarf so warm as a daughter's arms around the neck." He carried her to his saddlebag and brought out papers wrapping three round objects he gave to Letitia, keeping one box for Martha to unwrap, then spoiled the child's surprise by telling her what it was. "Tea set. Right from England." He set Martha down. "Lookee, two little cups and a pitcher. Fine china. Little painted flowers. So many interesting things in California."

"*Kloshe*, Papa. Pretty." She fingered the rose design on the porcelain. "Thank you." She blew him a kiss.

"That's more like the greeting a man expects when he brings a present."

He came to Letitia then, set Martha down. He bent to kiss his wife's cheek. He frowned but didn't ask her what had happened to make the scar, merely thumbed it. She shivered at his touch. She needed to be rigid as a bed key.

"It's good to be home, Tish. Place looks good." He scanned the room. "You did good."

He surveyed the cabin and Letitia looked too, seeing with his eyes. A cow's stomach was stretched wide and drying by the fireplace. A cabinet held dishes and pitchers and butter molds, purchased for her by Nancy when her friend went to town. Wild onion and parsley hung drying from the rafters. She'd washed clothes that colored the drying rack. Out the glass window she watched the herd graze with her brindled Charity clanging her bell in the distance. Deer hides were stretched on the split-rail fence. Betsy would work them in the spring, soaking them in the creek, then turn the hides into leggings and gloves and moccasins for the children. "I has good neighbors."

"Who's staying in the huts?"

"Kalapuya. Little Shoot and Betsy, they living in one of those."

"Good, good. You got everything under control." He opened his arms. "Now come to me. I missed you, Tish."

She couldn't bring herself to say she'd missed him too. She didn't move toward him, and after a silence thick as river fog, he went outside to tend to Fergus and his pack animals, took a fair amount of time cooling his horse.

That evening after supper, he told her stories of the gold fields, how he could make more money by packing her cheese and bacon south, selling it there. How his claim had been jumped and how he'd fought to get it back. That he'd run into the sheriff. "G.B. Smith and I met up last month. He told me he ran into you over that exclusion law and that he had to disarm you. Did you really pull a gun on him, Tish?"

"You didn't come back to see if we's all right?"

He swallowed once or twice. "I figured he'd a told me if you were hurting any."

"He tells you what he did to me, to Rothwell?"

"No. Where is Rothwell?" At the sound of his name the dog crawled out from behind a cupboard, his head lowered on one side. Sheepish, he slunk toward Davey.

"He think he at fault for it." Letitia patted the dog's head. "Smith struck him into this—wayward walk as Betsy call it." She scratched the dog's neck as he leaned into her leg. "He struck me too." She held her hand to her cheek.

"He did that? Why, if I'd knowed that, I'd a—"

"What you do?" It was the opening she needed. "You leave us to be struck by any man who care to. Keepin' us safe?" She laughed, hated the sound of her own anger.

"No, now. If I'd known, I'd have taken that man down a peg."

"He damage your . . . property." Fury like a geyser rose up through her, turning her insides hot.

"Oh, now, you're not my property. No, he had no right to hurt you or any woman." He reached for her, but she recoiled.

She touched her cheek. "Sulphur Springs and Nancy Read heal this." She ran her fingers then across the ribbed scar that jagged like lightning across her cheek.

"I am so sorry." His eyes watered. "I thought my going for gold would set us pretty and it will. But you did good without me." He looked around. "Say, where'd you get that cupboard?"

"You wants to talk about furniture?"

"I want to talk about something that won't rile you none, Tish. Surely sorry I am for what happened to your cheek. And to Rothwell."

"Joseph Gage." She answered his question. "They our neighbors north, in Polk County. With all them kids—double ones too—he needs beef and bacon. I gots that, so we trade."

"You done right well without me around. Probably wish I hadn't come back."

She didn't know what she wished. She'd worked hard these past months with a newborn and all alone. She was better off than some. The stories of men deserting their families and fields for a taste of gold were common as horseflies and just as irritating.

"Why you come back?"

Rothwell lay on his side, scratched the floor, chasing rabbits in his sleep.

"For you, of course. And they passed the Donation Land Act. I got to re-register this land with the surveyor or someone else could claim it. We get the land free."

"Not for the likes of me or even Betsy and Little Shoot. Their people here longer than any from the states and they gets nothin'."

"Yes, yes, I know. Well, I'm not letting anyone get their hands on this fine farm. And it'll be finer yet with this gold. Here." Davey opened the bag and dumped the ore on the table. He handed her two nuggets the size of his thumbnail. "You can go anywhere you want with that much gold. But I'm hoping you'll stay."

She stared at him. "Why you think I go somewhere? This my home. Maybe you take the nuggets and go."

He jerked back. "Why, Tish, I ain't going nowhere. We're married. I'm here to stay, to work with you like we did before. My wandering feet are ready to settle down. It was only a few months I was gone."

"'Cept you heading back to California."

"For us, Tish. Two weeks at a time, maybe a month, then I'll be back. Can make more supplying those miners than hunting up gold. Here, take the nuggets. Think of 'em as safety nuggets. Then any time you want out, you can go."

"What about that law? What if they come to send me away?"

"That ain't going to happen. You got to trust me in this."

"We gots to change how things are between us. You say, 'I doing something this way.' And if I have another way, you go in your mind and say to yourself, 'Well, that ain't a worry' or 'I can fix that,' but you don't say that to me. You just walk over me and do it your way, leave me sittin' in the dust. I tired of being trampled on. That's the way you went to California against my wishes."

He nodded.

"What that cost you, you suppose?"

He tugged at his beard. "A contrary woman when I got back."

"But what it cost you, inside?" She touched her heart. "It cost me, being contrary. Why I let it up, in time. But what it cost you?"

He was thoughtful. "I guess I miss out on things. Don't try things your way if I can't see the merit in it. End up feeling responsible if my way doesn't work out."

She nodded. "It cost you too, to not be the husband you promise to be. I ain't the wife I imagine either when I carries contrariness past the words that might settle our disputes."

She rose from the table and went to the cupboard, opening the tin-lined door. "I don't want your gold, Davey Carson. I wants you to consider my words even though you think they don't carry weight. That's what a partner does." She turned with a paper in her hand. "Micah Read. He write the words of our agreement. I knows you think it a waste of time, but I don't. You sign now?"

He seemed to be taking her words in, stroking his bearded chin. "It'll make you happy?"

"It make me happy knowing if somethin' happen to you, I gets paid for the work I do and for my property, like the cows. We got a contract. We gets something and our chillun be safe."

"Beside the nuggets, you mean?"

"Nuggets not make up for what I scour over, leave my sweat for. I worth more."

"Yes, you are worth more." He smiled at her then. "You are quite a woman. Get me something to sign with. I'll show you my better self and do the deed."

And so Davey slid back into her days like a mouse stealing past a sleepy cat. He did sign her paper. That night he stroked her arm as they lay side by side and whispered words to pluck her heart, sing songs of joy begging sweet forgiveness. Through the days that followed Letitia was surprised that she didn't feel the satisfaction she thought she'd have by squirreling away papers in a tin. Maybe because she'd spent all the years living with the uncertainty and had found a slender thread of trust apart from paper and men's words. Maybe watching how many things Betsy and her people got by without—expensive things like candlesticks to feel wealthy or guns and papers to feel secure. Like the sparrow, the good Lord would take care of them as he had all along. If only she could hang on to that hope.

"Junior? That be my son? Sure and it is!"

David Carson Junior sauntered out of the drizzling rain in time for Christmas. *Chile like showin' up for holidaying.* He didn't remove his hat when he passed through the door until he saw the dog. "Rothwell, isn't it? Good dog."

He tossed the hat onto Letitia and Davey's bed. It would have been the respectful thing to do, remove his hat for the lady of the house and not just her dog. The young man had thickened at the waist and his cheeks wore the red of a man who liked his liquor. He was clean shaven but for a bushy mustache he twirled at the ends. Letitia suspected he used beeswax or an oil, not unlike what she used to smooth her hair sometimes.

"Yup, it's me, Pa. Came on board ship like I said I would." He looked around. "Nice place you got here." He looked at Letitia. "See you still got your . . . woman."

"And a good one she is. You visiting or settling?"

"Depends. Partial toward settling."

"You're in time then. You can put in for 160 acres, being you're a single man. I'm gonna try to get my full 640 but not much chance of it."

"Why not?" Junior squatted to stroke the dog's head.

Letitia listened with a hollow pit in her stomach.

"People of color don't qualify for land. And since we ain't married under the law . . ." He shrugged his shoulders. "Our neighbors' wives, they'll get property in their own right under this claim. Add 320 acres to their husband's acreage."

Excluded. Betsy's people were excluded too. Couldn't claim the land they'd lived on for generations.

"So the 320 acres you've been fencing you can't have, I can file on it?"

Davey hesitated, like he might ask Letitia's opinion. "Don't know why not. It'll be good to have you around. Look after things when I pack into California. Or maybe come with me. You'll have to reside here for four consecutive years to get title, but traveling south now and then won't count against you." He patted his son on the shoulder. "Tisha, rustle up some grub here for Junior. Sure and it's a fine, fine morning when a man's son comes calling."

In February, Davey and Junior rode together to Oregon City to meet with the surveyor general to make their claims. Letitia suspected that was the real reason Davey came back when he did. Micah Read also went so the men could be witnesses for each other about how long they'd been in the Soap Creek Valley and the boundary lines they'd honored. He came home and said he'd met up with a David Davis who had property northeast of them. He's courting Sarah Bowman. Her husband died last year."

"Miss Sarah's widowed?"

"That she is. Seems to be an epidemic. Sure hope you don't catch it any time soon."

Neighbors came to help Junior raise his cabin late that fall. At last Letitia would be freed of cooking for Junior and cleaning his clothes. They fed his horse. He didn't seem to have much in the way of supplies to farm, so he borrowed their plow and spades and extra dishware too. Nancy offered a quilt; Frances Gage brought berry pies.

"What about those beds the Indians are using. Can't a man have one of those?" This from Junior the day after the raising.

"Make one for yourself." Letitia slammed the spider a little harder than intended, broke eggs for breakfast into the three-legged pan.

"Now, Tish. A man gets tired sleeping on the floor," Davey said. "Maybe Betsy'd give up that hammock she made."

"You give away my things but you've no right handin' off Betsy's."

"I'd ask first." He sounded wounded.

"They got no right being here anyway," Junior said.

"They here before any of us." She heard the biting tone and took a deep breath. Holding resentment was like stoking a fire while waiting for rain. "I makes you a hammock."

Junior scratched at his full mustache, his brown eyes held a hint of glee. "Sure and that'd be a kind thing, then, for a mother to give her son."

Davey smiled. "Good to see the two of you getting along."

Junior wasn't a grateful man, sour even when he appeared to have everything he wanted. Land. A cabin. A cow and pig given to him by his father—and her, which Junior did not acknowledge. His father's love and attention. He scowled whenever Davey bounced Adam—whom Davey started calling Jack—on his knee or had a tea party with Martha. At least if she made Junior a hammock it might be a little harder for him to make their home a place for every meal, carrying with him his poor disposition as a hearty appetite.

For the next two years, each spring Davey loaded the pack mules and took their goods south to sell. Junior went with him, and Letitia and Rothwell stood watching while the pack animals trotted after the men down the trail. It meant more work for her and Little Shoot to look after Junior's hog and cow, but she adjusted to the time without Davey or Junior around. She set her own schedules, made decisions that didn't have to be negotiated with him nor have surprises of plans he'd made with Junior he hadn't bothered to mention to her. She visited Frances Gage and quilted while Martha and Adam slept on the Gages' large bed. Her son had the same pecan color as his sister and he had Davey's high forehead and strong chin. The apple trees bore fruit. Letitia was asked to midwife more than once. At Nancy Read's, she marveled at the new additions she'd helped deliver.

"I thought Perry would be my last, but now here's Clara. I wouldn't have missed meeting her for the world. But really, Clara is my last."

"Wild carrot grows here. Using them keeps Clara your last. Or that sponge. Betsy tell me that."

"Oh, Micah would never approve. Goodness, I'll have to be strong and keep getting stronger."

During Davey's absences, Betsy stayed again near the cabin. She'd moved closer to the village of her people when Junior returned, but with the men gone, Betsy helped Letitia hang baskets of plants and herbs, roots and berries, and dried salmon from the rafters. The smoked fish cast a pleasant scent. The Kalapuya woman showed Adam how to hold a bow much too big for the two-year-old boy. She taught seven-year-old Martha to wrap hazel shoots into one of the bigger baskets for storing roots and vegetables from Letitia's garden.

Letitia would lie in her bed at night and consider how her life had changed in this country and all she'd learned about living in a family of her own choosing. Betsy was a school for her and her children, one she attended with anticipation when Davey wasn't around having her do things for him. Little Shoot became a young man before her eyes, once bringing a pretty girl to help make cheese. Everything changed. Letitia wondered if finding peace in the time Davey left her meant she loved him less, or if discovering strengths within herself made it easier to live with his warts and accept her own. Perhaps her enjoying the solitary time was a sign of greater love between them. Maybe even greater trust so she wouldn't really have needed that paper in her cupboard.

Letting Go

Davey kept his word that year and and was only gone for a few weeks at a time. The exclusion law stood and now there was a law forbidding persons of color to testify against a white man. If a white neighbor stole something from a colored man, the courts were no recourse.

Letitia had heard that G.B. Smith was back in the area and had married. Maybe that was why he'd left her alone after that last encounter. His young wife, Eliza Hughart, whom he'd sniffed around at on the overland journey, died in childbirth. Letitia hadn't midwifed that birth. She didn't know who did, but she was sure the midwife grieved the loss of the mother. The baby—named for G.B.'s brother—must have kept G.B. occupied, though the next year he married Mary Baker.

"He's put himself up as an administrator for public things, executing probates and wills," Nancy told her. "His brother died last year in Hawaii and he's been working on that estate." With a pulley, Nancy lowered her quilt frame from the ceiling while Letitia helped settle the frame on the floor. She brought cheese and butter for the small inn the Reads now ran. "Heirs aren't too happy with his handling of things, or so I hear. But the court keeps appointing him. Micah says he'd never do business with the man. He may not do illegal things, but Micah says he's on the edge of ethical."

Letitia wished G.B.'s new wife well and prayed for her at the same time. She put Greenberry Smith out of her mind and found quiet joy in the life she'd come to lead. A small village south of them named Corvallis had sprung up, with a blacksmith shop, an attorney, and a mercantile, but she had no interest in going there. She stayed at home. She was the keeper of the hearth who stoked the fires, served friends when they came by, and welcomed Davey back when he'd been gone. She fed her children and the dog. She listened to Davey's stories when he returned but had no desire to go to California or anywhere else. She was as free as she had ever been. She was at home in Benton County.

Davey always returned happy, lifted his children in the air and swirled them, one by one, until their happy giggles rang through the valley in the shadow of Coffin Butte.

"Don't know why I leave," he said. "Ain't nothing as nourishing as these hills, this farm, you and these wee ones."

It was on one of those trips south when Davey became sick and brought the illness back.

"Little Shoot, please go ask Mrs. Read if she take the children. They's got their own to look after, but they like mama and papa to Martha and Adam."

Little Shoot had become an extension to her very being, he and Betsy, always ready to help, like family.

"I take children. Bring back kasa with healing."

Letitia handed him a biscuit as he headed out.

She didn't want the children becoming ill and she didn't want to leave Davey, who moaned, sweat tiny beads across his forehead, face, and neck. He couldn't keep down even the thin gruel of boiled wheat she made for him. His body soured the room when he missed the chamber pot, but she didn't begrudge it. He'd have done the same for her, she was sure. He was too weak to reach the privy they'd built the year before.

"I ache all over, woman. Help me, aye, 'tis a sorry state I'm in."

He was a child in his sickness, a child who couldn't be comforted.

She cleaned the chamber pot, made herb poultices. Betsy arrived with a tin of the Sulphur Springs water. "This make him well." It was the burning month, though the Indians burned much less now with all the split-rail fences and land someone else claimed marking new borders. But Letitia still wanted them to burn the sections of their land the Kalapuya had fired before. She saw how it kept the blackberries down and brought game closer to their door.

Junior didn't want his acreage fired up nor the part that had once been any of Davey's 640 acres. "Smoke won't do Pa any good," Junior charged when he stopped by one time. "Make those savages put out those flames. Here, I brought him a twist of tobacco. Let him chew."

Davey declined and his son left with a pat on his father's shoulder.

Davey's breathing had become shallower.

"They almost done burning," she told Davey. She wiped his face with a spring-soaked cloth, cooling. "I boil apples. Taste good for you."

He shook his head, smiled a weakened grin. "We had good times, didn't we, Tish?"

"We did." She wiped his arms, his neck and chest. She didn't like the tone of his talking.

Martha ran in to show him a butterfly she'd caught in her hand and then on the floor beside the bed played Noughts and Crosses with little stones and a rubber ball. She'd brought the children back because Davey missed them so.

Something caused the child to stop playing.

"It all right. Your papa feelin' poor. He'll be better. You take your playin' outside. Look after Adam, now. You his big sister."

Obedient, she rushed out.

"You're a good mama, Tish. Couldn't ask for no better. The greatest gift to a man's heart. Worth more than gold."

"What you doing making pretty talk to me now. You'll be well soon and wonder why you say such kind things 'cause I'll remember." She pushed his thinning red hair back behind his ears.

"Oh, Tish. Don't be fooling yourself."

She felt her stomach tense.

The clearer September air didn't improve Davey's breathing. She asked Micah to please go for the doctor again, and while she waited she prayed for his recovery, staring out at Coffin Butte. She wanted him to see Adam and Martha grow up, for them to know their father as he grew older. He was her husband and, she realized, her closest friend.

"Just so weak. Can't . . . can't sit up." A few days had passed.

He'd been ill—they both had—last year in the winter of '51. Pertussis or whooping cough, Doc called it. They stayed with the Gages those weeks, recuperating, Frances loving the presence of Martha and Adam. Both children had a mild case and Davey had recovered first and gone back to the claim, hiring a man named Walker to stay and butcher. Later he said he hadn't realized how much work Letitia did until she wasn't there to anticipate what he needed done or doing it before he even considered. Junior hadn't come around to help.

She'd recovered with Frances's help and hadn't been ill since, though each time the fireplace smoked back into the cabin and she coughed, she wondered if the wrenching pertussis had come visiting again.

This illness of Davey's in September of '52 wore a different cloak, more threadbare, letting the coldness of the inside bleed through. Davey ached and his eyes watered and turned red. The skin of his face stretched across his cheekbones showing his skull. She'd shaved his beard to make it easier to keep him clean and the skin on his chin was pale as flat bread. Doc Smith didn't seem to know what ailed Davey.

"Can you. Feed me. Soup?"

Feed him, like he a chil'? The cowers so long gone came roaring back. "I . . . I soaks the sourdough in the beef broth, then you brings it to your mouth. You can do it. You feeds you self." She patted his hand, his fingers wrinkled now, the nails chipped and yellowed. "It good you keeps moving, doin' things."

"I . . . I can't. Please."

What was wrong with her? She couldn't feed her ill husband a simple savory soup?

And then she knew. She knew that spooning that soup into Davey's mouth would mean he was no longer able to tend himself and never would again. He was dying. She didn't want to do anything that said his days were numbered, that he'd be gone. For all his warts and willful ways, she cared for him. Loved this man who was the father of her children. She didn't mind washing his body, cleaning up his messes, trying remedy after remedy to help him through. But this . . . this need to feed him wound down her hope like a ticking clock. She took a deep breath. Tears pressed from the corners of his eyes. He reached for her hand; he was cold to the touch. She spooned the beef into his mouth, the broth seeping from his bluish lips.

"Findin' time like it was lost. I looked in nooks and crannies trying to find more time for us." She wiped the corner of his mouth. "Treasurin' the seconds, minutes driftin' like snowflakes meetin' on the taste buds. Did we forget to make time? Is that how I lost you, Davey Carson?" Her voice caught.

"You made time. It's how we found each other." He looked up at her and smiled. "Did my best, aye. Hoping the Lord noticed."

⬧⟳⬧

David Carson died on September 22, 1852. Letitia asked Nancy to put the date into his Bible and to add Martha's and Adam's births as well. He had neglected to include them. He neglected many things, but he'd done as he'd said: his best. Surely the Lord would ask for no more.

Doc Smith signed the death certificate, told her he'd let authorities know and the itinerant pastor when he came around, so she could have a service. "Best we bury him soon."

Little Shoot and Micah and his boys and Joseph Gage helped dig the grave beneath the apple trees while Roth lay with his nose upon his paws, watching. The children stood next to her, their slender bodies warm against her thighs. Martha wore a bonnet and Letitia a new flat-topped straw hat Frances Gage had picked up for her in Corvallis. Junior kept his hat off, didn't say a word though he listened while Micah read from the Bible, picking the verses she'd remembered giving Nancy when little Laura had died.

"'A time for mourning.' That be now." She thanked Micah, accepted the Bible back, folded it into her chest, and then she began to sing in her low range, "I want Jesus to walk with me . . ."

Those who knew the words joined in.

"Why'd we put Papa in the ground?" Martha asked. They were back at the cabin.

"His body was tired. His spirit be gone, Martha. He where he need to be. And we where the Lord want us to be too. Right here. Safe and sound." She looked to the cupboard. She patted her daughter's shoulder. "You play now, have a tea party with your brother with that set of dishes your papa brought back."

"Death part of living." Betsy fixed mint tea harvested from the wet ground when Soap Creek flooded each spring. They sat alone, the children playing as though they understood that grief settled better within silence.

Letitia had a little gold dust left, money not spent on buying cows and a bull and farm equipment and a good stove, all things Davey wanted. She had twenty-nine cows now. They belonged to her by Davey's hand. She had the agreement. She'd be all right when it came time to settle Davey's affairs. He had taken care of her and the children, like a good father would. That night in the cabin she let the light flicker in her candlesticks until they burned down to a nubbin.

26

Loose Ends That Never End

The next weeks found her lost in thought as she called each cow
in for milking morning and night. She made cheese, prepared for
the winter months. Their years together, seven in all, had been
shorter than she'd hoped for. Once she'd been uncertain, but she
and Davey made a good life together, did their share to mend the
wounded world being good neighbors, caring for their children,
fending for themselves with room to help others. A dozen irritations
through the years rolled through her mind, anger that he'd gone
to California then brought back what took his life. But maybe it
hadn't. Maybe as the Scripture said, there is a time for everything.
She wished Davey's time hadn't come so soon.

As the weeks passed, she remembered more occasions of joys
than irritations, moments that bled through the tears to stain her
heart. Those would be the stories she would tell her children. Those
would be the memories she'd let hold her hostage.

No one knew when the estate would be settled. For now, they
had the cabin and all the things bought to furnish it. The cattle

belonged to her, all from Charity's yield. Davey had claimed two old cows and a new calf. She expected she'd be paid the amount in the agreement, $200 per year since 1845 when they'd left Missouri. That came to $1,400. The land would have to be sold for that payment to be made. But if she received the $1,400 she'd be able to buy property somewhere, maybe in the Umpqua country in the southern part of the state. Maybe she could lease. When the executor was named, she'd give him the paper as a claim against the estate. That's what Micah had told her to do. And she'd tell them what was hers already, what property she had earned herself these seven years. She'd set aside Davey's watch for Junior when he came around, if he ever did. She hadn't seen him since the funeral. Until the executor rode in, she would be the sparrow, trusting in God's provision.

<hr />

Someone pounded on the cabin door. It was the dark of November, so early in the morning that if there'd been a clear sky the moon would have been a witness.

"Who—who be there? Shush now." Letitia spoke to Adam, who'd begun to cry. "You all right." His caramel-colored face dripped with tears. "You fine." She patted him, pulled on her knitted shawl to go to the door.

"What is it, Mama?"

"Nothin', baby. Go back to sleep."

She picked Adam up, held him on her hip. Roth stood, head at the twist, but he didn't bark. He hadn't barked since G.B. struck him.

The pounding began again and this time she recognized the voice telling her to "open up for the law."

"What—what you doing here?"

Greenberry Smith pushed past her with his former father-in-law and another man she didn't recognize crushing a letter at her chest. He jerked open cupboard doors, looked in trunks, counted dishes, his heavy brogans dropping mud.

"Why you here?" She set Adam down, clutched at her nightdress, his paper in hand. Both children cried.

"You two go out and count the stock."

"It's still dark, G.B. We can afford to let the woman get herself decent."

"Write down all the tools too. Make sure you get the bull and all those hogs they got."

"What you doin' here?"

"My job."

"You stop!"

"Why? You gonna pull a pistol on me? Here." He nodded to the letter that had fallen to the floor. "Not that you can read it so I'll tell you. I've been appointed executor of David Carson's estate. He had no will—"

"He sign an agreement. It like a will."

"Did he? Let's see it!"

Did she dare give it to him? Micah had said the executor would need it. "It in a safe place." She should have given it to Micah. At least he was a witness that it existed, though he'd never seen it signed.

"Come on. Give it to me."

The palms of her hands sweated. Thoughts like billiard balls rattled through her addled brain. *Should I? Shouldn't I?*

"Anything related to your husband's estate is court business now." This from one of the men accompanying G.B. He spoke softly.

"Get out there and count stock, I tell you." The men left and to Letitia G.B. said, "You'll be in trouble if you don't comply, woman. You aren't even supposed to be inside this state. Remember that."

Davey said the exclusion law didn't apply to those already here. She put Adam down; her hands shook as she opened the cupboard door and held a pottery canister to her stomach, pulling the paper out as she did. She handed it to him. He unrolled it, read it, and put it in the inside pocket of his vest.

"No!" She grabbed at him. "I keep that. Show the sheriff."

He pushed her away. "Sheriff and probate court have assigned me the duty." He grinned. "I'll see it gets to the right place. Now step back. We've got to make a list of all Davey's assets."

"Assets? I knows about assets. Some of what you countin' up is my assets. The furniture's mine. I pay Gage to make it. All the cattle 'cept Davey's three. The dishes—"

"Yours? You can't own property. You are property! The only reason I don't list you as a 'asset' is because no one's buyin' wenches these days in this *free* state. Rather humorous I'd say that you came all that way across the plains to find out that you're back where you belong. In the state of Nowhere and Worthless. That's your property."

The others returned.

"Ask Sarah Davis. She know I'm free. I belong to no one. Her father-in-law the one what free me. She know I'm not property. G.B. know it too." She turned to him. "You see my papers in Missouri. You know I free to come with Davey and work for him. He sign an agreement. Ask him!"

"What's she talking about, G.B.? She's got some kind of papers?"

"Let's leave Mrs. Davis out of this. We'll let the court know of our findings. You can remain here with your br . . . children until the auction."

"Auction?"

"No will." He raised his palms up as though he was powerless to do otherwise. "There'll be unpaid debts against the estate. Only way to pay them is to sell the assets. I'll set the date and after that, you're gone. What we reap from the auction will go to Davey's heirs. I already found them. Most back in North Carolina. Junior of course, but it'll all be divided among his *rightful* kin." He leaned into her. "Of which you are not one."

"That agreement say he pay me for the seven years I work for him, since 1845. That labor alone be close to $1,400 dollars. All the cows be mine. Twenty-nine."

"We'll see what the court has to say. Meanwhile, you won't

have much packing to do, because everything here is Davey's. It'll be sold."

"No! I buy this." She pounded her hand on the table. "I buy this!"

"With what?"

"My butter and milk and pork I sell."

"You sell? No, David Carson sells. Everything belongs to him. Don't you get that?"

"Where I go? Where I take our children?"

"No matter to the court. I've already got a buyer for the property."

Junior.

❧

It was like a summer storm rolling in with black clouds, lightning, hail, and wind. It happened so fast, the devastation unknown until it was over. G.B. set the date of the auction for January. She'd be turned out in the coldest, wettest month of the year.

"You stay with us," Betsy told her. "We build shelter. You be safe."

She sobbed at the kindness offered. She had to keep Charity. She had to make sure the agreement had been delivered to the court so they could see she had a claim not as an heir, a relative, but as an employee, as anyone else who ever worked for Davey and now had a claim.

Junior had never seen the agreement, said he knew nothing of it, and no, he wasn't planning to make his home open to the wench and her children.

"I do for you," she told him.

"What? What did you do for me? You took my daddy from me. I shouldn't even be talking to the likes of you. You put a spell on him. For all I know you poisoned him and that's why he's dead."

There was no reasoning with him.

With Nancy and Micah she tried to work the problem through, but it was like pushing a rock through the cheese sieve: it didn't go.

"She needs a lawyer, Micah."

"I can pay. I got a little money."

"The law doesn't allow a person of color to bring suit against a white person. Can't testify against them anyway." Micah bounced their youngest child on his knee. "I doubt any attorney will take your case with all the uproar about exclusions and lash laws and Oregon becoming free or slave, especially not in time to stop this auction."

"I can be there when they sells my things? I can buy some back?"

"You can. But a bigger problem is where you'll go after that."

"She'll come here." Nancy was firm.

Letitia shook her head. "You gots too many to look after now without adding mine."

Martha Hawkins sat beside her. The girl had grown so much and now held Letitia the way she'd once comforted Martha when her sister died. Adam and Perry Read played with wooden toys Joseph Gage had made for them.

"The Gages, maybe. They in another county. Maybe they willing to harbor someone supposed to leave the state."

In late November, she ventured into Salem and the probate court. She'd never been in the city before, but she swallowed her fears and asked to speak to the clerk about the signed agreement. She said she had a claim against the estate in the amount of one thousand four hundred dollars in return for her labor. "G.B. Smith has the contract David Carson sign." She heard the tremor in her voice. Would they send her away, she and her children? Arrest her? Put her in jail?

"There's no evidence provided in the material given to the court by the administrator," the clerk said. He wore a long coat and a string tie. She'd never seen Davey in a tie. "There are several claims here. Doc Smith wants $50 for his care and treatment of David Carson. David Carson is asking for $200 for four months of labor at $50 a month. Guess it's not *the* David Carson, deceased." He laughed at his own joke.

"I sees him take it. I gives the paper to Mr. Smith when he counts the assets."

The clerk pawed through more documents. "It's not here. Your claim's not on the list. I'm sorry."

"How I make a new claim, like Junior did for labor he wasn't paid for, he say?"

"Send a bill. Get a lawyer."

Get a lawyer? Raise the stakes, challenge white men? Maybe she could buy enough back at the auction to get by. G.B. wasn't a judge. He wouldn't make the final decisions, would he?

<hr />

Neighbors and others she didn't know rode into her yard, January 4, 1853, gouging wagon tracks in the mud. Rain slickers flowed over the backs of mules and horses like blankets at a picnic. A rare January sun break split the rain-soaked sky. Some buyers brought wagons to haul off what they purchased. The air felt cool, the clouds heavy as her heart.

Under a sopping canvas, Letitia watched, her belly aching, as others took her memories away. It was like she'd undressed in front of a window for all to see. Then, halfway through the bidding on the Bible she'd spoken her vows upon, she prayed to find another way to see this day, some way to hold her memories rather than having them hold her in this sorrowful place. She began to tell herself new stories.

That Bible going to the Wheeler family would bring them blessings and a comfort. They outbid her because the Lord wanted them to have that blessing. The plow, the gun, would be put in service to bring food to the Wheeler table. Her good clay pitcher would fill with nourishing milk for that family as it once had for hers.

It was harder to write a story for Mr. Davis, who bought cows. He'd married Sarah Bowman last year. She'd been widowed once too. He bought a cow, firkins, but not her Charity. Sarah would have something that Letitia's hands had held and that was good. A cow bellowed.

She hadn't seen the herd for several days. Even Charity hadn't come up to be milked yesterday. They did wander off, but she assumed G.B. Smith would have rounded them up for the auction. But so far, Davey's few animals and the bull were all that were corraled to be sold.

Junior showed up with a wagon into which he threw a shovel; had others help lift the harrow, plow, a thermometer, then placed her serving dishes in a blanket she'd given him. Her good copper kettle she used for making cheese Junior took too.

Letitia perked up. Five cups and saucers with little painted lilacs, the china set Davey had brought for Martha, came up for sale next.

"I buy those." She stood, stepped forward.

"Those are the children's things." Nancy raised her voice. "Goodness. Let her have those."

"Everything goes." G.B. shrugged as though he had no control. "What do I get for these? Five cents? Good china, looks like. Came all the way from California, I hear."

"I bids five cents." Letitia raised her hand.

"Three dollars. Those belonged to my pa. I'm entitled to his precious things."

"Sold!" G.B. handed the fragile pieces into the wide hands of Junior who dumped them in a heap amongst the blankets he'd also bought.

Junior also took a trunk full of Davey's shirts and drawers. She'd have given those to him if he'd said he wanted them. But the pots and pans and plates—and Martha's china—her heart broke at the carrying of those things out of her house into the mist and away to Junior's claim. He also bought the other half of the un-dug potatoes, then tied a calf to the back of his wagon. When the split rails came up for auction, Junior bought almost all of those. *Even the fencing go?* No more boundaries. A summer vest went to Mr. Hodges, who also bought the bull. Andrew Carson—a relative from back east?

She didn't know. But he stood with Junior and he bought Davey's only watch. *Fine. I's gonna give that watch to Junior but let 'em pay for it.* But she would not be a victim. She converted her anger, made another story. That boy needed time to grieve. A watch would do him little good, but it would do her no good either.

Nancy and Micah purchased sheets and feather pillows and chairs. "You'll get those back at least," Nancy said. "I brought cold chicken we can eat."

G.B.'s former father-in-law bought Fergus, the faithful beast. "You serve him well, now," she whispered as she held the velvet of his nose. She overheard men say there'd been private sales managed by the administrator, including the land that someone already expressed an interest in. He was to take possession in March. But who got Charity? And Blue and the rest? She didn't know. No sign of the hawthorn-engraved bell either.

She wanted to keep her large iron pot, her spider skillet with the lid, six plates, the pretty ones she brought with her from Missouri bought with her midwife money. In the end, she bought the bed, Davey's brindle cow and calf, and one roan cow. It was enough to start again. She paid $53.50 for the cows. None were Charity.

G.B. Smith bought one of Davey's good wolf fur coats and one velvet vest, never worn.

And at the very last moment—the auctioneer had held them up for last—she bid on her candlesticks. The brass sticks had represented her freedom. She needed to find a ladder to pull herself upward toward light. She started the bid at one gold beaver coin. Junior outbid her.

"He need light in his life," she told Nancy later. "Goes with Martha's tea set so her little dishes not be alone."

"Goodness. How can you be so generous, so philosophical?"

"I's free to decide how this day gets remembered. I say I let light shine inside me, keep the dark memories out."

By late afternoon in the fading light the men left. A few tipped their hats to her and looked sheepish, she thought. The hogs got

273

loaded, their grunts and squeals echoing in the misted air. Soon Nancy and Micah and baby Clara said their good-byes.

"You held up well." Nancy hugged her. "And you have your bed. That's good. The children can sleep in it."

Letitia nodded. She was as drained as a dishrag.

"Try to get some rest. Don't go to the Gages' tonight. Walk there in the morning."

Letitia nodded, waved good-bye. Stillness like a murky pond filled the valley. The emptiness threatened to choke her. She went inside the cabin, a place she didn't recognize now. All they'd worked for, all the possessions Davey had felt so strongly about, they were snowflakes onto fire.

She heard a sound at the door. "Rothwell?" She had no pistol. She forgot who bought it. "Junior? That you?" She prayed it would not be G.B. Smith.

"Ayee."

She sighed relief at Betsy's voice and opened the door.

"I's a paucity to offer but what I have is yours to share."

"My people give away things of those who pass on. That way no spirits are tied to this world. The dead have better places to go if we let them."

"I didn't plan to mourn my Davey the Kalapuya way, but I guess I have. Almost everything he touch, gone."

"You plant again."

"Somehow. I have a cow for milk. There's still cheese in the springhouse. They never looked in there. And one tallow candle. And the chillun's bed."

"We feast tonight." Betsy handed her a small basket with dried salmon, berries, and roasted camas root. The house was so bare there were few shadows. "Candles give warm light. Sister to the fireplace coals."

"As are we, sisters at the hearth."

Others had survived the loss of things, told themselves new stories. She would keep on keeping on.

"You have to contact that lawyer," Nancy told her as March approached. Nancy patched her husband's shirt, a simple act that brought tears to Letitia's eyes. Nancy pushed a legal solution, seeking justice.

Letitia hadn't seen any sign of the Mr. Fogel who was rumored to have bought her property.

"For Martha and Adam. That's who you're doing it for. You can't remain silent."

"I's a colored woman going to court, asking for money from a white man. What if I make myself known and they send us out? I can't go back to Missouri. My papers are gone."

"I know it's a hard thing to think, but it's what's right. Davey signed the agreement. After all that, don't you think he'd want his children taken care of—you taken care of?"

Letitia nodded.

"I didn't think I could ever look at Micah Read so soon after losing Zach, but if I hadn't done what I didn't think I could do, where would I be now? Sometimes a woman has to do what she thinks she can't."

Letitia trusted her friend, but attempting to bring a lawsuit would be too public, too risky, and she was too tired. It would be better if she stayed quiet, fit in, accepted the kindnesses of the Gages until . . . when? Until she could save money from being a midwife. Or maybe work for someone else.

Over supper that same evening, the Gages spoke of heading south to the Umpqua country. "Fewer people there. You could come along, act as midwife. Let this lawsuit idea go. We'll help you. Friends in Portland, Eliffs, they're heading south and they need a midwife. We'll wait until the roads are good this summer and take that trapper's trail. You can stay with us until you save enough to rent a place, start again."

What mattered was taking care of her children and moving on.

She'd lost this battle, and to pursue it risked them being sent from the state, and how would that help her children?

⟶∽⟵

"I'm so glad you've come with us. You haven't been to Corvallis at all, have you?" Nancy spoke to her friend sitting beside her on the wagon seat. "It's a growing town. Micah's getting supplies here now. It's much closer than Salem."

It did feel good to be away for a few hours from the Gages' many kindnesses that she couldn't repay, from the discomfort of being a guest in another's home. Spring herself seemed to like the idea of an outing as she showed off her budding trees and sent the rich earthy loam perfume to the nose. Letitia would have been planning her garden . . . but never again in the Soap Creek Valley.

Micah dropped the women off where the boardwalk began as he headed to the blacksmith's. Corvallis was doing well, bustling even, as Nancy described it. The women stepped along, stopping at the few glass windows displaying wares. A milliner with felt and feather hats. A boot maker and leather goods store. Their shoes tapped as they walked elbow to elbow. They met a man and woman, and Letitia stepped into the dirt street in order to let them pass.

"You don't have to make way for them," Nancy told her after they'd passed.

Letitia stepped back up. Some things didn't change. She stopped at the window of the mercantile. Her mouth dropped open in an O that turned into a moan. Her fingers pressed against her lips.

"Are you all right?" Nancy reached for Letitia wobbled. "What is it? What's wrong?"

"There! Lookee there."

The tea set Junior had bought at the auction sat in the window for sale, a chip in one cup, a crack through the lilac on the tiny plate. Beside it were the brass candlesticks she'd carried with her from Missouri.

"Those belong to me," she heard herself say, her grief spilling out over all the losses. "These belong to my children, *my* children. He have no right to sell—"

"He doesn't, Letitia. He absolutely does not."

In that moment Letitia knew that being free on the outside meant being free on the inside, having the courage to stand for what was right.

"For my children I—I must—"

"Yes! For your children's sake you file suit. Recover your money and your property. For Martha and Adam and for children of others who might be treated as you've been."

"No surety I win this case."

"No. But you have to try. Let's go inside. I'll buy those back for you."

"No." Letitia straightened her shoulders, adjusted her worn straw hat, and opened the door to the store. "Suh."

The clerk looked up from the string holder he refilled.

"I will buy that tea set and the candlesticks. In the window. In time. If you keeps them for me?"

"They're costly." He spoke the words with kindness. Did he know their story?

Letitia saw him look to Nancy.

"She'll pay," Nancy said. "And I'll pay for them myself if need be. Please keep them back, with her name on them, could you?"

"Got anything to put down?"

"I'll bring a firkin of cheese in tomorrow, if you keeps them back."

"Done. What name shall I write on them?"

She hesitated only a moment. "They belong to Mrs. David Carson."

A Light in the Wilderness

She returned the next day with Micah Read to deliver the cheese and meet the attorney. He'd arrived the winter past into the Territory and had a partner in Corvallis.

"He won't have any loyalties to G.B. Smith or anyone else, being new," Micah said. "But he'll be made aware that G.B. Smith has few friends and you have many."

"Not so many, but good friends."

"More than you'd realize. People are tired of the exclusion laws and property laws only allowing whites to claim land. We're tired of the constant slave-state talk. It's a matter of principle whether Oregonians stand for justice or power alone. People admire you, Letitia, for carrying on for your family. I don't know anyone who feels Smith was fair in his handling of the estate." He stopped before a door. "Mr. A.J. Thayer hails from New York. We'll see if he's up to the task."

The lawyer had kind, calming eyes, even if he did speak with short, clipped sentences. "This is an injustice. The law was meant to address this very kind of travesty." His office held boxes yet un-packed sitting beneath a table he used for a desk. Letitia wondered if Joseph Gage had made it. "If you'd been his legal wife, able to inherit, none of this would be an issue." He was thoughtful. "We'll make this a labor dispute case, requesting payment for services rendered. I've only been here two months and I've already heard things about Greenberry Smith I'd rather not know. I'll take your case, with pleasure."

In March, Letitia's lawyer posted a summons in the *Statesman Journal* to one Henry Walker (whom Davey had told that Letitia owned all the cows but seven) and Thomas Knighton (from whom Davey had purchased Charity with Letitia's money way back in Missouri—he was one of their drovers). "I've also seen who put in claims against the estate. G.B. is getting paid for his 'expenses.' Davey's son put in and was paid $242 for labor."

"What labor?" They were in the lawyer's office. "That boy rarely lift a hand to help his daddy. Maybe he claim he be paid for going to California. You heard any more about the buyer comin' in or when?"

"Not a word. No evidence that the land's been sold. Nothing about the larger herd either. I suspect Smith sold them outside of the auction or kept them for himself. We might not get those cows back."

"He must be keeping them somewhere. No one's seen 'em," Letitia said. "I goes back to look now and then."

"I can't get you the land, I'm sorry. But maybe we can get you money for your labor and those cows wrapped with a little justice."

What would justice look like, Letitia wondered. Her color kept her from being seen as a legal wife, as someone who could inherit, who could even testify against a white man. Her color and her gender kept her from ever voting to make changes in these laws that threatened to exclude her and her children or from making life better for all women and children. Letitia thought of Betsy. She too knew about being wronged. She too was as amputated from

279

the land as Letitia was. They were both staying when they'd soon be required to leave.

⸎

In February of 1854, a little over a year after the auction, her lawyer was ready to sue. He'd taken "witness statements" and she had witnesses to help her cause.

"Does I have to speak to the court against him? What if they takes me or my children away?" They sat in his office, now lined with bookcases and a shiny leafed potted plant at the corner of his desk.

"Where are you staying?"

"In Polk County, with the Gages. I never knew when G.B. come in the night and force us out so I took up the Gages' kind offer. I be going south to the Cow Creek Valley to help a family birth their baby, coming back and forth. You tell me when to be where and I be there."

He nodded. "I'll be speaking for you, Mrs. Carson." Thayer had never asked and she had never told him, but it pleased her that he called her by that name. "Much of this will go back and forth on paper. But you'll be sworn in official for the laying out of facts. I'll be the one to question Mr. Greenberry Smith. You won't have to say a word. I will ask the questions. Now that we've found Walker and Knighton, we have good evidence not only that you worked for Mr. Carson but that you were also the owner of those missing cows. We're going to sue him for $5,000."

She began to hope, though he warned her that the ins and outs of justice could take months, maybe even years. She had waited a long time to decide to stand out. But she'd also waited to find a man to love, to have two healthy children to raise; even longer to feel free and safe. She could wait to seek justice.

Letitia and her children lived in three places that year: with the Gages, then with the Eliff household where a baby was due in the Cow Creek Valley of southern Oregon, and then back to what had once belonged to her and Davey. She always visited the farm when she came for legal proceedings, walked the fields, checked the trees, chopped at blackberry bushes crouching in. Roth wobbled behind her, stood with her when the children raced among the apple trees.

The seasons changed. When it came time to roast the camas, Letitia and the children went with Little Shoot, traveling a few miles to where the clan dug the hole and built the fire to roast the roots. They stayed the day, watching the stick games and gambling stones pass between quick hands. Letitia knew she wasn't of these fine people, but she felt a kinship with them. In some ways the time with the group took her back to when she lived in the slaves' houses as a child, everyone kin, everyone looking out for each other. And despite the uncertainties of the future, she felt safe. Not just with the Kalapuya but within her heart. There was no certainty, no papers that could protect her. She had to live every day trusting that with friends and God's help she could put this latest cower to rest. It required repetition.

Later that fall, her attorney met her at the farm. He said he wanted to see what they had built together. The buildings stood empty, the barn door swung on one leather hinge. No one had moved there yet. Letitia and Betsy picked apples and put them in a basket as they waited for the attorney. Letitia looked for evidence of the cows returning. She'd seen a cow pie near the barn, and tracks but no animals.

Thayer arrived and looked up at the odd-shaped hill. "Heard about this landmark. It really does have a coffin look to it." He dismounted, removed his hat. "Hot." He wiped his wide forehead with his forearm. "But not humid like New York." He said the word like "New Yak."

She offered him an apple and he bit, the crunch clear and sharp.

"We've gotten a response from Mr. Smith's attorney. He's contesting any number of points. But we expected that." He was quick to reassure her. "A jury has been impaneled and we're going to court."

The palms of her hands began to sweat. "I needs to be there?"

"It isn't necessary."

But she'd already decided. "I wants to be." Like every woman of color, her life was a blend of fitting in and standing out. In that court, for her children and herself, she needed to model stepping up.

The months of waiting had taught her that she did not pursue this lawsuit out of desperation or fear; she could see her way through into the future and it no longer frightened her. She had a new story to tell. No, this lawsuit was seeking justice for her children and for Davey and maybe, one day, for another woman who fell in love with a man of a different color. It was one small way to heal a wounded world.

The courtroom was on the second floor of the new county courthouse. It housed linseed-oiled chairs and a large desk that the District Court judge sat behind. He looked tired from traveling the circuit to various inns and barrooms transformed into courtrooms. At least Corvallis boasted a proper site to conduct legal affairs. Along the wall twelve men fidgeted on spindly chairs. Letitia assumed they were hoping this wouldn't last long. The judge's name was Williams.

"Fair, wise. Politically astute. This is an important case for him to be assigned," Thayer whispered to her. "Look who else is here. Bois is a territorial prosecuting attorney, Wilson a deputy US district attorney, and there's even a deputy United States Marshal."

"They expecting trouble?" she whispered.

"Political trouble maybe, depending on how this all comes out."

"Do I . . . need to worry they remove me? That exclusion law?"

"No, no. They repealed it a few months ago. Maybe the news didn't reach the Umpqua Valley what with the Indian war going on there." He patted her hand.

"I knows one of those men." Letitia nodded to the jury chairs.

"Which?"

"Rinehart. He came in '45 with me and Davey. I midwife his boy, Charles, back in Missouri."

"Good, that's good."

"He know G.B. Smith too, come in that same company."

"Any others?" Thayer took notes.

"Maybe if I hear the names, but no."

"Fortunately several came recently, in '52. And from free states like Ohio and New York and Massachusetts. Most jurors are from slave-holding states. Kentucky, Tennessee, Alabama, Virginia." He checked off a list.

"None from Missouri?"

"One. Bounds, but he got here in '50 so I doubt he knows about G.B. Smith. I think we have a fair group." He patted her hand. His felt cool.

Visitors filled the chairs behind them. A man with a pad took notes. "The *Statesman*," her lawyer said. "This is a big case in the Territory, one that speaks to justice. Pro-slavery advocates are especially interested. We'll see what kind of state our Oregon intends to be."

G.B. Smith sat beside and across from Letitia and her attorney. His face flushed when he looked at her and she realized her lawsuit had embarrassed him, made him public in a way he didn't want. He wore Davey's vest bought at the auction. *Hope it keep him warm.*

Thayer presented their case, how he'd come up with the $5,000 claim based on her years of labor and the value of the cows.

G.B.'s lawyer, Kelsay, replied. "First of all, my client has a bill of sale proving that this woman was nothing but a slave bought by the deceased back in Missouri."

"No," Letitia whispered to Thayer. "I had free papers. He know that. He tried to take them from me back in Missouri on patrol. Sarah Davis know I'm free. We ask her." *Not being chased. Nothing to fear. Not going to die.* She caused her heartbeat to calm.

"Something wrong, Mr. Thayer."

"No, your honor." Thayer continued, "But if the defendant has such a bill of sale, would it not be helpful to the court for him to produce it? I suspect it is a myth. And we can produce a witness who would testify to the plaintiff's free status at the time of her overland journey."

"Mr. Kelsay?"

"We'll provide it to the court. Therefore," Kelsay continued, "when her master died she was owed nothing. Her emancipation is payment enough. Secondly, the seven and a half years she claims to have worked for the deceased as a free Negro under contract is a lie. We have witnesses saying she was often sick, so sick she stayed with Joseph Gage and family and the deceased paid for all her care during that time when he had no return in labor for six months or more. When she was delivered of her child, she did not work for months." He looked at his notes. "About the cows. When were the twenty-nine cows she claims are hers purchased? Are there bills of sale for said cows? No." Kelsay poked at his palm for emphasis. "In return, she's had the use of the deceased's ten cows for ten years earning money from cheese and butter and beef, so she's already been compensated well beyond the entitlement for labor that she claims."

Letitia shook her head. He was saying so many wrong things.

"Finally, members of the jury." Kelsay turned to the men, some looking like they'd like to be let out for a smoke, others wearing curiosity on their weathered faces. "The deceased also paid to bring this slave across the continent, at no small expense as many of you know, feeding, clothing, keeping her and her child safe. Then he clothed and fed her and her children for nearly ten years."

"Seven," Letitia whispered to her attorney. "We only had a little over seven years together."

"She's had enough compensation. She deserves not a dime more. I urge you to find for the defendant."

Thayer had objected and replied to many of the false claims. Neither she nor G.B. were called as witnesses and she watched G.B.'s face change from sneers to flashes of anger, then back to

284

satisfied. She was the only person of color in the room. She stood out, but for the first time she wasn't wishing she could sink into the comfort of a fundamentals circle. She was calm having her life splayed out, glad she was taking on a man who bullied her and others before her, she imagined. He was a marse in his heart and would always be unless someone stripped him of his whip. She had a written contract, that's what this suit was about.

The judge asked a few questions. Thayer presented Knighton's statement about Letitia's cow ownership and Walker's verifying that Davey told him Letitia had done most of the work, owned all but seven of the cows a few years previous. People had stood for her, stood with her.

The jury deliberated while Letitia and the Reads took tea in Thayer's office. Before the brew cooled off, they were summoned back.

"Do you have a decision?" Judge Williams asked.

The foreman stood. "We find for the plaintiff, nine to three."

A little chirp went up in the back. Letitia recognized it as Nancy's cheer of joy.

"We win?" she whispered to her attorney.

"Yes, indeed. But the judgment is yet to be considered."

What would they grant her? Whatever the amount, it would be helpful but not necessary now. They had won the point, won the day in showing that a white man could not simply abuse a colored woman without justice interceding.

~~~~~

The *Statesman* newspaper reported on the trial, stating that she'd lost and that it was a shame.

"He must have gone out to lunch," Thayer told her as he read her the story. "We won't wait for a retraction. They seldom come. But we know we won. Now we'll see how much of an award they'll make to you, and what they'll do about the cattle."

"I ain't seen those cows nowhere," Letitia said. "He's probably already sold them."

"You'll achieve some income from all this, Mrs. Carson. Can you hold out until they decide? It could be months."

"I hold out. I being held."

In January 1855, G.B. paid $529 as a portion of the judgment against him, anticipating a final award. He paid even before her lawyer Thayer received the notice. In May, the court ordered another $300 that G.B. paid to the court.

"But $800 isn't enough," Thayer told her. "I'll file a new motion saying that at the very least you are owed $1,500 reached by charging $200 per year for your labor from May 1845 until March 1853. You're entitled to a minimum of $700 more to meet the labor claim." For good measure, he also issued a summons for Sarah Davis as G.B. continued to contend that Letitia was a slave and therefore deserved nothing but her freedom.

"This may be all we'll get on the labor issues, Mrs. Carson." A.J. Thayer leaned back in his chair. "Your children are well behaved."

"Yessuh, they are good children." Martha wore a dress Letitia'd made for her and five-year-old Adam a suit she'd stitched herself. Both children sat quietly, gazing at the plants and shelves of books, their feet short of the oak floor.

"So I say let's sue him separately for the cows."

"Suh?"

"The cows are property that haven't appeared in the records. There's no evidence of the cows, yet everyone reports there were twenty-nine. He's absconded with them somehow. Those cows belong to you."

And so they went to court again, seeking $1,200 as the value of the herd. But with the money G.B. had already paid, Letitia stopped at the mercantile and asked for the box labeled "Mrs. David Carson" to be brought forward. She paid for the tea set and candlesticks . . . in full.

❦

They hadn't been able to reach Sarah Davis to testify about the cows. Funny, Letitia's journey west began in a way with the Bowmans and a cow. She knew the lawsuits would be settled and surely the farm would sell, and any money left would go to the heirs—Davey's sister, brothers, uncles—the fruits of Oregon being harvested in North Carolina. She'd learned that Smith Carson, Davey's brother, had died the June they'd left Missouri. She wondered if he had children.

She would take the money and stay in the southern Umpqua Valley. The Gages had already moved and she'd delivered Melvina Eliff of a girl, Alice. She'd been asked to remain with them, she and the children. As much as she'd miss Nancy, it was a good place for her, away from the memories of Davey's death. Nancy found someone else to midwife her latest, Sumner, born in May. Letitia made a new start in Cow Creek Canyon, hadn't waited for the outcome of legal issues to begin a new life. She had money G.B. Smith had paid. She'd have some left after paying her attorney. She wasn't afraid of the unknowns. She'd left her cowers behind.

❦

"He pay more?"

"He did." It was 1856 and Thayer filled his client in on their latest success at his office. "Another $780 to meet the demand of the labor agreement, so the full $1,500. And here's more. He claims now that the estate was worth $2,250 and it has claims against it of $3,250.79 with $300 cash on hand."

Letitia had stopped in Corvallis to see her attorney after finding what she hoped would be the perfect property in Douglas County close to the Eliffs and Gages.

"Davey's heirs get nothing? That ain't right."

"That's the executor of the estate figures. He's blaming you for putting the estate into debt. But no matter. If we win the suit for

$1,200 for the cows he sold, he has to make that payment out of his pocket, not the estate. The sale of the land he said was worth $2,000 by itself. That'll go into the estate value. The debts will be covered and heirs will inherit. Just not your $1,500 and the costs of securing justice."

"Property back in Missouri, Davey never sell it. His heirs take that. Me and my family only claim what we built in the Soap Creek Valley."

"You're a fair woman, Mrs. Carson. Fair, indeed."

⁓

In October, four years after Davey's death, the jury of twelve men met again and found for the plaintiff. They ordered G.B. Smith to make payment for Letitia's cattle. This time as an individual who had sold a herd of cows and never bothered to add that value to the estate. He hadn't even gotten money for that herd of twenty-nine cows; he'd sold them to himself. His only response to the $1,200 judgment of October 12, 1856, was that he only had twenty-eight cows. One had come up missing.

⁓

Nancy was there with her brood. Letitia would be leaving for southern Oregon the next morning. They'd dug up six apple saplings and took the table and child's bed from the cabin, all that had been left behind. She lingered at Davey's grave. She straightened the wooden cross Little Shoot had pounded at the head of Davey's mound. No one had yet moved onto the property though mice had moved into the house. Letitia hoped someone would come there who would love it as they had, who would plant their feet there and be nurtured by the encircling hills.

"You get the Gages to write." Nancy wiped at her tears. Letitia wouldn't be coming back and forth for court now. The case was settled and she had enough to begin a new life and keep her children safe.

"Frances teaching me to write."

"Even better. Birth those babies down south well, now. And goodness, if you marry again, you let me know so we can come meet the man good enough for you."

"I will." Letitia smiled. Leaving this valley saddened her, but she'd faced a cower and won. Power had been mated with the love of neighbors and good people and justice was the kin. Davey would be pleased, she thought. His children were being cared for, and as he kept saying it would, everything worked out fine.

Rothwell's howl, not heard for years, broke the conversation. Then, "Is that a cowbell, Mama?"

Letitia looked to where Martha pointed. She heard it too. No one seemed to be herding a cow down the trapper's trail, but here one came, bell clanging. *Can that be Charity? That possible?* Rothwell limped his way toward the bovine.

"Charity?"

The cow sped up with the sound of Letitia's voice, her bag swaying from side to side as she trotted, her back bones sticking out sharp against the landscape.

Letitia picked up her skirts and began running. "You old dear, where you been?"

That bell that Davey gave her on the day they spoke their vows, there it was, tarnished but still hanging around Charity's neck. The children hugged the animal, petted her nose, let her bristly tongue lick at their arms. Roth sat and howled.

"Will you look at that," Nancy said. "That old cow missed you all. She must have come around now and then looking for you."

"Can't believe the wolves or coyotes didn't find her before we did."

The cow's bony back was caved in; skin scraped off her face, maybe where she'd scratched against a tree. But it was Charity. Letitia rubbed her fingers on the hawthorn blossom engraved on the bell, fingered the velvet of Charity's ears. Next to the hands of her children and the holding arms of her husband, it was the most comforting touch in her world.

"It don't matter now if we don't find that whole herd or get the money for it either. I got the one cow I wanted back and justice. That's all I need. All I ever needed." She hugged her friend. "We sparrows be in good shape for the winter and all the winters to come."

Epilogue

Into the wagon they loaded the cheese items she'd not taken from the springhouse: firkins, large spoons, strips of rennet, churns. Then the tea set and candlesticks, and two new platters made of Pacific yew that Little Shoot had carved for her. Letitia, Betsy, and Nancy hiked Coffin Butte together. Letitia wanted to remember the view and remind herself to go higher when she faced a challenge, to let wonder be the air she floated upward on, to look back only to see how she'd fought fear before and won. The bed Letitia's children had outgrown she gave to Nancy for her youngest.

"It's such a beautiful oak," Nancy said, thanking her.

"It go with your quilt frame."

At the top of the butte Betsy said, "We all go at same time." Though the oldest of the three women, Betsy was the only one not huffing from the climb up Coffin Butte.

"I wish you come with us." Letitia made the invitation.

"And I wish you could find a place near here to stay." This was Nancy's plea, but the women spoke, knowing all had been decided. This was time to say good-bye.

"I go with my people to the Grand Ronde reservation. We all go. Little Shoot has a wife. Soon a baby. We stay together."

"But it isn't fair."

Betsy patted Letitia's back. "Fair is a flying bird settling on a waving grass, resting before moving on. It must fly again, light again. Fair needs much attention. We meet again one day."

Letitia couldn't dispute her friend's wisdom. She had a season of fairness and hoped there'd be other just moments in this quarrelsome place. Oregon hoped to become a state one day, join the Union. Maybe they'd leave the exclusion laws out for good. She hoped so. All along the way she'd had help with friends and strangers, people of many colors. Yes, she often had to ask for help. Thank goodness she had friends like Nancy and an attorney willing to take her case. But even the land sale had proven a gift. The new owner, a Mr. Fogel, planned to take possession that week. She'd met him. He seemed a good person, with farmer's arms and a friendly wife who asked if there was a trail up that "funny butte that looks like a coffin."

Letitia assured her there was, then showed her the orchard and told the story of its beginnings.

"I hope this place will come to mean as much to us as it does to you."

"I's hoping that too."

To turn over the care of land she'd come to love to someone who would respect it gave Letitia hope. She might find another land to give her heart to, if not another husband. Cow Creek showed promise. The children seemed to like it there, despite the Indian skirmishes. With Charity, Letitia was building up another herd.

She and the children said their last good-byes to Betsy and Little Shoot and his wife, hugging and holding until it was time. At the wagon Letitia spoke again, not only to the land that had held them and sustained them through the years but to Davey. "You did us well, Davey Carson. You did us well taking us to freedom."

Letitia drove the wagon and they stopped, leaving Nancy and her youngest off at her claim.

"I cannot tell you how much I will miss you." Nancy held her friend.

"Don't cry." Letitia wiped her own cheeks. "I's not so far away. I come be your midwife if you have another."

Nancy laughed. "I think those days are over. But you will come back to visit, won't you? And when Maryanne marries next month, you'll return for that, yes?"

Letitia nodded.

"I never did enough for you, Tish. Goodness. You were always so much more giving."

Letitia laughed then, held her friend's hand. She wished she could find the words to tell this woman what her life had meant to her, how her faith and absolute acceptance of Letitia's being had oozed strength into Letitia's soul. "You are the tree that a sapling looks up to."

"You're sounding like your Kalapuya friend."

"It could be. But I remember my mama saying it of her mama. We all need someone to look up to. It's a thing to remember."

The women laughed and then parted. Children reloaded in the wagon, a last hug between Letitia and Martha Hawkins. Then onward to a new beginning where a new candle would light the wilderness.

Author's Note

Letitia did go on to find new land to love in the Myrtle Creek Valley of southern Oregon. Once women—including widows, those with disabled husbands, and single women—were allowed to seek homestead patents, Letitia applied. She paid $11.92 on June 11, 1863, to apply. Six years later, on October 1, 1869, Letitia Carson received one of the first of seventy-one homestead patents issued in Oregon—one of only four women. From slave to landowner. Letitia (sometimes spelled Lutishia) spent the rest of her life in southern Oregon, acting as a midwife. Some say she ran a boardinghouse, and she was known as Auntie to many. She ranched and raised her children to adulthood and had grandchildren to spoil.

Adam, later called Jack, never married and stayed in that southern Oregon region his whole life working as a teamster. Martha did marry Narcisse Lavadour and moved with her husband to the Umatilla Indian reservation in northeast Oregon where many of her descendants still reside.

Letitia was born in Kentucky around 1818. We find her in Missouri leaving with David Carson and giving birth to one of the first mulatto children born on the Oregon Trail. (A nearly all African

American wagon train crossed the continent in 1844 under the direction of George Washington Bush, and it is likely a child was born on that journey. That group headed into Washington Territory where it was believed they'd receive a warmer reception than from a territory fond of passing exclusion and lash laws.)

We do not know if Davey signed any agreement, but the nature of that commitment was reported by Letitia and was the basis for her lawsuits. She did sue Greenberry Smith twice and won both times. The second jury trial was attended by prominent people in Oregon's history, including future Oregon supreme court judges, a US Marshal, and a US attorney, in addition to Judge Williams, who presided. Perhaps it was a test case or one that would wage the sentiment of the inclusion of Oregon entering the Union as a slave or free state.

Letitia died in 1888 and is buried in the Bryant cemetery on private land in Douglas County. Adam is buried next to her.

David Carson was born in Ireland. He did apply for citizenship in 1844 and it was granted in the fall of 1846, a year after arriving in Oregon. In December 1845 in the Willamette Valley, he claimed 640 acres under the provisional government rules and had to re-register in 1850 when the Donation Land Act was passed. Then he could only keep 320 acres because he had no legal wife, as people of color were not allowed to marry white persons. He was a patroller in Platte County, Missouri, and named a captain on the overland journey. He did fall asleep while on duty on the Oregon Trail and brought a lawsuit over the slave Eliza White. He made the Walk-up Trail around Mount Hood, getting caught in a terrible storm and milking a cow into her cowbell turned upside down. That precious liquid saved more than one life, as Mrs. Walden did indeed nearly die from the elements. People called him "Uncle Davey" for his generous spirit and heartiness, and he was also known as an old trapper for his exploration during his time in North Carolina. Davey died September 22, 1852, in the Soap Creek Valley. His grave site is unknown.

Evidence given by the witnesses (Walker and Knighton) is as described. Letitia owned the cows, had given Davey money to buy a cow from Knighton back in the states. So she must have either been free and earning money at the time, or a slave allowed to work outside, giving portions of her earnings to her owner. There is no evidence that she was owned by anyone nor is there evidence that she was free. G.B. Smith did claim he had a bill of sale for her, but he never produced it, and as the cases went against him, if he had such a paper, it would make no sense for him not to produce it. He did make the payments against the judgments as portrayed, and the issue with the herd is as conveyed.

G.B. Smith encountered court activity back in Missouri and may well have been a patroller there. Missouri as a state did not have large plantations and most slave owners had fewer than ten slaves. But the slavery movement was strong and intense and patrollers protected "the property" of white owners with active patrols. Davey was named a patroller in 1838. In Oregon, Greenberry Smith became wealthy and prominent and later active in the Golden Knight society, a form of the Ku Klux Klan active in Oregon after the Civil War. G.B. Smith went on to buy the entire town of Tampico, a rival of Corvallis, and then put everyone there out of business. One wonders at his motivations. Curiously, G.B. Smith planted an apple orchard in the Soap Creek Valley that still stands, the apples from a Missouri nursery.

David Carson " Junior" took a claim of 160 acres as noted, but he did not make the overland journey with the Carsons. Instead he arrived shortly before his father's death with an Andrew Carson, relationship uncertain. No evidence can be found to actually link him to David Carson except for G.B. Smith's documents referring to him as "Junior" and the land records showing his claim on what had been a portion of Davey Carson's original claim of 640 acres. He may have been a nephew, but I've portrayed him as Davey's son. The law permitted Davey to file on only 320 acres after the Donation Land Act of 1850. Davey may well have tried to continue use of the other 320 acres, even encouraging "Junior" to farm 160 acres of it. Junior was allowed to make a land claim as a single man who had not been in Oregon country for four years or more.

Sumner Read was not the last child of Nancy White Hawkins Read. Charles arrived in 1857, and Columbia in 1863, with Nancy raising twelve children, eleven to adulthood. A bed said to have once belonged to Adam Carson was handed down through the Read family via Charles Read. It resides now at the Benton County Historical Society. My thanks to Mary Gallagher and Irene Zenev of the Historical Society for their help in research and their encouragement. The story surrounding Dr. Zachariah Hawkins's death in Idaho is based on information in genealogical files and the work of Donna M. Wojcik in *The Brazen Overlanders of 1845* (1976). Nancy did remarry in the fall of 1846 and did not begin probating her husband's estate until February of 1847, perhaps the time when she truly believed he would not be coming home. Many widows quickly remarried as both a means of survival and potential land acquisition, as a wife was allowed 320 acres, along with her husband. Had Letitia been white and married, she would have inherited the farm she and Davey claimed. The Reads did settle at the southeast end of the Carson claim and were neighbors until Letitia's move to the Cow Creek Valley.

Sarah Bowman remarried in 1852 to David Davis, an apparent colleague or friend of Greenberry Smith. That the Bowmans gave Letitia her freedom in Missouri is author speculation. The court record does not tell us why Sarah had been summoned as part of Letitia's suit, only that she was never deposed. Both Letitia and the Bowmans came from Kentucky to Platte County, Missouri, so Letitia and the Bowmans may have known of each other. In Oregon, the Davis family did live 2.5 miles northeast of the Carsons. Could Sarah have confirmed the arrangement between Davey and Letitia? Unanswered questions.

Joseph and Frances Gage and their children lived north of the

Carsons in Polk County. On at least one occasion, the Gages provided respite to Davey and Letitia and their children when one of them was ill. They moved from the Soap Creek Valley to the Myrtle Creek area of Southern Oregon about the time that Letitia left and had claims within riding distance of each other there.

The Kalapuya woman, Betsy, and her grandson Little Shoot are composites of the Kalapuya people who lived for generations in the Soap Creek Valley. The lives of these peaceful people are graciously portrayed in *The World of the Kalapuya: A Native People of Western Oregon* by Judy Rycraft Juntunen, May D. Dasch, and Ann Bennett Rogers (published by Benton Historical Society, 2005). They sustained themselves from the land and were removed to a reservation area they were unfamiliar with (and where no shelters had been provided) in 1857, two years after the 1855 treaty signing of national tribes that created the reservations around the country. That Betsy could have met and lent sustenance and friendship to Letitia is speculation—but legitimate speculation. A band of the Kalapuya were allowed to remain on their land in the Yoncalla area rather than move to the reservation through the efforts of early pioneers Jesse Applegate and his family. I have come to believe that these women of color would have formed a bond to help them tend, mend, and befriend. It could be a model for us all.

Oregon did declare slavery illegal in 1844 while adding the famous "Lash Law." It was deemed too harsh—whipping a black person twice a year until they left the territory—and was replaced with forced labor in December of that year. It was repealed in 1845. In 1849 Oregon passed another exclusion law prohibiting persons of color from being in the state. It was repealed in 1854, then reinstated in 1857 by popular vote. On February 14, 1859, Oregon became the first state to enter the Union as a free state with an exclusion clause in its constitution, a clause that was not repealed until 1926, though the Emancipation Proclamation of 1863 would have taken precedence over the exclusion law ever being enforced.

Apple saplings were left behind at Fort Hall, but whether Letitia picked any up there or acquired seeds is pure speculation. An apple tree on or near the Carson land claim was named the Letitia Carson apple tree by Dr. Bob Zybach, completing an Oregon State University Forest Research Project, a fitting memorial to a woman who grew to be a strong and sturdy soul.

The historic Soap Creek Valley that Davey and Letitia settled in is encircled by Forest Peak, Smith Peak, Oak Hill, Coffin Butte, Glenders Hill, and Vineyards Hill. It's nourished by Soap Creek. The California Trappers Trail skirts the Carson claim. Davey and Letitia may well have made their living selling goods such as hides, butter, bacon, and beef to people heading to the gold fields or settling the southern portions of the state. Firkins were some of the items sold at the auction, suggesting cheese-making was a part of the Carsons' lives. Davey may well have joined the migration south in 1849 when the great gold rush began.

The settling of Davey's estate is as portrayed and based on actual probate and court records. Theologian Paul Tillich once wrote that "power without love is injustice; and love without an awareness of power will never achieve justice." That Letitia achieved justice in a hostile legal environment speaks to her courage, to her willingness to transform herself from fitting in to standing out, to her faith and the generosity of friends.

Acknowledgments

This book would not have been written without the passion, research, patience, organization, and goodwill of researchers and
Oregonians Janet Meranda and Dr. Bob Zybach. They discovered Letitia Carson's forgotten story in the 1980s while students
at Oregon State University and Letitia's story never let them go.
I am often gifted with story suggestions from readers, though I
rarely choose them for projects of my own. Instead I encourage
others to write the story of the man or woman calling their name.
Sometimes, they do just that. Dr. Zybach and Mrs. Meranda are
writing scholarly works based on Letitia's life and they hoped I
would consider a novel. A biography tells what and when something
happened, but it doesn't explore why or how that person might have
felt. Such is the realm of fiction. I hope I have done their research
proud; any errors in known facts are mine. The speculation of the
uncertainties are mine as well, though I welcomed Jan and Bob's
suggestions for filling in the historical unknowns. As Bob noted
one day in our ongoing discussion, "The yin and yang explanation
would be that you are using historical data to develop Letitia's

story, while we are using Letitia's story to develop historical data." I loved that characterization of our mutual work.

Dr. Zybach was especially generous in providing me a copy of his master's thesis on the role of storytelling on the landscape of that Soap Creek Valley. His passion for the place and Letitia's role within it was a constant enthusiasm for my efforts. A journey on the Soap Creek Auto Tour introduced me to the land where Letitia walked and the flora, fauna, and the Sulphur Springs where she might have found healing. Bob's interest through the years in the Kalapuya people of the region added to the richness of what he had to share, including videos of Kalapuya people baking camas and reports of old stone ovens near the Carson claim.

Mrs. Meranda and her husband John made the trek to our home more than once and to other sites around the state, carrying bags of material we referred to as "Jan's bag East" that she left with me and "Jan's bag West" for the material she kept with her. We walked where Letitia walked on land now owned by Oregon State University. They were both "local-Google," allowing me to ask questions they responded to in seconds. What warm and funny and superb researchers passionate about story. I couldn't have been in better hands.

Letitia's story moved me. The more I researched this period through the eyes of a black woman, the more compassion I had for her. Her triumph came years into her journey and after much hardship, out of which grew the resonant strength of this pioneering woman. I learned much about my own journey as a woman, as a westerner, about my adopted state and its exclusion and lash laws. But most of all I discovered the nature of freedom in the midst of chains and the strength of character it takes to persevere through the bondage of the spirit and the law. Safety is a state of mind, a matter of faith.

The Oregon Historical Society records, the Benton County Historical Society, and the Oregon California Trail Association are rich humus for details and the wonderings of Letitia's life. I'm grateful to the work of these fine historical sites.

Thanks go as well to Andrea Doering of Revell, a division of Baker Publishing, who when I told her of this story suggested that Letitia would have friends, perhaps both white and native. Thus grew the stories of Nancy Hawkins and The Woman that I interwove. Revell's acceptance of me as one of their newest authors has been welcoming and warm and I'm grateful for their support and encouragement in telling this story.

Greg Nokes, author of *Breaking Chains: Slavery on Trial in the Oregon Territory*, provided me with an advance copy of his book published in 2013 by Oregon State University Press. Greg's personal conversations about Oregon's exclusion laws, his insights into the lives of Oregon's African American community, and his generosity of sharing information proved invaluable to creating the story of Letitia with authenticity and care. I am deeply grateful. Near the end of my writing, Greg was contacted by a descendant of Smith Carson, Davey's brother. He put Lila Hyder in touch with me, and she provided new genealogical information and details woven into my story but also of great use to the biography being written by Janet and Bob. I thank her. Jenneane Johns of Myrtle Creek is a descendant of the Eliff child Letitia midwifed when she first moved to Southern Oregon. The Johns family has marked where Letitia's cabin stood with an apple tree. They are the keeper of yet another portion of Letitia's story.

Archivists at the Platte County Genealogical Society, the Ben Ferrel Museum docents, and members of the Weston Historical Society offered documents and speculation about life in Missouri when Letitia lived there and made us welcome as we visited Weston and Platte City. Gwen Carr of the Oregon Northwest Black Pioneers joined us for the hunt for Letitia and Adam's grave site. That organization works to uncover, honor, and preserve the history of black Oregonians. I am grateful for their research and education. They can be reached at www.oregonnorthwestblackpioneers.org.

Descendants of Martha Ann on the Umatilla Reservation, especially Joseph Lavadour, offered insights and photographs, though none of Letitia are known to exist. I'm grateful for their support in this true story imagined.

I'm grateful as well to a wonderful collection of colleague writers; my prayer team of Carol, Judy, Susan, Judy C, Gabby, and Loris; family, friends, and all editors, from my current and previous work, and readers: you act as wind chimes of creativity, bumping together in ways that I hope leave readers with the music of words worthy of their time.

To my readers, thank you for making room in your heart for my stories.

Finally, I am grateful to my husband who, despite medical issues, allowed me to rise early and live for hours in the 1840s and '50s. I look forward to our thirty-eighth year together and am so glad you're back to doing the cooking.

Jane Kirkpatrick
www.jkbooks.com

An Interview with the Author

What inspired you to write about Letitia Carson?

Her story is so compelling! How did an African American woman change her life from former slave to plaintiff, engage in a lawsuit in a state where a person of color was excluded from even being and could not testify against a white person, and where even a white woman had little status? How did she decide to stand out? How did she face the injustice of being a woman of color and decide not to be a victim but to become clear about what mattered in her life and then have the courage to act on that? That's what I wanted to explore.

Did you find it troubling to write about an African American woman when you are not of that race?

When I wrote about an Indian woman, Marie Dorion, I was asked by a reporter what business did I have writing of Indians when I wasn't one. I was a bit taken aback because I have male characters too and I'm not one of those either. But I said something like I had Indian friends, I did my research, I tried desperately to live inside her skin, and that we were first, together, women. Later I mentioned the reporter's comment to the tribal historian and he was thoughtful, then said, "You didn't write about an Indian woman. You wrote a story of a strong woman who happened to be an Indian." That's how I approached Letitia's story, about a strong woman who also happened to be African American.

What prompts you to choose a particular woman for a story?

Most of the historical women I'm drawn to lived in the West during the 1800s. I like that period of history, and history is the spine of my stories, with characters providing the flesh and blood of life. I especially like ordinary women—such as Letitia—whose stories resonate and allow a reader to ask themselves how they would deal with that kind of challenge and to see that the strengths these women demonstrate are present in all our lives. I think women like Letitia inspire us to greater things. I'm also drawn to ask where these women drew their courage from. My husband and I spent thirty years "homesteading" a remote ranch, and I knew that one day we would have electricity, running water, a telephone, maybe even email, or I wouldn't live there. But these women only knew what they had before them; they lived more in the present. I like to celebrate those women and let them teach me about living with what I have now.

Is there more to Letitia's story that you'll write? Her life in Southern Oregon, perhaps?

I think not, but then . . . one never knows. I usually tell readers that they get to finish the story in their hearts and minds. In the process they'll discover something about themselves they otherwise never would have known. The two researchers who introduced me to Letitia are writing a biography that will follow her through the remainder of her life. I'm looking forward to that.

How do you decide what to include in a story based on a real person?

I create a timeline of what is known about that character, the "who, what, where, when" facts. And then I explore the why and how of their lives: Why was Letitia in Missouri having been born in Kentucky? Why did she go west? How did she travel with Davey: as a laborer, a slave, a common-law wife? How did she feel being the only person of color in the wagon company? How did she handle the patrollers? How did she meet the desires of her heart? Somewhere in the answering of those questions I identify the character arc: what she wanted, what got in her way, how she had to change to accomplish what mattered to her. There are many details I may know both historically and within the genealogical record that I have to leave behind. Too many details will numb the reader's mind; too few and they'll question the authenticity. It's a balancing act. And I'm looking for the moment when I and, I hope, my readers will cheer for the character. I usually know where I'm going to end the story before I first begin.

Will you ever co-author a story?

Gosh, I haven't really thought about that. I've participated in novella collections, but we write the individual selections alone. I think I'm pretty quirky as a writer and I'm not sure a co-author would share the way I work or the lens through which I write. My threads are landscape, relationships, spirituality, and work, and having others write with the same threads could be a challenge. But I never thought I'd ever write a book in the first place, so twenty-six books later I've learned that anything can happen.

What's your favorite novel you've written?

The one I'm working on now.

What's next?

I'm working on yet another story of a remarkable woman. You'll have to wait and see . . . or follow my newsletter, www.jkbooks.com/ storysparks, or visit my website and blog, or visit me on Facebook and Twitter to stay abreast of the stories that steal my heart and that I hope will steal yours as well.

Suggested Readings

Nonfiction books on the African American experience that assisted in my understanding of Letitia's journey include the following:

Angelou, Maya. *Letter to My Daughter*. New York: Random House, 2009.

Kentucky Narratives, Vol. 7, of *Born in Slavery: Slave Narratives of Kentucky: Federal Writers' Project, 1936–1938*.

Larsen, Carolyn A. Bless. *We, Too, Lived: A Genealogy of the African-Americans in a Midwest Cemetery, 1850–1950*. 2009.

Lucas, Mario B. *A History of Blacks in Kentucky: From Slavery to Segregation, 1760–1891*. Kentucky Historical Society, 2003.

Mangun, Kimberley. *A Force for Change: Beatrice Morrow Cannady and the Struggle for Civil Rights in Oregon, 1912–1936*. Corvallis, OR: Oregon State University Press, 2010.

McConaghy, Lorraine, and Judith Bentley. *Free Boy: A True Story of Slave and Master*. Seattle, WA: V Ellis White Books, University of Washington Press, 2013.

McLagan, Elizabeth. *A Peculiar Paradise: A History of Blacks in Oregon, 1788–1940*. Portland, OR: Georgian Press, 1980.

Nokes, R. Gregory. *Breaking Chains: Slavery on Trial in the Oregon Territory*. Corvallis, OR: Oregon State University Press, 2013.

Oregon Northwest Black Pioneers, *Perseverance: A History of African Americans in Oregon's Marion and Polk Counties*. Salem, OR: Oregon Northwest Black Pioneers, 2011.

Pascoe, Peggy. *What Comes Naturally: Miscegenation Law and the Making of Race in America*. New York: Oxford University Press, 2009.

Ravage, John W. *Black Pioneers: Images of the Black Experience on the North American Frontier*. Salt Lake City: University of Utah Press, 2008.

Taylor, Arnold. *Rose, a Woman of Colour: A Slave's Struggle for Freedom in the Courts of Kentucky*. iUniverse, 2008.

Williams, Heather Andrea. *Help Me to Find My People: The African American Search for Family Lost in Slavery*, John Hope Franklin Series in African American History and Culture. Chapel Hill, NC: University of North Carolina Press, 2012.

Wojcik, Donna M. *The Brazen Overlanders of 1845*. Portland, OR: private printing,1976.

For further reading online, visit the Friends of Letitia Carson on Facebook.

———

For further reading about Oregon's Benton County and the Soap Creek Valley the following resources are suggested:

Fagan, David D. *History of Benton County, Oregon: Including Its Geology, Topography, Soil and Productions (1885)*. Portland, OR: Walling Printers, 1885.

Glender, Eugene. *Eugene Glender: Growing up on a Tampico Family Farm 1910–1941*. Monograph 9. Soap Creek Valley History Project. Corvallis, OR: OSU Research Forests, College of Forestry, 1994.

Hanish, James. *James Hanish: Biographical Sketch and a Tour of Berry Creek, Benton and Polk Counties, Oregon: 1930–1938*. Monograph 6. Soap Creek Valley History Project. Corvallis, OR: OSU Research Forests, College of Forestry, 1994.

Zybach, Bob. *Historic Soap Creek Valley Auto Tour*. Corvallis: OR: Oregon State University Press, 1990.

———. *Using Oral Histories to Document Changing Forest Cover Patterns in Soap Creek Valley, Oregon, 1500–1999*. Unpublished master's thesis, Oregon State University, 1999.

Zybach, Bob, and Kevin Sherer. *Oral History Interviews*.

The Benton County Historical Society and the Oregon Historical Society provided important reminiscence and histories of the area where Letitia and David Carson chose to live.

Other works about the Oregon Trail providing detail and depth:

Holmes, Kenneth L., ed. and comp. *Covered Wagon Women, Diaries & Letters from the Western Trails 1840–1890*. Glendale, CA: Arthur H. Clark Company, 1983.

Mates, Merrill J. *The Great Platte River Road*. Lincoln, NE: University of Nebraska Press, 1969.

Unruh, Jr., Jesse. *The Plains Across*. Champaign, IL: University of Illinois Press, 1979.

The work of the Oregon California Trail Association www.octa. org whose lecturers, books, and web material are invaluable to the historians and novelists passionate about this period.

As I am a novelist and believe deeply that story reveals truths sometimes hiding in the most factual of histories, I include these novels that informed me about both the journey west and the challenges of a woman of color:

Bateman, Tracey. *The Color of the Soul*. Uhrichsville, OH: Barbour, 2005.

Crew, Linda. *A Heart for Any Fate: Westward to Oregon, 1845*. Portland, OR: Ooligan Press, 2009.

Jones, Edward P. *The Known World*. New York: HarperCollins, 2003.

Kidd, Sue Monk. *The Invention of Wings*. New York: Viking, 2014.

Margolin, Phillip. *Worthy Brown's Daughter*. New York: HarperCollins, 2014.

Morrison, Toni. *Beloved*. New York: Vintage, 2004.

Perkins-Valdez, Dolan. *Wench*. New York: Amistad, 2010.

Pitts, Jr., Leonard. *Freeman*. Evanston, IL: Agate Bolden Publisher, 2012.

And the poetry of Maya Angelou, Mary Oliver, and Gwendolyn Brooks, especially "To Be In Love" from *Selected Poems* by Gwendolyn Brooks (New York: Harper Perennial, 1999).

Book Discussion Questions

1. Pulitzer Prize–winning author Willa Cather once wrote that the emotions that drive great stories are passion and betrayal. What were the passions in this story? Where was the betrayal? As you think of your own life stories, how are passion and betrayal a part of them, or are they?

2. The author suggests that two other desires are present in all stories: a character's desire for acceptance and forgiveness. How did Letitia seek acceptance? Do you think she found it? What about forgiveness? Did Letitia seek forgiveness? Did any other characters demonstrate a desire for acceptance or forgiveness?

3. How did Letitia overcome her cowers? Where did she draw her strength from? What were Nancy Hawkins's desires? Did she have her own kind of cowers? What about Betsy, the Kalapuya woman? What were her worries and how did she resolve them?

4. Were there other ways Letitia could have dealt with her stepson, David Junior? How did Letitia's race complicate her role

as a stepmother? Was her sense of intrusion by Davey's son warranted? Why or why not?

5. Could Letitia have found a better way than a lawsuit to confront Greenberry Smith? What choices did women of color have during that time period if they experienced an injustice?

6. Letitia says at one point, "Maybe that was what freedom meant, being in a place where one didn't fear." Later she notes that freedom is having the courage to do what must be done. How would you define freedom? What about justice?

7. Does the turmoil around slavery in this far western territory surprise you? How might Letitia and Davey's life have been different if they had remained in Missouri? What about going north to what eventually became Washington Territory, where historically African Americans received a warmer welcome?

8. Letitia notes about her traveling companions on the Oregon Trail that "they might be in new territory, but it would be with the same people bringing what they knew to wherever they were going." How did that insight reveal itself once Letitia and Davey made it to the Willamette Valley?

9. Nancy notes, "Power without love is never just." Do you agree? Why or why not?

10. Did Letitia come to accept the promise of the sparrow? Why or why not? Was Davey's attitude of "not to worry" justified? Was he a good partner? Why or why not?

11. How do Letitia or Nancy or Betsy's lives speak to women's lives today? What autonomy did these women have and how did that affect how they survived when injustice entered their lives?

Jane Kirkpatrick is the *New York Times*, CBA, and Pacific Northwest bestselling author of more than twenty-six books, including *A Sweetness to the Soul*, which won the coveted Wrangler Award from the Western Heritage Center. Her works have been finalists for the Christy Award, Spur Award, Oregon Book Award, and Reader's Choice awards, and have won the WILLA Literary Award and Carol Award for Historical Fiction. Many of her titles have been Book of the Month, Crossings, and Literary Guild selections. You can also read her work in more than fifty publications, including *Decision*, *Private Pilot*, and *Daily Guideposts*, and in her Story Sparks newsletter. Jane lives in Central Oregon with her husband, Jerry. She loves to hear from readers at http://www.jkbooks.com and http://Facebook.com/theauthorJaneKirkpatrick.

Grace Hathaway must rescue a dear friend from a remote and notorious clinic that promises healing but delivers only heartache. In a place laced with deceit, where lives hang in the balance, whom can she trust to help her?

NOW AVAILABLE AS EBOOK ONLY!

Four unexpected letters. Four intrepid women.
FOUR LIVES CHANGED FOREVER.

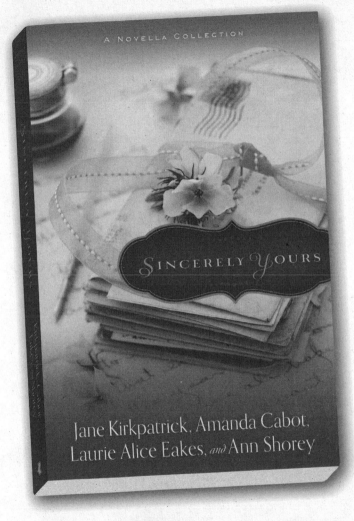

In this inspiring collection of historical romances, four
young women each receive a letter that will change their lives.
Four novellas in one.